D0640663

COUNTRY COUSINS is the tragic
story of a man's confrontation with re
and as such is universal in its impact
man's name is Martin Kilbanky. The
ity is an isolated farmhouse made up of
kitchen tables and tire irons, experimental
television and strange red wigs at twilight,
just outside of the town of Winosha Falls
somewhere in the American heartland.

The story begins with a legal squabble
between Martin and the authorities of
~sha Falls. As this conflict gra⌐
⸢artin begins to discover
⸢ons in reality, UFC
⸢ that have neve⸢
e. Obie⸢

Country Cousins

Also by Michael Brownstein

Highway to the Sky
Brainstorms

Country Cousins

A NOVEL BY

Michael Brownstein

A VENTURE BOOK

GEORGE BRAZILLER New York

Acknowledgment is made for lyrics from "Not Fade Away" © 1957,
  McCartney Music, Inc. Used by permission.

Published simultaneously in Canada by
  Doubleday Canada, Limited

For information, address the publisher:
George Braziller, Inc.
One Park Avenue, New York, N.Y. 10016

Standard Book Number: 0-8076-0749-5

Library of Congress Catalog Card Number: 74-79059

First Printing

Printed in the United States of America

DESIGNED BY RONALD FARBER

for Anne, Dick and Ron

Country Cousins

PART ONE

Poor Martin

1

A Rude Awakening

Martin Kilbanky wore trousers on Sunday. He walked to the cement place and said, "Give me five tons, please—I need them for a house I am building."

The little man behind the counter glowed with appreciation. He made arrangements for the load to be delivered free to any site of Martin's choice within the vicinity.

Martin took his time getting back home, since the load would not be delivered until three. Whistling to himself, dreaming against the windowpanes, he walked the early morning streets of the town. He stopped in at a malt shop, a sweet shop, and a machine shop, and then as the streets began to fill with people who stared curiously at him and made remarks among themselves, he decided to look in unexpectedly on some old friends of his—the Parsons. He thumbed a ride in a pickup truck heading out of town.

Bill and Marge Parsons lived in a new housing development outside town in a ranch-type dwelling much larger than they ever dreamed of four years earlier, when Bill had just been released from the army. Bill was a rangy fellow with light brown bristly hair. He had no idea, then, what to do with his life. Wayne Buddins, an old high school buddy of Bill's, offered him the position of fat-separator at Wayne's new meat packing plant up in Clipsieville. And Bill—out of plain just not knowing what else to do—was all set to take him up on it when Marge arrived on the scene.

You see, Bill's younger brother Digger had been going with a girl named Fontessa Margins for some time: in fact, Digger had more than once wanted his freedom back but so far had been unable to break off his relationship with the bouncy, stubborn, big-boned Margins girl. And when he went so far as to find himself interested in someone new, Fontessa up and claimed their baby was on its way and threatened suicide if he did her the public humiliation of running away from her. After they were engaged, however, Digger found out that she wasn't pregnant after all, and this revelation soured and embittered them toward each other before they ever stepped one foot down the aisle at Holy Christ Methodist. By the time Fontessa did become pregnant and gave birth to a set of jolly twins, she and Digger hardly spoke.

But actually, back in the days when they were still sweet on each other, right during when Bill had returned from the Service and was sitting on the porch on those sweltering July evenings, counting the bumper stickers on his brother's pickup and wondering what he'd do next, Fontessa's aunt and three cousins arrived from Spartanburg to visit the Margins, and Marge was among them. She was the oldest Margins cousin, a sturdy nineteen with naturally ruddy cheeks and a suddenly insistent touch-football air about her. Digger just laughed, but something about the sturdy girl made Bill look twice. He was not yet twenty-four himself, but he could feel the bald spots coming.

Over the next few weeks Bill became captivated by the big girl from Spartanburg. She seemed to see it the same way, so they got married—although Marge was to feel forever embittered toward her cousin Fontessa and toward Fontessa's mother Sheila because they refused to let the two couples have a double wedding ceremony even though both Bill and Digger thought it was a great idea. Marge felt certain Fontessa was snubbing her, whereas in fact Fontessa secretly was making a heroic and romantic gesture by refusing to taint the presence of true love (Marge and Bill) with the already-doomed union of herself and Digger. Fontessa hinted at the real reason in what she thought were obvious ways, but the fact that Marge never understood this soured Fontessa toward her in the years to come, so that in the course of things when Bill made advances to Fontessa (who was living alone at the time), she didn't feel obliged to refuse them. When within six weeks or so Marge realized what was happening—that Bill was shacking up with her own cousin—she formed a permanent crease above her lips that never disappeared, even after she died. Almost immediately she confronted Fontessa about it—just letting her know she knew, nothing more, not saying a word about it to Bill.

Fontessa at the time was living in a house-trailer with Peggy (one of her twin daughters by Digger) and seeing lots of different men. She was working as a checker and bumper at the tri-county airport, keeping irregular hours and not sleeping much, when Bill re-entered her life. She had always felt something for him, though up until the moment he knocked on her trailer door and she opened it and saw that look in his eyes she had always felt slightly uncomfortable with him. Sometimes he seemed purposefully slow-witted and without motivation to her, like so many of the men she knew, but at other times she felt he was OK—life was tough and she knew just *how* tough, too. And Bill was nice, an important consideration with men. He wasn't nasty and cruel like Digger. Technically still her husband, Digger would still come by and try to give it to her, and if she refused to sleep with him he would beat her up, sock her around a few times (in front of Peggy, too!), and just walk out the door.

But Bill treated her right. When he had the money, which admittedly wasn't often, he would buy her candy and little gifts, or take Peggy and her out to a really good diner for supper. Not many people in Winosha Falls who saw them together thought a thing about it at first, because it's natural for a man who's practically her brother to be looking after her a little. But although he said he loved her and Fontessa knew that was true, he refused to leave Marge because he simply refused to subject her to the unbearable pain he thought she would suffer if he told her about Fontessa and himself. He felt Marge was a noble being although he no longer loved her. He also knew Marge packed a nasty wallop and secretly he was unsure he could survive her wrath. Besides, he'd gotten used to his life with her. Fontessa was aware of Bill's affection for Marge and therefore couldn't bring herself to tell him that Marge *already knew*, that Marge deliberately was keeping that knowledge from Bill.

So it was these three people emotionally entwined the day Bill's old friend Martin Kilbanky looked in. Martin himself had suffered a severe nervous breakdown or crack-up—nobody seemed to know *what* to call it—the day after graduating from high school with honorable mention, and had spent what would have been his college years gibbering and half-naked in the fields on his terribly embarrassed father's farm a few miles outside Winosha on old Route 41. He gradually recovered just enough to form this grand plan in his head to build a house—his very own house that would consist of five tons of concrete. He decided the best way to build would simply be to have the cement delivered at the site of his choice. Then, and only then, would he begin to think about designing it. He would mix the cement right there on the spot, lay a foundation, and do whatever came into his head after rapid reflection at that precise moment. He was able to initiate this extravagant oddball project so easily because his father had died that past winter and had left the entire farm operation in Martin's name, including the bank accounts. Martin's mother, who was never able to admit to herself that her only son might be addle-brained, lived with him on the farm after her helpmate died and in fact had been the one to convince old Ike Kilbanky that his son's mental condition was temporary and had been greatly exaggerated by gossips. Up until that point, Ike had been planning to leave the farm to their runaway daughter Chartruse, who was four years older than Martin, but the mother hated the daughter for her insolence and promiscuous carrying-on: they heard from her but rarely, and each time practically all she did was praise some new man she was crazy about. Chartruse had left home in the first place pregnant from one drifter and hanging off the heels of another . . . Sleeping around with every damn horse in the stable . . . Louise Kilbanky weighed her two offspring carefully and decided she would rather live out her years with her lightheaded son even if he proved to have a screw loose rather than turn the farm into one big heavy make-out parlor.

So Chartruse got nothing when her father died, not one penny. Of all the members of her family her father was the only one she really loved, so when she heard the news—that in spite of the fact he had known how hard-up she was, he still had left her nothing—she felt hurt and confused, and further estranged from her mother and brother. She returned to attend the funeral but left the next day vowing never to write or visit either one of them ever again; to make it on her own in the Big City, no matter how difficult it was or how alone she felt. Sometimes her body would just shake with the emptiness of her city life, whether it was secretary-ing, or waitress-ing, or hostess-ing, and she'd get so scared! What else was there for her to do but run into the arms of some awful *man*, who would more than likely step all over her than love her?

Martin Kilbanky was navigating tremendous waves of vertigo and gaiety when he knocked on Bill and Marge's door that morning. He knew he'd probably be waking them up but he was so overjoyed about his deal with the cement-mixing company that he just had to share it with *someone*.

Bill staggered to the door in his pajamas. He and Marge were sore from living on pins and needles lately, though neither would admit what the other knew, and the last person Bill wanted to see was a nut like Martin Kilbanky. And on Sunday morning, too!

In high school Bill and Martin had been friends, but Bill shied away from him like the plague ever since news of Martin's breakdown became gossip. Bill wasn't the sort of guy to play Florence Nightingale and try to retain friendship with some nut who lived out in the bushes, usually, and grinned at trees.

In spite of that, though, they had seen each other in town dozens of times since Bill returned from the army, and he always said hello rather than act as if Martin didn't exist. The result was that Martin, rather than catch Bill's true feelings about him, simply thought they had "gone their separate ways" but still remained good friends and even buddies.

Martin stood beaming in the doorway. "Hi, Bill!" he shouted enthusiastically. "Guess what I just did—I bought five tons of cement down at Schwartz's and it's gonna be delivered to that pasture out behind the pond today. Wanna come over and watch?"

Bill Parsons stood staring at Martin in disbelief. His first impulse was to tell him to beat it, but at that very moment Marge walked into the living room in her bathrobe and sleepily invited Martin in for some late breakfast. She knew how uncomfortable Bill was around Martin and seized the opportunity to make him suffer, since she had awakened that morning convinced she was holding the rotten corner of the triangle: Bill and Fontessa seemed to do what they wanted, making love repeatedly, while she was left with the questionable joys of plot and intrigue.

Marge stepped up with a smile and pumped Martin's hand. "Come on in and have some eggs," she said.

7

"Sure, old buddy, step right up," Bill hissed sarcastically. "Welcome to the Bright Street Annex of the State Funny Farm—we're open all hours so don't be shy!" He stepped aside theatrically and waved Martin over to the breakfast table. Martin beamed happily. He rejoiced in this purported scene of domestic tranquility he was about to share—the toaster, the coffee pot, the empty Coke bottles from the night before, Marge's poodle wagging its tail by her side as she broke six eggs into a bowl. He sat down rakishly on the edge of a kitchen chair and began decorating the back of his left hand with strawberry jam. The dog, a big black standard poodle named Donnie, leaped up and down barking furiously, and Martin joined in, hooting and swaying back and forth. Bill disappeared into the bedroom. Marge decided to let it all ride. She busied herself preparing eggs, toast, juice and coffee.

Martin was wiping big spoonfuls of jam onto the poodle's coat when Bill reappeared, still dressed in his robe and carrying an axe. His face seemed contorted.

"Get out!" he shouted, swinging the axe above his head like a tomahawk, and Martin leaped back against the wall in terror.

Marge swiftly took control of the situation, however. "Goddamnit, Bill, you quit that!" She wrestled the axe free from his grasp. "Now sit down and eat your breakfast—you must be joking, waving an axe at a friend of yours . . . Come on, Martin, the eggs are ready. Bill was just fooling."

With some difficulty the three sat down at the table. Martin stared wildly away from Bill. His fork shook his first bite of eggs all around the table, but soon he decided Bill simply had got out or the wrong side of bed that morning. Martin calmed down and grew intent on the food in front of him. The dog sat forlornly rubbing his jam-covered coat onto the lower kitchen cabinets as the three sat, their sinuses dried out by the uncomfortable baseboard heating, and ate and drank and talked.

Martin subsided and ate calmly, occasionally however putting his left hand into his mouth and sucking on his fingers. He was feeling good that morning, and he realized as he sat eating that he had been feeling good, really good, for three or four days already . . . He concluded it must be due to his plan to build a house, which had come to him suddenly a few days before and which he had been thinking about ever since. A sudden rush of creative energy and enthusiasm overtook him. He felt transformed—a new person. In the past seven years few things had moved him to put on his pants and confront the world like this plan for the house had. Above all he now felt substantially free of the mysteriously gyrating depression he had known for so long . . . Freedom (maybe!), freedom at last! . . .

Martin's head reeled, the room turned upside-down, his fork stabbed at a stray piece of hot buttered toast, then in a reflexive physical shudder sent the toast flying across the breakfast nook where it hung in the doorway for a second like a butterfly and then was gone.

Bill couldn't believe it! He had worked himself into such a state before breakfast, at odds with his wife and in a frenzy over Martin's appearance, he was so nervously keyed-up and strung tight inside, that when Martin interrupted their briefly blissful eating and erupted with a twitch, the flash of the fork upon the table, the toast literally exploding into the air—well, something snapped inside Bill and for the first time he caught a glimpse of what Martin's world could be like, what Martin saw from inside his head. Bill's eyes bulged out over his bathrobe as he saw Martin sitting, day after day, or rolling and rolling on the grass: he couldn't believe it! Bill let out an abbreviated howl. He spilled his bowl.

Marge followed this outburst at the breakfast table with shouts of disbelief. But actually Martin was an unknown commodity to her. She was vaguely but definitely intrigued by his strangeness; and his stroke of turning up after six or seven years out in the fields as the owner of a prosperous farm made her laugh delightedly, inside. To herself. (A whole world in there, inside her head. Who else hears it? she wondered.)

Eventually Bill quieted down. As for Martin, from the moment the toast left his fork and Bill howled, he was a changed person. He sat in a corner brooding, polishing his shoe with a shirtsleeve, defensive and solemn. Then Marge put up another pot of coffee . . . Out the window they all watched as massive, beautiful storm clouds swiftly occupied the sky. Soon the trees and surrounding ornamental bushes began to bend in the wind, then whip erratically from side to side as the day grew dark and rain began to fall.

The rain slid down like pie. A solid sheet fell for several minutes, but as abruptly as the storm appeared it was gone, an April shower

. . . Now the clouds broke and the sun lit a path across the lawn. Martin stood up as if to go. At that moment the coffee was done, however. Marge turned to him with a steaming cup and a smile and Martin sat back down, still uneasy, sighing to himself like a broken pony.

"Well, Martin, you gonna vote for Howard Magnuson for State Senator this year?" Marge asked as a joke. Bill was looking downright morose but she knew he'd crack up at the idea of Martin voting for anybody. And somehow the fact that it was *Martin Kilbanky* voting for *Howard E. Magnuson*, made it especially funny. Bill burst out laughing, right on cue. Marge joined in.

Martin smiled happily: finally these two people seemed to be coming around! Up to that point he had been traumatized by his experiences in the Parsons house, and anything that might release any laughter at all—well, he was for it.

"Yes, Marge, I do believe I will."

"You better register, then, or when the time comes to vote everybody else'll be let in but you. They won't let you through the door."

"Register?"

"Yes, Martin. And you'll have to do it this week. It's the last week."

"I'll go right now," he announced soberly, and stood as if to go. Bill laughed: "Today's *Sunday*, man . . . they don't do registering on Sunday, Martin. You gotta go tomorrow morning. Right, Marge?"

She nodded.

"But don't worry none," Bill deadpanned. "If you miss it this year you can vote for Norton Magnuson next year." He couldn't resist guffawing, though no one else joined him.

"But listen, Martin," Marge asked sincerely. "How'd you get in the cement store on Sunday, anyway? I can't believe you bought all that stuff, five tons of cement, that really kills me, but how'd you get in there in uh first place?"

"Well," he replied evasively, "the door was open so I just walked in."

Bill was still laughing. The cigarette burns on his institutional bathrobe grew larger.

"I mean, that old cement store's run by Jews, ain't it? It's Jewish people," Martin continued, "that's bought out the Hundleys, ain't it, who used to own the store, right? Them Jewish peoples'll stay out till all hours to get your money, ask anybody," he drawled.

Bill looked over at him in surprise, nodding in agreement and adding testily: "That's the truth, too. And they'll be open every dad-blamed Sunday of the year, too, right?" He pronounced the last word "rat," mock southern-style, and they all laughed heartily.

Martin has a lot of sense in him after all, Marge thought to herself. He's crazy, no doubt about that, but still and all he has sense. . . .

She was growing more and more interested in her life as the partly cloudy day progressed. She put her brain to work, too, since she and Bill had almost no money left and as usual Bill refused to look for work.

2

Digging In

Martin finished his coffee quickly. It was nearly twelve o'clock and the cement men would be at the farm at three. He had to make arrangements. His mind worked desperately. What were the arrangements he had to make?

"Now tell us about this house you say you're building, Martin," Marge said. "Are you gonna—"

"You and Bill," he shouted back. "It's Sunday, ain't it? What the hell. Come out to the farm with me and watch. Mother ain't seen you, Bill," he continued, turning to Bill with a significant nod of his head, "it must be three or four years!"

As if for the first time, Martin realized how long he and Bill had been out of touch. He seemed embarrassed by this fact. His face turned crimson.

Bill was still extremely touchy about Martin in general and any reference to them both in particular he took as a personal affront.

"Fuck you!" he screamed violently, and also rather incoherently.

"Bill!" Marge was furious. She understood at least in part that he was being so defensive because he felt threatened by Martin's craziness. But it infuriated her beyond words to see him give in a second time to such a ridiculous emotional display. She ran to the stove, picked up the coffee pot (which had been cold for some time now) and suddenly shrieking like a wild animal (Bill's such an asshole! she thought) she threw the pot in his face.

"Agh!"

Martin remembered later, when he thought back on this scene, how when Marge, who previously had been so nice to him, so warm and comprehending, changed into a seething wild animal right before his eyes, her hair frizzing out and standing on end, her eyeballs rolling white in their sockets, her body shivering with fury where only seconds before it had been calm and even serene—well, Martin's whole being seemed to blow some kind of fuse. He would never forget for the rest of his life that feeling, an explosion that spread through his veins to every part of his body like being caught by a huge wave at the ocean, upended and thrown into the foam. His vision whited out and he tingled like a foot that had been asleep and was now violently awakened.

Most puzzling of all, he remembered distinctly that he had felt that way for what seemed at least ten minutes—but when he revived and looked around the parts of the percolator were still clanging to the floor, Bill was running out of the room again, and Marge had collapsed sobbing horribly at the kitchen table. Cold coffee and coffee grounds were strewn across the kitchen tiles and cabinets.

Martin Kilbanky may have been crazy, but he was no fool. Obviously something was going on between the two of them, the nature of which at first eluded him. He sensed that Marge was not crying because of Bill, for example, but simply out of embarrassment. That in itself complicated the situation enormously. Martin knew Marge was the stronger and wilier of the two—he just sensed it—and he concluded she would be the one in control of almost any situation involving Bill, including any hypothetical home, car or office situation. The explanation must be, then, that she was embarrassed by her lack of control over Bill—and that she was not embarrassed for Martin's sake but for her own!

He almost fell out of his chair when he realized what was happening: Marge wailed because Bill wouldn't accept her version of—of what?

"Of me!" a voice inside Martin answered, and he slapped his forehead in surprise.

. . . Now, Martin Kilbanky was not accustomed to deliberations of this sort. In fact, normally he didn't think about other people at all—or if he did, the thoughts were simple spin-offs of how various people he encountered treated him and acted toward him. Most people acted like shit toward him and Martin knew it. But he had a sunny disposition and the truth is he just didn't care. Since early childhood he had been subject to a certain hallucinatory dreaminess

—abrupt visions whose nature he did not attempt to understand and which occurred more and more frequently as time went on, as he became fascinated and turned his attention to them. Highly detailed and pictorial, they intruded upon his everyday life without warning, monopolizing his attention as he sat at his desk in school or played with his classmates, and by the time he entered high school he had given up resisting them. He surrendered to them immediately, in spite of how dull-witted this made him seem to others, in spite of how he was teased and abused.

In fact, he felt himself immune to the growing sarcasm he had to endure. He led a carefree, solitary life most of the time, though on the other hand for days at a stretch he would be plagued by a vague emotional depression leaving him in a state of total listlessness. Lethargic and devitalized, he would sit in the fields out of sight of the farmhouse, day after day on occasion, rolling slowly at the bottom of an ocean of spring rye or else just sunk in weeds, going nowhere, covered with bugs and feeling like a sack of manure.

But these moods—these states—came and went like violent thunderstorms: at the end of it would be a terrible state of affairs, beyond belief really, but suddenly giving way to simple sunshine. What a welcome relief!

. . . Martin looked out the window. The rain was stopping, the storm seemed over. Soon the sun would be out again for good. He had to be getting back to the farm: it was getting late.

Sheepishly Bill crept back into the kitchen. He was still jumpy and edgy, but he seemed truly apologetic when he offered to drive Martin out to the farm. Marge would come along too.

Marge whistled and hummed to herself as she sponged the cold coffee grounds that were strewn all over the kitchen. Bill put on a fresh white T-shirt and brand-new Levi's. Since it was Sunday he changed into his dress shoes, incongruous oxblood cordovans. He clipped his nails and cleaned them with a coat hanger.

Marge reappeared wearing a bright cotton print dress and carrying her best shiny patent-leather pocketbook. Everyone seemed to be in one piece again.

The car seat was warm and sunny. Martin loved sitting on a warm and sunny old-fashioned straw-weave seat cover, the windows down, driving and driving through the low hills around Winosha Falls, preferably in a used Ford or Chevy or an old Mercury, or even an old streamlined Hudson or Nash . . . Martin disliked the newer model cars he saw on the road, with their gratuitous decorative fins and phony bucket seats . . . Thinking of a Hudson brought to mind the boxes and boxes of Hudson paper napkins his father used to hoard in the cellar of their farmhouse—what were called "dinner napkins"— and he chuckled to himself remembering how as a little boy he had gone downstairs one day and turned the water tap on full force until the cellar floor was flooded under twelve inches of water and the paper napkins were ruined. The strange thing was that his father discovered what he had done that very afternoon but never said a word about it. In fact, he realized excitedly as he climbed into the back seat of the Parsons' car, those dozens of boxes of soggy paper napkins were probably still down there! After all these years! He strained his memory, telling himself not to forget to see if they were still there when he got home. . . .

Bill was behind the wheel and Marge beside him. They backed out of the driveway on wet gravel and turned onto the road toward town. The brief rainstorm had given way to a beautifully vibrant, sunny spring day, partly cloudy and partly alive with playful, sudden alternations between cold and warmth, when you were convinced at first that you still need a coat, but it was warm and cool all at once and the last of the snow pockets under dwarf pines had receded two weeks before. Rubber-boot weather, but not sloshy really since it was late spring, April 19th, in fact . . . The rain had caused the pine needles that carpeted the lawn and driveway to radiate their lonesome smell. The stray brown and grey leaves on the ground blew in a fresh little wind and fat clouds scudded through the blue.

Bells were ringing in the distance as they set out.

"Must be twelve o'clock," Martin said. "Lunchtime. That's probably old Gorsley Towers, flicking the switch on that siren. Soon everybody'll be pouring outta the tack factory for lunch. Listen: there's the siren right now."

Marge turned to him with a gentle laugh.

"It ain't Gorsley, silly. That's the bells over at the Church. It's Sunday, Martin, remember?"

Bill turned on the radio. Surprising modern jazz came out of the speaker.

"What is that shit?" Bill asked heavily as he gripped the wheel.

"Must be some sort of modern jazz or something."

Marge and Bill looked at each other.

"I know a lot about modern jazz," Martin announced, then laughed to himself.

They both turned toward him and Bill asked, "What in the world are you talkin about?"

Marge mumbled something about "coon music" and played with the dial for awhile, zipping past stations that were mostly gospel or church music but also included earnest country voices selling hog seed oil or fertilizer, a show about how to organize a knitting bee which consisted of a taped interview with "The Queen of the Knitting Bee," and finally the Casper State Teacher's College radio station. The laconic student announcer introduced the college's special Sunday Afternoon Concert, "Experimental Devotional Music of Twentieth-Century Dutch Composers."

"God!" Marge wailed, wrenching the knob. "Where's the music?" At that moment a distant station flooded by static came through briefly, loud and clear: *My love is bigger than a Cadillac, I try to show it and you drive me back—*

The Parsons lived in a burgeoning prefab suburban development called Crestview Developments, the first of its kind in the region. Although its size was relatively small—several square blocks, some fifty or sixty replica houses—it already had created its own unique environment with chunky asphalt roads, monotonously bare lawns supporting small new transplanted trees above a sewerage and drainage system so moronic and self-serving in conception as to have created in a few short years great yawning gullies and eroded canyons where once the rich red soil stood carpeted with meadows. Now bags of fertilizer were a popular item with the residents, in a bald attempt to ignore the facts. The smell from some of the conduits on rainy days was enough to make the gorge rise. Chronic eye-irritation was endemic in the area.

However, two or three minutes' driving time for Martin and the Parsons and they were free from all that, riding instead through the narrow strip of rural countryside that separated Crestview Developments from the town of Winosha Falls. To get to Winosha they had to drive through this brief strip of country, and though it never occurred to any of them consciously, they were grateful for that fact. Deep inside they needed that wide old country sky.

Approaching Winosha brought the three of them down to earth. Bill remembered he had forgotten to bring his money, though on the other hand he tried not to remember that he had forgotten to bring his money because he had no money to bring. He started thinking then about hitting the bottle.

And Marge, in turn, was forced to remember her own problems, which were indeed prodigious: Bill, for one, and how she more and more actually felt about him; then that whore Fontessa; and to top it all off was the fact that if some miracle didn't occur soon she and Bill would be completely destitute. Damn!

Marge turned in her seat, jerking all the way around so she could see out the rear window, catch a glimpse of the countryside, and the hills and fields and clouds called her name—or, at least, they were calling Martin's name for sure and Martin suddenly felt they could be calling Marge's too if she only would listen. . . .

Bill swerved to the right and stopped the car. "I just want to smoke a fuckin cigarette, that's all."

They got out of the car and sat on a bank of grass by the side of the road. The beginning of Winosha Falls proper was the old abandoned stone flour mill on the river, no more than a half-mile farther down the road from where they sat.

"I gotta get goin soon," Martin said anxiously, squinting at the sky to see what time it was.

"Man, I know that," Bill threatened. "Just cool off, we'll get there before they deliver your cement." Then his face brightened maliciously. "And with the asshole project you got in mind, I wouldn't be surprised if it was little men in white coats that showed up instead." He thought of himself at that moment as terribly witty and cutting-'em-dead.

"Bill, you're such a lame-brained jackass I can't believe it," Marge shouted.

"Oh, screw you!" he roared, and leaping over Martin who sat between them he viciously burned Marge's arm with his cigarette and then half-falling over Martin began to pummel her. Instantly they were all wrestling and shouting, Marge shrieking with pain and rage, Martin sobbing and trying to separate his two desperate friends.

The scuffle was violent but brief, though it left an ugly aftertaste.

Martin whispered hoarsely in Bill's ear, "You oughtta be ashamed of yourself," and Bill suddenly subsided, a strange unpleasant smile, however, lingering on his lips. His shirt was torn.

Marge lay weeping heavily, a hole painfully raw on her forearm, her face and legs muddy.

Martin found himself losing his patience, which was such a rare sensation for him that at first he didn't even recognize what it was. Then he found himself saying, "For Christ sake, you two are worse than babies—let's go, goddamn it!"

He enunciated the words, which were so unfamiliar to him, in such a way that both Bill and Marge broke out laughing.

"You better watch out, Martin, or before you know it you'll be the boss!"

"Ha ha ha," said Bill.

"What do you mean, the boss?" Martin asked uncertainly.

His voice suddenly took on an anxious tone; he felt frightened and out of place. Dizzy. All of a sudden Martin wondered where he was, what he was doing with these two violent people. Who were they? What did she mean when she said he might be the boss? Her voice had sounded mocking—it confused Martin, set him on edge. Was she teasing him? Threatening him?

He turned uncomfortably toward Marge, and the frizzy light brown hair outlining a corky, determined face made him uneasy. But at the same time there was a definite memory of this woman being nice to him, of this girl treating him with respect. Did this face belong to the same person that had invited him in for breakfast? He couldn't figure it out. He got scared.

"What do you mean?" he repeated, the blood surging up to his eyes.

Marge looked at Martin, fascinated by the transformation taking place. She was surprised beyond words by how quickly he had become afraid, off-balance, uncertain of himself. But by the time he asked his question Marge's intuition told her to act gently and reassuringly with him . . . A certain total absence of aggressive behavior . . . Wipe baby's chin and rock him slowly . . . Open the pantry window to the sweet coloring-book breeze, and add one part pure pearly spittle . . . Hold him close to your voice, the warmth of your voice like your serene small white breasts. . . .

"Mar-tin, Mar-tin, oh Martin is my friend, umm . . ." Marge hummed softly, cupping her knees in her arms and rocking back and forth, back and forth, as the three of them sat on the hillock.

Marge's voice mesmerized him: he snapped to attention like a toy.

"Humm, hummm, the baby is asleep . . ." she continued, as Bill stared on in disbelief.

Martin alternately tensed his muscles and relaxed. He was in a state of extreme stress. His neck and shoulders knotted up and pain shot down his back. He began rotating his head this way and that, trying to relieve the pain, when he noticed a pickup truck parked on the road nearby, its engine running and two burly-looking figures hunched inside the cab. Martin flinched and turned to signal Bill, who out of embarrassment over what he was witnessing had been staring off into the woods. "Somebody's here," he called out.

Marge stopped singing and looked up. Bill swung around. Instantly the three of them fused together, united into a team to confront the unknown. For the time being Marge put aside her singing, Martin his listening, and Bill his facing away.

But then Bill announced, "That's just Big Willie from down at the Esso station. He probably thinks we done run out of gas or something." Bill loosened up, strolling over to the pickup with a lazy country stride that said to the casual observer, "Howdy, I'm OK. . . ."

He stood laughing and talking for a few minutes with Willie and Willie's unidentified sidekick and then ambled back to the car. Marge heard Martin's name mentioned and was sure Bill had been cracking jokes at his expense.

Willie's battered truck pulled back onto the road. With a wave and a honk it was gone.

"Says it's two fifteen at least," Bill volunteered. "We'd better get goin—although they didn't have no watch and I don't see how it could be *that* late."

Martin seemed shaky but the three of them climbed inside the car and drove into town. Bill knew where he could get a bottle of whiskey even though it was Sunday, and Marge wanted some ice cream. Martin shivered awhile and mumbled but finally seemed alright.

Winosha Falls (pronounced *wi-NOH-sha*) was a town much like Circleville, Ohio, except it was a little bigger and wasn't located in Ohio. Also it was busier, almost as if it were an industrial town, which it wasn't, though, either. Smudged small fry wandered at will through the unkempt grounds of the town's one industrial park, which was now functioning at one-third capacity. Pretty white picket fence maple-leaved side streets gave place with no warning to a deadly-looking red brick Catholic church squatting off to one side, or big gray clapboard Pentecostal houses of worship catching one blind-side from between glazed-doughnut shops. The mature maroon-slab presence of the Baptist Church of the Redeemer virtually exhausted Winosha's devotional possibilities, sharing its own quiet side street with a row of rubber tire establishments and R. Lemaster's Funeral Parlor. Several large town houses, fine old structures of stone and wood graced with wide verandahs, large airy rooms, high ceilings and broad winding staircases leading up to the bedrooms, completed the scene. The front porches were equipped with various types of chairs, including sturdy platform rockers, and generally had a swinging-settee suspended by means of chains from hooks in the ceiling.

Winosha Falls itself is located five miles SE of the town that bears its name. The town proper is basically flat, and without a river. The Falls, however, are quite beautiful—a dramatic drop through lime-stone shelving of a good forty-five feet, briefly churning white river water, and the eventual return to a placid unbroken flow.

The principal downtown business in terms of acreage was Neil Lord's Triple-A Ford franchise. The principal industry, the tack factory located out at the industrial park. The primary alteration of the town's essence was the spanking-new, city-block-square discount warehouse a few miles outside of town called The Plastic Elephant. The "Elephant," bringing business to Winosha from all over the tri-county area, had recently introduced a flood of commercial bargain merchandise for the first time, and the townspeople and surrounding farm population were about evenly divided for and against the chain operation. Cheap Japanese baseball gloves and plastic flowers from Hong Kong were starting to replace the native wares, though finally no one much cared. Although life for the residents often led to early calcification, for the most part it was neither barren nor dangerous. Most people seemed content. Summer corn was big and sweet.

"Don't Go To The Lord For a Ford" joked three-foot-high posters wrapped around each telephone pole on Main Street. Neil Lord was also the town's mayor and the closest thing Winosha had to a "big man." He had eyes for state politics—maybe a gubernatorial appointment—but so far nothing had jelled.

Main Street, which was the name of Route 41 in town, led to a sleepy town square surrounded by the County Courthouse (Winosha was Wayne County's county seat), the insurance building, two banks, the five-and-dime, several hamburger restaurants and a structure saying "Moose" that housed the Boy Scouts' and Girl Scouts' local offices as well. The shady tree-filled square was flanked by parking places not busy enough to necessitate parking meters, in one of which Bill Parsons stopped the car and parked.

"Hey, Chester, what's happening?" he sang out to a passerby. Bill had decided to accept the fact he'd be seen in public with Martin by joking about it at every opportunity and otherwise acting natural about it. Although he didn't understand why, he detected something in Marge's demeanor and actions since Martin had shown up that morning that made him play along. Marge had something up her sleeve besides her elbow, and Bill was in no position financially or emotionally to contradict her, at least for the time being. He disappeared down an alley to go buy his fifth.

"Hey, Chester, what's happening?" Martin repeated the words light-headedly as he stood alone on the sidewalk. No one answered. Marge had disappeared as well as Bill.

He stood next to the streetlamp on the north corner of the square, fiddling vaguely with his shirt and pants, buttoning and unbuttoning, playing almost coquettishly with the zipper. Schoolgirls taking a Sunday stroll giggled. Martin began rubbing himself. They broke into laughter and skittered off across the square. Sweet little birds, he thought. But where were Marge and Bill?

Martin's eye fell on a copy of the regional Sunday paper, *The Triangle Observer*, its crumpled pages peeking from a wire trash basket. He separated the soiled and soggy pages with considerable effort and squinted down at headlines proclaiming:

GROWERS SHOW INTEREST IN SOYBEANS
EISENHOWER NOW SHOOTING IN LOW 90's
DOG TO TAKE STAND: LAWYER

Soon his eyes began to smart and he threw the paper aside, glimpsing one final paragraph announcing in sepulchral tones that former Governor Hoople was slipping deeper into a coma and appeared near death . . . A special liquid diet and constant supply of oxygen . . .

Martin tried to remember who Hoople was but the harder he tried the less he could recall, until he was left with the following images: a pair of wire-rimmed spectacles, a wiry little man crushing a hazelnut, and his own mother lifting up her gingham skirts long ago to cross a spring-time-muddy front yard, her dainty boots squishing as she ran toward the road calling his name . . . "Martin, Martin—come in for your lunch!"

Martin's stomach rumbled.

Would Bill and Marge ever return?

Martin's condition was such that, in situations such as this one, a 50-50 chance obtained that there would come a time when he literally did not know, for example, whether or not Bill and Marge would ever return. Becoming anxious he looked around the square and nearby side streets for any sign of them . . . Where are they, where are they? . . . He was quite upset now, moaning aloud but at the same time in an effort not to be noticed by everyone in the square, discreetly burying his face in his hands. Finally he tried to bury his head in the wire trash basket affixed to the lamp post and a small crowd gathered, mostly young boys who started to pester him. Martin alternately threw bits of newspaper at them and turned away, shivering silently.

The village clock struck three.

Martin's mood changed abruptly when he heard the clock strike. He frightened the kids away with a vigorous hoot-owl hoot they wouldn't forget for a long time, if ever. He brushed off his clothes and grew impatient. Where the hell *are* those two? he thought darkly.

Then a space opened up and he saw light. It was all clear to him now: it was fudge ripple.

Three cones.

Marge held them unsteadily in one hand, balancing a box of hair-curlers on two rolls of toilet paper with the other. Martin ran to help her. He took the rolls and box. An accolade of ripple then soothed his grateful brain.

Naturally Bill's cone melted over Marge's hand and then was eaten without him, since Bill had become involved with friends in the alley. He knocked twice at a transplanted stable door barbed-wired between two tool sheds and walked into Sonny's place. Sonny, Billy Howells who worked the tow truck, Marvin and Jeffrey Staples (the latter nick-named "Sonny" as well) and Dr. Lester the town chiropodist, all sat around an old pool table now stacked with cases of beer and whiskey, used as a combination bar and shelf space.

"Whaddya say, Billy? How's it goin, Doc?"

Bill knew all these boys since his childhood, though neither Sonny nor Dr. Lester qualified in the least as boys, being 61 and 66 years old respectively.

Sonny James had run this place, as well as a shifting panoply of other bottle houses, legitimate bars, whore bars and roadhouses, at a profusion of different addresses in Spartanburg, Speedunk, Virdon and Clipsieville as well as in Winosha Falls, for years and years. By now he was virtually a town institution, someone the Calvinistic town supervisors could not touch in spite of how much some of them might have wanted to. But Sonny was a regular old boy who supposedly knew some powerful people further upstate and across the state line, too, probably, so nobody messed with him. And since Sonny liked to drink and shoot pool he could do that too, as long as he made it a point to keep enough on hand for the bottle trade and did it some place out of sight.

Sonny's brother lived over in Virdon, his sister and her husband and kids lived here in Winosha, and so did Sonny's old mother, in fact: eighty-eight years old now and still clipping the buds from her hedge with the same huge pair of cast-iron garden shears she bought in 1889. The shears had even made her a kind of celebrity some years back when a stranger driving through the area spotted her using them, got out of his car and chatted, photographed the shears, and had the photographs deposited in the State Historical Museum up at the state capitol. Although she was nearly ninety now she was still scheming to open a real antique store that could compete with fat Mrs. Yancey's "Cast-Iron Wagon." She sold antiques of her own on the side, a big hand-lettered cardboard sign was in her window, and everyone in town knew right where she stood on everything, because she told them. The bank refused to lend her any money, supposedly because Sonny had a prison record but actually because she and old Tom Dowd who ran the bank had hated each other since they were kids. So she was still waiting in her heart for Sonny to strike it rich and set her up in a store of her own. . . .

Bill knew all this, of course, and he knew lots more as well, but he knew it all without being aware that he knew it—automatically, so to speak. He was incapable of recording these local anecdotes and in fact it never occurred to him (or anyone else in town) to even try, so that the people to whom the events referred grew faint as the years passed, until one day all their stories would be gone.

"Gimme a bottle, Sonny, I got Marge waitin down at the square."

"Lookit him," Marvin Staples cracked. "He's in such a hurry you could give him a bottle of window cleaner and it wouldn't make no difference."

"Marvin, you're a sorry son, but you happen in this case to be right: I'm gonna set down for awhile and have a drink. I sure as hell need it."

"Whattsa problem, Billy boy?" Sonny James warbled with a smile, winking at Doc Lester and the others. "You got woman trouble?"

They all laughed, Bill included. He knew that his escapade with Fontessa—"partaking of his brother's meat" as it was jokingly referred to—was tacit knowledge in some parts of town. He also knew the protocol of the situation allowed him to ignore the remark if he wanted to, and that if he did it then would not come up again for discussion, at least until next time. According to an unspoken but universally accepted code, whatever woman anyone could get was alright, with a few very rare but very real exceptions, such as when Jesse Edwards took his own father's new bride away just to play around with her and then taunted and shamed his own dad about it in public . . . Jesse's jaw was broken twice and shortly thereafter he moved to Ohio . . . But otherwise practically anything went, since without this underground electricity the town would have been truly destitute of any action whatsoever.

"Old Marge'll keep for a minute, anyway," Bill remarked as he unscrewed a bottle of cheap bourbon and ran tap water from the sink. He added something about sweet old cherry wine, everyone laughed and the topic changed.

Sonny sighed. "I don't know, man. It looks like rain to me."

Marvin Staples chortled. "Better plug your buckets, Sonny, or you'll be dry soon no matter how much it rains."

"I'll plug em, alright," Sonny answered significantly, and they all laughed.

"Well, guess I'll go step on a few toes," Doc Lester cracked, taking a farewell shot from Bill's newly opened bottle and putting on his hat. "Don't lose your marbles before the new ones roll in," he quipped, and ducked out of the shack into the alley.

"Wanna shoot some odds-n-evens? Eight ball? Lucky sevens?" Marvin's younger brother Little Sonny asked apathetically. They had obviously just finished a game.

"No, just a few more tugs and I gotta go," Bill said.

He wiped his face with the back of his hand and grimaced. The cheap bourbon ate through his innards. "This sure is tough juice," he added. "Turpentine?"

Sonny became mock-serious. "Well, if you had more'n ten cents to spend on a bottle you might have a right to complain."

Bill nodded morosely. "Yeah, that's the truth. 'Fi don't get somethin soon . . ." he trailed off. "Just like old times, huh, Sonny?"

They all laughed.

Billy Howells who worked the tow truck rose to go.

"Sit down," Marvin ordered facetiously. "You can't escape us that easy."

"Aww, shit," Billy lisped. "Won't you guys *ever* let me go? What are you gonna do to me? Fuck me up the ass?"

This coarse attempt at humor was greeted by guffaws.

A few moments of silence then intervened.

"Wanna go out to the lake and shoot duck? It's Sunday, ain't it?"

"Now *there's* an idea!" Marvin shouted. "I ain't been duck huntin since last fall. Let's go, man. We'll go in the damn tow truck! I can borrow my cousin's gun, I know for sure, if I give im a duck when we get back. Let's go!"

They all felt convinced that was what they were going to do. Even Sonny seemed to consider locking up his place although Sunday was his busiest day.

In the end, however, Sonny decided not to go, and although the idea definitely appealed to Bill he knew he couldn't get out of driving Marge and Martin to the farm. He mumbled something about maybe seeing them out at the lake later, and Billy Howells and the Staples brothers departed.

Sonny and Bill continued drinking in silence.

The flies buzzed and capered in slats of dusty sunlight.

They drank some more, then Bill paid Sonny and pocketed the

bottle. His eyes squinted painfully in the sunlight as he left the inky shack. He hopped back down the alley to the square.

Marge was drumming impatiently on the steering wheel with her fingernails when Bill finally reappeared, tossing his bottle into the back seat and playfull, elbowing Marge in the ribs. He started the car. Martin sat in back eating graham crackers that Marge had bought as a treat for him.

They left town heading north on Route 41, riding slowly in the opposite direction from which they had come, since the Kilbanky farm lay north of Winosha and Bill and Marge's house roughly southwest. The wind was clocked at the WRRL-AM Weather Tower as eight to ten miles per hour out of the northwest. Temperature mid-50's. The forecast was partly sunny with possible brief showers, turning colder toward evening. Marge finally paid attention to the radio when an advertisement pushing a special lawnmower for use on the new carefree plastic lawns got scatological. Barely touching on the two-seater's handling ability and blade selection, the announcer almost immediately began a long involved paean to the glories of the mower's custom foam-covered seat which became so filthy Marge was shocked into changing stations.

"I'm surprised they allow that kind of stuff on the airwaves," she said. They listened instead to WDDV out of Virdon broadcasting faultless caterpillar music. Marge turned it up. When this sort of tape-loop background music was loud enough, and if she accompanied listening to it by smoking many cigarettes and sipping coffee, it gave her a kind of oblivious buzz capable of drowning out whole sections of a humdrum afternoon.

Listened to while riding in a car, however, its potency was reduced to simply coating the over-familiar streets and houses with a half-inch layer of cozy aural wax. . . .

They rolled past the familiar sights, passing last of all the Town House Inn at the north edge of town. The Town House Inn was Winosha's only class eating establishment—too expensive as a rule for the likes of Marge and Bill—serving glazed duck and beef stroganoff to guests first dazed by drinks in the Trophy Room. Jim Ross, "The Smiling Scotsman," ran the Town House Inn strictly for the moneyed members of his own advanced generation. Nothing more recent than "Because" sung by Deanna Durbin was allowed on the jukebox, and this fact combined with the prices meant that only plaid-shirted elders sporting manicured nails were truly at home there. One left one's rod and reel at the door. Bill and Marge had eaten there once or twice, Martin never.

The modest low hill country's cream and grey formations now began to roll by. "Howard E. Braniff for District School Supervisor" election posters were stapled to the telephone poles along the road-side. Large groups of dairy cows became visible at almost every turn.

Suddenly Bill veered left on two wheels off 41, laughing thickly at Marge's squeals. The car headed rapidly up by-pass 41—known lo-cally as "old Route 41" and even more locally as "the Clipsie-ville highroad," since long ago it had been the horse track to Clip-sieville.

As they drove into the Kilbanky property Martin peered intently at the house he knew so well and sensed his mother's head at the win-dow, behind milky gauze curtains in the front room. Nervously he picked at his ear: it must be at least 3:30 by now, but the cement truck was nowhere in sight. . . .

Mrs. Kilbanky was a short squat sharp little woman who had worked on a farm in perfect health and contentment every day of her life until two catastrophic events took place within three weeks of each other—her crippling attacks of arthritis (which was what she called it, having no idea what else to call it) and the sudden tragic passing away of her husband, old Ike Kilbanky. Ike's was the rough and simple heart she had come to love and know well, and she suffered badly. Although she was only in her sixties it seemed her hearing began to go. For the first time in her life she found herself not wanting to get out of bed in the morning, suffering bouts of melancholy. She felt old and weary. Ike's unexpected death nearly broke her heart.

Also, the decision she had had to make concerning who would run the farm as Ike lay dying had been a difficult one. To protect herself she was forced to cut off her daughter Chartruse without a penny and place the survival of the farm in Martin's hands. Almost his first official act as head of the Kilbanky household had been to order five tons of cement to be delivered at once, and the reckless self-assurance with which he initiated this scheme frightened and disoriented Mrs. Kilbanky even further. She didn't like the look of things. But for the first time in her life, really, she didn't know who to turn to for help. Her heart beat rapidly in such uncertain times.

Which was the real shame of it all, because—what a lively, wonderful woman Louise Kilbanky was underneath all her troubles!

3

The Bottom of the Barrel

Even before meeting them, Louise Kilbanky took an instant dislike to Bill and Marge Parsons. Seeing them all drive up to the house was enough. Something in Bill's manner of driving and Marge's manner of sitting annoyed her, and the sight of her son munching graham crackers in the back seat of a strange automobile upset her. Who were these people? What did they want with the Kilbankys? She had no way of knowing that Martin himself had sought these two out and brought them with him.

She peered through the curtains as the car came to a halt. She saw a bleary, devious-looking fellow emerge from behind the wheel and her lips tightened. She saw a frizzy-haired woman and her eyes narrowed. Her knees chattered against each other as she stood up and made her way to the front door. The house shook slightly in occasional gusts of wind.

"Care for some beanies with bark tea?" she asked, smiling guardedly, for nothing would make her forget the amenities. Marge answered politely for all of them saying yes they would, Martin was grinning from ear to ear, but Bill merely mumbled or even croaked, and moved off to the side sitting down heavily on the porch steps.

"Mom! Mom!" Martin called out dizzily, "This is Marge and Bill Parsons, they live over in the Crestview Developments, you know? Bill's the same Bill I went to school with, remember? He came by here a few times?"

Martin seemed eager to establish this previous connection between them, so out of respect for her son Louise Kilbanky turned toward Bill and remarked politely that yes she did remember him, when in fact she was sure she didn't.

"Of course I remember Bill," she said graciously.

"And this is Marge!" Martin was becoming more excited.

"Hello, my dear."

"I'm *so, so* glad to meet you, Mrs. Kilbanky," Marge simpered sweetly. "Martin's told me so much about you," she lied.

Mrs. Kilbanky laughed. "I'm sure he *hasn't* done that: but come inside and we'll have some tea and some nice fresh beanies. I might even have a slice of cobbler left somewhere."

They mounted the porch steps and walked inside, Bill and Marge last of all. As they were walking up Marge discreetly pumped Bill in the ribs, signaling him to shape up. She was furious that he couldn't control himself and had to go get half-looped and rubber-headed, especially on a day as important as today. Marge exchanged a burning glance with Bill, mutely threatening him with her personal retaliation if he didn't sober up and try to act common-denominator-neighborly. Bill, who was in a syrupy half-stupor at the time, and who openly viewed the Kilbankys as a joke, caught Marge's imperious stare like a clap of cold water on his face. He shook himself together temporarily. But Mrs. Kilbanky, who in her place as hostess was still angled half-in and half-out the front door, saw the woman poke the man and signal him dramatically with her eyes! This conspiratorial behavior sent chills up the old lady's spine.

The four sat down to tea in the kitchen. Or rather Marge and Martin sat, while Mrs. Kilbanky boiled water on the vintage Swedish porcelain wood-burning stove and Bill paced around the roomy ground floor of the big fine old farmhouse. It was a simple, sturdy old house, built some time during the last century by a sea captain beached in his old age on this distant inland incline. The original structure had been altered and expanded by each succeeding generation.

Some of the rooms were said to date back to 1847, though Louise Kilbanky doubted that was true.

But the planking on the floors was rich and fine and wide, the checkerboard windowpanes glittered in the sun, the pump in the kitchen looked out over the pond, the cows and horses swam across the fields and God's merry homespun arms leaned powerfully down to cradle it all.

Bill was impressed. The place was a little seedy, probably from not being worked every day as a farm needs to be worked or soon it isn't a farm anymore, but the house's two stories made Bill feel moderately baronial, an emotion he hadn't experienced, he realized now, in months! Moodily he paced around the ground floor, through the parlor and the dining room, into the pantries and tool room, the kitchen and the greenhouse. He became oblivious for the time being of what went on around him and wandered, completely wrapped up in himself in thought. This was such an unparalleled thing for him to do that Marge stopped her small talk in shock, then resumed it smoothly, vexed to the hilt that Bill was acting so unsocial and at the same time flabbergasted by the way he was going about it.

Mrs. Kilbanky didn't miss a beat of all this, she was sure. Covertly she kept tabs out of the corner of her eye as she made the tea. This man just was not acting right. She decided he might even be a thief.

Bill was pacing around wondering how he ever was going to feel on top of things again. Until recently life had been partly bearable, not working and enjoying two tough women simultaneously. Now suddenly he was behind an eight ball. He realized for the first time in his life that neither woman really trusted him, *really and truly* loved him—or something like that . . . He couldn't figure it out. . . .

Also, he was absolutely and definitively broke: he had no money whatsoever and since Marge had stopped working their funds dried up while their tempers flared, which gave Bill a headache. Primarily his attitude toward all this, his reaction to it, was one of resentment. Deep resentment. Why did *he* have to get caught like this? Why should *he* be singled out? Why couldn't he just do what he wanted to do, even if that were nothing?

But Bill also was pacing up and down because he felt uneasy with the Kilbankys. He kept thinking of going duck hunting. Images of reeds and cold lake water, red flannel shirts and high rubber boots, game bags and flasks of good rye or bourbon, ham sandwiches in the hamper and explosions in the sky, brightly-colored ducks falling to the water, the golden retriever's flash of gold as he retrieves . . . Bill reached convulsively around his person until he found his cigarettes . . . He lit one as he walked, and when he found himself in the greenhouse again his thoughts finally turned to Fontessa, and there among the heady hothouse foliage he sank back and beat his lonesome meat.

Meanwhile Marge was chuckling to herself in the kitchen. She had worked like blazes to get Mrs. Kilbanky loosened up and finally the old lady was responding as Marge talked woman talk, anecdotes learned under the hair dryer, innocuous gossip about people Louise Kilbanky seldom saw, recipes for fudge cake, how to can your favorite vegetables . . . Marge had to strain her talent to the limit in an effort to remember recipes used maybe once six years ago, or anecdotes she felt would be proper for the old lady and yet spicy enough to hold her attention.

The three sipped their tea and smiled.

Martin, totally in his own world as he sat at the table, could have been a mile away as he laughed to himself about hair-dryers, the way they stood up on legs like music stands or even people.

Bill suddenly entered the kitchen. Feeling purged and clear-headed he glanced apologetically at Marge and sat down with every intention of taking part in the conversation.

"Would you like some tea, honey?" Marge asked evenly.

"Sure . . . Sure is a fine house you got here," he added, turning abruptly to Mrs. Kilbanky with a brusque encompassing sweep of his arm.

She was startled slightly, and moved back.

"Wh-why thank you!" she answered. "We try our best to keep it going—that is, my husband, uh, we—" she couldn't finish.

"Oh. I know," Bill said. "I heard about that and I'm extremely sorry. Uh, it must be a whole lot of work, this place, uh—"

Marge kicked him under the table and he subsided, staring glumly into his cup of tea. They all drank or sat for a moment in silence.

A low rumble was heard in the distance. It was replaced by a coagulated roar and groan that grew louder and louder. The cups and plates on the shelves began to shake. Martin jumped in his seat as if he'd been shot—the cement truck was here at last!

Martin leaped up from the table with a shout and ran outside. There he saw not one but three cement trucks (cement mixers) straining up the final slope before the house.

Three trucks!

He hopped up and down in the yard in his excitement, tearing away at his windbreaker. The trucks pulled into the farmyard one by one, and the picture these immense noisy monsters made falling into line and rumbling straight toward Martin was more than he could bear. It was sensational, sheer intoxication! He could barely contain himself, and in fact he might not have contained himself if he hadn't noticed the expression on the face of the first truck's driver. The scowling unshaven face—the large fleshy head wrapped in a red bandana—meant business.

Martin's throat contracted in sadness as he struggled to understand this man's obvious ill humor . . . What's *wrong* with people anyway? he wondered . . . Why are they always so stiff? We could have so much fun with these beautiful red trucks. We could pour cement together day and night! . . .

The trucks came to a halt in tight formation.

Three drivers jumped down from their cabs.

Martin felt panicky. The front door opened and Marge, Bill and his mother all stood on the porch in hesitation. Martin couldn't stand the fact that they were behind him, looking on and obviously feeling sheepish and embarrassed for him. It made his blood boil.

"Get back inside!" he shouted, and they all flinched back a step. "This is my operation, this is my operation! Back inside!" Martin was so jumpy now that he forgot he had invited Marge and Bill out to watch him build his house in the first place. At that time he had even hopefully looked forward to them taking part in it with him, helping him build, but now their presence unnerved him completely.

"Go away!" he shrieked, and they popped back in and shut the door.

The drivers stood in the yard. They each wore overalls, grimy shirts rolled to their biceps and red bandanas around their necks. They each needed a shave. And they each were glowering: they had been called away from their one free day a week, forced off their Sunday afternoon beer sofas to load up cement for a lunatic! They cursed their Jewish bosses and vowed to finish the job as quickly as possible.

The first driver spoke. "Arg, arg, arg!" he barked. He was so heated up the order form shook uncontrollably in his hand. Finally he waved it in Martin's face.

"What the hell is this, anyway," he roared.

Martin fought back intense insecurity and nausea that threatened to wash him under and said in a contorted but somehow forceful voice: "I order that cement. You deliver it. I pay for it."

The drivers looked at each other.

"Take it over there!" Martin ordered, pointing around behind the house in the vicinity of the pond.

"Let's go, let's go! It's late! Where were you guys, it must be 4:30 already! Move it over there! Where were you guys? No, no—out *there*! Come on, let's go! Let er go, let er go!"

Martin hounded them back into their cabs.

He yelped as they started their motors and ran ahead of their deafening noise to the pond.

"Move it over here! Let's go! Let's go!" Martin barked like a sheep dog until the trucks had navigated the vegetable garden and stood grumbling in neutral, their cement mixers like three huge metal barrels against the darkening sky.

A chill wind sprang up and suddenly Martin felt cold. He felt the butterflies beating their wings in his stomach and prayed he wouldn't lose his nerve. The entire operation including materials, truck fees and drivers' overtime was very costly. He had refused to divulge to his mother exactly how much money was involved for fear she might somehow abort the proceedings. He told her instead he had negotiated a discount. The fact that three trucks showed up instead of just one upset him further.

Mrs. Kilbanky had meant to check up on her son during her next visit to town, but that visit had not as yet taken place. When she forced herself to think about it (which she preferred not to do) she somehow arrived at a figure below one thousand dollars—that is, her grasp of the situation combined with Martin's sketchy information led her to believe a sum not higher than eight or nine hundred dollars was involved. Sooner or later, Martin knew, she would be in for quite a surprise: the substantial amount he spent was actual savings-account currency and could never be replaced.

Martin ran back to the house for a sweater. He was shivering uncontrollably now, and Bill and Marge both wished they had never answered their doorbell that morning. As they watched him feverishly poke his arms through a lumpy red sweater they felt intensely embarrassed, and their only thought was given over to how at this point they could possibly get away with making a run for their car and leaving the scene immediately. They started for the door but Martin, who assumed they meant to oversee his actions again, turned and ferociously ordered them both to be seated. With tears in her eyes Marge obeyed. Bill looked up and stared at the ceiling. Mrs. Kilbanky was nowhere to be seen, probably upstairs "resting."

The sun behind late afternoon cumulus offered little warmth as the men worked at positioning their machines. It seemed more like March than April, in fact. A stiff wind was blowing now and when the sun did reappear it lit husky bodies tugging on stiff metal toggles, steam puffing from cold faces, and wintry steel-grey ripples on the surface of the pond. The men beat their gloveless hands together and cursed. All three trucks vibrated heavily, emitting a loud unearthly whine. The first driver separated himself from the knot of men and approached Martin, who stood by the pond wrapped in thought.

Martin was deliberating his next move desperately. What kind of house was he going to build? What was it that he wanted? His idea— his inspiration—had been to postpone all preparation or plans until the cement actually arrived, at which time the presence of the cement and the pressure of the situation, he had reasoned, would force him to unparalleled architectural heights. Now that it was all happening, and there were three trucks instead of one, and these horrible men were menacing him, and Marge and Bill acting grotesquely embarrassed, and the wind was so cold—Martin's brain froze. He didn't know what to do. What was he going to do? OK, OK, he couldn't stand it! OK, OK!

He leaped to his feet as the driver approached and bawling "Ahhhhh . . ." ran off into the field. The driver stopped in his tracks, his immense stubbly jaw open wide in disbelief. The other two drivers opened their jaws as well. It was apparent they took their cues from the first man. With their identical trucks, their stubbly chins and red bandanas, they seemed to be carbon copies of the first. But even carbon copies had never witnessed someone like Martin before. The three men stood riveted in stupefaction. Several blackbirds approached, landed on their chins and hands and pecked at the laces of their boots, and like statues the men were not aware of this. All that moved were their eyes as they watched Martin stumble back and forth across the fields, yowling hysterically to himself.

Soon came the moment of truth, however. Martin knew the afternoon was almost over. He shuddered to think what might occur if for any reason the cement went undelivered. Mr. Schwartz at the hardware store had explained to him the cement could not be returned once it was mixed; on top of that, no refunds were permitted for any reason on any materials bought at a discount. And Martin, as he understood it, had realized substantial savings by purchasing the entire batch of cement at a discount. So he was stuck. He *had* to act now!

He strode firmly across the fields. As he approached the trucks he saw the three men sitting in their cabs. The motors of the trucks were running and the lights were on. Little drops and pieces of cement shook loose from the mixers and scattered on the ground, making tiny piles and smears, plicking here and there on Martin's pants.

He gesticulated and the men climbed down from their cabs. The motors were still running so they all had to shout to be heard.

"Let's go!" Martin bellowed.

The men snickered among themselves.

"C'mon!"

They looked at him facetiously and the first man even gave him a mock salute, but then one of them climbed into all the trucks and turned the engines off. They were plunged into silence. The wind blew fairly steadily now, and small branches and twigs were becoming disconnected. Somewhere in the distance a German shepherd barked. Martin could see the little splashes of cement harden on the ground at his feet. The time had come.

"Listen, you guys," he said matter-of-factly. "I know you think this is an insane operation, but it isn't. Take my word for it. I'm doing something here that will be remembered and talked about and visited years after you guys are dead and buried and forgotten. I'm building purely—get it?"

"Get it?" he repeated, looking them in the eyes.

His stance and manner and complexion were cool. He seemed confident and in control. The three drivers were still convinced he was a lunatic but on the other hand they were all perfectly aware of what would happen to them if they returned to Winosha Falls with the cement undelivered—that is, if as a result of any act on their part Mr. Schwartz did not receive his money. They shuddered in their boots at the prospect of being blackballed from the Mixers-Drivers Union, of going hungry, of losing their self-respect. Deep down these coarse bruisers knew fear. They would do whatever Martin asked.

The wind stiffened, blowing loose the droplets of hardened cement from Martin's pants. Assuming an air of control he pulled a slip of paper from his pocket and barked directions to the men while looking down at it, as if the paper contained a hastily-scribbled plan of operation.

"I want each truck at the corner of an equilateral triangle whose base runs parallel to the east shore of the pond and stands forty-five feet from it," he announced authoritatively. Since none of the men understood he repeated these instructions, scampering around the flat land east of the pond, driving stakes in the ground at three equidistant points and clearing the site of any debris or memorabilia. He seemed like a lunatic indeed at that moment, since the steadily failing light forced him to rush frantically from point to point of the triangle, at the same time carrying and dropping and retrieving an assortment of objects including a broken umbrella, shredded newspapers, half-eaten toys, a metal stool, a plastic telephone, bottles, caps and wires. Mrs. Kilbanky, who had awakened from her nap upstairs, came to the window in time to see her son skittering erratically around the yard while three strangers stood by and mocked. She couldn't bear it. Raising the window she wailed his name in the gathering darkness.

"Martin! Martin!" She sobbed bitterly and beat her fist against the sill.

Martin looked up. "Stop that, mother!" he shouted. "There's no time for crying. I need your help. I can't hold on to this trash!"

"What?"

"I said I can't hold on to this trash, it's too cold! Bring me my gloves!"

The men interrupted noisily, clamoring that they were freezing as well. It was getting too cold for their hands to grip the toggles and prongs. The ratchets might stick, the quadrants become twisted. The crank disc might slip! The guide plates and control rods had to be operated manually and the drivers could not be held responsible, they said, unless they were furnished with gloves.

"Mother!"

Her keen head reappeared in the window.

"Go up to the attic and get more gloves! Do we have any extra blankets? Bring down blankets and gloves for the men!"

The kitchen door opened cautiously and Martin saw Bill's face behind the screen.

"Come on out!" he shouted. "I need your help."

The door banged shut.

Dropping the garbage he had collected Martin ran into the kitchen and discovered Bill and Marge hiding under the kitchen table. He implored them to come to his aid and after much coaxing Marge joined him at the site although Bill would come no closer than the back porch. He knew the drivers personally, he claimed, and so he refused to get involved.

But whenever Marge was roped into something she gave it all she had. She would do whatever Martin wanted, though she fought off deep crevices of vertigo whenever she drew back from the situation and realized the hopeless unreality of what was going on. It scared her like nothing else had scared a woman ever before.

Mrs. Kilbanky came to the door with blankets and gloves.

She stepped proudly into the freezing gloom and distributed blankets and gloves to the participants. The men liked the gloves, while Marge preferred a blanket. She stood huddled mournfully with Mrs. Kilbanky as the trucks roared to life, three sets of headlights pierced and sliced through the property, and Martin skipped like an inspired sculptor among the moving hulks.

Each truck pulled up backwards at the stakes driven in the ground so that their enormous mixers pointed to a spot in the exact center of the triangle, where Martin now stood. He held a flashlight in his hand. "When I raise and lower it three times, open your mixers at quarter-speed and start pouring!" he shrieked.

None of the drivers heard him above the roar of their engines. Martin waved the light up and down. Nothing happened. He jumped up and down on the spot. One of the men finally released his toggle, the noise increased as the mixer strained to life, and wet cement spurted onto the ground. Martin yelled that he wanted them all to pour in unison—and also that the first truck was pouring too quickly —but none of the men could hear him. With two shovels he had stashed for the operation he began slapping the cement from the first truck toward the center of the triangle, meanwhile imploring the men to pour in unison at quarter-speed.

He begged Marge to take a shovel and, pondering for a second, then instructed her to try and steer the rapidly expanding pool of cement toward the center of the triangle. Feverishly he explained that he would do the same with his shovel for the cement from the second truck. The third would be allowed to spill freely. If he was successful, he shouted above the groaning engines, Marge's cement would harden into a grand embankment that would meet his own embankment at the exact center of the triangle, flaring out in the direction of the third truck. The undirected cement from the third truck would then collect in a pool until it accumulated above the level of their two hardened embankments, whereupon it would wash over the edges and form a vast esplanade. If Marge and Martin could join their two embankments successfully, they would ascend to a point approximately fifteen feet above the ground, forming three sides of a pyramid. The fourth side, or face, of the pyramid would be left open to receive the cement pouring from the third truck in such a way as to form—not the fourth face of a pyramid—but (Martin concluded masterfully) a gently sloping esplanade that would spill gracefully down past where the truck now stood to the pond itself! At the rear of the pyramid would be a cave-like opening and a chute made from two-by-fours that would rise up inside the pyramid to its acme. From the top of the pyramid one could rest facing the pond, or one would be free to roll or tumble smoothly down to the water. It would be great for swimming and playing in the summer!

Marge thought she was going to pass out. Black spots and rich red globules formed inside her eyes. She couldn't believe what she was hearing. She knew there was no chance for this preposterous operation to succeed. With tears in her eyes she realized that in addition to everything else Martin had not even given the drivers clear instructions. Cement was pouring steadily onto the ground from the third truck now, while the other two stood rumbling in neutral. The last straw was that as far as Marge could see the lay of the land was all wrong for such an operation. At first glance it looked like flat land, but when you examined it closely the ground broke into a series of gullies and sandy pits tucked between at least a half dozen small conflicting inclines. Some sloped off toward the pond, but others went in different directions, and often they intersected with each other forming crazy echoing indentations and reverse trenches. A lumpy shoulder of basalt was working itself free in one corner of the plot, as well. Marge couldn't stand it. Her head spun around and she felt she was going to throw up.

However, Martin pulled and shoved and entreated her until she took her station, shovel in hand, at a point mid-way between "her" truck and the center of the triangle. Martin waved at the first truck to stop pouring cement, which it did not do. He then ran' to the other two drivers, shouting details of the overall plan and their individual instructions up at the cabs. The drivers nodded and opened the gates of their mixers. Over the noise neither had heard what Martin said and neither cared. It was getting colder and darker by the minute and all they could think of was emptying their loads and going home. They opened their mixers at full speed and looked on. They refused to slow down their mixers, no matter what Martin said.

The cement from their two trucks soon spurted together and formed a huge pool that dwarfed the pool previously released from the third truck at a slower speed. Martin succeeded temporarily in getting the third driver to stop pouring cement so that he and Marge were left free to deal with their own respective trucks. Rapidly they began trying to press the hardening waves of wet cement into steep inclining walls for the pyramid. The pool of cement was too fast for them, however, and rose above their shoetops as they worked. In desperation Martin abandoned his plan for an interior tunnel and used the two-by-fours to try and contain the expanding cement. Bill condescended to bring him hammer and nails and Martin feverishly constructed a retaining wall out of the remaining lumber he had set aside previously for the tunnel. He dammed the flow of cement at a forty-five degree angle, then built a smaller wall out of his two remaining boards for Marge's side. The result was that although most of the cement from the two trucks spread freely over the pock-marked site and hardened into an uneven pool eight to twelve inches thick over an area extending in some directions twenty or twenty-five yards, a substantial amount was nevertheless dammed up by the makeshift walls to harden into two very irregular embankments. Neither embankment was over four feet tall or extended more than five or six yards, and also neither met and joined the other as had been planned. In fact, at no point did they come closer to each other than ten or fifteen feet. As these two shattered fences of concrete took shape and Martin saw the remainder of the cement harden into an aimless lava flow that reached the pond, he realized that he had failed.

Miserably depressed, not caring anymore, he slumped to the ground and with the last ounce of strength in his arm waved the third truck to release its load. In freezing near-darkness Martin, Marge, Bill and Mrs. Kilbanky watched as the driver worked his toggles and the wet grey mass appeared. The cold was quite intense now, and as the cement sluggishly appeared and grew behind the truck, Bill and Mrs. Kilbanky retreated to the kitchen while Marge stood, teeth chattering, her arm on Martin's shoulder.

As they looked on, the truck shuddered and the mixer groaned like a tortured mastodon. The cement, which emerged from its gate in a thick uninterrupted flow like taffy, slowed and slowed until it hardly moved at all, while the engine raged furiously and the driver panicked and climbed back into his cab. He tugged and pulled at the switches but it was too late. The cement had accumulated behind the truck, dammed up by Martin's embankments, and had hardened vertically until an unbroken mass of cement reached from the ground to the truck like a cascade of frozen diarrhoea. With a sudden clunk the mixer shut off and slipped toward the back of the truck chassis into the hardening mass below, tilting the truck onto its rear wheels. The front of the truck was raised completely off the ground. The truck froze into place like that, as the agitated drivers pounded and hammered with shovels and axes to no avail. The entire fore part of the truck was in the air: cab, front wheels and hooded engine. The headlights shot up into the trees. The headlights shot up into the night.

The drivers shouted and cursed but no one knew what to do. Eventually they climbed into the two remaining trucks and drove off.

4

P. S.

Martin decided in a tearful scene later that night that he was incapable of running a farm—witness the debacle of the unrefundable cement—and that if the Kilbanky farm were to survive, someone else would have to oversee its activities.

In a climactic scene in the kitchen Martin begged his mother to allow him to hand over the administration of the farm to his old friend Bill. Martin cried that all he wanted to do was build his house, and if he could not do that he would not do anything. Claiming he had a plan whereby the five tons of cement in the yard might be salvaged, he refused responsibility for the normal maintenance of the farm, declaring those activities were too much for him. Bill, on the other hand, with Marge's help, possessed sufficient ability to make the farm work again. Finally, Martin declared, he himself would retain sole financial responsibility. He promised he would not relinquish control of the family's remaining bank money. He would not allow Bill direct access to the Kilbanky accounts. These would remain in Martin's hands.

Louise Kilbanky had dreaded something like this from the moment she saw them drive up that afternoon. Now, six hours later, spattered with cement, hungry and frightened and cold, shocked by the day's events, she had to fight with every ounce of her strength merely to retain her self-possession. Visions of handles flying off doors accosted her sight. Her heart beat like a rabbit's. What was she to do?

Here were these strangers who, she was sure, were responsible in some horrible underhanded way for Martin's offer to relinquish control of the farm. Yet Martin himself was on the verge of collapse or worse. The last six hours had been traumatic for him. In addition, he obviously considered Marge and Bill to be his friends—if she refused outright, or blurted out her worst suspicions about Marge and Bill while they were there, how would Martin react? Would she be forcing him to take sides? If so, would he take their side? Would he go against his own mother?

She couldn't stand the pressure of the situation, and claiming to be weak and faint begged to put off a decision until the morning.

Martin exploded, saying he was the boss and Bill would move in that very night!

Mrs. Kilbanky began crying horridly, and it was at that point that Marge tactfully intervened. Using diplomacy she first suggested to Martin that she and Bill had their own lives to lead, they couldn't simply drop everything and come running. Secondly, negating in a way her first point, she asked Martin to understand how his mother must feel: she had lived on this farm most of her life proudly and independently, and so naturally she was upset and suspicious at the thought of someone else taking charge of things . . . Marge smiled at Mrs. Kilbanky.

"Martin's so impatient, ain't he?" she said softly to the older woman, as if in commiseration. "We ladies have to slow these crazy menfolk down a bit, ain't that the truth?" she drawled.

Bill looked on nervously. The events of the day had taken their toll on him as well as the others. He was shocked by Martin's proposition, and even more shocked by Marge's obvious interest in it. He saw it was Marge's way of resolving their financial difficulties: she probably didn't care in the least whether he was actually capable of running a farm or not. Martin volunteered the idea out of nowhere and now she was all for it! Bill had worked on farms at random times during his life as had nearly everyone around Winosha, but that was just picking corn, cleaning out stables or working the thresher at harvest time. He knew how to drive a tractor but that didn't mean he could administer an entire operation! He was only vaguely aware of what kind of farm Ike Kilbanky had run in the first place. Was it crops mostly, or crops plus cattle? Was it a dairy farm? How many chickens were there? Were eggs important? Bill was certain it wasn't a dairy farm, but beyond that he knew nothing. He didn't *want* to know, either. . . .

His mind raced on and on. He realized resentfully that he was being railroaded. Farming was hard work—backbreaking work—that paid little and made you old before your time. Spring planting was the toughest work of all, and that should have started a week ago. He knew what Marge had in mind, of course—they'd move in but no one would have to work very hard, they'd worm money out of Martin one way or another and maybe milk a few cows, or sell off some chickens. Plant a few rows of corn and beans. Lettuce and squash and watermelon.

But her plan hinged entirely on Mrs. Kilbanky relinquishing her power—even Bill could see that . . . And what guarantee was there the old lady would do that? What was to keep Mrs. Kilbanky from causing trouble? She was a well-known, well-respected member of the community: two or three words to the right people and Bill might even wake up behind bars! He would bear the responsibility for any heinous swindle that saw the light of day, not Marge! Suddenly the thought occurred to him that this was all a trick to get him put away in jail. It was an act of revenge on Marge's part for the heartaches she had suffered due to Bill fooling around with Fontessa. Bill slapped his forehead: "You're tryin to frame me!" he shouted, and the other three stopped arguing and crying and looked up.

"This is a frame-up! Fuck you! I'm going home!"

He ran out of the kitchen into the night. Soon the car engine roared to life and Marge realized Bill was so steamed up he was going to leave without her. She jumped to her feet, grabbed her pocketbook, and before she whizzed out the door she whispered to Martin, looking him fondly in the eyes, "We'll clear this up tomorrow. I'll call you on the phone." Martin's head jammed with the smell of her perfume.

Shortly after that Martin went up to bed. He left his mother in the kitchen all alone.

Mrs. Kilbanky ate one last beanie and sadly went up to bed.

PART TWO

The Way Things Work

5

Down on Tanner's Farm

Martin Kilbanky awoke the next morning and stared at the ceiling for thirty seconds. He rubbed and stroked himself delightedly. Then he jumped out of bed and ran to the open window. Fresh morning sun and chirping sparrows, robins and flickers lit the air. Enthusiastically he opened his chest of drawers and took out the aromatic lilac sachets from each drawer. Transported by their smell and humming to himself in a superior mood he placed the sachets on the window sill. Soon four or five small birds fluttered near the exquisite packages. Martin pounced on one of the birds, a young robin, catching it by its tail feathers, and as it trembled and pee-peed in his hands he carried it into the bathroom and wrapped it in toilet paper. He splashed cold water on his face and brushed his teeth. Then he returned to his bedroom and dressed.

Martin felt elated that morning. The debacle of the night before never crossed his mind. Selecting a bright orange V-neck sweater and newly-ironed Levi's he vigorously inhaled the fresh April air circulating in the room. At the exact moment the robin worked itself free from its bundle of soggy toilet paper Martin reappeared in the bathroom. He caught the bird again and, whistling happily to himself, tapped on his mother's door.

"Look, mama—a bird!" he announced, as the sleepy woman brushed past him in her morning robe. Mrs. Kilbanky was preoccupied with the previous day's events and hardly took notice of her son. Then her toothbrush fell to the carpet.

"Release the poor robin immediately!" she sang out. "Just think how *she* must feel!"

Martin, his elation fading, tripped downstairs and opened the front door. He tossed the bird into the air. Watching the grey and red speck grow smaller he vowed to himself to remain cheerful. He would remain dressed today. He would not take off his clothes and roll on the ground. He was hungry. He inhaled sharply. The fresh spring air cut into his nostrils, enlivening them. They quivered in the sun. Martin felt like a man today. "Time for me to grow up," he said to himself. "Quit fooling around. I'm no baby anymore. I have immense responsibilities."

He sucked in a mighty breath, squared his shoulders, stiffened his back and marched into the house.

When he saw his mother boiling water for tea in the kitchen it finally came back to him: he remembered the painful scene of the night before. He remembered his offer to Bill, and that Marge had said she would telephone him in the morning. He looked at the wall phone. It wasn't ringing. Martin felt a pang of uneasiness.

"Is the telephone ringing?" he asked, his voice quavering.

Narrowing her lips his mother replied negatively.

Martin promptly dropped the subject.

"I'm starving, mother!" he complained. "Do we have any jelly doughnuts?" He pounced on the remaining jelly doughnut even though it was totally stale. As he munched it and sipped his tea Mrs. Kilbanky made a large breakfast: large fried eggs, a large glass of frozen orange juice and finally, one after another, homemade buttermilk pancakes smothered in butter and imitation maple syrup. Finally she appeared in the pantry door with an immense ball of red and white fat.

"Still hungry?"

"You bet!"

The mother smiled fondly at the boy. She unwound from the ball a strip at least four feet long which she draped along the stove and over the top of the refrigerator. She cut eight-inch sections from the strip and fried them on the griddle of the old Swedish stove. She placed the greasy, shriveled strips on the table under Martin's saucer-shaped eyes, and as fast as she put them there they disappeared. She replaced the ball in the pantry.

It was nine-thirty in the morning, which was late for farm people to be eating breakfast. They were farm people, and farm people usually were up at dawn. But since the husband and the father had died the mother and the son lingered in bed a little longer each day, until by April 20th the climactic exertions of the day before kept them hammered between the sheets until well past eight-thirty.

The day's farm chores stretched before them.

Stuffing a final strip into his mouth Martin took six pails and went out to milk the cows, of which there were six. It was the one farm chore he positively looked forward to every day. He loved to milk the cows and consequently fell into such a smoothly-oiled reverie while milking them that he saw, heard and thought absolutely nothing. It was like a dream. He knew each of the cows intimately, each had her own idiosyncrasies and personal character that Martin had grown over the years to respond to automatically. Chucking one playfully behind the ear he would turn to the next with a stern kick in the rump. To a third he whispered sweetly his mother's maiden name.

In each case the cows gave their milk freely and calmly, chewing on bundles of shredded hay and processed agricultural wrappers —papers and oats and corn, slices of cloth and green peppers. They were Class AA Cloth Herefords, a breed most dairymen would be proud to own, though some said Cloth Herefords were susceptible to blockage. These cows, however, were not blocked.

Martin loved them and understood them, as much as they loved and understood him. To him their chocolate brown markings afloat on a creamy white sea of hide spelled heaven. He sailed with them in the sky every day.

He slung the pails brimming with fresh milk two at a time on a sapling and carried them into the house. His peaches glowed from the exertion.

Martin looked around him: what else needed to be done? He knew the hogs had to be slopped, the chickens fed, the eggs collected. Most of all of course the complicated task of spring planting lay ahead, and Martin grimaced at the thought. He had always hated the endless days filled with drudgery, first straining on his knees and then seated on a tractor. He had always given his father much difficulty at this time of year in the past, and now that his father was dead the impetus was gone. Deliberately he put out of his mind the hulking bags of seed and fertilizer that were stacked row upon row in the barn. Bill would take care of that.

He walked into the barn, however, and continued walking until he had emerged behind it and faced a long, squat apartment building made out of tarpaper and riddled with a series of tiny air holes where beaks flashed and from time to time a feather popped out, small and white. An unholy smell radiated from the apartments and turned Martin's stomach. Cackling and squawking, too. Martin was not enamored of a certain unnamed quality of life that permeated the entire chicken and egg evolution. The hens seemed like fractious robots, surrendering with petulance their oval treasures. Martin just wasn't in tune with them, but his mother was getting too old for all the stooping over involved, and cleaning out racks covered with chickenshit in a fog of feathers was no longer an appropriate task for her either. The chickens seemed to encourage Martin's sense of dislocation around them and never failed to make things hard for him, pecking at his hands or even rolling eggs back and forth among them with their beaks while Martin, egg basket in one hand and feed bag in the other, struggled to keep his balance on the slippery boards.

On past occasions he had become angry enough to choke a few of the hens in rage, something his mother never knew, of course. He buried the birds or if she had gone to town for the day he cooked and ate them.

Now, however, they were on their best behavior, and in no time Martin emerged with a basketful of big brown eggs smeared with hay and excreta and returned to the house.

Martin was in the most carefree of moods that morning, but Louise Kilbanky was not. She couldn't forget the extraordinary, shocking event that had occurred the night before—that had occurred *after* the cement debacle, *after* the drivers had given up the third truck for lost and had gone home . . . Martin screaming back at her in defiance . . . That horrid Parsons woman and her dark schemes, and her awful husband . . . And to top it off, by this morning Martin himself apparently had forgotten it: because it had been highly disturbing for all concerned. While she fixed his breakfast she expected him to say *something*, but no.

. . . Now she was wide-awake and brooding over the night's events, unable to forget how Martin had spoken to her in spite of the broad smile on his face this morning as he brought in the milk and eggs. She sat in the front room—the parlor—sipping her tea and sighing, half expecting the phone to ring and hoping it would not. A minor but nagging sense of dread spread over her features. She tried to sort things out, to see all that had happened to her in these last brief weeks sequentially, so she might establish an orderly progression from them, but she could not quite bring it off. They failed to fall into place.

She sat before the old-fashioned phonograph in the parlor, staring sadly at the small mementoes of her life that filled the walnut whatnot beside the piano—photographs of her husband and herself when they were young, wedding pictures, dim snapshots from the sturdy part of her life, photos of Martin and Chartruse as children, Martin's high school graduation portrait . . . The tears came to her eyes as she fought back unsuccessfully the images of what used to be but was no more, of time passing and her life itself, passing, passing . . . In spite of herself she began crying—softly, struggling to keep the tears mute so Martin would not hear. Her shoulders shook soundlessly in the room.

Mournfully she turned to their record collection, stacks of old battered 78's she and Ike had grown up with and loved, songs she had known as a child, dances she had heard her Uncle Dave play on the fiddle, dances and songs she had known and loved by the Carter Family, the Monroe Brothers, Wade Mainer, the Stanley Brothers . . . Weeping unrestrainedly now (thank God Martin happened to have gone outside again!) she went through the collection of brittle old records with trembling hands and stopped at what had been her favorite of all—such a sweet farm-country melody, so sweet and innocent and true—"Down on Tanner's Farm" recorded by Gid Tanner and Riley Puckett way back in 1934. The tears coursed down her cheek as she separated that record from the rest and started the ancient 78 phonograph she had kept in good condition all these years just so she and Ike might listen to the songs they loved, after working long hours together in the fields.

The machine warmed up, Louise running her finger across the needle until she heard that sound in the room. She placed the simple, bittersweet song on the turntable and lay back in her chair. Moist-eyed and trembling she listened once again to the familiar words:

> Well ladies and gentlemen, sing this song
> It's not right but I know it ain't wrong
> Just alive and mean no wrong
> Hard times in the country, out on Tanner's Farm

Haven't got a penny left in town
Moved to the country in a little log house
Had no windows and cracks in the wall
Work all summer and they rob you in the fall
Hard times in the country, out on Tanner's Farm

Hard luck in the country, go back to town
Hands in your pockets and your head hung down
Put you on the chain gang, won't pay you at all
Hard times in the country, down on Tanner's Farm

But it was the melody that moved her especially, even though it was sweet rather than lonesome and melancholy like most country music. So innocent and vulnerable. . . .

The needle scratched its way through the last sweet guitar and banjo, then came up against the center of the record repeatedly—clunk, clunk, clunk, clunk. She replaced the record in its sleeve and closed the cabinet door. It wouldn't do to keep playing these records, she thought to herself sadly. They didn't mean the same thing to Martin or his friends as they meant to her—as they had meant to her and Ike. . . .

Now deep waves of sadness for the days that had gone by washed over her and broke all resistance. She could hear Martin slamming around in the kitchen now, she knew he would hear her weeping but she couldn't control it any longer. It seemed as if she could control nothing any longer. She was a simple woman who had been physically active and spiritually in control of herself for as long as she had been a woman, but now she wasn't sure. She might not be able to control it any longer. For whatever mysterious reason, she knew life would no longer give her peace. Life, life, life!

She wailed aloud, the tears ran down her face and her body shuddered pitifully, and in the kitchen Martin dropped what he was doing in horror and ran to the front room. It galvanized him that his mother was weeping miserably, so utterly thrown into weeping by forces not under her control. He couldn't bear to look on. He didn't understand—what forces were responsible for transforming her like this? Where were these evil forces? What did they look like?

Having substantially forgotten the events of the night before he was at a loss to understand; and of course the special lonely pain, the torment and the sadness of being separated from her helpmate, of growing old alone, were inconceivable to him. He dashed to her side in total alarm: What was wrong? What was going on?

His mother wept and shuddered but Martin never had a chance to plumb the flood to its depths. In fact, before he could do more than cry out, a loud peremptory series of knocks on the front door startled them both into silence. Mrs. Kilbanky shook like a willow leaf as she hurriedly dried the tears from her cheeks and smoothed her dress. Martin turned to face this new uncertainty.

Knock! Knock! Knock!

Who could it be?

Since he woke up Martin had been wondering when Marge would call. He never for a moment thought she and Bill would appear at the farm without first telephoning, since he sensed his mother's determination to keep them from settling in. So it was with uneasy surprise that he opened the front door to find Marge's cute freckled face and also her determined frizzy-haired face both confronting him. And he could see Bill in the background, struggling with suitcases at the car door. Obviously they had come to stay.

It was all very awkward. Martin was still in a traumatic state from finding his mother weeping and all he could think as he looked at Marge's extra-friendly smile was that he had betrayed his own mother. He had defied and even belittled her wishes the night before —suddenly that entire scene returned to his mind—and therefore he and he alone was responsible for her unhappiness, for those awful tears and that strangled, desperate weeping he had heard from the kitchen only minutes before and which he was convinced were the most horrible sounds he had ever heard. The situation, then, was clear. He knew what he had to do. Without a word of greeting he shut the door in Marge's face.

There was an electric pause, after which the knob turned very slowly and the door opened again . . . Marge was trying to push him around! . . . Martin became incensed.

"Get out! Go back home!" he said shrilly, all the while avoiding her eyes.

Marge froze in place, her hand on the knob and her eyes calmly searching for his. The four eyes played a quick game of hide-and-seek. She knew if she could establish eye contact she would be well on the way to reversing the situation. She was convinced Martin had a soft spot for her. In other words she figured he was sweet on her, or at least she knew he *might* be, and if that was the case nothing on earth was going to stop her from establishing herself at the farm. As far as she could see, for her and Bill in their present financial state, no pleasant alternative existed.

It was either the farm or finding herself out on the road, because Bill was becoming more surly and erratic every day. He refused to look for work, claiming no one would give him a good job and that the bad jobs, like fat-separator or bowling boy, were beneath him. He had never held down a real job for more than a few months anyway, and since being dismissed from the army he had come to see the pre-fab split-level Marge was able to rent because of a small inheritance, as being his inalienable domain. He was king there, and deeply resented the possibility they might be kicked out on their ears if he didn't get a job. To him that equation was humiliating. And although Bill usually had been a thoughtful considerate husband the first few years of their marriage, he had become more and more mean and unpredictable since taking up with that bitch Fontessa . . . Marge knew him well enough to have a graphic estimation of his temper tantrums, too. She knew what he was capable of if she tried to cut loose from him, tried to throw him out. Being twenty-seven rather than twenty-three years old didn't help matters, either.

So it was with considerably more hard reality riding on the line for her that morning than Martin had ever even *conceived* of that she met his feeble power-play with all the devious force she could muster . . . No two-toned nitwit was gonna drive *her* to the wall, that was for sure! Marge was the more desperate of the two at that time, so there was no question at all who would prevail.

A pushover, as far as Marge could see.

They pawed at the porch with the toes of their shoes like two big bull moose, the steam flaring from their invisible nostrils. They confronted each other balanced on a line as fine as silk, and as white and strong as surgical thread. The chrome danced in the sun. Time stood still, like a button raving in its hole.

Pop!

Martin felt the hidden potency she possessed spurt over him. With a shudder his eyes met hers. His foot jumped spasmodically, and as he stood there in the doorway with his mother peering uncertainly behind him and Bill gawking in the yard, a change came over him.

His brain rippled—or riffled. He ceased pawing at the floorboards like a bull at the very instant, too infinitesmal to measure, when he began pawing sheepishly . . . Suddenly he found himself pawing sheepishly while Marge stood unfazed, and the brief psychic skirmish was over. Marge had won.

Wow, thought Martin giddily, what the hell just happened?

His knees wobbled.

"Oh . . . Martin," Marge whispered conspiratorially. "Oh . . . Martin," she hummed, as if he'd been a naughty boy but it was alright. She understood and forgave. (Behind him he heard his mother gasp as she saw part way into what was going on and refused to believe it.)

A stunned silence followed, but soon it was replaced by normal breathing. Climactic conditions by their very nature cannot extend themselves indefinitely in time. Instead, a return to some less demanding, less revealing level of energy is unavoidable, and this was no exception. Almost as if the entire scene were a dress-rehearsal abandoned because it did not sound just right, Bill turned away to face the car, Mrs. Kilbanky turned away to face the parlor inside the door as she dried the final tears from her eyes, and Marge faced Martin simply and honestly, without a trace of tension. It was as if Martin had just now heard the car drive up, just now for the first time heard the knock on the door.

"Why didn't you call first?" he asked.

"Oh . . . Martin!" Bill teased in a ghostly echo of what had come before. He climbed the porch steps and chucked Martin playfully under the chin. Martin recoiled. He was amazed that he absolutely disliked Bill touching him. He had never felt that way about anyone before. He hated the touch.

Marge saw this in his face, and neutralized it by touching him quickly on the cheek and smiling.

"Aw," she answered gently, "we just decided to come on ahead, Martin, that's all. I'm sorry. Bill can be so impatient sometimes. I was gonna call but he was jes rushin me so I couldn't get to the phone . . . Anyway, here we are, right?" she finished, looking him firmly in the eye.

Martin's head spun, and that instant of dizziness was enough to make him dismiss his mother's mysterious misgivings. What in the world was wrong with her anyway? Here Bill and Marge had arrived with their belongings, just like he had wanted, to help him run the farm. What was wrong with that?

He felt better already.

He gestured to Bill and Marge expansively.

They all walked inside, Bill lugging two overstuffed cardboard suitcases tied together with two army belts. The buckles of the belts glinted sharply in the morning sunlight as Bill struggled with the bags.

Martin's face lit up: the glinting brass buckles reminded him of playing in the high school band, marching smartly across the crisp football field surrounded by chubby excited fellow band members as the crowd roared in the bleachers. Martin had played French horn.

"What instrument did *you* play, Bill?" he asked out of nowhere.

"Huh?"

"Didn't you play in the band, too? At the high school?"

Bill set down his luggage and laughed.

"Why, shit, I played the foot-long hot dawg, Martin," he drawled, "Don't you remember?"

Then he continued.

"The band! Shit, Martin, we was just babies then. This is the real thing now, man." And waggishly poking him in the ribs he added as he pulled the luggage clear of the steps: "I didn't play shit in the band, Martin. Unless . . . let's see . . . maybe I *did* come to think of it perform on some kind of instrument, I can't remember which or what, though . . ." He set down the suitcases again and began to think. Tuba? Trumpet? Bones?

Martin was dumfounded by this. His mind normally prevailed at such temperatures that much of his memory simply melted on him, but even *he* could remember playing in the high school band!

He was about to pursue the matter further but Bill skipped up the steps into the house leaving the bags on the porch.

The belt buckles were no longer lit up by the morning sun, and Martin's head spun further.

He was remembering—how awful it had been actually, playing in the high school band. Those insanely awkward uniforms and the stupid military medleys played over and over. Most awful of all, he remembered, had been the bandmaster himself—Mr. Heller, the only wholly obnoxious person Martin had ever encountered, and the only sadist too.

Mr. Heller was notorious for having tortured his clarinetists behind the bandstand after school hours, perpetrating with Prussian fervor and surplus batons the most unspeakable acts upon the hapless youngsters. Consistently he had favored boys over girls in auditions for membership in the band, and he had made life miserable for Martin when the boy steadfastly refused to be sucked and fondled by the vicious old corpse.

Ugh! Martin shuddered aloud at the memory. Mr. Heller was the only person he hated, in fact, and somehow the fact that Bill's army buckles had called all this to mind left him fuming.

He stormed into the house—

"WHY'D YOU LEAVE THE SUITCASES OUTSIDE, BILL?" he bellowed ferociously.

Bill, who was leaning against the mantelpiece in the front room, recoiled convulsively from Martin's sudden loud entrance. He broke a treasured heirloom blue glass vase that his elbow had been propped near before he jumped in surprise. The chips of priceless glass fell into the upright piano nearby and onto the floor. Marge was aghast. Mrs. Kilbanky's lips narrowed.

Bill was deeply flustered and embarrassed. He couldn't believe the bossy tone with which Martin was addressing him. Exactly who did this little twirp think he was? Bill was about to respond in kind, when he thought better of it and swallowed for the time being what he thought of as his pride. He clenched his fists but contained himself. No doubt he would get even in the future.

Fumbling apologetically he retraced his steps to the porch and returned with the two bags.

Mrs. Kilbanky stooped through a shower of apologies from Marge and swept up the shards and smithereens of vivid blue glass.

The two women then sat down again in their upholstered chairs and Marge resumed the conversation.

"So what's new?"

"New?" the old lady asked suspiciously.

Marge persevered.

"Yeah—you know, like *new*, you know? Like that truck stuck out in the yard is new, ain't it?"

Bill laughed.

Louise Kilbanky's eyes took on a worried expression. Mention of the truck brought difficult problems to the surface.

"Yes," she answered hesitantly, "it's just dreadful. I don't know what to do. I'm so confused about it, really." She was incapable of acting frostily toward anyone forever, and she realized—unhappily —how determined Martin was to have Marge stay on at the farm.

"What do you suppose will happen?" she continued, referring to the truck.

They all went to the window and looked at the huge red machine, its chassis semi-dislocated and its mixer wrenched off the chassis. A solid bulk of hardened cement like frozen custard, four or five feet in diameter and proceeding from the gaping mouth of the mixer down to the ground, completed the picture. Nothing looked more bizarre than that truck in its present context, and Louise wondered to herself how she possibly could have forgotten about it all morning!

Martin wondered the same thing. He hadn't given the truck a thought since the night before. Now it presented itself before him as in a dream, a huge problematical presence. He hadn't the faintest idea what to do.

Radiating around the truck lay an irregular pool of hardened cement altogether covering an area roughly twenty yards square and spread out across the ground like hardened lava. The two pitiful attempts at "embankments" formed an insane rampart midway between the truck and the pond. The scene was so flagrantly out of place it begged to be erased. As they looked out the window the very countryside seemed in a semi-permanent state of shock.

A black leather glove lay half-submerged forever in one corner of the dismal pool.

"Hey, that's my glove!" Marge exclaimed.

The others, however, were silent, and the sight of a renegade cement truck tilted forty-five degrees to the sky sobered them all. Some vague foreboding took shape in the air. A sense of imminent disaster, or at least ill-repute.

Marge put an end to that, though. She laughed raucously.

"Imagine!" she squawked. "My hand sunk into that cement last night and I wasn't even aware of it. I must have been asleep on my feet! Ha, ha . . ."

She went outside and tried to retrieve the glove, tugging at it while the others watched through the parlor window.

The wind seemed to grow colder. Marge gave up and returned to the house. "I'm cold," she announced peevishly. "Let's have some tea."

It sounded like a suggestion but everyone else seemed to understand that in reality it was an order.

They all filed to the kitchen for their tea.

6

The Confidence of Control

The next few weeks rolled by relatively smoothly for the new Kil-banky household.

Bill sneaked back to the house in Crestview Developments that he and Marge owed two months back rent on and collected the rest of their essential valuables, things that were important enough to them to risk a confrontation with the real estate agent. On successive trips he brought back with him to the farm Marge's big black poodle Donnie, her portable hair dryer and emery boards, her copies of National Geographic and aerosol makeup cans.

Marge also possessed various mysterious bottles and cartons clearly labeled and sealed with heavy tape which she insisted Bill retrieve for her . . . Many times over the past few years Bill had found himself staring at these labels, some of which made sense to him but most of which did not: JIMMY CREAM, for example, stenciled neatly on one of the half-gallon jars, greatly puzzled him. He would grow curious about these labels to the point of plotting how best to open the cartons and bottles undetected. But then, ten minutes later, his mind on something else, he would remember them only for the strange and various sensations reading each of them aloud produced in him. What did they mean? Lids and sides of boxes and jars were labeled PELLET QUALITY, MARGE'S POODLE, SALVA SPASTICA and GENETIC SAFETY; METAL TEETH, ROLL-BACK FEEDER DEVICE and VERTICAL CORRUGATIONS

... The patchy allusions intrigued Bill no end, so that if he happened upon them when Marge was not at home contemplation of the various phrases which to him made no sense at all would throw him into a kind of cryptic reverie—a pleasurable daydreaming he never otherwise experienced. Rooted to the spot, his fists thrust deep into his pockets, he would run his eyes over and over the jumble of half-cosmetic, half-psychotic names, bobbing and weaving back and forth until he nearly lost consciousness ... After a few minutes of this Bill would suddenly look up as if an alarm had gone off, staring off into the racks of old ties and bundles of used clothes and torn magazines that otherwise clogged their modest attic storeroom. The dust and heat and sheer desolation of the nonventilated space would always overwhelm him at this time, changing his mood from detached curiosity to its more normal state of irritated distraction. The names on the jars merely irritated him now. Fighting his way through the jumble of broken hula-hoops and stepping by mistake on one of Marge's fancy dress hats and completely destroying its veil, in a rare moment of lucid self-appraisal he would become angry with himself because he lacked the minimal cleverness necessary to open and examine one of the boxes or jars without leaving a trace of himself behind.

He was simply too dumb to do it. Too stupid to pull it off. There could be no other explanation.

This in turn left him cross and ill-humored, so that when he finally fought his way out of the attic and down the stairs it was with the conviction that the bottles and jars and cartons meant nothing—just various objects of female vanity. Snorting at Marge's congenital weaknesses he would head for a cold bottle of beer with a newfound smug self-confidence. Weeks would go by before he once again became curious about the labels, whereupon the entire process repeated itself almost exactly. This continued from the day she brought home the first labeled jars until the day he moved their belongings out to the farm. . . .

Bill was sorely tempted to open one now and examine its contents but he knew Marge was a fanatic when it came to guarding her secrets well, and that no matter how painstakingly he retaped the package she immediately would see that it had been tampered with. So, grumbling but acquiescent, he loaded the boxes in the back of his jalopy without examining them.

He made several trips back to their abandoned house in Crestview, mostly after dark, salvaging kitchen utensils, clothing, furniture bought on credit that didn't belong to them and the 26-inch black and white Motorola that did. This heavy console-model TV was Marge and Bill's prized possession and although it weighed nearly two hundred pounds Marge awaited its arrival at the farm impatiently, complaining to Bill each time he returned without it. Finally on his last trip she went along with him, and together under a full moon they hoisted the monstrous object out of the house and into the car. Their neighbors, the Wilkens, who had been unfriendly ever since the Parsons had moved in, stood on the patio of their own nearly identical prefab ranch house and hurled insults at the two figures laboring in the dark. Mrs. Wilkens, a particularly repulsive overweight presence in her house robe and slippers, her hair-curlers glinting like armor plating in the moonlight, was especially vehement in her denunciations.

"Trash! Flim-flam! Scum!" she shouted. "If I wasn't so glad to see you gettin out I'd call the agent. Don't think I don't know what you're doin. You ain't got a chance!"

"Fuck off," Marge spat over her shoulder.

"Why, my God, Amos," Mrs. Wilkens implored her husband, a meek cardpuncher at the tack factory, a time-server whom Bill loathed. "Are you gonna let that cheap whore talk to me like that! What about the children?" Her brats were there beside her, lending moral encouragement by turning scarlet with shame.

Amos Wilkens moved decisively from his patio grasping a twenty-inch barbecue fork, only when he was certain Bill and Marge already were leaving.

"C'mere and say that, you bums," he shouted as Bill's car backed down the drive.

Bill slammed on the brake and tore open the door. He was all too willing to settle a score with this little runt. He jumped out of the car with a tire iron in his hand.

Amos stopped in his tracks. He was dressed in pajamas and the cold wet earth numbed his bare feet. He coughed and nearly choked in terror. He was all set to drop the fork and run when Marge called Bill back.

"C'mon Bill, you'll just break his nose and then he'll sue us. Let's forget it."

Bill grumbled but gave in. He and Marge were more satisfied each day with their new living arrangement at the farm and Bill didn't want to jeopardize it. He knew he had enough on his hands merely avoiding Jim Backus the realtor. He and Marge fully intended to pay their back rent when they could afford it but he knew they'd be in trouble if Amos Wilkens called attention to them. The Wilkenses had no idea where Marge and Bill were moving to and Bill preferred to keep it that way.

"You little creep," he concluded at the top of his lungs. He and Marge then drove away.

Meanwhile at the farm Mrs. Kilbanky made every effort to swallow her suspicions and trust her son. She went out of her way to be helpful and accommodating, clearing out Ike's upstairs storeroom so Bill could store Marge's bottles and cartons there, and in general bending over backwards to act graciously toward two people she did not trust. She tried to make them feel at home, which wasn't very difficult since Marge and Bill insisted they already *were* at home. In fact, Louise realized unhappily, if she made clear her feelings about them it would make no difference: they were determined to stay no matter how she felt. This sobered and saddened her, and instead of challenging the two interlopers she preferred to avoid them, hoping that in time Martin would come to his senses or they would get bored and leave of their own accord.

Otherwise, however, the farm property seemed the very picture of contented, purposeful activity. Bill refused to farm the fields that spilled north of the house acre after acre, but on the other hand he made a great show of plowing four acres directly behind the house and seeding the moist rich furrows with white and yellow corn.

He insisted Martin's chore was to ready the big family garden for planting, and so while he rode back and forth on Ike Kilbanky's tractor Martin worked himself to death pulling rocks and roots from the earth and planting lettuce, onions, peas, summer squash, pole beans, tomatoes, carrots, radishes, spinach, beets and melons. This was backbreaking work but it took his mind off the problem of the cement mixer and his guilt at having perpetrated that disaster.

The garden also gave Martin a focus for his more unique activities, and as long as he confined himself to the sloping terrain inside the chicken-wire fences Marge and Bill did not complain. There, after working for a while with the garden tools and dried manure he would rip off his pants and roll around in the mud, singing to himself or merely rocking back and forth in fetal position, his elbows hooked over his knees, the wide blue sky his only company. Eventually he would get hungry and, trying to control himself, hitching his pants up over his muddy ass, he would appear at the kitchen door for lunch. Marge had grasped his state of mind intuitively that Sunday when he first rapped upon her door, and so now she simply handed sandwiches and tea out to him with a smile.

Before three weeks were out the entire garden had been cleared and all the vegetables planted. The seeds were torn from their packets and sown at random and as a result many of the plants came up in chaotic swirls and clusters, but most of them did come up. Marge knew she couldn't ask for more than that.

Mrs. Kilbanky, on the other hand, spent more and more of her time in her bedroom on the second floor, coming down only often enough to seem part of the group. She missed Martin, too, among these strangers, and so she came down for that too.

. . . And when no one else was around she came down to listen to her records, to play the old songs like "Red Rocking Chair" and "Little Maggie," and sigh. She began playing songs by the Stanley Brothers over and over again that she hadn't heard in years, especially "Death Is Only a Dream." But she had many other favorites as well. She handled the worn old 78's carefully.

She took to going through collections of memorabilia she had saved from the past, collections of specific things (such as postcards, snapshots, personal belongings, clippings and receipts) as well as the random accumulations of years gone by that now resided in the attic, as well as in the basement and out in the barn . . . Everything from Morris chairs to mustache cups, and including hand pumps and high-lace shoes, razor strops and snuff boxes, fly swatters and scarecrows, a dry sink and a lard kettle, a churn with plunger and a galvanized tub, woolen and cylindrical foot-warmers, a box-foot-warmer, half-eaten leather buggy seats and the whip for the old grey mare, the mare her own mother raised and that was long gone, now . . . Her head reeled . . . What about the waterproof collars?

And what about the leaching tubs? Soap was another essential item, she remembered gravely, that used to be made on the farm, whereas now it was purchased in food stores and drug stores. Tallow was obtained by melting the fat of cattle or sheep, while the lye was produced by leaching wood ashes. Ashes from fireplaces and stoves were collected in a stone ashpit, usually located in the basement of

63

the farm house. When a sufficient supply of ashes had been collected they were leached in water in special tubs kept for that purpose: but no more.

She realized that even scarecrows were going out of fashion because it was decided they didn't accomplish their purpose. Their disappearance makes one wonder what will become of the expression "She looks like a scarecrow" as applied to a dowdily-dressed female, Louise thought. Members of the younger generation who never have seen a scarecrow will hardly grasp the full significance of the term.

Louise wept for the disappearing scarecrow. She also wept for the good farm life gone down—luckily for her she lived on what was still a working farm, but she knew it would never be the same . . . But at least they still milked their own cows every morning, at least they ate their own eggs. Soon the garden would start growing and she could can again this year, if she had the heart. . . .

For the heart was the problem, rather than the cans. She saw herself as she went through the complicated ritual in years past, doing all the gardening herself while Ike worked the fields; buying the cases of mason jars in town on credit and swapping can tales with the neighboring farm wives; deciding on those delirious summer nights when the crops reached maturity which ones she would can and which they would eat fresh . . . Those wild nights and days, working ten and twelve hours at a stretch in the big kitchen completely given over to the canning procedure . . . Boiling down the tomatoes in big vats, cleaning bushels of cucumbers for pickles, running her fingers through quarts of bruised raspberries for jam, scraping and sealing and packing, her hands blistered red and her arms rubbery with fatigue, the sweat stiffening her ringlets as she bent over the quantities of vegetables and fruits still to be dealt with before they became too ripe to can . . . And finally the grand, delirious trashing ceremony at the very end—on the very last summer night—when, too tired to work anymore, or out of cans or good fruit, she and Ike would drag the bushels of remaining sour vegetables out behind the barn and make a huge bonfire, and drink corn liquor and really lose their heads, letting go with glorious great shrieks, dancing half-naked around the sheets of flame and exploding apples, slipping at some point dead tired and drunk into each other's arms as the fire died down and the first birds chirped in the elms above the cool dawn mist. . . .

Oh, those days were gone forever and she knew it, and Louise

Kilbanky couldn't stand it. She dreaded the future more each day and she knew dread must take precedence over the rows of jars filled with sweet harvest bounty. Besides, it had been no picnic slaving like a nigger all those years over the big vats: by no means was she certain she possessed the stamina necessary to tackle such a project anyway. And all the years of canning just for the family had left a surplus on the pantry shelves and in the basement sufficient to feed four people for six years, she calculated uncertainly . . . In any case, rows and rows of jars remained, shelves sagging with pickled corn and beets, cardboard cartons stacked in the basement some before the Second World War and not touched since. She wondered if the jars in those cartons were still good, if she might eat green beans from the summer of 38!

Probably not, she thought dejectedly. Even if they were edible, time must have taken its toll in other ways. She shuddered as she puzzled over what those other ways might be. A pervasive loss of color, of nutrition, a deadening grey? Incorporeality? Insubstantiality of the filaments? Deceptive fiber substitutes? Ghosts? . . .

Brrrh, it's cold in here! she thought. So sunny outside, such a beautiful spring day, and yet my feet are freezing, my hands never warm up no matter what I do, my neck's stiff and my joints ache . . . Where is Martin? Where is my son? I haven't seen him for days . . . Maybe I'll go outside now and watch the men planting . . . I'll try to make friends with that woman downstairs . . . I'd better get a hold on myself soon, she thought . . . I won't give up. I won't spend the rest of my days in this cold spooky room paralyzed by nostalgia. I've got to live!

With a brave jolt she threw the muffler from her shoulders and ran down to the kitchen for tea. She stepped outside and watched Martin's muscular back strain in the sun as he pulled up roots and rocks. Her eyes stung in the unaccustomed sunlight, but she would not go back inside, she vowed. This farm belonged to her and she loved every inch of it. She was determined to work it again. The least she could do was help her son in the garden.

The days and weeks after the Parsons moved in saw Mrs. Kilbanky oscillate between these bouts of arthritis and melancholy when she would see no one, and brave bright days filled with activity when she would work in the garden or go to town for supplies, clean out the stables and groom the two horses they still owned—Silver and Butler—until they shined. Marge always gave Louise a wide berth, doing her best to stay out of her way, since she knew the delicate nature of their living arrangement depended on Martin's peculiar state of mind, and that this might buckle or snap if his mother collapsed or revolted. As long as their daily routine survived intact, however, Marge felt she and Bill were home free.

As each day passed Marge radiated more and more confidence—she knew she had the power. This feeling transformed her entire sense of self as well. Her body grew stouter and more imposing, she flexed her muscles and gritted her teeth unconsciously as she walked around the house, she even gave in to believing she had grown two or three inches taller. Nothing could stop her now. She had to struggle with herself in ways the others never even conceived, restraining the heady impulse that grew stronger each day to dress in black leather and high-heeled boots, to swagger and strut around the grounds, horsewhip in hand, cutting down the rampant milkweed with a single regal stare!

These easy fantasies were entirely new to her and she had to struggle to keep them hidden. Something inside her warned that people could not understand—people in town as well as the simple farmers who lived nearby would not tolerate costumes, would not tolerate a big female swaggerer! On the other hand, Marge shivered with glee at the prospect of finally meeting up with Fontessa and settling the score with her rough-and-tumble cousin. She didn't think about it from day to day, but deep inside she could hardly wait. Meanwhile she would dress and look and act the same as always, she decided. And in a way she *was* the same. The same pretty cotton dress, the same determined face, the same big black poodle.

As for Bill, each day Fontessa increased in his mind until he saw nothing else. In bed each night he pushed Marge aside, feigning fatigue from farm work, and fell asleep. Finally after they'd been at the farm two weeks he couldn't stand it any longer and sneaked off into town after an especially busy day when the others fell asleep from exhaustion around nine p.m.

Bill pushed and rolled the car a good half-mile down the incline in front of the farm before starting it. He surprised Fontessa as she was washing out her socks, but her little twin daughter Peggy was visiting

Daddy that week and with a gasp they realized they had the house-trailer to themselves. Bill was delirious. They rocked and socked, making all kinds of love till dawn. Bill told her all about the set-up at the Kilbanky farm, and in spite of how much she loathed Marge she couldn't help feeling genuine admiration for them both for having pulled it off.

Fontessa herself was depressed lately with the kind of work she'd been forced to do. She saw no way out. Driving every morning thirty-five miles to the tri-county airport to be a checker and bumper for the creepy businessmen who flew their light planes in from Pittsburgh and Cleveland and Louisville, from Columbus and Charleston and Roanoke, cheap booze on their breath and dirty sex in their eyes! Ugh, she couldn't stand it. Her boss at the airport, Jack, was a nice enough guy, but the job itself soured on her. But what were the alternatives? Working at the local dry cleaner's, where she'd have to put up with Mrs. McCloskey's insane penny-pinching? Or behind the cash register at the Five-and-Dime? And even those jobs probably were no longer available. Winosha Falls was a small town, and what's more a small town that was dying rather than growing. Aside from the tack factory, which had a policy of hiring men only except for cleaning ladies, there was no "heavy industry" in the area. The dairy farmers had their Co-op office in town, it was true, as did a half-dozen other organizations like the Elks and the Boy Scouts and All-state Insurance. But the turnover for women at any of these places was limited and slow—all you could do was secretary, anyway, and everyone knew what that usually entailed. Most of the men who ran these enterprises were either horny hypocrites who pawed a girl to pieces as part of her job, or old fogies who peed on their blue-veined hands as they slept. Ugh! If she had the cash to stake herself to "looking money" maybe she would have gone to a bigger city and looked for work, but she didn't. Fontessa suspected it could only be worse in the cities, anyway. She had no special skills that would guarantee her a job. She had her daughter Peggy to worry about, too . . . No, she would stay put in Winosha . . . Maybe someday. . . .

But that Marge Parsons with her collosal nerve sure had it easy! Fontessa hardly believed Bill when he told her all that had happened in the last few weeks. She almost would have risked a confrontation with Marge just to see it for herself. But if Bill could sneak into town every few nights and they could make it together, Fontessa was content. She had learned to take the good with the bad before—in fact, she had learned that mixing the two together like that in this life was the best a poor girl like her could expect.

Bill was wary of Marge's intuition and let a week go by before he visited Fontessa again, but the second time was even better than the first and he could contain himself no longer. For a while it was every other night that he schemed and racked his brain for lame excuses about "getting more beer" or going to town to "meet the boys and shoot pool".

Marge knew Bill had always been an indifferent pool player but she soon would have guessed his secret anyway, since lately Bill had taken to wearing a very distinctive smirk when talking to her. His was the sort of cunning, or intelligence, that operated only intermittently. At all other times he lost track of the fact that other potentially dangerous sensibilities still existed that needed to be dealt with to carry off whatever trick it was that he had in mind. In other words, Bill just somehow sloppily assumed his tricks and ruses worked, so that while he went through the motions of making an excuse his eyes gave him away. Looking smug and superior he mouthed the same words about "pool" and "beer" time after time, grinning to himself about what a pushover Marge had turned out to be after all.

Marge meanwhile was hopping mad, but when she realized precisely what was going on she decided it was the wrong time for a showdown—with either Bill or Fontessa—and that the most she would do was prevail upon him to "play pool" only twice a week. Life on the farm had turned out much better than she had hoped. If she forced the issue with Bill, lashing out at him for the two-faced liar he was, she knew he might very well bolt the farm and leave her there alone with the Kilbankys. As far as Martin was concerned, Bill was the man of the house to whom he had delegated much of the authority for running the farm, and although all of them recognized that was not so, that it was Marge herself who was in control, she was uncertain how Martin would react if Bill left. She was unwilling for the time being to take the risk of finding out. Also, if she told him to his face what a liar he was and that she truly hated him it might result in sheer violence on his part. He might flip his lid and try to punch her out. Marge did not look forward to that.

So for the time being she sat tight. Bill resumed making love to her again, too, so that was something. In addition, he grumbled constantly but he did perform the minimal tasks and chores to keep the farm routine going. He plowed, raked, cleaned out the barn, ran and fed the two horses—even attempted to fix the roof which leaked in several places, though Marge nervously demanded he forget the repair job since she knew how inept he was. It took him nearly a week to maneuver the sheets of tar roofing onto the roof, whereupon a stiff May wind sprang up and blew the roofing into the trees, and rolled Bill yowling down the steep incline, where he saved himself from a nasty fall by clinging to the rainspout until Martin and Marge rescued him.

To prove he was a man he started to climb right back up the ladder, though the roofing was gone and his tool box had overturned, but Marge insisted he forget about it. They would hire somebody from in town who knew what he was doing—Bill Rigley the carpenter, or Tony Ab, or even old Mike Magurk.

"What about those Swedes up near Hurleyville?" Marge added. "Those potato farmers. I hear them dumb jokers are really hard up: the nut sedge keeps worming into their crops and yet they refuse to take any agronomical advice. Can you imagine that? I hear they ain't got more'n a month left before they're dispossessed. I'll bet if we drove up there we could get one of 'em real cheap. All Swedes are good carpenters," she concluded. "They're dumb, too. Hell, we could probably get em to build an extension on the house for free!"

"Well, *you* can go up there if you want but I ain't dealin with no damn Swedes," Bill retorted peevishly. "Screw the roof, anyway . . . I'm goin into town for some more beer, we're almost out," and before Marge could stop him he jumped into the car and drove off, tires squealing in the hardened mud.

"There goes a true asshole," she swore under her breath, as she and Martin stooped over in the long grass to retrieve the tools. Later Martin climbed the elm and threw down what remained of the roofing caught high in its branches.

The Kilbanky homestead was in essence a traditional country box. As in all country boxes the floor plan was simple and easily recognized, the silhouette the box made against the sky repeatable, so that farmers visiting each other crossed stretches of corn or wheat only to come upon structures greatly resembling the one they had just left. As a consequence, when visiting neighbors they felt right at home.

Most houses were rectangular two-story structures finished in white or grey clapboard or shingle and topped by fish-scale roofing, aluminum gutterspouts, and a series of glass and steel lightning rods along the uppermost beam. Often a delicate cock or bull swerved in the direction of the prevailing wind, pointing to a W or an S-E, or trembling at an N. Almost every house had one of these weathervanes, and the Kilbanky home was no exception.

Farmhouses were built individually, however, by men and women proud of their own independence and resourcefulness, so that unlike the prefabricated "country-look" of today, each house varied in some basic distinctive way from its neighbors. Each house revealed a life of its own. The general structure was the same throughout much of the countryside, but each particular one was unique. In fact, often it was only the most universal characteristic of all that was shared by every house in a given district—and that characteristic was the box. No one built a house that was not rectangular. No one did not live in a box.

As a result, when television began to make its appearance as a popular-priced commodity in the late 1940s, very little resistance was encountered in the strongly traditional farm communities that crisscrossed the American homeland. Winosha Falls was no exception. Farmers who had disfigured their daughters for life with pots of scalding water for flirting with a stranger, eagerly snapped up the flickering little boxes with their images of idle chatter and flirtation, as soon as they hit the market. They apparently were not fully aware that these boxes wrought violent changes in the minds of their viewers, destroying their delicate regionalism almost invisibly, making parochial attitudes quaint before disposing of them altogether. Though this process took several years its seeds were planted without fail on the very first evening a network television program was seen. All across America this strange new crop was growing, but the men and women whose lives were given over to the magical process of fertility, of sowing seeds and reaping their reward, were the very ones who could not detect its final manifestation. They failed to make the connection between the airwaves in front of their very noses and the crops that stood ripening in the earth outside their door. As a result, this small fluorescent box spelled doom for the larger clapboard box in which it stood.

In the television receiver, the incoming impulses were fed to the control electrode of the picture tube (cathode ray tube) in which an electron beam was zigzagged across the fluorescent screen synchronously with the beam in the camera tube, and with an intensity varying with the strength of the electric impulses. In this way a pattern of luminous points of varying brightness was produced on the screen in rapid succession, thus making the picture that the viewer saw.

However, some who could afford it still refused to buy a television set, either because picture quality was poor where they lived or because television destroyed the orderly rural silence and peace of mind in which they thrived: they sensed the threat though not its maganitude.

Ike Kilbanky was one of these persons. He flatly refused to purchase a television no matter how his neighbors teased him, saying he preferred the radio for news and music and that the picture hurt his eyes. Louise for some reason also couldn't have cared less, and Martin followed suit—as a child he saw all the TV he needed when he visited friends, and after he went "ape" it mattered even less. Why would he need an irritating ray-gun apparatus to watch gilded hucksters sell facial hair-removing cream and crack senseless jokes, when he could roll around in the grass under God's blue sky, and squash insects, and chirp with the birds for free?

It's true that in high school he had been an avid football fan. Now that he was in his present condition he rarely got into town, and much less was he able to see a good football game like the ones he used to watch. He had attended all Winosha's home games, and he had even been reduced to attending some of Casper State Teacher's College's, that had such a wretched team. He heard football games were broadcast on television, and he longed to see one. People spoke about the Green Bay Packers, a professional team that were world champions. Martin was in awe of this fabled team and longed to see them, even go to Green Bay in person, wherever that was, and watch the great team play.

For Bill and Marge, though, it was decidedly another story. They enjoyed television immensely—or rather, they watched it often. They bought the biggest television set they could find.

This Motorola was a monster.

Furthermore, although Marge didn't indulge in too much daytime viewing, regarding with disdain the soap operas and other pap fed to housewives, she liked to watch TV regularly for several hours every evening no matter which programs were on. She even liked the news, though it made no impression upon her one way or the other. President Eisenhower was a favorite of hers, both because he furnished excellent material for jokes and because Marge was sincerely fond of him and believed he was the real thing—he acted the way a president should act, he spoke with the natural gravity and decorum expected of him, he said the right things. The old general reminded Marge of a plate of hot biscuits on Thanksgiving Day, and Marge loved home-made hot buttered biscuits. They tasted exactly the way she knew they tasted.

Otherwise she liked the comedy and variety shows best, The Garry Moore Show and Ted Mack's Amateur Hour, but she watched it all, and so did Bill. Near a TV, Bill could sit in an easy chair with a can of beer forever.

So naturally the night they drove to their previous residence and succeeded in making away with the huge, walnut-finish console was a night for celebration and rejoicing. Bill stocked up on beer and Marge painted her nails and dusted her hair in anticipation. They moved the set right into the front parlor, convincing Martin that the old upright piano no longer functioned by first cutting a few wires and then suggesting they move it into the hallway until it could be repaired. Mrs. Kilbanky protested meekly.

The TV now occupied the place of honor. Bill rearranged the furniture so the most comfortable chairs fanned out around the huge immobile screen. Entire evenings were to pass uninterrupted before its ghostly glow, but the first night they had the television at the farm was especially thrilling. President Eisenhower was about to deliver an important address to the nation the very first time they turned the set on!

But first McNaughton Bixby, the self-made food-services million-aire, appeared in a brief advertisement for his original company. Bixby, the inventor of "Champagne-In-A-Can" ("Just mix with soda water and serve ice cold"), liked to appear personally in his own ads. He usually showed himself relaxing on an arbored terrace over-looking the Mediterranean, a forceful image of perpetual springtime engulfing him. A brief low-keyed speech extolled the virtues of his canned champagne-concentrate, and then Bixby challenged an obvi-ously aristocratic Frenchman who appeared at his side to distinguish between Bixby Champagne and the costliest native variety. Naturally the man could not do so, swearing through an interpreter that their taste, their fragrance, their bouquet were identical. American audi-ences that watched this ad were perfectly aware of its fictitious nature but they loved it anyway. Bixby Champagne was a popular item in many parts of the country, especially during the summer when on festive occasions enormous bowls of it were concocted, along with fresh fruit, bourbon, milk, and nutmeg into a perplexing but deadly brew nicknamed Cypress Punch. At about the time hula hoops enjoyed popularity Cypress Punch became the rage, and many of the new split-level houses and tacky pre-fab replicas springing up all across America in the 1950s were witness to strange involuntary rites of lubrication on their front lawns. Often in full view of the neighbors, what started as an innocent Sunday brunch with two or three families participating, evolved into a messy argumentative spectacle of slobbering hula-hoopers erupting their stomachs of Cypress Punch onto each other as they weaved drunkenly across the lawn in their hoops, mortally embarrassed by their sudden loss of control.

Be that as it may, Bixby's commercial soon was over and a network newsman asked everyone to stand by: the President of the United States then appeared on the screen and immediately began to speak.

7

The Gravy Thickens

They were all eating breakfast in the kitchen the next morning. The tea had tasted soapy so Mrs. Kilbanky was washing out the teapot when the telephone rang. She put down the teapot and answered it.

"Hello?" she said normally.

"Yes? . . . Yes? . . . Yes? . . ."

A solid fifteen minutes elapsed, during which time her face changed from fresh early morning energy and purity of mien to wizened effort of concentration, and finally downright sickened, hopeless despair.

She dropped the receiver with a heavy clunk.

To the others she lifted a face bright with tears, torn apart by concern.

"It's the lawyer . . . Mr. Sisley . . . down at the Courthouse . . . no alternative but to . . . Schwartz says he'll sue . . . two earthmovers and maybe a crane? . . . Martin! Oh, Martin! What'll we do!"

She fell back against the sink in a swoon.

They all rushed to her side, calmed her by applying pressure to certain points along her neck and shoulders, and made her sit down at the table. Marge made another pot of tea.

"What is it, mother?" Martin asked anxiously.

"Mr. Sisley, don't you know who he is, Martin? He's the County

Prosecutor—I think—good heavens!—or maybe he's not . . . But he called from the Courthouse just the same . . . It's all on account of that accursed cement truck!" she wailed.

"They—or, that is, Mr. Sisley—it's got me so flustered I can't even think—Mr. Sisley claims they'll have to sue us—that is, Mr. Schwartz at the cement store is suing us—that is, he's suing *you*, Martin—for the loss of his truck . . . and . . . and for the cost of hiring earth-movers . . . and a crane if . . . if necessary," her voice blurred and blubbered, broken by sobs. "A crane if necessary to come and extricate the mixer from its present situation, he said . . . from its present position. . . ."

She swooned but then continued in a whisper:

"Mr. Sisley, he says that *you* are legally responsible, Martin . . . You are being subpoenaed, or something, I couldn't get it straight . . . Oh, dear! . . . to appear before the court—no, that's not it . . . Damn! . . . To appear before Mr. Sisley at the Courthouse tomorrow morning to answer charges and defend yourself!"

She began wailing once more.

"To defend yourself! Oh, Martin! How can you defend yourself? . . . And Mr. Sisley, Mr. Sisley insisted you had to appear alone, Martin . . . That I couldn't come along . . . He said *he* would serve as lawyer in all aspects of the case . . . *He* would constitute adequate representation . . . So no other lawyer need be present in the courtroom . . . or rather the room where they'll take you . . . Room 11! At 7:00 sharp in the morning. Seven sharp, he said. And I am not allowed to accompany you!"

Mrs. Kilbanky couldn't go on.

Bill and Marge stood scratching their heads over this latest development.

Marge was especially upset that they wouldn't allow even his own mother to accompany him. His own mother! And Martin being in the condition he was, which nearly everyone in Winosha Falls was aware of, and which was no condition for defending himself in a lawsuit, certainly. That was very strange. Marge became suspicious. This damn Mr. Sisley sure had his nerve!

She tried to calm the old lady down by talking in a low, soothing voice. Mrs. Kilbanky had worked herself into a state, however: she was incapable of further discourse and went up to lie in bed. So that it wasn't until much later in the day—around four in the afternoon

when they all found themselves in the kitchen again for more tea—
that Marge was able to learn the exact details of the phone call.

Throughout the remainder of that morning and early afternoon neither she nor Bill were good for anything, as they sat around the front
room nervously awaiting Mrs. Kilbanky's reappearance.

Marge tried to concentrate on a crossword puzzle while Bill tied
and untied various sailor knots he had learned as a Boy Scout long
ago. Neither could muster the necessary concentration, however, and
coils of rope proliferated across the parlor floor. Bill cracked his
knuckles incessantly until Marge growled and threw a coaster in his
direction, whereupon he was reduced to carving his initials in the
woodwork and waiting.

They both were very concerned, needless to say. Any brush with
the law seriously threatened their situation, since a nosey lawyer
would be the first to impute some sort of wrongdoing in the innocent
new household at the farm.

The effect on Martin was traumatic. As soon as his mother
collapsed he pulled a long, long face and wordlessly left the house in
leaps and bounds. Bill watched from the window as Martin ran along
the property in a discontinuous manner, stopping here and there to
beat his head with his fists and finally climbing up into the limbs of an
old elm a half mile from the house where he sat unmoving, staring
vacantly like a gorilla for more than six hours.

But finally they all gathered in the kitchen and Louise Kilbanky
related in more detail what she had been told over the phone.

It seems that the men who delivered the cement that Sunday had
insisted to Mr. Schwartz afterwards that the catastrophe was all Martin's fault; that he had deceived them as to the lay of the land and the
manner in which they were to dispose of the raw cement, at the same
time berating them in a cruel manner and under the threat of force
obliging them to unload the cement . . . In obviously disastrous circumstances, for fear of life and limb, each driver in addition now felt
himself deeply bound and constrained to sue Martin personally for
the sum of $75,000 each for unusual cruelty, deception, and humili-
ating working conditions, viz., excessive cold and excessively strong
wind.

These suits came under the category of personal injury suits for a total of $225,000, Louise was told—but Mr. Sisley was quick to add that such a figure was required by the courts before they would handle such cases, and that in reality the men would settle for much less ...A technicality....

Secondly, however, it seems Martin was being sued by Mr. Schwartz himself for the total market value of the cement mixer and truck ($8,000), plus "any fees due for the recovery of the wreckage," by which, Louise insisted, was meant the rental costs for the two earthmovers and a flatbed truck; as well as possibly for the cost of renting and operating a crane, if it was found the earthmovers could not do the job. This, Mr. Sisley assured her, would not amount to more than $3,500, even if they were forced to call in the crane.

But thirdly—and here her face reflected frank alarm—Mr. Sisley had hinted darkly that a "certain anonymous party" was considering "putting a lien" (or *something*—she just couldn't remember the exact phrase) on Martin's bank accounts, or rather on the Kilbanky accounts as they now stood in his name. This last threat seemed the most hideous of all, because in mentioning it Sisley had implied that due to the past events Martin's mental state—"his present mental and future mental condition"—might very well be called into question, or "examined by the proper authorities," or something, she couldn't remember what....

She was nearly as upset now as she had been in the morning, so Marge tried to comfort her with the fact that Martin had done nothing more than spill a little cement.

"They can't lock you up for that," she reasoned irritably. "And as for those three jokers suing you for personal damages, why that's ridiculous. Sheer bullshit! Pardon my language, but those bruisers couldn't have cared less—I remember, I was there...."

"Don't forget, Louise, we were all there. We're witnesses. You, me and Bill. If they wanna try anything on Martin they gotta take us to court, too, and we'll just tell em what happened, that's all. All we gotta do is tell the truth."

"Those shysters have some nerve!" she continued fiercely. "They won't get a penny outta Martin, anybody can see that. If they wanna go to court we'll hire us a lawyer and beat em cold."

But Louise Kilbanky was thinking of the other words she had heard from Mr. Sisley, dark phrases like "peripheral vision," "psychosurgery," and "voluntary personality retraining," and she was worried.

She also was deeply embarrassed. This entire situation had mushroomed out of nowhere and she really felt it was too much for her. She might keel over and die any day!

And what must the community think, as well . . . She felt too humiliated to show her face in town ever again. It was awful!

Marge paced up and down the ground floor hallway in thought. She knew the only chance for Martin lay in her feeding him lines—giving him lines now which he must memorize and not fail to repeat, word for word, unswervingly, when Mr. Sisley tried to grill him the next morning.

Sentences like: "I am a free white adult, aged so-and-so many years, in full possession of my faculties."

And, "You cannot question me without a lawyer." "I have the right to one phone call and one lawyer." "Take your hands off me." "I cannot incriminate myself." And, "The charges brought against me are utterly without foundation."

Marge wracked her brain to come up with more appropriate phrases: "The law is only as good as the men who defend it." . . . Or, "Time and tide wait for no man or woman." . . . But her head filled with static and she couldn't think. In any case, it didn't look good from where she stood.

"Here we were, rolling along so smoothly, and now *this* has to happen!" Marge barked to herself in an impotent rage—because for once there was nothing she could do.

Too nervous to attempt anything else Bill, Marge and Martin stayed up that night as late as possible watching TV. The last show on the air was a documentary on Anton Lisch, the famous concert pianist, presented on Casper State Teacher's College's educational station, Channel 43.

The program, "Anton's Hands", consisted of an interview at the great master's home in New York City. A student interviewer from Channel 43 sat at the maestro's left on his living-room sofa and asked various questions. However, Lisch said very little other than continually returning to praise the gleaming pair of enormous gold-plated hands that reposed on the coffee table before them.

The hands, stretched out to their fullest as if hammering out a final impossible chord, were slightly larger than life size: a gift from a famous sculptor-friend of the master's.

"My hands—aren't they wonderful?" the great artist kept repeating. "I can't take my eyes off them—what a marvelous surprise!"

"Aren't they marvelous?"

Marge hissed at the screen. "Boy, these big time ar-teests sure have got it bad, ain't they?" she drawled. "Why don't he play us some music if he's so hot? They oughtta send him out here, we'll take care of him. Make him do a little honest work. Shore would be a sight to see him shuckin corn, now, wouldn't it?"

Marge guffawed and turned off the TV. They all luxuriated for a moment in the sudden silence and listened to the distant sounds outside in the night.

Then they yawned and went up to bed. Marge decided she would give her advice to Martin in the morning, he was too tired to remember it now. She'd be sure and pump him bright and early, right before he left.

8

A Rainy Day at the Courthouse

The next morning at ten minutes to seven Martin found himself alone on the Courthouse steps, stamping his feet in the early morning rain and wondering about the ball of fright in his stomach, whether it was going to enlarge itself painfully the moment he encountered Mr. Sisley.

Martin was certain the morning was going to end darkly for him and it had taken a superhuman coaxing job on Marge's part while she and Bill drove him into town to convince him to meet this challenge head-on rather than turn tail and run away, which would have been so easy for him. Above all he was instructed that under no circumstances should he mention Bill or Marge's name.

He bit his lip and shivered. The rain continued to fall, soaking his sweater. Presently the tall metal doors clunked and slowly swung open, and a pair of white cotton gloved hands joined a rasping voice and pointed down at him.

"C'mon, son, let's get goin," the voice informed him, "although it's true we got all day." The cotton hands encouraged Martin up the steps.

Martin recognized the voice as belonging to old Burton Hennesey, the Courthouse guard, whom he had known as long as he could remember. Burton was a crippled World War One veteran, crusty and feisty, and Martin liked him. He was one of the few people in Winosha whose manner toward Martin hadn't changed drastically upon learning he might be crack-brained. Old Burton treated him exactly the same as before, in fact, telling uncouth rapscallion stories from the horse and buggy days. To him everyone else was a listener, and all listeners were the same: they existed to be told.

Martin skipped up the stairs. (Oh, boy! Old Burton! he thought happily.) But Burton was gruff with him this time: "Mr. Sisley's waitin, boy. Up the ramp to the second story balcony, see?" The white hand pointed across the courtyard. "Room number eleven, see?"

Eugene Sisley, the Wayne County Prosecutor, stood in Room 11 waiting. His body followed closely the physical description of a stovepipe and his face was hard and thin and grey. He grew a thin black mustache in a paper cup. He realized it was raining.

He was conscious of many other things as well. His nose, for example, was itching horribly, but instead of relieving himself immediately he prolonged the agony to the last possible moment, until delicious tears of frustration misted his eyes and his nostrils quivered at the edge of explosion. His ass itched too, now, and all along his spine and the balls of his feet, behind his left ear and even the roof of his mouth, all itched horribly. Sisley swooned. Finally he was a primitive ball of itch. The supreme instant of repression had arrived. He could stand it no longer and releasing a muffled howl he collapsed on the carpet, scratching himself all over, rolling back and forth and moaning.

Knock! Knock! Knock!

Sisley immediately regained possession of himself with a single grunt and snapped to a standing position. He brushed off his suit and steadied his face, combed his hair and mopped his brow. He blew his nose vigorously. He allowed two full minutes to go by (good for the boy's shaky self-confidence, he thought) while he reviewed the Kilbanky case in his mind. He heard Martin breathing heavily on the other side of the office door.

He then walked over to the intercom on his desk and spoke to the receptionist for the entire group of offices on the second floor: "Miss Haynes—this is Mr. Sisley speaking . . . Please come get young Kilbanky at my door and have him wait with you in the waiting room. I will fetch him myself as soon as I am free."

Sisley chuckled to himself, then lay down on his brown leather sofa and took a nap. He slept for forty minutes.

While Sisley slept Martin was fidgeting in the waiting room, becoming more and more distracted. He could hear the rain beating steadily on the roof. Rain always made him dreamy and left him sluggish and tongue-tied, and he knew he wasn't going to be able to say the right things at the right time, like Marge insisted he should. He couldn't remember *any* of the sentences she had coached him with. What was he going to say?

Just as he became thoroughly distraught and was jumping up to leave, Mr. Sisley shot into the waiting room with a grave expression on his face and grabbed Martin by the elbow. His fingers pinched at the boy's arm like pincers. Martin yipped aloud.

"C'mon, son," Sisley said impatiently as he dragged him down the hall. "We're very busy people here, you know. In spite of what you might think we definitely do *not* have all day. I have big responsibilities and many things to do. If you try to use up too much of my time," he added as he pinched Martin's ear, "I warn you I won't like it!"

"I have more important things to do than fool with lazy no-good layabouts like you!" He threw Martin into his room and slammed the door.

"Now then!" he demanded. "What can I do for you?"

. . . Martin was struck dumb. His face twitched spasmodically. What should he say? The pressure was just too much and he started sobbing. Sisley realized he had overdone it.

"OK, son, OK . . . *I'll* tell *you* why you're here. But stop that crying, for God's sake, it's completely disgusting!"

Overcome with shame Martin became mute, burying his face in his sweater. Soon he calmed down enough for Sisley to resume.

"Now, Martin," he said in a reasonable voice, "let's be friends. I understand the shape you're in, believe me. I called you in here this morning *precisely for that reason*, don't you see, so you could talk about all this unfortunate business to a friend, rather than defend yourself cold against a stranger—and a Jew, too, of course . . ."

Martin looked up, a flicker of trust returning to his eyes. Mr. Sisley can't be all that bad, he thought. Desperately searching for a way to explain the painful situation he found himself in, Martin was all too ready to fall back in his childlike manner on Mr. Schwartz's ancestry.

"My stomach hurts . . . I don't feel good . . . what should we do . . . I knew I never should have dealt with Jews in the first place . . .

Mommy . . . my stomach hurts . . . I wanna go home . . . how come we can't just forget about it? . . . I didn't do anything . . . what are we gonna do. . . ."

Martin continued disconnectedly, slobbering and shaking, until Sisley became exasperated and slapped him squarely on the face.

Whap!

"Get hold of yourself!" he barked. Whap! Whap!

The sound echoed around the room. Martin's cheek burned and his face turned scarlet. This man was slapping him—

Springing to his feet he slugged Sisley on the jaw and screeching in a contorted voice, "Nobody slaps me but my mother!" tore open the door and ran down the hall. Unfortunately, a retired policeman rounding the corner as part of his job collided with the frantic youth and both went sprawling across the parquet. Two minutes later Martin was seated again in the County Prosecutor's office—only this time his arms were bound to the arms of the chair by handcuffs, and his legs were bound to the legs. Sisley stood over him quaking in anger and rubbing his deeply bruised chin.

The skin had split in two places and with each drop of blood that fell to the carpet Sisley's face became more suffused with rage, until when the patrolman returned with bandages and first aid cream Sisley looked like he had suffered a heart attack. His long thin face was bright red and the shiny purple bruise at his chin spread upwards toward his mouth.

"You little moron," he whispered between his teeth. "I'll kill you for this!" While the patrolman affixed the bandage Sisley never took his eyes off Martin's face. As soon as the man left Sisley glowered like a maniac, his eyes darting around the room until they spied the polished chunk of pink Tennessee marble he used as a paperweight reposing on his desk.

"Umumfgh . . ." Sisley lunged for the paperweight and turned to face Martin, laughing savagely and seeming to have lost all control.

"Agghh, agghh, grahrr . . ." he roared, and then the County Prosecutor fell heavily across the manacled boy, hammering and pummeling him with the paperweight but doing so with such uncritical abandon that he tore the back of the chair apart. His most savage thrusts therefore missed their mark, but nevertheless when it was over Martin's arms and chest were raw and bruised, a small cut had opened above his eyebrow, and the state of nameless panic into which he had been plunged was unequaled in the annals of his lifetime.

For five minutes after Sisley subsided Martin existed as the literal embodiment of terror. His brain became a single white sheet of panic repeatedly torn in two like a sheet of paper, and his eyes swung in and out of phase in their sockets. Foam dripped down his orange sweater. His hands shook like palm trees in a hurricane.

But the most startling result of all was the fact that Sisley's uncontrolled onslaught had sizzled Martin's being to the point that substantial portions of his hair turned white, or grey. From a great distance this dramatic change was unnoticeable, but forever after his hair would be peppered and streaked with white. Martin of course was not yet aware of this, but when Sisley looked up from where he had fallen to the floor and saw a grey-headed boy rocking back and forth in trauma, tugging in vain at manacled wrists and gurgling like a cornered beaver, the County Prosecutor yelped involuntarily and shaded his eyes.

The shattering sight sobered Sisley quickly. He had meant just to scare the boy, break down his resistance with a view to obtaining more easily his signature on certain pieces of paper, but being slugged on the jaw had provoked Sisley into forgetting himself. He had overreacted. The streaks of grey were frightfully uncanny, and in addition Martin was in a state of panic such as the County Prosecutor had never before witnessed. He sighed to himself as he wondered what to do.

"OK, son, OK, OK . . . I'm sorry . . . C'mon, Martin, I'm sorry . . . Just lost my head . . . But you shouldn't have slugged me, you naughty boy . . . Don't you know men like myself in positions of power are unable to react calmly when slugged by farmers? . . . After all, Martin, this is the twentieth century! . . . I'm an important man . . ."

Sisley tried to reason with him but Martin had vacated the verbal level seemingly for good. He rocked back and forth, glassy-eyed and unresponsive. At a loss as to how to proceed, Sisley finally decided to act as if Martin had been the victim of a natural holocaust or disaster, such as a flood or fire, automobile accident or hurricane. He ordered Miss Haynes to fetch blankets and a hot water bottle from the Courthouse dispensary. When bundling him up warmly had no appreciable effect Sisley released his handcuffs and rubbed the wrists vigorously with witch hazel, at the same time ordering a doctor. Soon Dr. Tom Rice, G.P., appeared from his office across the town square, and while Sisley fabricated some excuse for a boy whom everyone assumed to be off his rocker, Dr. Rice took one look and gave him an injection. The grey hair he simply refused to acknowledge.

"It's a medium-strength sedative," said the doctor. "He should be awake and feeling refreshed in two or three hours. Just let him sleep, Gene. The chemical will do the rest."

So while Martin slept on his brown leather couch Eugene Sisley initialed various documents, ordered chocolate-covered doughnuts and coffee, read his mail and then took a short snooze himself. Finally Martin woke up and looked around. Sisley wondered with some irritation whether he was fit to continue with business—sign his name, and so on. The boy still appeared groggy. Sisley felt enough time had been wasted already, but on the other hand he was extremely relieved to see that Martin apparently had forgotten the details of their explosive encounter.

Martin stared around the room trying to orient himself—he obviously had difficulty remembering where he was. Although he felt his bruises and the cut above his eye he did not directly ascribe them to Sisley, who sat across from him now with a look of fatherly concern on his face.

The County Prosecutor breathed a sigh of relief. Maybe they could proceed with business after all!

Martin tried to clear his head by shaking it strenuously, and this made Sisley laugh. Martin joined in, and soon the two of them were chortling heartily. Martin remembered little of the attack he had survived just a few hours before, although certain things disturbed him—he eyed the marble paperweight with a growing uneasiness and could not look down at his raw red wrists without feeling a temporary surge of anxiety.

But Mr. Sisley smiled sympathetically, Miss Haynes gave him two nice hot cups of cocoa, and before long Martin seemed to have completely forgotten, except for an unpleasant emptiness in his stomach whenever he happened to look Mr. Sisley directly in the eye.

Sisley did his best to avoid what he took to be these pathetic attempts at normal human contact and proceeded briskly with the matter at hand. He took a bulging folder marked *KILBANKY* from a desk drawer and opened it with a flourish. Soon Martin was trying to concentrate as the County Prosecutor droned on and on with a technical description of the cement truck in question: its physical features, dead weight, condition, as well as a lengthy enumeration of every single one of its parts down to the last bolt and screw.

The cocoa combined with the sedative and the hypnotic sound of ever-falling rain to lead Martin more than once into a half-dream, half-waking reverie where he hardly was aware of the endless stream of words leaking from the Prosecutor's mouth. He began to hallucinate lightly, for some incongruous reason first seeing a bunch of ripe green celluloid bananas floating directly behind Mr. Sisley's head . . . Bananas turning slowly in the air as if suspended from a length of string . . . Strings of words pouring from a cruel stovepipe . . . Tarbabies tumbling off tarpaper shacks, tumbling off roofs . . . Bill Parsons, at the farm, tumbling off the roof and into the sky . . . Bill Parsons slicing bacon and popping bread into a toaster . . . Bill Parsons eating bacon and tomato sandwiches . . . Rows and rows of fresh-baked rolls, as if at a bakery . . . Great slabs of bacon, racks of cheeseburgers, sides of ham . . . His mother, dressed in a gingham dress from long ago, peering down at him gaily as she stood in a meadow and uncovered picnic baskets . . . as she drew away red-checked dinner napkins covering apple pies . . . Rows of frosty coca-colas . . . Barrels of ice cream. . . .

Martin awoke with a start, interrupting Sisley who was still reading out loud.

"Food!" Martin begged. "Food!" He began to salivate.

"Hungry! Food! Me! Now!"

Sisley stifled an urge to belt the boy across the face again, instead calling out wearily to Miss Haynes to bring them both lunch. Hot turkey sandwiches and french fries from Polly's Cafe down in the town square. He was reaching the crucial point in his elaboration and it wouldn't do to have Martin distracted. Obviously the boy has little control over himself, Sisley thought disapprovingly with a shake of his head.

"I could really use a Turkey Special myself, though, come to think of it," he said to himself, suddenly ravenous. Where the hell was their food? Angrily he rang his secretary's buzzer, but Miss Haynes stood across the street in Polly's tucking hot platters into brown paper bags and coughing. She had a bad cold, and all this rain and aggravation wasn't helping. In addition, *she* was hungry too, but the boss came first. She began to hallucinate lightly as well, although all she saw as she stared down at the aromatic sandwiches and waited for her change was one single, intermittent image: her own legs from the knees down, but with the shoes and stockings kicked off, resting on a luxurious ottoman on the other side of which a hooded figure dressed in black stooped and licked her feet. The figure licked and licked, as

Miss Haynes dizzily navigated her way across the Courthouse parking lot and up the stairs to Mr. Sisley's office. Her hair and dress were soaking wet. She plopped the sandwiches onto his desk and immediately ran from the room.

With infinite precaution, performing a labor of love, Eugene Sisley removed the Turkey Specials from their brown paper bags and freed the piping-hot open face sandwiches and cups of french fries from their temporary aluminum foil prisons. Generous helpings of turkey and stuffing drowned in a pool of rich brown gravy. The gravy had already soaked through the two slices of white bread that supported the bird meat, disintegrating them in the process. Smaller cups of mayonnaise, ketchup and cranberry sauce had been squashed in Miss Haynes's grip as well, mingling their forthright flavors in a smashing peach and pink blob that rode the surrounding dark brown gravy ocean with insolent pride.

"Piss!" Martin exclaimed. "Now what am I supposed to do—I don't like mayonnaise and it's mixed all in my sandwich! I can't eat this now," he whimpered crossly, as if at any moment he might cry.

Sisley set down the sandwich he had been attempting to hold. His hands were covered with a greasy brown mess, mushroom-flecked and glowing alarmingly in the light, more like oil-base paint than gravy.

As he craned his neck around the room looking for napkins the gravy-paint began to harden. He wiggled his fingers uncomfortably. Soon he could feel only one finger of his right hand.

"Martin, I'm surprised at you . . . Here I thought you were a grown man, a man among men like myself, a man like your father was—and instead you keep acting like a baby . . . You ought to be ashamed of yourself . . . What would your mother say?"

Martin began shaking with anger.

"You leave my mother out of this! And leave me alone, too. You asked me up here hours ago and then beat me up, I remember now . . . Now you're trying to make me think I'm a baby—but this mayonnaise has spoiled my sandwich for me, don't you understand? I refuse to eat it!"

"Oh, come on, Martin. Don't be such a baby."

"I'M NOT A BABY! GODDAMNIT! SHIT!"

He stood up shrieking and threw the open-face sandwich into Sisley's face. It splattered, though the County Prosecutor avoided part of it by ducking.

"YOU EAT THE SANDWICH THEN! HA HA! HA HA!" Martin let out a splendid laugh and ran for the door. Again however the on-duty patrolman proved to be his nemesis, apprehending him in the hallway and forcibly seating him once again before the man of authority in his gravy-spattered office.

Sisley was livid. McGurk, the retired policeman who served as Courthouse patrolman, declared himself more than willing to beat Martin senseless as fair punishment—as just retaliation—but Sisley had other ideas. He needed a napkin desperately.

"Run get me some paper towels, McGurk; I'll take care of Kilbanky."

Once he had cleaned off his face and hands the County Prosecutor resumed eating, consuming his sandwich with obvious relish, smacking his lips and smiling to himself. All the while he was eating, however, he looked wordlessly into Martin's face with cold hatred. He eyed Martin coldly while he ate away happily, and the spontaneous appearance of these two contradictory expressions terrified Martin and struck him mute. He realized that this dark man was in a position of power, that he was capable singlehandedly of determining Martin's fate in some way that nevertheless escaped him. He might take all Martin's money or sell his poor mother's farm. Or worse!

Several minutes elapsed during which Sisley ate greedily and silently while Martin cowered in his chair. The sound of heavy rainfall was all that intruded upon this apprehensive scene. Martin didn't dare to ask for a bite of the Prosecutor's sandwich.

His testicles ached badly and he longed to stand up and stretch, free his balls from the tight blue jeans and limber up his legs, but he found himself too scared to move. He glanced around worriedly: how much longer was this going to last?

He was a statue whose eyes could move—nothing more. The clock ticked away. He could hear the mechanism somewhere in the room, a quickly beating heart. He felt his own pulse getting louder and louder until the sound suddenly became a pack of wild horses. The galloping heartbeats pounded down into his brain. He gripped the armchair and shut his eyes tightly in terror.

Sisley continued eating.

Then, slowly at first, Martin's pulse grew fainter and fainter until it was no more than the hypnotic breaking of a tide against some distant shore and he became thick and sleepy-headed. His mind fogged up. A drapery of fatigue fell softly from above and hung itself between his eyes and the outside world, a spacious drapery made of the finest cool white linen. Stirring softly in the breeze . . . An arm of sunlight moved through the drapes, playing with the rich white material and illuminating it . . . Outside Martin heard the school bus from long ago, taking the elementary children to school . . . He himself was sick—was it the mumps? scarlet fever?—and had to stay home . . . A soft, sweet breeze . . . The cool clean sheets . . . A kitten played on the floor with a big ball of blue yarn. "Shame on you," Martin thought. "You naughty kitten!" . . . The clouds peeked through from outside, then the drapery closed over them. Someday, he knew, those drapes would close over them for good. . . .

His head slumped onto his chest and for a few blessed minutes Martin slept.

And for his part the County Prosecutor was startled anew by the streaks of grey and white that he saw covering Martin's head— streaks that he himself ultimately might be held responsible for by Mrs. Kilbanky, and by the whole community for that matter, unless he came up with a good explanation . . . The hair certainly was uncanny-looking . . . He shuddered as he imagined what a mother's reaction would be when her only son was returned to her looking shattered and grey. He had to think of something.

He stared uncomfortably at the sleeping head. Should he pretend Martin had suffered a "psychotic attack"? (He wasn't too sure what that might be.) That Martin had seen a ghost? That he had stuck his finger into an electric outlet? A wall outlet?

He was still puzzling over the problem when Martin awoke for the third time that morning and looked around.

Sisley decided his best course lay in keeping firm control of the situation, proceeding as if nothing had happened and then surprising Martin at the last minute with his image in a pocket mirror. He was still unaware of his condition, of course, and might be convinced almost anything had caused it.

"Let's get down to business, son," he said briskly. "We've wasted enough time."

He turned to the KILBANKY file that lay on his desk and started reading aloud from one of the documents therein:

". . . Whereas the culpable party, Martin Galworth Kilbanky, did on Sunday, April 19th, 1959, solemnly and in good faith make legally-binding contract with Mr. Emanuel Schwartz, sole owner and manager of Hundley's Hardware and Concrete Co., Inc., Winosha Falls, to deliver x amount of freshly-mixed cement to such and such a predetermined site upon the Kilbanky property; and whereas said Martin G. Kilbanky, born on such and such a date and aged so many years, failed to give adequate protection and instruction to the drivers and operators of the three (3) cement mixers duly dispatched by Mr. Schwartz to the aforementioned site; and whereas, due solely to said Kilbanky's clear and delinquent negligence one (1) of said three (3) trucks was lost at the site, causing great mental anguish and financial stress to said owner and operator of Hundley's Hardware and Concrete Co., Inc., Mr. Emanuel Schwartz . . . And so on and so forth. . . .

"Therefore, said Mr. Schwartz is herein obligated and obliged to sue said Mr. Kilbanky for the full market value of said vehicle in question were said vehicle to be appraised as new and sold on the market today; plus full recovery fees and workmen's compensation as detailed below in Paragraphs 8, 8-A, and 9-C. The full monetary amount of the civil suit herein described is to be found, computed in detail, appended to Paragraph 19-C below . . ."

The County Prosecutor read this document slowly and carefully so Martin would be sure to understand.

He was led to believe by the boy's furrowed brow that he had in fact, if not in full, understood.

He dropped the document on his desk and looked sympathetically in Martin's direction: "It's an expensive proposition, I know, son . . . Obviously you weren't prepared for certain facts when you undertook to build your house . . . For example, do you know how much cement weighs? Well, it's very heavy, Martin. The five tons of cement you ordered actually weigh fifteen tons. What they call 'actual weight' as opposed to 'apparent weight'. . . ."

He scribbled a note to himself and then continued.

"Now, Martin, I'm not going to read the other two suits aloud to you at this time, since I summarized their contents over the telephone to your mother yesterday and she led me to believe she transferred this information to you. Did, in fact, your mother so transfer?"

Mr. Sisley leaned forward in his chair.

"Well—did she?"

Martin did not know what to say, so he said, "Yes."

"Very well, then," Sisley continued. "Rest assured there's no real need for us to read these final suits aloud. I'll just summarize their contents for you. One group of suits are comprised of the personal damage suits filed by the three truck drivers for seventy-five thousand dollars each—and as I told your mother yesterday the men will certainly settle out of court for much less money . . . Already we have gotten them to settle through this office, through me. . . .

"Whereas the final suit, brought by an anonymous party as suit to obtain possible lien on your family bank accounts, by means of possible concurrent voluntary incarceration in a state institution, state hospital or state sanitorium . . . As to this final suit, I say, Martin, we cannot involve ourselves any further at this time . . . Suffice to say it's being taken care of. . . ."

He emphasized the ambiguity of these final words.

"That is, perhaps this final suit will be suspended and perhaps not. Perhaps the party involved will see fit to suspend the intent and thrust of the action as intended," the Prosecutor mumbled deceptively, "and perhaps not."

"Maybe, that is," he suddenly shouted, his voice taking on a brittle urgency, "that is, most likely and in all likelihood there will be no need for such an act on the part of said anonymous instigator . . . Said instigator being compassionate by nature and all too willing to suspend said suit against Martin Kilbanky if said Kilbanky is," and here he lowered his voice and stressed the words clearly, "if said Kilbanky is in the judgement of the Court and of the County Prosecutor—" he repeated the words, "—in the judgement of the Court and the County Prosecutor ascertained to be in good mental health and capable of carrying out his duties as responsible head of the Kilbanky household . . ."

He leaned back in his chair to observe what effect if any these words had on the defendant, so to speak.

Martin was perplexed and a little scared. He understood at most a third to half of what Sisley said, so that the County Prosecutor's dark hints of "incarceration" and "anonymous instigator" left him more confused than alarmed. There was no doubt, however, that Sisley's final words had put Martin at a disadvantage: the ball of fright in his stomach quickly expanded, and red and white dots pulsed in front of his eyes. He felt woozy, as if he were going to faint. He experienced difficulty breathing.

Sisley leaned across his desk and slapped him lightly on both cheeks to bring him around. "Now, Martin," he warned, "we must make an effort to listen calmly and carefully *and we must not black out*." He barked these last words very crisply, one by one, and Martin stiffened in his chair and sat up. Sisley tapped him once more on the cheek and then proceeded.

"Now what I'm going to say at this point is very important, so please pay attention. . . .

"We've made official inquiries and subpoenaed the records at Tri-County National Bank here in Winosha, so we are fully aware and cognizant of the precise extent and nature of your liquid assets, as it were. In other words, we know how much money you have left in your Kilbanky accounts. Namely, all assets considered come to a grand total of nineteen thousand five hundred and nine dollars ($19,509) . . . Now, the County has decided that in view of your present condition but also taking into account the genuine hardship presented by the spectacle of your mother at her advanced age being forced to run the Kilbanky farm all alone if you were to be—uh—incarcerated—uh—and appreciating therefore that your mother has no one else on whom to depend, on whom to rely . . . And in view of several additional momentous facts taken into account by this office, we have decided the following: to release you, Martin Kilbanky, from any further obligation on your part of any physical or mental servitude in a prison or state institution upon fulfillment by you of two conditions. . . .

"One—a signed statement agreeing never again to order freshly-mixed cement to be delivered in bulk anywhere. . . .

"And two—" he continued in an exact measured voice, "your release from any further obligation on your part to be effectuated immediately upon prompt payment by you *of a single overall fine and fee* covering all legal suits pending, either civil or criminal, against your name by the aforementioned cement company, its owners or employees (including the three drivers), or any governmental suit against your name filed by any city, county, state or federal authorities with regard to these developments, either retroactive to include the past or postdated to include the future. . . ."

The County Prosecutor paused.

"Also, needless to say, the removal of the cement truck from your farm will no longer be your responsibility upon payment of the fee and fine. You need not concern yourself with it in the slightest. The appropriate men with the appropriate tools will come to take it away at the appropriate time. Your only task in this regard will be to ignore the truck until it is removed."

Finally he was finished. He leaned forward. "Now, do you agree, Martin? OK? Do you understand? . . .

"Please think about this carefully before you sign your name on the dotted line. That is, before you sign *this blank check made out in my name* . . . This blank check which shall be made out for a sum to be determined by this office to adequately cover damage done to all parties, *and payable to me personally,* as County Prosecutor of Wayne County, this 1st day of June in the Year of Our Lord 1959, at 3:45 P.M. in the office of the County Prosecutor, County Courthouse, Winosha Falls, Wayne County, I Martin Kilbanky hereby do freely and voluntarily agree. . . ."

"Well, do you so agree, Martin? Will you sign over this check and consequently be released?"

Martin tried to clear his head and think.

He knew he understood what a "blank check" was, although he saw no connection between that blank check and the cancellation of all his problems.

"You mean if I sign over a certain amount of money to you I'll go free?" he asked.

Mr. Sisley smiled. "Hell, son, you're not in jail here! The payment is merely a fair reimbursement to all the parties involved, don't you see? We haven't determined the exact amount yet, of course, but I have my assistants working on it," he said, sweeping his arm around the room to indicate his assistants presumably working in another part of the Courthouse. "That's why it's a blank check, don't you see? As soon as the correct amount has been determined, we simply fill in the check for that sum of money and cash it in your name . . . It's all very simple and above-board, Martin. It's what has to be done."

Martin slumped back into himself and wrinkled his brow. He strained every muscle in his brain to comprehend fully the situation and be on top of it, but he couldn't seem to concentrate. He longed to step outside and refresh himself by means of deep breathing and exercise. He wasn't able to connect more than two or three points— "Kilbanky," "bulldozer," "check"—without losing the thread. He sagged in his chair, digging his fingers into his biceps as he tried to think. Where was all this leading? What other alternatives did he have?

He couldn't make it.

Finally Mr. Sisley, sensing the kill, feigned impatience and even ingratitude.

"Martin, I'm surprised at you! I'm truly disappointed. Here we've gone to extraordinary lengths in this office to help you out of this mess, to see you don't land in jail or an institution or something, to save your mother's name and help her in her infirmity and dependence upon you," he modulated convincingly, "and all we're rewarded with in return is your inability to make up your mind, your lack of decisiveness, your damn mistrust!"

Standing up dramatically from his chair he added: "Do you mean to say you don't trust us?"

He shouted: "IS THAT WHAT YOU'RE TRYING TO SAY?"

Martin curled into his seat in damp confusion. He started trembling again in spite of himself, and the ball of fright pushed at the walls of his stomach. He felt he was going to puke. That would be awful. His entire body ached, all he wanted was to go home. Sometimes he felt so disorganized.

"OK, I'll sign . . ." he said uncertainly.

"You will? Really? Oh, that's fine, Martin, just fine . . . I'm really proud of you at this moment . . . Here, sign once on this page," feverishly he pushed the document toward the boy, ". . . that's it . . . And once on this check . . ."

Martin signed the check and felt an enormous burden lifted from his shoulders. Not knowing exactly why, he breathed a sigh of relief.

Sisley was nearly hopping up and down in delight.

"Now, Martin, we'll have some of the boys drive you home in the Sheriff's own patrol car, won't that be nice? . . . A nice ride with the red light flashing? . . ."

"But I just want to show you one more thing, son," he said, suddenly becoming serious. He took out his pocket mirror, uncertain whether to show Martin his streaks of white hair now or let him find out for himself at home. He decided to risk it.

"Now don't get alarmed, boy," he warned. "It must have happened when you mistakenly stuck your finger in that wall socket, remember?"

He proceeded carefully, uncovering Martin's image a bit at a time, but Martin responded unequivocally:

"Yeeeooowww . . ." he screeched as soon as he saw his new blasted head of hair, blasted and sprinkled with grey and white; and jumping up from Sisley's desk he ran howling out of the darkening building into the rain.

He was rather taken with the hair, actually, although it had scared him silly when he first looked in the mirror.

He wondered how his mother would see it; he hoped she wouldn't become alarmed.

Above all he wondered about Marge—would she like it? Would she make fun of him?

He shuddered. The prospect of Marge belittling him had never entered his mind before and he didn't know if he could stand it. As he hitchhiked home alone in the rain he hoped and prayed with all the fierce desire he possessed that she would like it.

He could think of nothing else.

The rain had finally stopped and Marge was sweeping out the hog feeder on the back porch steps when she heard a car pull into the yard in front of the house. A door opened and shut and then the car shifted into reverse and whined back down the drive to the road. She heard swift footsteps slapping across the puddles in the yard. Replacing a strand of hair that had fallen into her eyes she let a puff of steam escape from her mouth . . . "I shoulda got Bill to clean out this damn feeder . . . didn't realize it was so big . . . Damn . . . That must be Martin now . . . Must a got a ride home with Akie Jake or somebody . . ."

She dropped the big rusty metal basin that had the words THE NU-GROW COMPANY stamped in one corner, and turned to go back into the house.

Just as her right foot caught in the step planks and she was looking down at it and tugging vertically on her leg the porch door whapped open and Martin shot toward her with a low whoop.

First she saw his shoes—or rather, those darned mudstained sneakers he persisted in wearing, *why* Marge would never understand. She started to laugh at herself, all the while tugging impatiently at her imprisoned foot, so that when Martin skidded into her and her foot popped free they both exploded and went sprawling down the steps into the yard. They laughed as they slipped and rolled in the wet grass. Marge laughed playfully, but Martin's laughter shot up like a Yellowstone geyser to extreme over-excitation, and without warning he was suddenly rubbing and squeezing both himself and Marge and moaning to himself with feeling.

Shocked, Marge realized he had been sexually aroused by their collision! She rolled away from him with a squawk and stood up, and it was then that she first saw his hair.

White streaks dappled with grey!

She was speechless.

Martin sat up and saw Marge looking, and embarrassment juiced his face apple red.

"It—it just happened," he said sheepishly.

"I was at the Courthouse all day and now I've got grey hair."

He rolled his eyes like a clown and began a nervous laugh.

Marge looked down at him and chuckled. She liked it! The hair shocked her when she first saw it, but he seemed so handsome now, she thought . . . She was surprised at herself to be thinking that, but he looks so distinguished! Even if he is just twenty-six!

"I like it, Martin," she said in a dusky voice, and his heart jumped in his chest.

She likes it! Martin swooned. He was so glad. His body hummed and crackled with physical sensations he had almost forgotten about. When they rolled in the wet grass he had smelled Marge's fresh sweaty body, her fragrant ringlets flat up against his nose, and he had breathed deeply of that perfume and gone euphoric. Her hips and breasts had left their imprint. Marge now had difficulty calming him down. She managed it by complimenting him on his hair, which he had been so anxious about, and by getting him to tell her what had happened at the Courthouse.

In excited tones Martin related an increasingly vague tale of blankets and electric shocks, turkey gravy and blank checks . . . Marge made no sense of it. She started to cross-examine him—after all, she had a direct interest in what had transpired—but she saw from his clouded eyes and drawn cheeks that he was hungry, and as a matter of fact the distant rumble in her own stomach echoed down to her socks.

Martin's had a long day, she thought to herself. He can't talk straight. We'll go eat dinner and let him rest up. He'll tell us about it later. Obviously things didn't go that badly or he'd be in jail tonight . . . And I should go upstairs right now and change my clothes, she added to herself huskily . . . I got so damn hot just then, everything's gone and soaked itself clear through!

PART THREE

A Jury of His Peers

9

The Chain-Link Fence

In the days that followed everyone at the farm adjusted to Martin's new hair. Marge in addition was concerned with forgetting their moment in the grass.

Bill couldn't have cared less about grey or brown, and Louise Kilbanky seemed to have gone through the same string of reactions as Marge and Martin himself—first shock, then a blip of uncertainty followed by acceptance. The acceptance itself was first self-conscious, then enthusiastic. Now she thought Martin looked more mature this way. Such a distinguished-looking man!

That night after dinner, Martin had related to them as best he could what had occurred with the County Prosecutor. It was clear he did not fully comprehend what had happened to him: he kept referring to how hungry he had been all day and to Mr. Sisley's "sixth sense." Mention of paperweights, handcuffs and Miss Haynes merely complicated the matter. They eyed with alarm his raw wrists and black and blue shoulders.

But above all they were confused by Martin's explanation of how he had come to sign a blank check made out in Mr. Sisley's name, although they were relieved to hear that the County Prosecutor had absolved Martin of any further guilt and had guaranteed he stood no chance of being detained or sent to jail. This was good news. But the blank check? The two ladies weren't so sure. Marge in particular was quite suspicious. She was further upset by the compromising situation she found herself in, which made it impossible for her to come to his defense. She and Bill could remain at the farm only on the sly, for the time being, at least.

However, Martin had judged himself lucky to have escaped Mr. Schwartz's clutches.

"After all," he reminded them, "that cement truck's still out there and somebody's got to pay for it. I guess it's gotta be me. . . ." He had lowered his head in shame and then all four had gone to the window once again and peered out at the huge upended vehicle. The truck still pointed at the sky. The scene endured unchanged as it had for weeks, the pool of cement and unfinished barricades so uncomfortable to look at that they all turned away from the glass with headaches. Soon afterwards Mrs. Kilbanky had retired for the night and the other three had lapsed into silence. The gathering darkness somehow merely increased the truck's presence in their minds. They all saw the red machine at least once that night during sleep.

The next few days found them going through the motions of farm maintenance while their real concern was news of the blank check. By then all four realized what Martin had done: Mr. Sisley was free to make out the check for any amount he wished, plunging them all into poverty in the process. Marge just couldn't believe it. She grilled Louise repeatedly on the subject of the Kilbanky accounts—how many accounts were there, how much money did they actually have? But the old woman refused to divulge the information. She still didn't trust Marge or Bill, and casting around mentally to relieve her sense of helplessness had led her to deduce that in some way the Parsons were responsible for the whole mess. She refused to surrender what little power she still possessed. The more Marge questioned her the more uncommunicative she became, until at last her tight lips became a daily feature of the house, a house emblem.

So they waited instead for some word from the Prosecutor. Marge attempted to convince Mrs. Kilbanky to telephone the Courthouse and speak with Sisley directly, but she would not.

Marge was exasperated. Bill had reacted to the problem in an entirely predictable way, spending more and more time in town with Fontessa, until Marge felt she owed it to him to confront him with her knowledge of the affair and then kick him out on his ear. She hated him actively now and could hardly bring herself to share the same bed with him.

Somehow, however, the brute's sexual potency was increased by his illicit encounters, so that he became a lion in bed and Marge continually postponed a showdown. She was angry with herself for it but couldn't resist that rod of his. The past year or so had seen their sex life dwindle to a splutter—she couldn't afford to pass up such a big surprise. The bed rocked and bumped in their corner room while Marge allowed her hate to build up deep inside.

During the daytime she worried about the blank check and their future on the farm, and it also upset her that apparently she was unable to control Mrs. Kilbanky. The old lady was being stubborn and refused to give in. Marge could hardly swallow such insolent behavior but she avoided using force because of Martin.

. . . So her old daydreams of omnipotence began fading, the fond jackboot and cracking-whip sequences grew dim. With this psychic change her body altered as well. She felt softer and more frail than before. She began wearing frilly lace tops and baking cupcakes and other little treats with newfound enthusiasm. Her nipples constantly seemed to stand erect. Her eyelashes grew long and sulky. Her fingers seemed so small and petite, now. Her old friend the poodle was so smelly now: out on the porch naughty Donnie must go!

Six days after Martin returned from the Courthouse, that would be the morning of the sixth day after June 1st, warm rain splashed on the windows of the Kilbanky farmhouse and a listless grey partition was in the air. It was an early summer rainstorm but the feel in the air was that the hot muggy weather might linger for hours, if not days. The land was green now, had been for weeks, since the gusty days and cold nights of March had long surrendered to the charm of April and the widening exhilaration of May. Now came the heady indolence of early June, when the dew piles up thick and sweet on the bluegrass and masses and stacks of honeysuckles clog the streams and cover the walls with their tasty drops of summer's essence hidden in a profusion of sexy white cups, honeysuckle blossoms and beds of June roses too, and the lovely sheen and foxy teenage fuzz on everything —the hills and meadows and fields magically excreting their green. The warm spring sunshine gradually burned into the first hot days of summer—the preceding day, for example, had been their first *really* hot afternoon on the farm, when time for a second had stood perfectly still, until Bill stepped on the teeth and whacked himself in the mouth with the rake.

For the first time, the day before, the sun had been around long enough to dig deep inside and warm the veins and bones. All over the county people lay around in languorous clumps. Schoolchildren were late for school, the postmasters put off franking their mail, the engineer forgot to start his train and then at lunch neglected to eat his hearty buckle stew.

That morning, then, the glorious warm rain came down, and for the first time since this household was formed no one got out of bed. Louise Kilbanky in her room and Martin in his, Bill and Marge Parsons in theirs, all lay abed charmed and transfixed by the rain. It didn't even occur to them to get out of bed and start the day's string of activities. Just dally abed near the rain, the windows wide open and the curtains thrown back, as the warm green leaves of the apple and pear trees, as well as the other farm trees, made their marks against the stormy grey enclosure.

For once, without human sounds to compete with them, the sounds of the farm were left all to themselves in the wind, creaking and popping and sighing, all the melancholy snorts and peeps of deserted farm country, the hybrid animals and crops left to themselves, the fields of rye as they blow in the wind, already at this date nearly six feet tall, and the primary growths of shrubs and bushes and young trees alive with their first carpet of crickets and beetles and slugs, and already the first swarm of mayflies has come and gone, a month early this year, the small exquisite bodies with their huge transparent wings smashing against the north wall of the house in wave after wave, countless millions of mayfly replicas already come and gone, and the moths of every type in the light in the kitchen at night, and the secret semaphores of the lightning bugs at dusk, weaving in and out among the snakegrass and the peas. . . .

So that morning all four lay prostrate and listened to the rain. Tufts of moist air fell into their faces. They all hung back in their respective beds sighing deeply. The warm storm buoyed them, carried them up and out above the modest farm landscape in which they lived for a split-second view of what the storm saw, the cold flashing pocket of unstable clouds and rain, floating its magnetic ball inside the warm June current surrounding it, the sunny June consensus.

"Jesus!" thought Bill to himself unexpectedly. "I don't understand this but I don't ever want to move: this is too full and too fine. . . ." He lay like a sheik on his carpet in the air. It carried him up above the clouds . . . Azure angel babies blew their conch shells and mussed his hair . . . The sky, the lordly sky was all around him and forever there. Forever! . . . Why, he could—

BRING! BRING!

What was that?

BRING! BRING!

—The telephone! Damn . . . Bill couldn't believe it. Marge's heart dropped. Louise Kilbanky's lips pursed in resentment. Martin buried his head in his pillow and groaned.

BRING! BRING!

BRING! BRING! BRING!

Somebody had to answer it so finally Marge—the strongest of the four—tore herself away from the sweet oblivion and the rain and ran down the hall. She knew who it was before answering, but she picked up the receiver and sadly worked her mouth: "Hello?"

"Hello, hello? Who is this?" Mr. Sisley's weasel voice demanded.

Marge fought off the impulse to slam down the receiver and instead cupped her palm over it. "Louise!" she shouted, "Better come downstairs, it's for you!"

Mrs. Kilbanky dressed herself shakily.

Marge wiped away a tear as she handed the poor woman the phone.

She then remained within earshot.

Louise cleared her throat.

"Hello?" her voice wavered pathetically.

"Ah . . . Mrs. Kilbanky? Hello. This is the County Prosecutor's office, Eugene Sisley speaking . . . How are you and your son? . . . Who was that woman with whom I was just speaking?"

She said the first thing that came into her head: "Oh, just a girl to help with the cleaning . . . comes in once a week . . . I'm not as young as I used to be, you know." She gave a weak laugh.

Marge bristled but held her tongue. Cleaning lady indeed!

"Well, Mrs. Kilbanky, I won't procrastinate . . . you *do* know what that word means?" There was a low snicker on the other end of the line.

Louise Kilbanky had never been so insulted in all her life.

"What do you take me for, Mr. Sisley, a country bumpkin?" She lashed out with all the spirit she could muster and it sounded surprisingly tough and spunky. There was a pause during which Sisley obviously was attempting how best to restructure the conversation.

"Of course not," he finally answered meekly. "I just thought you might not know the word—I myself just yesterday discovered what the goldurned word meant when it occurred in official correspondence from my Assistant District County Supervisors . . . Those assistant D.C.S.'s," he chuckled. "Always trying to show off their college ed-jee-cation," he drawled carefully. The last thing he wanted to do was antagonize her.

"Well . . ." she hedged suspiciously. She refused to laugh with him. She stood looking at the telephone receiver as if at any moment she might drop it to the floor and walk away.

"Enough of this," Sisley called out, sensing her impulse. "I'm a busy man and this case already has cost the county more time and money than it should have. I'm calling you for one reason and one reason only, namely to inform you officially of the results of the legal and financial inquiry made in the Kilbanky-Schwartz-Mixer case. As previously arranged with Martin, criminal and civil charges are dropped conditionally upon payment of the amount for damages and services as determined by this office . . . I am calling to inform you of that determination," he repeated, building up to his climax.

"AND THE RESULTS ARE AS FOLLOWS!" he shouted suddenly. "WHEREAS official investigation of the Kilbanky accounts reveals all assets considered come to a grand total of 19,509 dollars, both checking and saving; AND WHEREAS this office duly has determined and affixed the amount owed by Martin Kilbanky for his culpability in the entire incident as 16,452 dollars; THEREFORE, I hereby make and give fair and ample warning that the blank check so signed in my office on the afternoon of June 1st has been filled for said amount—namely, and I repeat, 16,492 dollars. . . ."

Louise Kilbanky gasped and fell back against the kitchen cabinets. Marge rushed to her side.

"I repeat, Mrs. Kilbanky, that the check has been made out to the sum of 16,572 dollars. It has been deposited in my own bank in my name. Please do not attempt to withhold or in any other way attempt to circumvent due process of the law. Please keep in mind, however, that your son is now absolved of all guilt. The cement truck currently stuck onto and imbedded in your property will be removed in due time at no additional cost to you. . . ."

"I am more than happy to have been of service," he concluded, his voice growing thin and distant, "—to have been of service during these troubled times to such a fine, eminent member of the community as yourself. I hereby recommend myself to you, dear lady; and to your son Martin, who has had the opportunity to learn much about himself and others from this unfortunate affair; and finally, to the memory of your dearly beloved husband, the lately deceased Mr. Ike Kilbanky, a man among men whose likes will not soon again walk among us, and whose death weighs heavily upon us all . . . I join the entire community, I am sure, in once more paying my deepest heartfelt respects to the widow of this great agricultural man . . . I weep, I tear my hair, I throw myself about, and I hereby say to you, dear lady, thanks and goodbye . . . If I can be of any service in the future don't hesitate to call and I shall do everything in my power to respond, given the full schedule and heavy workload of a man of my stature . . . Thank you again and goodbye. . . ."

These last words were barely audible but in any case Louise was in no condition to reply to them. She had long since swooned and dropped to the floor, leaving an alarmed and awe-stricken Marge to summon the others and carry her up to bed.

Somehow Providence had tricked them. They all spied the glum face of poverty directly ahead. Marge simply could not believe it. Bill took to drinking more and more. Louise neatly folded her hands in her lap and wept.

Martin alone seemed not to care, although Marge tried to convince him that when money is gone life looks grim. He understood, or thought he did, but he just didn't care.

He had little grasp of what was in store for him. His principal feeling was relief at not having to return to the Courthouse or deal with the law. It was impossible for him to take the future seriously. The simple joke was that others did. In fact, all he really grasped with conviction was that soon the cement mixer would be taken away. He might even be able to start all over again, he thought excitedly. Build a whole new house!

And what kind of house would it be? Although Martin surrendered himself to that question, he found no easy answer.

10

Passion Pit

Marge was exasperated. Her arms hung at her sides. She walked with a slouch, or sat in a corner of the sun running straw through her teeth and staring blankly. She couldn't figure it out. How could Martin possibly have done such a thing? She knew he was batty, but she also knew he possessed more sense, in a certain surprising way, than anyone else she had ever run across in her brief life as the miraculously-escaped parallel to a small town truck-stop waitress. That is, Marge had circulated among people economically and socially as if she were a waitress at a Clipsieville truck stop, but all the time in which she participated in that world naturally she also indisputably was not a waitress. Marge Parsons was simply Marge Parsons.

She cupped her elbows in her hands and sat on the split-rail fence in a reflective mood. Carefully she nursed a forbidden cup of instant coffee . . . Coffee: the one thing from town she missed since coming to live out at the farm . . . Or were there other things, too? Things even Marge would never admit to herself? . . . She shifted her weight uncomfortably. The lumpy rail dug into her butt.

Yes, were there other things she missed too, things she was unwilling to repeat to herself—or were there? A secret life even Bill was not aware of? A tragic love affair that could never have worked anyway? The long, lonely walks down floodlit streets at night; sipping mugs of coffee in the Allstate Insurance Office after hours with mature, forty-five-ish Ward Birdwell, seated on his fancy new aluminum-tubular couch before the artificial log fire he had purchased the week before in Spartanburg? Or else their wool-socked feet stretched out gratefully before a real fire, out in Ward Birdwell's hunting cabin in the woods, their bodies exhausted from a long hard day tracking beaver in the marshes, their hip-length rubber boots drying by the fire, their hands warming big tumblers of brandy: then the tumblers are knocked over brusquely, they tumble to the floor, and a scarf and hunter's rubberized shirt followed by twill slacks and huntress's calf-length skirt and wool plaid shirt are thrown feverishly aside so that two people who hunger for each other but whose fate decrees they cannot have each other more than a few times, tear at each other's enflamed bodies with desperate longing? . . .

Marge leaned forward on the fence, her inner eye bugging out at this reverie that had suddenly accosted her. Wow! she thought. I've got to get hold of myself!

She jumped down from the fence, buried her coffee cup under some bushes, and walked off into the burgeoning fields surrounding the farmhouse. It was a hot summer afternoon, one of the first they'd had, and Marge was overdressed in a corduroy shirt, winter under-shirt, stiff new jeans and heavy white tank toppers. Soberly she worked her mouth on a stick of gum. She had many problems, even just taking into consideration the farm and the blank check; and Martin . . . She cursed because of the heat and took off her creased and soaked topper. "Fuck!" she ejaculated bitterly.

Marge felt bitter and disappointed because a beautiful nest egg, a once-in-a-lifetime set-up, had plopped right into her hands only to break apart when she least expected it and leave her fingers covered with runny yellow phlegm. Disgustedly she wiped them on her jeans. What a chance, what an opportunity, and now it seemed all gone. Down the drain! Nearly twenty thousand dollars—enough to keep them neck-high in steak for years! Where would she ever see that kind of money again? She'd never dreamed they were worth that much. And Martin hadn't had enough sense to hold onto it for more than a few weeks . . . and the day Marge's dream was born was the very same day unbeknownst to her that it lay poisoned. How ironic!

"How ironic!" she laughed aloud. Marge's mouth hardened in re-sentment. Goddamnit . . . "Oh, goddamn you God!" she bellowed out loud in an onrush of bitter disappointment. "Goddamn you God I hate you!"

But this was too much for even Marge to take, and she sprawled sobbing into a bank of high grass, pounding her fists in a blind rage into the warm earth. She worked herself up into a major tantrum, pummeling the earth and tearing away at the surrounding turf and grasses, until finally she subsided and lay completely alone, exhausted and whimpering in the noonday sun.

Ten or fifteen minutes went by, during which time several bugs apparently of the crawling variety bit and stung her. Through her spent rage and dried tears she wondered where these bugs had come from so early in the summer—even the bugs won't leave me alone! She cursed again. And it's so fucking hot!

Straw and twigs worked their way into her shirt and underpants and the sun burned her nose. Damn! she thought . . . I gotta get outta here!

She started to pull herself up from the sizzling weeds when an airborne bug flew into her gaping out-of-breath mouth, causing a paroxysm of coughs and choking noises. Suddenly the insect attempted to hoist itself back up Marge's larynx and Marge went wild, coughing and choking until she passed out. Her last memory was a deep sense of frustration followed by a bulging sea of red dots that bubbled and swam before her eyes. As her gorge rose the dots became huge skittering metallic-blue globules, then angular gunmetal spokes that lashed out at her eyeballs, and Marge dropped from consciousness asphyxiated. . . .

She might never have rejoined her companions here on earth had not Martin happened to be traipsing home to lunch at that very moment and spied her crumpled body in the grass. He dropped his sack of garden tools and ran to her side. Frantically he turned the blue-faced woman on her side and began slapping her face. Opening the spittle-covered jaws he looked inside and saw something small, black and shiny waving at him from deep in Marge's throat. He panicked and almost blacked out, but at the next moment he realized a bug was trapped in her throat. Marge herself looked awful. Her face was clammy, hot and purple—while deep inside her throat a tiny being cried for help. Two antennas, one broken, waved feebly from the mountain of hot wet throat that threatened to crush it to death. Martin jabbed two fingers down the hatch and freed the terrified insect. It fluttered off between Marge's teeth, some sort of thin black fingernail beetle.

Martin clasped her lifeless body to his own, beating and lifting it off its feet in his grief, unknowingly forcing a modicum of breath down to those comatose lungs, breaking the death-spell of that fear-stricken esophagus. Marge hacked and choked alarmingly but color flushed her cheeks and suddenly the dim machine sparked back to life. Blubbering and weeping and gasping for breath she fell into his arms.

He was so traumatized by what had occurred that he embraced her in a state of frenzy, frightened out of his wits. Without realizing what he was doing he began kissing her arms and face and squeezing her flesh with all his might until she yelped and dug her fingernails into Martin's eyes.

"Raaowrrgh!" he howled, and then they began embracing each other in earnest, both oblivious to their surroundings, crazed by waves of passion, madly tearing the clothes off each other's bodies and falling into a gloriously frightening tear-stained embrace. Martin's eyes popped open wide in amazement. His mighty engine, so long neglected, roared to life. He plunged the splendid member deeper and deeper into Marge's steaming pocket and moaned deliriously. Marge—on the rebound as she was so precipitously from dizzy black unconsciousness—gasped and shuddered and responded to Martin's frantic plunges as never before with any man or boy. She wailed vertiginous joy and amazement at the apparent size and lasting power of Martin's cock. Her white-haired boy with a cock of steel!

Oblivious to their situation Marge and Martin furiously made love on the bush-covered incline, rolling and tumbling in their embrace down the gravel into an adjacent field of waving green rye stalks, already six feet tall this early in the season, at whose ghostly furrowed bottom, insulated from the sky above by the thickly-sown stalk profusion, they explored and madly fondled and touched each other, or else coupled feverishly like storks, madly rolling among the stalks and snapping them with their thrashing bodies. Rye fluid spurted out everywhere.

They made love there at the bottom of the rye for nearly two hours. The heat was intense. Finally depleted and exhausted they fell into deep sleep, knotted in each other's arms, absolutely afraid to wake up and look into each other's eyes to see who they were and what they'd done, afraid their dream might burst.

After very little time had passed they did awake, however, and immediately they resumed making love. Neither could look the other in the eye, although rarely was that necessary. Navigation proceeded underwater as usual. Eyes closed, hair streaming, legs flailing; together in that watery dream.

Martin at any rate was completely caught up in what he was doing, since it had been seven full years since he last made out—and that was as far as it went—with a girl named Peggy Stubbs in high school. He had therefore never before experienced intercourse with another person. His was an untapped horniness. Since he graduated from high school into his present condition his sexual urges had lain partially dormant: that is, deep down he had felt too embarrassed by what other people took him for to walk into town and approach the girls he had gone to high school with, most of whom were married off or regarded him oddly and would not talk. So who was he to talk to? Who was he to make out with? The little girls who, as opposed to their older sisters, often adored him? Hardly.

So the moralistic credo fed to him by his society prohibited any normal dating and necking activities for the likes of "the new Martin Kilbanky," the Martin Kilbanky of the last six or seven years. He responded to his social and sexual ostracism by the obvious ploy of a healthy red-blooded fellow in his unfortunate situation. He loved to horse around with the little schoolgirls in town and thought about any actual encounters for days afterwards, playing with himself a lot. Now at last Martin had stumbled on the real thing, and the depths of his potency seemed to have no bottom.

Twelve, fifteen times he came to climaxes that amazed even the poor grasshoppers that the lovers' crazed bodies rolled over onto and quickly crushed to death. In her brief but varied sexual experience Marge had never felt or heard of anything that could compare. She herself came time and again, stupefied by this sudden surfeit of pleasures which she had hardly suspected to exist from the evidence of her previous lovemaking. Marge surrendered herself that afternoon as she never would have believed possible before, and as a result she had her hands full and her lips too. Their sweat-drenched bodies gradually became coated with the juices of their love and combined with the dirt and pebbles and the squashed bodies of insects to form a thick ambrosial paste, sweet and red and stiff.

When they finally stopped loving they were so sore they could hardly move, and when they awoke after dozing off they found the paste on their bodies had hardened like clay. The aromatic factor was overwhelming, too. One sniff was all that was needed.

They struggled like mud ducks back up the embankment for their clothes. Marge was shaking and Martin could barely control himself. His embarrassment and sense of foreboding were intense. He felt something monumentally out-of-place had just occurred between himself and Marge. He didn't understand at all but he shuddered nonetheless, fuzzily reflecting that somehow what they had done was catastrophic, or would have catastrophic consequences. But . . . wow, had it felt great! Martin discovered that he loved sex beyond belief, and all considerations paled before that discovery. All he could really think of was doing it again immediately. As they struggled with their clothes he eyed Marge hotly, and it was at that moment she cleared away the tidal wave of passion from her eye and saw clearly the strategic position she now found herself in—a precarious one, to say the least. She looked at Martin uneasily: how was she ever going to be able to control the floodgates that obviously had broken open in this semidomesticated creature? She realized there was a good chance he would simply flout the laws of accepted social behavior no matter how strenuously she demanded he keep their intercourse a secret.

The fact was that Martin couldn't control himself in any truly dependable way, Marge realized groggily . . . What was she going to do? . . . He was perfectly capable of agreeing if she asked him to keep their love a secret, then half an hour later whipping out his whanger without warning just as they all sat down to tea. She imagined what Mrs. Kilbanky's reaction would be and laughed in spite of herself. And Bill, that poor jackass! Ha ha ha, Marge laughed silently, and even somewhat clumsily. She was having trouble getting her thoughts together. Her legs and cunt and in fact her whole body—deliciously sore, to the point that every muscle ached when she moved. Her brain whirred and her fingertips crackled. Martin started running a love-juice-coated finger up and down her left leg as she struggled with her jeans and Marge swooned and thought she'd pass out. Compulsively she grabbed for his rod, then turned away . . . This is no good—no good, she thought in mounting desperation . . . She hated being out of control . . . feeling like a slave—and hell, people might be watching! What if Bill were watching?

That thought sobered her quickly, like a slap on the snout. She jumped to her feet and looked around. She saw in the distance the house and the pond and the upended cement truck. Nothing suspicious. They were over a half-mile from the house, so unless someone was walking in the fields nearby they would not have been seen, at least would not have been seen in detail. From that far away they might have been pulling up stumps. But what if Bill were somewhere nearby? True, he almost never left the house when he was at home, but Marge craned her neck anxiously in every direction . . . There might have been quirk trespassers or bystanders on the county road . . . The unknown factor . . . Marge didn't like it . . . She didn't like it one bit. . . .

They were both fully dressed and on their feet now—Martin seemed to understand well enough what the problem was. He scouted around the vicinity, but except for a vexing profusion of horseflies he found nothing. Marge decided they had not been seen. "We're lucky, Martin," she said, turning to him, and he responded by sinking to his knees and burying his face in her muff. She moaned and wriggled free. "Damnit!" she pleaded as sternly as she could. "We just can't have this. You gotta realize, Martin . . . people won't accept it. They just can't understand. We *must* restrain ourselves . . . What about your mother, Martin? Whaddya think she would say if she saw us this way?"

"My mother?"

This seemed to wake him up, and in a state of apprehensive exhaustion they walked slowly back to the house. It was still a sweltering summer day. The sun burned and burned in the sky.

That evening Marge and Martin were so sore and worn out that they could hardly keep their eyes open. Mrs. Kilbanky regarded with suspicion her son's inability to properly masticate his food, and the dinner table was the setting for quite a scene during which the old woman momentarily spent her frustration on what she took to be further evidence of Martin's inability to cope with everyday life. She bawled him out in front of Marge and Bill, calling him "spastic" and at one point when he protested with tears in his eyes she dared him to prove himself by eating his food like an adult. "Like a regular person," she said. Martin was so exhausted, however, that try as he might he could not master with any regularity the movement from plate to fork and from fork to mouth, spilling buttered lima beans and mashed potatoes down his shirt as Marge giggled like a schoolgirl and Bill snorted sluggishly.

Even Louise Kilbanky had to smile at Martin's frantic vaudevillian attempts to please her, and she responded to a successful foray of meat loaf and potatoes with a facetious round of applause and a lightly mocking, *"That's* like a man!" Marge and Bill laughed. Martin was deeply humiliated to be the butt of his own mother's jokes, but one glance across the table told him Marge was enjoying herself, and that was good enough for him. He smiled and continued eating.

Walking home from their orgiastic conflagration earlier Marge had warned him not to exhibit openly his emotion for her, pleading with him that any false move might well destroy their happy home. It would be as hard on her as on him, she confided. How she longed for him, how she burned! She added that if his mother discovered them together she probably would not be able to withstand the shock, and it was this last consideration that convinced Martin to try and "play dead" as he phrased it.

He agreed and swore on his honor not to betray their secret love, but all he really acknowledged by so doing was his state of complete physical exhaustion. Marge eyed him uneasily as he half-ate and half-slobbered his fifth and then his sixth helping of tapioca pudding. Marge knew tapioca pudding was his favorite dessert and she hoped, crossing her fingers under the table, that eating such great quantities of it would not immediately restore his virility . . . She had enough difficulty subduing her own newly-fired urges. They surfaced when she least expected them, causing her to pinch her own nipples in spite of herself, or rub her thumb against herself and swoon. She seemed oddly distracted and giddy. Through his own fog of beer and self-absorption Bill wondered vaguely what was going on, but he was too thick that night to see.

It was very hot that evening and no one felt like sleeping. They all repaired to the front room after dinner to watch TV, and in the monster console's ghostly blue light Marge and Martin blew furtive kisses while all four watched a succession of programs, capped by their favorites, Batman and the Garry Moore Show.

Martin's grey hair glowed in the phosphorescent light. Everyone was in fine humor at twelve-thirty that night, Mrs. Kilbanky dozing off in her Morris chair, Bill drinking himself onto the floor, when all the network channels signed off for the night with the playing of the national anthem and Marge was forced to tune in the only station still broadcasting, Casper State Teacher's College's educational station, Channel 43. She giggled as an inept student moderator dressed in a badly-cut Robert Hall suit and thin black tie introduced the final speaker of the evening, a Professor Hurdle from some big eastern university.

Professor Hurdle, an overweight, determined-looking man in goatee and horn-rimmed glasses and wearing a white lab coat, stood before twin blackboards in an empty classroom and announced the topic of his lecture: *Instantaneous Transmission of a Signal Is Impossible,* or *Your Own Line Spectra as Messengers from the Micro World.*

He began abruptly:

"This age dedicated to change for its own sake has also discovered the simple hierarchy of the replicas that fill the world. Since the universe remains recognizable from one moment to the next, each instant is nearly an exact copy of the one immediately preceding it. Every action belongs in a series of similar actions. The copies vary by minute differences. The act of discard corresponds to a terminal moment in the gradual formation of a state of mind . . . Discarding useful things differs from—differs from the discard of pleasurable things in that—in that the first operation is—is more final . . ." He closed his eyes as if slipping into a reverie, then opened them slowly and tried to resume. He fumbled with his papers. Something had thrown him out of balance. He started to signal off-camera but then changed his mind and spoke again:

"In other words, there are only two significant velocities in the history of things. One is the glacier-like pace of cumulative drift in small and isolated societies when little conscious intervention occurs to alter the rate of change. The other, swift mode resembles a forest fire in its leaping action across great distances, when unconnected centers blaze into the same activity. . . ."

But something was wrong. The professor looked disgruntled. It was obvious he had misplaced a good part of this address, so there was no alternative for him but to change horses in midstream. He clearly was not pleased by this predicament, and Marge chuckled softly.

Without any transition or explanation the professor abandoned his first topic and continued the lecture with a new one.

He cleared his throat and began speaking very rapidly in a loud, serious voice:

"Mathematics alone is not enough," he began rather disconnectedly. Soon however he found his stride: "They build a model. They stick it in a wind tunnel and hope they've got all the basic data correct, that the arithmetic is good. Sometimes it is. Sometimes it isn't. Think of a drop of water hanging for hours off the end of a faucet. There is a decided limit to the size of that drop. You couldn't take that drop of water as a true indicator as to how a ton of water would act. I doubt if you've ever seen a ton of water hang off the end of *anything* for very long . . ." He paused for a second, and in the farmhouse parlor in the dead of night Bill began snoring. Marge giggled, a trace of her old hard-boiled self returning as she blew an unmistakable fart at the television screen and Mrs. Kilbanky gasped aloud at her crudity.

Martin, meanwhile, stared at the screen with total uncomprehending absorption. His eyes grew huge and empty. His mouth hung open. "Maybe he'll learn something," his mother said to herself.

". . . Now it happens that a cubic foot of helium will lift about one ounce," Professor Hurdle continued. "The ratio between the surface area and the volume of a cylinder is not constant. Fill with helium a small, rigid, cloth-covered aluminum-framework cylinder, and nothing happens. It is too heavy. Fill a large cylinder built the same way, however, and it rises into the air . . . How large?" He looked around the classroom, but since no one was there no one answered. "HOW LARGE?" he repeated petulantly. A trace of irritation crossed his face. "Very well, then, since no one has come prepared I'll have to give the answer myself. . . ."

Dramatically standing back from the blackboard he announced: "Eighty feet!"

He drew the number 80 on the blackboard and continued.

"An example may serve to clarify the distinction between the small and large cylinders: the totality of all the bodies in the universe determines a reference system possessing the property that any body turning with respect to this system will experience centrifugal forces. Thus these forces are a consequence of the rotation of the body with respect to the other objects and so are of purely relative origin. It makes no difference if the earth turns and the heavens stand still or—on the contrary—if the heavens turn about a stationary earth."

Martin's face twitched as he looked on.

"Consider for example a perfectly rigid rod extending from point P_1 to point P_2, the distance between these points being as long as we please . . ." Martin felt his cock grow hard and, shifting his weight against a coffee table leg as he sat on the floor, he began to massage it.

". . . The rod constitutes a signaling device that works faster than a telegraph system, since a blow applied to the rod at the end P_1 apparently can be delivered immediately at point P_2. Thus, with the aid of an absolutely rigid body, it should be possible to transmit signals with infinite speed over arbitrarily long distances."

"However," Professor Hurdle waved a meaty hand in warning, "in order to rule out this possibility the theory of relativity must make the additional assumption that there is no such thing in nature as a perfectly rigid body—"

Marge laughed outright at this. "No such thing in nature as a perfectly rigid body," she mimicked. "Ha ha ha . . ." She looked over and saw Martin's stiff cock in the TV light.

"Actually," the Professor continued, "because every body is composed of atoms it must be deformable, since the relative positions of the atoms will change when stress is applied to the body. In the experiment with the rod, what actually happens is that the blow applied at P_1 is not transmitted at once through the whole body,"— Martin began shivering and breathing harder—"but produces an elastic wave of compression that travels from P_1 toward P_2 with a speed quite small compared to the speed of light."

"A speed quite small compared to the speed of light," Marge mocked again and Martin laughed loudly in an over-excited falsetto fashion, temporarily waking both Bill and Mrs. Kilbanky.

"Huh?" Bill grunted, and they all laughed again. Martin crawled across the floor to the far side of the sofa and resumed rubbing his cock. He grew increasingly abandoned, moaning to himself, until his mother leaned over drowsily with, "What did you say, dear?" and Marge signaled him to quiet down. Something very vaguely dawned on Bill.

Professor Hurdle drew a cylinder and a rod on the blackboard behind him and then drew a circle. "In carrying these notions over to three-dimensional space," he continued, "it can be said that a space is either flat or curved according to whether it shows a behavior similar to that of a plane or a curved surface . . ." Marge's tongue curled lasciviously in the TV's blue light, exciting Martin even further. He threw all caution to the winds and wrestled furiously with his member in the corner of the floor. ". . . In particular, a spherical space has the property of being *self-closing*." The Professor emphasized the words. "This means that a line which otherwise gives the impression of being straight will, if followed far enough, eventually lead back into itself!" With a triumphant flourish he drew dozens of tiny circles like bubbles very swiftly on the blackboard.

At that moment unable to contain himself any longer Martin groaned aloud and came, thrashing back and forth in one brief explosive flurry. He moaned and shuddered as the orgasm ricocheted along his synapses and waves of pleasure broke all long the shores of his body. "Uh uh uhahhhh . . . wuahh . . ."

"What, dear?" asked his mother in concern. She could hardly see him in the darkness but some knick-knacks were falling to the floor accompanied by the sound of material being torn, and she was worried. "Is something wrong?"

"Uh uhahhhh." Martin sloshed against the far corner of the room but could not reply.

"He's all right, Louise," Marge said in a husky voice. "It must be this program. It's got Martin all upset."

"Well, let's turn it off, then. We should all be in bed by now, anyway."

Martin lay gasping on the floor but then recovered in time to watch Professor Hurdle finish his lecture. He listened in rapt fascination, unable to comprehend a word.

The professor concluded by saying: "From consideration of the dual nature of radiation and of matter, we are able to formulate a general and far-reaching principle called *complementarity*. It says, essentially, that every experiment that allows the observation of one aspect of a phenomenon denies the possibility of observing a complementary aspect. For example, the wave and the particle descriptions are complementary—they are never manifested in a single experiment or encompassed by a single description . . . And so it *is* possible to interpret the facts perceptually, *but only by using two mutually exclusive pictures*. These two pictures must necessarily clash; and on every such occasion one picture comes into power while the other loses its validity . . . So that when mankind today truly first inf—"

But he was forced to cut himself off in mid-sentence as his allotted time apparently had run out. Omitting the intervening explanatory material and shaking with consternation the professor concluded by bellowing hurriedly: "But as William Blake the great poet was inspired to say—and don't you ever forget it—'Eternity is in love with the products of time!' That is very profound and generous and, but—but I see my time is up . . . I see my time is up . . ." He was glowering off-camera now but was left with no alternative. "Thank you and good night," he said.

The picture tube went blank, then snowy white. Bands of black lines traveled slowly from left to right across the screen, an ocean of lines.

"Eternity is in love with the products of time, eternity is in love with the products of time! Yahoo! Yahoo!" Martin crowed, jumping up and repeating the line over and over again in jubilation while Bill and Marge laughed and chased him around the house a few times and finally up to his room where he collapsed on his bed fully dressed. The other three retired for the night in high good humor.

But once she was prone Marge hardly slept at all. She lay awake in the heat and stared at the ceiling.

She tried to sleep but just couldn't. Her soul was on fire—and besides it was a hot night, muggy and oppressive. A warm front complicated by a stout low pressure system had settled over the area late that afternoon, a brooding low pressure that refused to be displaced. It hung over the countryside like a washcloth, trapping the heat that had been refracting and refracting off the sunny fields all day . . . It refused to rain, the wind had died to nothing, and the heat of the day was trapped under a thick stratus cloud cover, holding down with it the normally expansive perfumes of the night and making them heavy and sweet. The lovely nimble exhalations of the living beings of the day—the trees, grasses, insects, birds and flowers—combined with the brusquer exhalations of people, the darker tobacco-colored or ruby-red ones, to accumulate under a constantly falling pressure center as the night wore on and the cloud bank held them down, held them down, until by two o'clock in the morning you could cut it with a knife and the dogs and horses out in the yard were wheezing and Marge lay awake in her bed. She couldn't sleep. Drifting in a daze, or more accurately that nameless, "other" state suspended between waking and sleeping, she looked up at the wallpaper islands and then down at the big clear panes of glass stacked up neatly by the bed: the panes of glass like blue fire that had resulted when the storm windows were taken down and abandoned . . . The windows that had been taken down two months before and lay stacked beside the bed all that time . . . The windows that had been abandoned. . . .

Marge dropped down through a glass ocean . . . The wind whistled at her feet, and in that deep-dropping blue-fire ocean Marge at last was free.

The next morning at 5:48 the sun came up and over the horizon. A hundred thousand tons of beer and cheese per second hurtled outward from its burning core. But due to atmospheric conditions, principally the low pressure system, this summer sun could not be seen or felt directly. A thick pearly cloud bank hung motionless over the Wayne County area, and though it got hotter and hotter as the day progressed until by noon steam rolled off the telephone poles and pencils in the houses stuck to tables, no direct sunlight fell on the people. Not a peep of blue sky was seen. The clouds dropped lower and lower. All day it could have rained but didn't. The muggy humidity trebled. In Clipsieville and Morton's Corners, in Winosha Falls and Lunenburg and Virdon, the townsfolk stood in bunches gaping for air. By four o'clock that afternoon the sensation was highly oppressive: the low pressure system had not budged. Short-sleeve shirted seed salesmen and door-to-door Bible salesmen fought with their tightly knotted ties and turned purple. The blackbirds gasped for breath on the wires. The telephone lines hummed with pleas for relief. Wayne County now lay sweltering. The dairy cows became queasy and had unprecedented dreams of eating meat. Horses neighed and kicked their stalls, and the pigs lay prostrate in their pens. Frantic slugs did their utmost to advance themselves one inch. The ponds all bubbled. In the swamps and gullies eggs hatched in profusion and clover bloomed, while under the porch steps dank delirious fungi dormant for years flared up out of sleep. It was, in short, the first real dog day of the year. Marge's poodle Donnie would be a miserable tick- and flea-ridden ghost before the day was through.

At 7:00 A.M. the four members of the household were already awake, though drugged by the increased mugginess. In their three respective beds they lay soaking their sheets clear through but too dazed by the heat to move.

Marge watched the white-gloved hands on the Mickey Mouse clock Bill had given her for their third wedding anniversary . . . 7:14, 7:15, 7:19 . . . 7:34, 7:38, 7:46 . . . She lifted one arm but couldn't get up. This must be some kind of record for June! she thought . . . But she was in no hurry to get out of bed anyway. The problems she faced were enough to make her *never* get up. She had brooded over them the night before and she was brooding over them now . . . Yesterday's erotic explosion, which she was afraid might recur in a situation out of her control. Even now she had difficulty believing it had happened . . . And the blank check Martin had signed, all that money gone, and that slimy County Prosecutor involved in the farm's affairs . . . Out of control, out of control . . . She was extremely depressed by the ease with which fortune had slipped through her hands, like water . . . Apparently she just didn't have what it took. . . .

The sweat poured down her brow, between her breasts. She shifted her legs then kicked off the sheets. Bill woke up and looked at her momentarily, then rolled over and faced the wall . . . And Bill! she thought. That cold distant look in his eyes . . . She knew they were finished with each other . . . Through . . . Bill rolled off the bed and hit the floor with a thud. Instead of laughing as she normally would have done, Marge growled in disgust . . . She hated him . . . Her skin stuck to the sheets . . . Without saying good morning or looking at her again he stood up and wobbled into the bathroom. Soon he returned and without saying a word dressed in brand-new Levi's and white T-shirt and left . . . Marge could hear him fumbling with the teapot downstairs in the kitchen. She felt positive he would drop it. Instead, she heard the screen door open and shut, the car door open and shut, the engine roar to life . . . So he was going into town, was he? Not awake for ten minutes and all he could think of was Fontessa . . . Too lame even to make up an excuse.

But then it dawned on Marge that perhaps that wasn't the correct explanation. She realized that Bill knew she knew about them by now, and *still* didn't care. It no longer seemed to bother him, and therefore any confrontation Marge herself was looking forward to between them was pointless now. Marge had looked forward to grilling him, tripping him up on his own words, making him squirm and then letting him have it. Now she knew he'd just smirk . . . "So what?" he'd say . . . She steamed and dripped with frustrated revenge . . . It's all falling apart anyway, she thought . . . What's the use? It's all over . . . She had no reason to get out of bed . . . No energy either . . . To hell with it. . . .

She might have remained in that state all day if Martin had not acted. He was unable to get the bathroom door open in the hallway and stood tugging and kicking at it and making such a racket that Marge was forced to get out of bed and come to his aid. Had Bill somehow locked the door behind him when he left the bathroom? Groggily she stumbled down the second-floor hall to the bathroom door, joining Martin there in a damp skimpy nightgown. He was half-asleep himself, and when he turned suddenly and saw her standing right next to him (she had padded silently down the hall in her slippers), when he smelled her steaming body and felt her presence like a magnet so close to him, it was more than he could resist. He lunged into her arms. His mouth dropped accurately onto her breasts.

In a matter of seconds they had fallen to fucking madly up against the banister, Marge gurgling to him in vain that his mother in her room would hear them. But she responded passionately to his embraces, digging her teeth into his shoulder so that her hoarse cries might not give them away. Martin grunted in pain but did not cry out, and soon they were rocking carelessly against the modest wooden banister. Martin grew harder as time went by until Marge wondered deliriously whether she had awakened some kind of force she might not even be able to survive, much less navigate. He seemed to have become permanently horny. Finally the banister splintered, and in their mad scramble to avoid plunging fifteen feet through the air to the ground floor, their bodies came apart accompanied by cries of fright. Marge already was plastered with sweat and lovejuice. Martin lay on his back like an upended figurine, his marble cock standing straight up. It was then that they both heard an unmistakable gasp and high-pitched shriek. Freezing in panic they looked up from the floor and saw Louise, her hair undone and her mouth quivering agape, standing framed in the bathroom doorway. It had been she who had locked the bathroom door, because it had been she who was inside it. Tears were coursing down her cheeks now, however, and her entire body shook with shame and rage.

"Oh, Martin—what have you done, what have you done?" she bawled, and the two glistening bodies leaped to their feet.

"M-Mother—" he began, mortified.

She cut him off with a wave of the hand, however, and dashing at Marge with surprising agility punched the groggy girl squarely on the jaw. As Marge went down Martin pulled his mother away and shouted, "Please, Mother, don't worry—it's alright, I love her!"

Louise Kilbanky turned on her son with fury in her eye.

"Martin!" she spat out, "You can't even tie your shoes and you say you love her. Don't be a fool! . . . Ah, I can't stand it!" she wailed, beating her head with her fists in her grief. "You're so innocent!"

"I am not innocent," he countered automatically. "Marge is a fine person, mother," he pleaded. "She's—"

"Oh, son, you're a fool. She's a whore and a nymphomaniac and—"

Martin slapped his mother across the face, instantly wishing he hadn't.

"Martin!" Even Marge was shocked. Desperately trying to salvage some sort of normalcy in the household she took Louise by an arm, put her arm around the weeping woman, tried to comfort her.

"Really, mother, everything is alright," Martin said softly, afraid of what he had done. "Please believe me."

His mother stopped wailing long enough to look her son directly in the eye. Instantly they both looked away.

Silently Mrs. Kilbanky turned and walked away from them back to her room. She closed the door behind her and locked it.

They stood pensively for several minutes, mulling over the scene they had just lived through. Marge was afraid Martin would go to pieces—begin wailing on his knees for his mother's forgiveness or else turn on Marge, seeing her as the evil person his mother accused her of being. After all, Martin's attachment to his mother was very deep. He relied on her implicitly and his love for her seemed boundless. Now he had just slapped her, and Marge wondered uneasily if that act would release a violent reaction in turn toward Marge herself. She shrank back against the wall.

Martin, however, aside from slipping into a more reflective, inward-looking mood in which his previous behavior no longer had a place, did nothing to alarm her. He seemed to brood, to have grown older (and maybe wiser) as a result of the terrible thing he had done. His grey hair was now that of a distinguished warrior emerging from one of the most severe tests in his life with equivocal results but with an unshaken resolve to carry on. He had neither won nor lost, it was true. But how handsome he was in the muggy light . . . How distinguished! . . .

Marge's heart melted at the sight of him and soon they were making love again on the carpet, although with a new sobriety, a more mature sense of purpose—even a strange reverence and acknowledgement of what an unpredictable, humbling force love could be. She felt she and Martin were like gods, temporarily freed from the limitations and inhibitions of mortal life. In her mind's eye she saw their figures become enormous, gargantuan. Stubbornly and calmly Martin worked away, his hips rising and plunging; calmly and fully Marge gave of herself. Soon they lapsed into an erotic episode that lasted for hours: in the hallway, on the stairs, and on the floors of all the rooms below. Occasionally they paused and Martin would lift his voice plaintively: "Don't worry, Mother. It's alright!"

"It's alright, Louise," Marge would add, her voice echoing in the deserted hallway, but there was no reply from upstairs.

Saddened by this granular distance between mother and son they would return to their lovemaking with renewed sense of purpose, renewed conviction.

Soon they completely lost track of time. In a dream they navigated the downstairs rooms, standing, rolling and tumbling, an enraptured oblivious couple drawn into each other like moths by their passion . . . Marge gasped in amazement as young god images floated in and out of her consciousness like rippling gauze curtains in the milky light . . . She even remembered a few specific names from her high school ancient history class . . . Adonis, Apollo, Venus, Pluto . . . Whoever it was. . . .

Martin for his part revolutionized his physical universe, keying on Marge's entire body plus his own as one continuously overlapping erogenous zone submerged under repeated jets of abandon. His newly-awakened sexual urge seemed to know no bounds. He pulled and tugged at his member trying to make it longer and nearly pulling it off in the process. Waves of hair sprouted up and spread over his body while Marge's breasts grew larger, in addition to being bruised red and rubbed raw.

After several hours more her electrically frizzy cunt hair began to glow and pulsate faintly rust-colored and then lemony-chartreuse in the shadows, driving Martin crazy with desire . . . Steam rose from the toiling maroon bodies . . . Deep curves of alabaster flesh, silver torsos gleaming, whisking through the parlor, agape on the kitchen floor, up against the sink, rolling along the hall, running and climbing, biting and licking, losing track of time altogether in their perpetually extending dream. The sweat poured off their bodies and somehow the heat, which remained oppressive all that day and night, *released something inside them* that delayed their fatigue indefinitely. Though the cloud bank did not lift and no breezes refreshed them they continued unabated that entire day and night. Except for them and the mother hidden upstairs the house was deserted. Gradually the light faded and it grew dark. They stumbled outside into the yard naked, playing with each other in a mosquito-plagued reverie until they lost consciousness very late, locked in each other's arms. Bill did not come home at all that night, though Marge had not noticed one way or the other. She and Martin were oblivious to everything except their love.

During the night they bumped into each other several times under the clouds. Startled awake, they embraced in a dazed manner and then Martin began to tell her of his great dream. Prompted by the tilted hulk of the cement truck that loomed out of the darkness nearby Martin became suffused with inspiration, until by the first hint of dawn's light he was striding manfully along the border of the irregular cement pool, chipping away at its surface with a rock or standing abstracted, straight-backed and naked, declaiming the long-forgotten substance of his dream, his plan. With grandiose gestures that for no accurate reason brought the names "Rousseau" and "William Burke" to Marge's mind (more chance memories from her high school history textbook), Martin spoke with conviction about his great dream to build a house. An arm swept out over the cement waste partly visible in the waning darkness: "I have a magnificent dream . . ." he began rhetorically, and Marge could almost see the high-heel shoes and powdered wig.

Martin's eyes brimmed with tears. Suddenly the great purpose and life's challenge he had forgotten for nearly two months came back to him in agonizing clarity and he wept aloud for the time he had lost, the time it seemed as if he had wasted . . . After all, he was a man: he still had his self-respect.

He stamped a bare foot in vexation.

"My destiny awaits me," he enunciated firmly. "I must build!"

Marge saw he was getting more and more worked up. In a last attempt to salvage what was left of the farm she used all her persuasive power to explain to him that any new grandiose schemes—ordering tons of cement or wood and dressed stone, building houses and such—would certainly ruin them all financially. She begged him to postpone any new operation for the time being: by not building, by making that sacrifice, he would be saving them all, she said. Surely he would not ignore his responsibility toward the others as head of the household.

"What about your mother?" she added, falling back on a ploy that had worked for her in the past.

"Mother?" Martin echoed uneasily. He was still troubled by what had occurred the day before. He couldn't easily dismiss having slapped his mother in the face. His and Marge's glorious and unforgettable day and night together had been marred only by his mother's refusal to respond, to answer them when they called up to her. Even Marge had begun to wonder if the old lady was alright, though most of the time, of course, deeply involved in their exploration of ecstasy, she never entered their minds.

"Mother?" Martin repeated, wondering if he should go inside the house and look for her. He stood hollow-eyed at the edge of the cement pool, idly stroking his cock and staring up into the surrounding muggy dawn opacity. Somehow the mere word "mother" was enough to make him temporarily forget his architectural inspiration —or rather, to forget he had been thinking about it. The grand inspiration was still there just as it always had been, but now it slipped from his mind, he was no longer looking at it, no longer seeing it. Instead, he was seeing the opacity.

Marge blew a sigh of relief. That was close! she whispered to herself. Her instinct for survival had prompted her to distract him from his ambition, because even the measly two or three thousand Kilbanky dollars that remained were vastly better than nothing. If she somehow could prevent him from spending blindly, somehow keep him from throwing his money away—which unfortunately, however, was legally his and his alone to dispense . . . If she could do that they should be able to live for eight months to a year on what was left, with a little luck . . . But Marge too had difficulty focusing on this topic . . . All the time she had been convincing Martin to postpone his architecture she was fighting against the powerful urges that had burst loose from inside her twenty-two hours earlier. . . .

Martin stood repeating "Mother?" and stroking himself, his eyes narrowing to slits as the engine grew long and hard. Marge dropped to her knees and with a sigh ("Oh, it's so pretty!" she couldn't help exclaiming) she closed her mouth around it and gave Martin the first blowjob of his life with infinite, protracted skill and care. Before long, his eyes bugging out and his tongue lolling onto his chest, he fought to keep his footing while she gave it to him. In spite of nearly twenty-four hours' strenuous lovemaking he had never been harder than at that time, never had it thrilled him so. Finally he lost control of himself and obliterating her slow expertise almost tore Marge's head off as he jammed it down upon his cock until she gagged and rolled back onto the cement gasping for breath. This occurred just at the moment Martin was about to come. He howled in frustration. His member, swollen and purple, nodded up and down with the beat of his pulse like the head of a snake in the early dawn light. Marge looked on in fascination. She rolled over onto her back and in a voice eroded by passion garbled, "Give it to me, baby, give it to me!"

Martin moved forward with a shout, but just before he leaped onto her he came in spite of himself, the hot white substance spurting through the air and splattering in Marge's face. "Damn," she growled in disappointment; but then, pulling him down onto the harsh cement surface she rolled him over and spread her legs, panting and trembling so hard she could barely speak, and whispered: "Eat me, honey —c'mon, eat me!" Thumbs and forefingers fastened on his ears she yanked his face directly into her joint. Before he knew what had happened his nose was submerged and his lips and teeth filled with hairy, pungent wet flesh. He choked and raised his head. "Whaddya mean?" he asked, quavering with surprise.

"You don't think it's just a one-way street, do ya?" Marge snapped. But then her resentment vanished and she became very affectionate and understanding, patiently explaining what she wanted him to do. She explicated quickly, pointing out her vulva and clitoris and explaining how stimulation of the latter by means of a tongue gave her great pleasure not unlike the pleasure he felt when he was stimulated, and by way of brief demonstration she closed her mouth over the engine once again for several seconds. Martin immediately understood, and burying his face in her muff began to suck and explore, pulling her back and forth by the hips until she tore open her back in several places thrashing on the rough cement. He ate and ate until she lost all sense of herself, bucking and humping in a mad abandoned frenzy. She had never expected anything like *this*! Martin was burrowing in so hard he lifted her into the air. They rolled off the cement into the nearby grass as blood trickled down her back and over her buttocks into Martin's mouth. The new taste surprised him but he had no idea what it was and did not stop his rabid mouthing. His cock stood on end once again, this time rolled tight between Marge's knees. Her loud ghostly moaning and sounds of abandonment woke the animals in the barn. Off in the distance, porcine grunts and belches pierced the air. Roosters near and far crowed with all their might into the hot inky sky, which was brightening into day by imperceptible degrees . . . The cloud bank and humidity still had not lifted . . . Her cries and entreaties grew louder ("Don't stop! Oh, Martin, don't stop!") as Marge, losing all self-restraint, came and then came again and again . . . It was a totally unprecedented experience for her . . . The men she had known before had at most merely dabbled down there, whereas Martin waded into it with mounting involvement. By the time she was submerged under wave after wave of orgasm he hardly retained consciousness himself, his jaws frozen wide and his tongue and teeth working up to such a pitch of uncontrolled frenzy that he nearly tore her cunt right out of her body.

Finally they fell back into the weeds, totally exhausted. Marge's heart beat at twice the normal rate. Her body clenched and unclenched convulsively, something she was unable to regulate. Martin hallucinated large multicolored globules, globules whose striking colors he could taste and which zipped effortlessly back and forth in his field of vision as if lubricated. Then a flotilla of oblong white lozenges shaped like cough drops, hundreds and then thousands of them, steadily progressed from left to right under their own steam, crowding out the previous globules. They reminded him of the bands and dots of static he had seen on TV two nights before. Soon the lozenges dissolved, replaced by vague sheets and swirls of metallic blues and deep blood reds. His mouth felt as if it was on fire, and panicking momentarily he sank his teeth into the bed of a small puddle of water nearby. His mouth filled with mud and twigs and he gagged.

Jumping up in confusion he lost his place and ran directly into the side of the cement mixer, bloodying his scalp and nearly gouging out both eyes on the toggles and switches that projected from the body of the truck. He fell to the ground spewing mud and clutching at his face and lost consciousness . . . Ten yards away Marge lay exposed, spreadeagled in sublime oblivion, dead to everything around her . . . A leg twitched, then an arm . . . Grasshoppers, beetles, crickets, worms and butterflies crawled and buzzed over them . . . Gradually diffuse light of day seeped through the cloud cover . . . Another fifteen minutes and they were both clearly visible —two torn, wasted bodies smeared with lovejuice and squashed bugs that looked as if they had been raped and beaten by a madman.

They awoke several hours later to a day just as muggy and overcast as the one before, but nonetheless a day like any other with its assemblage of beings and objects clearly visible at ground level—the trees and fields; the house and pond and cement truck; the questioning eyes and cold wet noses of the farm animals, several of them grazing and ambling into the lovers' immediate vicinity. An ancient mare, Silver by name, stood nibbling at Marge's toes, running a thick sandpaper tongue along her instep. In her comatose state she assumed this to be Martin starting to make love to her again, and turning over still half-asleep she spread her legs open wide. The horse moved forward.

It was then that she fully regained consciousness. She looked up to see a dark muzzle burying itself in her loins. Barking in surprise she rolled out of range and the horse shied away.

"Silver! You oughtta be ashamed of yourself. Horses ain't allowed in there."

She wobbled to her feet and stroked the old mare's nose. Then she stroked the shank.

Martin was still sprawled out in the weeds sound asleep and Marge noticed as if for the first time the blood mixed with dirt that coated his body. He looked awful! She then reached up over her neck and ran her hands along her shoulder blades, wincing in pain. Obviously her own back was in worse condition than his. The bloody strips of flayed flesh stung her from behind, while one opening continued to drip blood down her back onto the ground. She felt dizzy. Wondering if she and Martin had really gone too far this time—if there remained any chance for them to resume daily farm activities in a normal manner—she stooped gently in the grass and shook him until he awoke. It must be at least seven o'clock by now, she calculated. Broad daylight! In their present position they could be spied from the road except when lying completely flat on the ground. Obviously that was no good, no good at all. She tried desperately to get hold of herself . . . Somebody'll see us . . . We've gotta be able to stand up! . . .

As soon as Martin woke, however, she knew they had no chance.

He wiped the sleep and crushed grasshoppers from his eyes and stood up, and as soon as Marge saw those inquisitive eyes again, saw that same body with its limp bloodstained cock, that same childlike head surmounted by the same shock of grey hair—as soon as she saw him in all his irresistible actuality she knew they would not be able to separate themselves from each other. Her hollow-eyed expression returned and mingled with his own, and soon they were wandering arm in arm around the property again, their minds slowly but surely returning to that trance-like erotic focus so powerful it swept away all sense of caution. They had not eaten for nearly twenty-four hours but they felt no hunger. They had slept very little but fatigue no longer affected them. Marge was afraid of the only conclusion she could draw from all this: obviously they would go on making love forever, or else screw themselves to death!

Physiological changes seemed to be occurring, too. Marge was frightened by the alterations taking place in Martin's body. His body was hairier and heavier than before. Thick tufts of wiry light-brown hair had sprouted on his chest and shoulders. His genitals seemed larger. Marge couldn't believe it. Her own body was undergoing some sort of physical transformation as well. Her curves accentuated, the entire corpus feeling perpetually kittenish and sexually responsive to a fantastic degree. Her breasts radiated heat, the nipples huge and red and sore. Her tongue flicked in and out like a reptile's. Her toes and fingers were totally elastic.

But the most dramatic change of all had taken place in their eyes. By this time their faces were drained of color and the huge saucer-like eyes dominated, hollow and unyielding. Color and warmth returned to them only when they looked on each other with passionate desire. Otherwise the eyes belonged to ghosts. On the back porch steps Marge sank to her knees once more and the erotic scenario they had enacted again and again in the past twenty-four hours began to recur. She closed her mouth around his rod. He looked up into the grey cloud cover and moaned. "Oh, Marge," he said for perhaps the fiftieth time. But then he added, "All these years I've been rolling around in the grass here . . . I never knew it could be this way . . . I never knew that—"

"Oh, God! . . . Oh God oh God oh God!"

A loud shrill voice manic with unhappiness tore between the two lovers from out of nowhere. Martin stared around wildly. His cock popped out of Marge's mouth and she stood up. The screen door slammed open and there stood Louise Kilbanky—red-eyed and weary, trembling grievously, her poor face creased and crumpled by great despair. Obviously she had spent a good part of the previous day and night crying. Crying to herself alone up in her room.

"Oh my son, my son, what are you doing?" she erupted. "What are you doing to me?"

. . . Mrs. Kilbanky had come downstairs that morning to fix her breakfast as usual in the hope that if she resumed her daily routine the rest of the household would click back into place. She had assumed—had hoped without thinking about it—that Martin and Marge were still asleep in their respective rooms, that Bill was back from town as well, asleep beside his wife as usual. She was still considering whether or not it would be possible for her to call in the police at this point and salvage her son and herself, and a modicum of decency and self-respect. But could the sheriff be relied upon to handle this horrible incident with discretion? She had known Fred Handle the Wayne County sheriff since childhood, but she was uncertain whether she could prevail upon him to forcefully evict Marge and Bill from the premises without revealing to all of Winosha Falls the exact nature of the scandal taking place on Ike Kilbanky's farm. She decided it was too chancy: even if the sheriff were successful Marge herself might blab to everyone in sight as an act of revenge. Besides, Fred Handle was just human, like everyone else: his curiosity only would be made keener by what he saw at the farm. The more he learned, the more he would want to know . . . And besides, Martin simply was not reliable . . . He seemed to have become strongly attached to this awful Parsons woman, she reflected, in which case he might cause an unbelievable scene if the sheriff attempted to drag the Parsons away . . . Any revelation of Martin and Marge's horrible fornication would ruin the Kilbankys forever, Louise decided. She just couldn't take the chance . . . But on the other hand, how could she allow such things to go on? She didn't know *what* to do, and consequently her only recourse was to hope that overnight things had returned to normal. . . .

As she put the tea kettle on the stove she happened to look out the screen door, and instead of seeing the usual amalgam of early morning green trees and fields she saw two naked bleeding figures performing some act of rank perversion in broad daylight, as if they were on another planet.

When she realized in the same instant these two were Marge and

Martin she lost her head, and even now out on the back porch Martin was having difficulty restraining her. The old woman seemed determined to disfigure herself in her agony with nearby garden tools. Finally, however, Marge dragged her back into the kitchen. They cleaned the blood and sweat off their own encrusted bodies with hot towels. Marge found two pairs of pants for them to wear, though she remained bare-breasted. Although Louise was physically unable to look in Marge's direction the three sat at the kitchen table drinking tea. They attempted to make scrambled eggs and bacon, to carry on with breakfast as if nothing had happened. But it was impossible. Half-way through a jelly doughnut Martin took his pants off, and before another five minutes had gone by they were both naked again, fondling each other and kissing. Louise couldn't stand it. She was in tears.

"Don't you see what you're doing?" she pleaded.

But Martin only smiled and tried to reassure his mother. "We're perfectly OK," he insisted almost smugly. He and Marge got up and walked outside, arm in arm, Louise following close behind.

"But you can't do this—you can't do this!" she shouted. The veins stood out in her neck and forehead.

"What about the neighbors, Martin? People driving by will see you from the road. Hank Diggler and the Henley brothers drive their tractors up and down that road every day. And the school bus! And Sandy Buckey rides by on his bike!"

Her words had no effect. Marge Parsons, who should have known better, smiled at Mrs. Kilbanky reassuringly, as if humoring a child, and for the first time Louise became terrified. Obviously both of them were dangerously out of control. They looked like zombies. They'd lost all sense of time and place.

"What about the neighbors?" she repeated sorrowfully. "Somebody'll see you!"

"Oh, mother," Martin answered playfully. "The neighbors are so far away . . . Far away . . . We'll stay back out here . . . Back behind the house . . . Nobody'll see us. . . ."

"Nobody'll see us, Mrs. Kilbanky," Marge echoed dreamily.

Louise turned to her. "And you! Where is your so-called husband? Where's Bill? That no-good sponge. Is he in town getting drunk? Didn't he come home last night?"

They looked at her silently, without a reply. They blinked their eyes and smiled, and continued to smile.

After pleading with them once more, threatening to call the sheriff, threatening to kill them, threatening to kill herself, she suddenly fell silent and stared at the two somnambulent lovers. Even while she carried on they had been fondling each other, and now they sank into the weeds in a passionate embrace not fifteen feet from where the old lady stood.

She lost her senses and thought of racing up to the attic for Ike's old shotgun and blasting these two devils clear to hell. She could kill them both easily with one shot, bury them out behind the pond, no one would ever know . . . Or would they? . . . Her head reeled and she burst into tears . . . How could she even have *thought* such a thing?

Completely confused and terrified, now, disgusted by the spectacle of Marge and her son, afraid to call the sheriff and unable to bear any aspect of the situation a second longer, she turned and fled back into the house inside a straightjacket of indecision. She ran up the stairs and locked herself in her room. She cried and cried and cried, until eventually she cried herself to sleep. All that day the curtains remained drawn over her windows, the door to her room locked from within.

Outside, the low pressure system that had plagued the area for two days at last seemed to be lifting. A breeze stirred the elms and refreshed the squatting lovers. At least now the summer heat would be bearable, the awful humidity was lessening . . . The undifferentiated cloudbank gradually resolved itself into discrete grey rainclouds . . . The wind picked up . . . Soon it would be raining, or more likely the warm front would pick up speed and blow over Wayne County entirely. The sun would break through at last. Once again blue sky would reappear. . . .

Meanwhile, the oppressive weather of the past two days had taken its toll on other residents of Wayne County as well. Bright and early the morning before, Fontessa Margins had struggled to wake up in time to catch her ride to work as a checker and bumper at Jerry D. Eisenhower Memorial Airport (the tri-county airport), but to no avail. The heat and lack of circulation in the little house trailer she and her little daughter Peggy rented were too overwhelming, and in spite of herself she swooned back into sleep. At 10:00 A.M. her eyes opened again and she cried out. Three hours late! In desperation she dressed well and stood alluringly in the road, but it was twenty minutes before someone stopped to give her a ride and nearly eleven-thirty by the time she arrived at the airport.

By then it was too late. There had been an accident, and the men were swarming all over the field.

A brisk wind was blowing as Fontessa stepped out of the car. The men who raced with long white canvas hoses to put out the fire raging on a single-engine Delta Tip Flyer wrecked on the runway were continually losing their caps in the wind. Racing Indian-file eight or ten of them trotted each holding a section of the hose until one lost his cap in the wind. He reached for it awkwardly, couldn't hold it, couldn't keep his balance, fell across the hose, sent the others sprawling . . . Meanwhile the Delta Special burned rapidly. Thirsty flames shot up on every side.

Holding a hand to her aching side Fontessa ran as fast as she could out onto the runway. She saw her boss, a man named Jack, among the others—a clump of men standing as close as possible to the burning plane. But when she caught up to the normally gruff, friendly, baseball-cap-wearing Jack, she was in for the surprise of her life.

"You lousy bitch!" he tongued at her, giving her a growl and a hateful sneer. "You're more than three hours late!"

The other men in the circle, all fellow employees of Fontessa and all actively friendly toward her up until that moment, went out of their way to identify themselves with the boss. They stared angrily at Fontessa as if at a stranger. Everyone suddenly seemed to hate her. For Fontessa the shock of it all was hard to bear. She had to fight with herself to keep from bursting into tears. She felt guilty. She had heard the fellows shouting before that two men were trapped in that burning plane.

Things were going badly. Barely seconds after the firemen reached the site with their canvas hoses the airplane exploded—the gas tank had caught fire. A large explosion took place which sent pieces of airplane and bodies hurtling in every direction, and blew most of the onlookers—people like Jack and Fontessa—onto the ground. It was very frightening. Several of the firemen were burned (two requiring extended hospital care) and almost all the scorched men reacted by becoming frantic. Some suffered concussion while others went temporarily insane: they foamed at the mouth and rolled on the ground whimpering to themselves. Their socks showed. Their eyes rolled in the sockets until they went dead white. It was very hot out on the airstrip, the weather and the flames combined, so several people fainted from that. Plus, thousands of dollars worth of damage was suffered by the cartons of merchandise stacked on the runway at the time of the accident, which also had caught fire. In fact, it appeared that the accident never would have occurred in the first place except for those very same wooden and cardboard containers, which should not have been stacked on the runway at that time. The airplane had collided with the giant boxes and caught fire.

Warren County and Braxton County fire trucks reached the scene well before Wayne County's own antiquated fleet, but for the entire tri-county area the fire was a major catastrophe. Two men killed and two firemen burned badly. Many witnesses at the site came away from the accident changed persons, but none of them were changed the way Fontessa was, because Fontessa had been fired. She lost her job. And not only that, but the company announced through Jack that it was considering suing her for criminal negligence! Fontessa was beside herself—she didn't know what to say. It had all happened so quickly.

But she had lost her job!

She was judged negligent in the line of duty. What was worse, Fontessa alone was being held directly responsible for the tragedy. Her job as checker and bumper called for her to be at the airport and in action no later than eight o'clock every morning, six days a week, without fail. The airport being located thirty-five miles from Winosha meant she had to get out of bed at 6:30. It was thankless work and Fontessa would not have taken the job except that no other employment opportunity existed for her.

As checker and bumper she was personally responsible for checking the commercial packages, cartons and containers of every size and type that arrived via air freight each night and were deposited on the single runway of the small rural airport. Often, the containers completely obscured the approach to the airstrip and blocked the runway so that no airplanes could land or take off until they had been cleared away—and that was Fontessa's job. Bright and early she had to be out on the runway, in all kinds of weather, taking inventory and opening and inspecting the containers, whose destination might be any commercial enterprise in the tri-county area, and which must be correctly examined by her for county tax purposes, as well as for the proper levying of local airport handling and shipping charges.

The freight then had to be moved from the runway to one of several outbuildings near the terminal, where later in the day it would be transferred onto flatbed trunks and transported to its destination. This entire operation was Fontessa's responsibility. The trucks were unable to drive onto the airstrip itself, so after taking inventory on the airstrip Fontessa was obliged to "bump" the containers from where they had been deposited overnight to their respective outbuildings. Each container went to a different "outbuilding," which in reality was nothing more than a loading platform protected from the elements by a makeshift tin roof. These platforms were located, on the average, forty or fifty yards from where the packages were deposited on the runway, and it was Fontessa's job—unaided—to clear them from the runway before the private planes upon which the tiny airport depended for most of its revenue began landing on the field, usually no later than nine-thirty in the morning.

Many of the cartons were quite heavy, some weighing as much as two hundred pounds. It was this part of her job Fontessa hated most. Often while she struggled with the bulky wood or metal containers, or single-handedly shoved huge cardboard cartons along the pock-marked runway, the gross businessmen who frequented the airport on pleasure excursions would gather at the door of the terminal bar while their planes were being refueled and make foul and insulting remarks. Bronx cheers, catcalls, and atrocious obscenities hounded her while she bumped the containers down the runway. The containers had to be checked and then "bumped" (bumped with her rump) off the runway. Fontessa wore special heavily padded hip-guards strapped over her rump so she could bump the cartons without injuring herself, but as a result her hips and butt were made to look enormous. The paunchy, alcoholic pilots of their own light planes—a despicable breed of half-civilized pigs most of whom had amassed their fortunes in the most treacherous manner possible—never missed the opportunity to make Fontessa's life miserable either through insults while she worked, or by assaults upon her person after hours. Some caught her and forced themselves upon her in the most revolting way imaginable. They pushed her up against the side of an outbuilding and forced her to kiss them, or even pressed five dollars into her hand and forced her to give them blowjobs while their buddies watched from their cockpits and cackled.

Empty beer cans and hip flasks littered the field as well. But the management at the airport always looked the other way at these abuses, since the men who perpetrated them were its best customers. Fontessa was told to escape if she could, but never on any account was she to turn on her assailants in violence. The company itself was powerless to defend her, she was told.

Fontessa herself was a strapping, big-boned girl physically superior to many of the men who tormented her—half of them she could have beaten to a pulp in any fair fight. But her job was to check and bump freight before these men landed their planes at the airport, not to challenge the customers. If she did her job right, she was told, she would be on her way home from the airport before any of them even showed up, though invariably there was too much freight for her to process for that to be true. Usually, in fact, she had to work until three or four in the afternoon. But the pay was good, and in spite of the abuse and exhaustion she valued her job: she had a small daughter to support, a house trailer she paid rent on, food and clothing to buy, and a no-good bully of a husband who had deserted her but who showed up periodically and demanded money. Digger would not think twice about socking her around if she had no money to give him, either. And though Bill was Digger's older brother and claimed to be in love with her, he refused to challenge or reprimand Digger in any way. After all, Bill reasoned, Fontessa *was* Digger's wife. . . .

And now her job was gone, just like that! She had been three hours late to work, it's true, but the muggy weather was so oppressive she simply had overslept—you'd think someone would understand! . . . Give her another chance . . . Show some compassion . . . But no. Apparently the two men whose plane had exploded and who died in the flames had landed their plane that morning in spite of the unmoved containers on the runway, which had made for a hazardous and hair-raising landing. The men, green around the gills, had immediately disappeared into the airport bar and emerged dead drunk two hours later. When they saw the containers *still* had not been removed they became incensed and insisted they would take off anyway. In vain Jack and the other workers sought to dissuade them, pleaded with them, saying they had no chance. There simply was not enough room on the runway for them to gather the necessary speed to put the plane in the air. But the two men, drunk and ill-humored, had insisted. Climbing into their plane they cursed and spat at the airport employees and opened the throttle all the way in an effort to gun their single-engine Delta Tip Special up and over the containers. The airplane swerved and hit a massive group of wooden boxes, crashed, and erupted into flames. The boxes burned as well. In a matter of minutes the men were dead. And they had been among the airport's best customers. . . .

So Jack was tight-lipped and adamant. Fontessa lost her job as of that morning, and not only would she be ineligible for unemployment insurance of any kind but also the airport authority was considering suing her for criminal negligence.

Badly frightened and shocked, feeling guilty for the death of the two drunkards but also seething with anger at the spineless men who had fired her, Fontessa collected her things from her locker and left the building. No one said good-bye. The tears streamed freely down her face as she walked along the shoulder of the road and stuck out her thumb. Although she was in no condition to talk to strangers she would have to hitch-hike back to Winosha Falls all alone.

When Fontessa arrived at her house trailer shortly before four o'clock that afternoon Bill was slouched on her bunk bed drinking warm beer. He had opened the tiny ineffectual port windows as wide as possible but was sweating profusely. Stripped to the waist, empty cans on the bed and grimy linoleum floor, he had spent that morning shooting pool in town, although the heat was so bad even in Shorty's Pool Hall that about noon everyone quit playing, and he had been drinking steadily since then in Fontessa's trailer, waiting for her to return from work. He knew little "baby Peggy" would be spending that particular day and night with her grandmother, Fontessa's mother and Marge's aunt, Mrs. Louella Margins.

While they both perspired uncontrollably Fontessa tearfully related that morning's catastrophe. She was without a job now, could not even apply for unemployment compensation, and had lost all chance for a favorable recommendation from her previous employers if she were to find work somewhere else. Winosha Falls was small enough so that anyone she might ask for a job would discover her record at the airport almost immediately: she felt certain, therefore, that she would never be able to find work. Gloomily she counted and recounted the measly fifty or sixty dollars she had stashed under her mattress: the total extent of her savings!

Becoming morose she cursed her fate, cursed the heat, cursed Digger for being such a swine, cursed Marge, and especially cursed and condemned her sallow, cowardly ex-fellow employees at the airport. Bill pawed at her breasts, grunting that he wanted to make love, but the sturdy Fontessa shoved him to the floor saying she needed time to think. However, five to seven minutes yielded no solution to her problems. Soon thereafter, more out of an intense need for release than out of sexual desire, she gave in to Bill and they embraced, rolling around the cramped aluminum cabin like caged hippos, the perspiration gushing freely from their bodies. They made love until dehydration, and then Fontessa dressed, went out and purchased more beer—breaking down, in fact, and buying a fifth of bourbon for herself—whereupon they spent the evening drinking themselves senseless. They awoke in the trailer next morning to the same unbearable mugginess, the same cloying heat. Glum and despondent, feeling like a cornered water rat, Fontessa grimly went over her economic and social status with Bill once again, and in a rare moment of candor he delivered himself of the opinion that she definitely had no chance of finding another job in Winosha.

"Everybody'll swear that if old Jack fired you, you just ain't no good," he said. Fontessa agreed and then admitted she simply did not know what to do. Peggy was scheduled to come home that morning, so Fontessa telephoned her mother and explained the situation, begging her to take care of the little girl for a few more days until Fontessa figured out what she would do. Her mother, who was growing more ill-tempered as the years passed, bawled her out for losing her job—"I don't care *whose* fault it was or wasn't!"—but in the end agreed to look after the child until Fontessa found work. She made it clear, however, that "that definitely *don't* mean forever."

Fontessa's back was against the wall and she knew it. After arrangements had been made to take care of Peggy she tackled the problem of what to do next in earnest. Bill at that point made as if to go, mumbling something about having to buy horse liniment for Silver's infected fetlock, but she refused to let him pass.

"You gotta help me, Billy," she pleaded. Her big hard biceps barred the door.

Bill stopped in his tracks.

"I'm just a hired hand, Fon," he said bitterly, wrenching free of her grasp. "I ain't even lord of my own pigsty, much less my own manor . . . whaddya expect *me* to do? I can't get you no job—I ain't worked since I got outta the army and you know it. You know real well what most *self-respectin* folks around here think of me," he spat out.

"Well, what am I gonna do, Bill? How'm I gonna get work? I'll get kicked outta this trailer in two weeks if I don't find something, and then what? What about Peggy? You know that lousy brother of yours ain't gonna help me none. Christ, when he finds out I lost the job he'll be over here quick as a flash and ransack the place. He knows I got a few dollars hidden away. He'll turn this place upside down until he finds em. And if he don't, he'll come lookin for me, you know it . . ." Parenthetically she added, "Your brother's a real bastard, you know that? I can't figure out how I ever fooled myself into marrying him . . . Imagine! Back then, when we was courting, it was *me* that wanted *him*, can you believe it? I must've really been cracked. Remember? It was *me* tricked *him* into marriage—and now just look where we're at! He's a bully and a crook. I don't see how you can put up with him, Bill . . . even stand to be called his brother. . . ."

"He's a mean one, alright," Bill agreed lackadaisically. He couldn't have cared less. He and Digger steered clear of each other, more or less. Neither paid much attention to the other's exploits. Digger's life was his own affair.

But while Fontessa complained Bill had been thinking.

"Listen, Fon: why don't you come out to the farm and live! What the hell. Marge won't like it one bit but I don't see how she can say no. I mean when the chips are down she knows I could blow her cover in a second. Just one little phone call to the sheriff and she's gone . . . All of us is gone . . . That moron Martin threw all his money out the window, anyway," he added contemptuously, and related once again for her the details of the cement mixer fiasco, the civil suits, the loss of sixteen thousand dollars. The more he thought about it the greater was his resentment toward Martin—"that stupid lunatic"— for having blown the best setup of Bill's life.

Fontessa too was incredulous. But as for moving out there herself, it was out of the question, or so she thought. She and Marge were cousins—when they were little girls they had been quite close, though Marge lived up in Spartanburg. But since their respective marriages to Digger and Bill they had grown further and further apart. Fontessa shacking up with Bill had been the last straw, and although the girls hadn't seen each other since then they were now sworn enemies.

Fontessa didn't see how she could do it. She and Marge were both fighters, big strapping girls. She visualized the scene that certainly would take place if Bill brought her out to the farm. Marge would go wild with jealousy and hate, Fontessa felt sure, and they would be obliged to fight. Although Fontessa was the bigger and stronger of the two—at five feet nine inches and a hundred fifty-five pounds, hardened by months of checking and bumping at the airport, there probably weren't a dozen *men* in the entire county she couldn't whip in a fair fight—nevertheless Marge was no pushover. Fontessa didn't like the idea.

"And what about Martin, and the old lady, Mrs. Kilbanky? You think I can just show up on their doorstep with my suitcase? Howdy do, Mrs. K., I've come to stay? You expect you and me to shack up together, right under their noses? You gotta be jokin, Bill . . . This is America, after all. Your wife has every right—"

"SCREW my wife!" he shouted, turning red. The veins stood out in his neck. "I hate her, she's two-faced! She's known about us for months, I'm dead certain of that, but she prefers playin this game with me, seein if she can double-cross me one way or the other, thinkin she'll trip me up on one of my alibis and catch me red-handed. Well, she can kiss my ass! How do you like that? I don't care if she knows about us or not. I'm sick and tired pretending, Fontessa . . . And as for Mrs. Kilbanky and her son, I don't give a hoot in hell for them either. Why, you could run a whorehouse right under their noses and they wouldn't know the difference. He's cracked, lost his marbles, spends his days rollin around in the mud—it's disgusting—and as for the old lady, she don't even come down out of her room anymore . . . Pining away for her dear departed Ike," he concluded sarcastically.

"Lord God almighty," he chuckled, "you could set up a condom factory in the kitchen sink and those two donkeys wouldn't know the difference . . . No, there's no problem there. The only trouble will come from Marge. We can tell the Kilbankys you're an old friend of the family," he explained. "And as for Marge . . ." he hinted ominously, leaving the sentence unfinished.

Fontessa was impressed. She looked at him, studying his face with new respect. His determination surprised her. It seemed to be for real. Maybe there was something more to Bill after all than the charming but shiftless no-account she had known previously. At any rate, it might be worth taking the chance. Apparently Marge was the only thing standing between Fontessa and security, even if the security proved to be temporary.

She bit her lip and tasted blood. She really had no other alternative. She flexed her muscles and stomped on the floor, gritting her teeth and breathing heavily, forcing the air in and out of her lungs, in and out, in and out, working herself into a state. "If it's a fight Marge wants, then by God I'll give it to her," she thought, already champing at the bit. "It's either that, or me and Peggy thrown out on the street."

She and Bill collected her nightclothes and other essentials and threw them into an old leatherette suitcase. The noon heat was so bad, however, that the leatherette suitcase developed a case of blisters and they decided to wait until late in the afternoon before driving out to the farm. By the time they climbed into the car Fontessa had reached such a pitch of supercharged excitation she could contain herself no longer. As they drove through Winosha and up Route 41 she sat quivering with anticipation, tearing chunks of upholstery from the seat with her bare hands and tossing them through the open windows. Bill's meek protests only increased her agitation. She dug into his ribs and punched him repeatedly while he drove. Twice he lost control of the wheel and they ran off the road, narrowly avoiding collisions. Bill gulped and wondered what he had started.

In any case, never in his wildest dreams could he have foreseen what awaited him at the Kilbanky farmstead.

What they saw when they drove up late that afternoon simply buggered description. Bill swore he was having difficulties with his vision and stood next to the car, blinking and squinting up at the house in horror. Fontessa gasped and buried her face in her hands. Up on the porch, her bloody legs spreadeagled wide over the porch steps, Marge lay submerged under Martin's naked bulk. From where they stood below all they could see were Marge's legs and Martin's bare flayed back and buttocks smeared with grime, but that was more than enough. Flinching under the blow of an image indisputably real and right there before his eyes but also completely inconceivable to him even in jest, Bill stood like a man who had just been shot. He staggered sideways. Shock waves generated deep in his bowels welled up out of his being. They were physical, as if he were shitting and pissing in terror, except that sheer disbelief rather than danger or fear had released them. The waves poured from his body, wracking it with tremors.

When Martin turned his head around, with its hollow obsessed eyes, at the sound of the car and the people behind him, Fontessa saw for the first time his shock of grey hair—something Bill had neglected to mention to her. The sight of those shameless eyes with their dreamy unquenchable look combined with the grey hair and torn convulsive bodies even now fornicating out of sheer momentum, even now that their possessors knew they were not alone—Fontessa fell whimpering to the grass. Her mind was stunned and refused to process what it saw. Blinding pain flashed across her forehead and she lost consciousness. Waking up a few minutes later she looked again, then vomited on the ground between her knees. Ten feet away Bill did not fare much better. He too passed out, or so he thought. He was gurgling monotonously to himself. But finally Marge realized the nature of the situation and stood up, toppling Martin off her torso and down the steps, and in a matter of seconds all four stood facing each other, equally terrified (though for different reasons) and revolted. It had taken Marge thirty seconds of staring at the intruders before she realized who they were, and another full thirty before she reacted in any way.

Marge and Martin were so immersed in each other, so deep below the threshold of their normal names and lives, that these other faces appeared at first as faces in a dream . . . "New bodies, new men and women?" she wondered inarticulately . . . She and Martin had reached a state of free-floating erogenous animation, bubbling in an infantile libidinal fixation deep in the tar pit of their bodies. After Mrs. Kilbanky had run upstairs to hide from them at nine-thirty that morning they lapsed into a single uninterrupted coitus, indoors and out, that proceeded to infinity like fish in a dream fishtank of unlimited dimensions, free from fatigue and the force of gravity—supine along the hallways and in the rooms of the house, upright against the TV and on the porch and in the weeds outside, washed up against the side of the house, knee-deep in mud in the pond, sprawling in abandon under the elms, to the point that even their male-female polarization was obliterated. Luckily, whenever anyone drove past on the road they happened not to be visible, though the fact of road or cars never occurred to them.

So it was just as much a physical shock for their bodies to suddenly break off as it was for their minds when they recognized Bill and Fontessa, when precisely who those two shapes were dawned on them. Marge wobbled to her knees. The look on her face was indescribable. Martin stared off in the distance like something not quite human, a satyr or a sprite. When Bill and Fontessa managed to catch his eye they saw nothing. He seemed to look through them into the landscape. His sex swung slowly in the wind. They were appalled.

Martin's grey-topped head swung vaguely back and forth on its neck. It appeared as if he might never talk again. Fontessa wondered how she had gotten herself involved in this. She felt acutely uncomfortable even looking at Martin, though since they all stood so close together that was unavoidable. What she saw repelled her. He seemed a maniac or worse. And Marge . . . Fontessa couldn't understand or accept what she had done, either. Marge seemed alien and what she had done totally unacceptable. Fontessa would have given anything to believe Martin was an interloper, that he had escaped from an institution and forced himself on Marge, that he was a mad rapist. But the evidence before her testified to the contrary—indeed, it appeared that Marge had sunk willingly to a level of bestiality Fontessa never previously entertained as being even remotely possible. She was revolted. The only way she could explain it was that Marge had become a monster, sinister and satanic. "A beast, a whore, a monster," she kept repeating to herself, backing away from the slit-eyed, spittle-covered pair until she backed herself against the side of the car and could go no further. Marge looked at her defiantly. In an act of supreme contempt and abandon she thumbed her nose at Fontessa and then proceeded to excite herself—right in front of the others! seemingly without shame!—by fingering her clitoris. She spread her legs and soon became excited, all the while peering over at Fontessa with cold disdain. This was another world to Fontessa, hideous and equivocal, and she panicked.

"Bill!" the tall muscular girl called out, "Bill, let's go. Take me outta here: these people are possessed!"

But if her mind worked painfully in the attempt to explain what she saw taking place, at least it had worked. In the most favorable circumstances Bill's reasoning powers were modest. In this case his mind simply refused to function. Jaw open he stood rooted to the spot, frozen and insensate. He failed to respond to her entreaties because in spite of how she raised her voice to him he did not hear her. Deaf and dumb to all around him except his hollow-eyed wife, he stood staring at her thumb as it worked inside her until she began to moan and Martin's rod responded to the call of duty. It rose like a dowser's wand. Marge dropped to her knees, her eyes shut tight by the finality of whatever was overwhelming her. She opened her mouth. Martin stepped forward. He seized her by the ears and yanked her open head onto his member.

But Fontessa could stand it no longer. Shattering the pressure that built up inside her she moved across the yard with a shout and pushed the pair apart. Since she was the strongest person there to begin with, the force with which she exploded sent the lovers sprawling. Martin in fact hit the side of the house with such speed a tooth was chipped: a small piece fell to the ground beside him.

Calling her a monster and a pig Fontessa then fell upon her naked cousin, pummeling her breasts and scratching at her face. In a matter of seconds they were fighting in earnest, pulling each other's hair, kicking and biting. Yowls of pain rent the air. Teeth marks gave way to the salty taste of fresh blood. Bill remained paralyzed in place, unable to move. As the two big girls rolled and scrapped he watched with the same unseeing eyes as before. For his part, Martin lay slumped against the side of the house. He had struck his skull squarely against the windowsill. He rocked back and forth holding his head and whimpering.

Finally the two girls rolled apart. Fontessa obviously had the best of it so far: Marge's mouth was cut and bleeding and purple bruises disfigured her hips and breasts. At that moment Bill's speech mechanism sparked to life and he lurched between them, not so much breaking up the fight as momentarily obstructing the view. Both girls were now on their feet. Bill turned to his wife and said as distinctly as possible:

"I've decided to tell you, Marge, I don't love you anymore. I love Fontessa. Either she moves in with us or I leave!" He then fell silent.

Marge merely laughed. "You're an asshole, Bill—you always have been," she said scornfully. Being torn from Martin's embrace and finding herself locked in mortal combat with her cousin brought Marge to her senses all at once. The urgency of the situation demanded that she defend herself, act aggressively, and with that came the rest of the psychic paraphernalia she had abandoned for the past two days: speech, sense of self, and cunning.

Backing away from Bill and from Fontessa who was pulling Bill aside she ran up the porch steps, stopping just inside the doorway and addressing Fontessa menacingly:

"I'll be back. You have the gall to insult my lover and me while you spend your life double-crossing your own husband and cousin—your own flesh and blood—just to get a bite to eat. You're a piece of trash and everybody knows it. You'd go down on your own baby daughter if it could pay the rent!"

Fontessa had never been so insulted in all her life.

"I'll kill you," she roared, tossing Bill aside like a bag of potato chips and starting up the steps. "You have the nerve to insult me after you've sunk to the level of a pig and a goat, debasing yourself in broad daylight with a mentally-deficient monster. He's just a gibbering idiot," she added, jerking a finger at Martin across the way. "It's the most shocking thing I've ever seen—you're both sick! You oughtta be locked away!"

"You just wait," Marge threatened thickly, and slammed and locked the front door behind her. Fontessa started up the porch steps after her but then stopped and swung around.

"Has she got a gun, Bill?" she demanded. "Is there a gun in the house?"

Once again Bill was speechless.

She jumped off the steps and slapped him across the face. "Bill, answer me. Is she going for a gun or not? Snap out of it!"

He finally came around. "No, she doesn't have a gun. We ain't got a gun in the house, unless the Kilbankys got one . . . Old Ike musta had one, come to think of it." He creased his brow. "But I don't have the slightest idea where it would be, and Marge neither, I'm sure. . . ."

He looked around himself vaguely, as if any second he might make a run for it.

At that moment, however, the front door banged open and Marge reappeared at the top of the steps, her eyes hastily painted black with mascara and a large, pink fright wig planted squarely on her head. Still naked and covered with blood and excreta, with the frizzy hot-pink wig obviously made of artificial hair—nylon or something—she looked like a hulking, strutting Little Miss Queen of Darkness, risen from the bowels of the earth with a puff of pink smoke and a shriek.

Fontessa backed away in confusion. For the second time in ten minutes she was confronted with something she could not assimilate. The wig crinkled and glared in the sunlight like some kind of devil-amulet, totally foreign to her realm of experience. With her distended nipples, smeared torso and dramatically accented eyes Marge inspired terror in her beholders. Fontessa felt the ground buckle underneath her. Bill began running toward the frog pond.

"She's got her fright wig on, my God, she's got her fright wig on," he blathered, hardly in control of himself. He had never seen the wig before but suddenly he remembered with astounding clarity that day months before when Marge had come home (to their Crestview Developments home) carrying a big parcel she wouldn't let him touch. She had added it to her collection of other mysterious cartons and jars that were off limits to Bill, but on that one occasion she had responded to his query with a smirk and the words, "Fright wig" . . . Bill had forgotten about it until this very moment.

"She's got her fright wig on!" he repeated over his shoulder as he disappeared around the side of the house at a dead run. Martin lay dazed next to the house, massaging his head. Marge and Fontessa were now alone.

Coldly Marge stared down at the bigger girl, and for the first time Fontessa was afraid. The wig startled her, but if it hadn't been for Bill's display of terror she might have forgotten about it and assaulted Marge once again. Now, however, she eyed her cousin uneasily. Marge was what—a witch?—or something . . . Fontessa couldn't make it out. She felt physically oppressed, as if she might suffocate.

Marge jumped from the porch to the yard in a single bound. She stood not four feet away. Opening her mouth wide and tilting her head back she let loose a fierce primal scream like a war cry—so fierce, in fact, it was an eerie, deafening caricature of itself. The trees turned to cardboard and briefly the sky was blue cardboard. And then, in a gesture of supreme insult, though more like something a rhinoceros might do than a girl from the tri-county area, she swiftly turned her back and bent over until her ass stuck up into Fontessa's face. Forcing out another war cry she then proceeded to fart and defecate. It all happened so quickly—the entire progression from porch to asshole—that Fontessa had no time to move. Lumps of liquid-covered excrement splattered against her and dripped down her shirt-front. Gasping and retching she fell to the ground and at that point Marge wheeled around and dropped on top of her, punching and flailing with all her might and attempting to scratch her eyes out. Fontessa went under.

The fight was now in Marge's favor.
Bill was nowhere to be seen.

In a fit of violent perceptual activity a succession of startling trans-
formations took place before Martin's eyes. Numerous starbursts
were followed by the single, heroic image of two large women,
fiercely determined, locked in mortal combat.

Cords of toiling muscle stood out in their necks and arms like
rope. Their bodies shined in the sun like bronze ropes. Then they
were snakes. Then he lost track completely and they were snorting
stallions ready to challenge each other to the death, stamping their
coal-black feet and steaming at the nose. Behind them materialized
a high alpine valley in winter, or rather the first days of spring . . .
The two oldest stallions, leaders of the pack, turned on each other
crazed by the first chemical splurges of the new mating season;
turned on each other with an ancient score to settle, a sudden challenge taken up, a struggle filled with fury until one emerged the
victor from a circle of bloodstained snow. . . .

However, Martin was seeing things, hallucinating as it were. There
were no stallions here and certainly no snow. Soon the two women
came back into focus.

For the first time he realized how *seriously* Marge and Fontessa
were fighting. Martin had led a fairly sheltered life up to this time, so
the hatred and massive amount of energy released by them as they
fought scared him. They snarled and sank their teeth into each other.
Most of the clothes had already been torn from Fontessa's body.
Patches of bloody hair lay on the ground. Eyelashes and chips of
teeth sped through the air. Part of an eyebrow disappeared. But the
last thing Martin would attempt to do was intervene. He understood
they were mortal enemies, enacting something ancient and irreversi-
ble at a level of sheer wrath he might never live to see repeated. Their
struggle took place inside a magic circle.

Martin then slapped his forehead as he hallucinated a backdrop of
polar blue skies, vivid and cold, supported by a desolate cold stony
shore where slate-grey waves rolled in behind them from the arctic
sea. The two women stood together now, locked in combat, black
shapes against a polar sea. Martin's head swam. He fought hard for
clarity, but the shapes became two hulking armor-clad prehistoric

birds, their beaks slashing furiously, darkening the sky with their shadows. The waves pounded against the stony shore. Martin gasped for breath, then blacked out . . . His face and hands numb from the cold. . . .

BEEP-BEEP!

Sharp talons tore jagged holes in the frozen blue sky. In his vision he looked on helplessly as the shredded blue sky-material fell into the sea.

BEEP-BEEP-BEEP!

The holes in the sky grew larger, and puffy middle-aged faces appeared in them, peering down at the battle on the shore below. Their chubby faces gazed down on the scene in horror. They were faces Martin did not recognize.

BEEP-BEEP!

Who were these people? Had they come from somewhere behind the sky to rescue Marge and Fontessa from each other? Were they friend or foe? He couldn't tell. The suspense unnerved him, but in another few seconds the gaping sky disappeared and he was wide-awake. The faces belonged to people in the real world. Two heavy balding men stood over him, shouting unintelligible words and waving small engraved calling cards in his face.

He struggled to his feet.

"Are you Martin Kilbanky?" one of the men demanded, while his companion stared in disbelief at the female figures, one entirely naked, that were fighting in the weeds. Marge's bright pink fright-wig had been torn off in the scrape and lay at Martin's feet.

"What's going on here?" the man shouted. "Are you Martin Kilbanky?" He could not accept Martin's grey hair. He tried to avert his eyes from the boy's bloodspattered nudity but his mouth kept popping open and in spite of himself he stared down at Martin's discolored sexual organ.

So embarrassed he was unable to speak, Martin looked away from the men and down at the wig. He nudged the pink thing with his foot.

Suddenly losing patience the man shook him by the shoulders. "Is one of these women Louise Kilbanky?" he demanded.

"N-no," Martin finally stuttered.

"Well this is disgusting—it's awful. What the hell is going on here? I'm gonna call the police! C'mon, Bud," he said, turning to the other man. "Let's drive back up the road to the goddamn pay phone!" He started toward their panel truck.

But the word "police" worked wonders. Marge and Fontessa instantly rolled apart like gymnasts at the completion of a routine, united in purpose now before these strangers. In an exaggerated show of modesty the girls grabbed for pieces of clothing, tittering and turning red with coquettish embarrassment. Whereupon the two intruders —who seemed to be quite gullible, Marge noticed thankfully— immediately slipped into their role as intruders. Delicately they shielded their eyes from the naked girls. Squealing and chirping like young maidens caught unaware while river-bathing, Marge and Fontessa skipped up the stairs into the house. These simple honest workingmen seemed relieved to adopt the role of intruder, any other interpretation of what they witnessed being so disturbing to them their minds refused to countenance it.

However, this left Martin alone with them, still stark naked and covered with a gamey two-day patina of squashed bugs, lovejuice, dirt and blood. He looked like a wild man, a maniac, and if it hadn't been for the fact that one of the men—the one who addressed him earlier—had been to the Kilbanky house once months before, was acquainted with Mrs. Kilbanky and knew of Martin's reputation as a near-lunatic, their intuition of unspeakable orgiastic horseplay would have gone on unchecked in spite of their wish to ignore it. Martin looked as if he had just emerged blinking from a basement den of squalor and criminal depravity. Why, he looked like nothing so much as a cannibal—in fact they all looked like cannibals!

Gus Wormsley swallowed hard. He had never seen anything like it, and in spite of knowing about Martin's condition he was still suspicious. Those girls! They had been fighting to the death! Naked and smothered in filth . . . But now they were gone—inside the house— and Gus had only Martin to confront with his suspicion. Three minutes of the boy's disassociated gurgling were all he could stomach, however.

"Go put your clothes on!" he finally bellowed. "I'm gonna puke, I swear it." He shoved Martin up the steps. "GO PUT YOUR CLOTHES ON, FOR CHRIST SAKE! TELL YOUR MOTHER SOMEONE IS HERE TO SEE HER!" Gus howled with such force he blew Martin up the porch steps. His blood pressure mounted dangerously.

Turning to Bud Jacobsen, his assistant, he propped an arm against the shorter man's shoulder and whispered: "That's the most disgusting damn thing I've ever seen, I swear to God . . . I feel sick."

But Bud was unable to offer his sympathy. Sweating profusely and twitching from head to toe he stood speechless, staring up at the deserted front porch.

All this time Bill was nowhere to be seen.

The two men, as it turned out, were employees of the State Historical Society. They had been sent to the Kilbanky residence to rephotograph the Kilbankys' antique Swedish porcelain kitchen stove, which Gus Wormsley had documented for the Society a year or so before. He had come to the farm, received a warm welcome from Ike and Louise Kilbanky, had photographed the stove and spent a pleasant afternoon chatting with them. He grew to like the old couple and was glad he had taken the assignment. Occasionally Martin would appear outside one of the windows like a ghost, and sadly Ike and Louise explained to him as best they could the nature of their son's plight. Their affliction—as parents—had moved the three older people to tears, Gus remembered fondly.

Subsequently, however, it was discovered that the photographs were missing. A routine check of the files at Historical Society headquarters in the state capitol turned up a folder labeled KILBANKY-SWEDISH STOVE-STOCKHOLM, 1786?, but otherwise empty. Wormsley was called in but could offer no explanation, so he was sent straightaway to Winosha Falls to rephotograph the stove. The Historical Society curators expressed interest in many objects at the Kilbanky home—the very chairs they were sitting in, for instance—but apparently the stove was considered something of a rarity. The curators had eyed the previous photos of it hungrily and already had made overtures to Ike Kilbanky about it. Quite a correspondence developed. The Society was willing to purchase the stove for six hundred dollars, much more than they could hope to get from an antique dealer, and it would be exhibited proudly in the state capitol in the lobby of the State Historical Museum. A card afflxed to the stove would name the Kilbankys of Winosha Falls as benefactors.

When Ike refused this offer on the grounds that he needed the stove to cook with, the Society promptly replied saying that it understood perfectly, that Mr. and Mrs. Kilbanky had every right to cook on the stove in good health and prosperity and enjoy the stove as an object of great historical significance and aesthetic beauty right in their own home, but would Mr. Kilbanky be so kind as to will the stove to the Society so that after his death it might not fall into the hands of private speculators?

At that time Ike Kilbanky was a man at the peak of health who nevertheless because of his age was forced to consider the future termination of his stay here on earth; but it was a topic on which he was quite neurotic. Death scared him. He never allowed it to be mentioned in the home. Therefore the letter from the State Historical Society irritated him, and he was just about to compose a harshly negative reply when the sudden heart attack did him in. He died scarcely a week after receiving their last letter.

In the pain and confusion that followed his death Louise Kilbanky had forgotten all about the stove. Now she lay in her room, the curtains drawn and salty tears caked on her cheeks, listening to her son's shouts from below that two men from "the state society" were here to see her, and wondering what she should do.

How on earth could she possibly go downstairs? The last two days had been a living hell for her, hell on earth beyond compare and beyond endurance. She was sure she was going to die soon. Life had become impossible, contorted by sorrow beyond recognition. The fact that her son and "that woman" had been together in an unspeakable manner for such a long time was too much to shrug off. They were animals—hideous and revolting—and furthermore she was *certain* they had been seen from the road. It was so humiliating! She longed for release, for oblivion . . . She had been only faintly aware of Bill's arrival, and that another woman had come along with him, and that she and Marge had been fighting in the yard. It was all so ghastly anything was possible. And now these men from the State Historical Society were calling for her. How on earth could she go down to them?

She managed with much difficulty to pull herself together, however, and ten minutes later wobbled down the staircase to greet her old acquaintance from the Society.

Gus Wormsley hardly believed his eyes, which filled with tears. What a change had come over the poor woman. In ten or twelve short months, how she had aged! Gus was aware that since he had visited the farm Mr. Kilbanky had died, and he easily surmised how the burden and grief would age the old woman—but to such a degree! Previous to Ike's death she had been the absolute personification of a farm woman—self-possessed, self-reliant, suffused with energy and good will, glowing with health. Now she stood before him, the expression of sorrow and defeat in her eyes so prominent that Gus was forced to look away. With a lump in his throat he explained to her the reason for his reappearance and respectfully asked if he and his assistant might rephotograph the stove. Mrs. Kilbanky, who had liked Gus Wormsley from the moment she first met him, saw no reason to refuse. She was terribly upset by her domestic situation but there seemed to be a tacit agreement between the two visitors not to further embarrass her by calling attention to the grotesque acts they had witnessed outside. Louise sensed this, and was grateful. A certain propriety must be preserved at all cost, without which civilized intercourse between social people would be impossible. Gus Wormsley guessed something dark and disagreeable was taking place on the farm. He had been so unnerved by what he saw when they first drove up, however, that when the two women straightaway disappeared his first impulse was to put it out of his mind. This impulse was reinforced by Mrs. Kilbanky, who betrayed with every move she made her desire not to acknowledge or discuss what might have taken place. With his innate sense of decency and his overriding concern to get the job done—to photograph the stove —Wormsley was the last person in the world to ignore her wishes. He was, therefore, to be forever left guessing as to exactly what *did* occur out in the yard that day. Martin's bruised, naked body he eventually ascribed to a worsening of the boy's mental condition. If that were so, it would have been the height of indiscretion to question the poor lady about Martin. He simply must assume everything is under control and go about his task. . . .

With a sigh he turned to Bud and began issuing instructions, and soon the two men became engrossed in their equipment, unpacking it and setting it up. Battery packs, cameras, floodlights and scrims soon cluttered the sitting room floor. Each piece of equipment was meticulously labeled and inspected, and as needed each was carried into the kitchen, taken apart and reassembled, checked and checked again. The photography of rare objects was a difficult business, more so than the untutored layman might realize, especially for such men as Gus and Bud. The successful completion of the process demanded their fullest concentration. Nothing must go wrong this time or the curators would be very upset.

Finally they assembled all the equipment in the kitchen, so intent upon the task as to be oblivious of what went on around them. Marge and Martin came and went, skulking sheepishly at first, with thick slices of meat and cheese from the refrigerator for sandwiches. Their two-day ordeal had left them ravenous when they finally came to their senses—literally ravenous. In spite of their distrust of the photographers they could contain themselves no longer, and as the men worked with their grips and supports the lovers tore hungrily into their food, grunting hoggishly in the light from the open refrigerator door. Realizing Gus and Bud were too busy to pay attention to them they abandoned themselves completely, peeling then stuffing whole cantaloupes and cases of liverwursts down their gullets. Strings of sausages disappeared down the hatch. Gus looked up in consternation only once, when an empty plastic liverwurst case fell from Martin's mouth into one of his lamps and broke the bulb. Soon this little matter was cleared up and they were ready to begin shooting.

But one detail remained, however—the full length, four-color "Farmer and Mrs. Jones" cardboard cut-outs had to be taken from the truck outside and propped up against the stove. Bud struggled with them at the front door while Gus leaned back and drank a Coke, all the while proudly explaining to Mrs. Kilbanky—and to Marge and Martin, too, since they stood nearby—this most recent innovation of the State Historical Society. The Society had decided that greater charm and realism would result from the objects to be documented if they were photographed in their original surroundings, as far as that was possible. Local color must be promoted. Therefore the men were now sent off on their field trips with an assortment of life-size cardboard people dressed in a variety of regional costumes from different historical periods and constructed with movable joints to allow several postures. The original flavor of frontier life was to be recreated as far as possible, so that a spinning wheel or mustache cup or lye tub might be shown as it was originally used by the folks who originally used it. Gus himself was especially proud of Farmer and Mrs. Jones, and demonstrated the figures to Mrs. Kilbanky with a twinkle in his eye. He sat them at the kitchen table, or had Farmer Jones peeling potatos in his authentic overalls while Grandma Jones whipped fresh butter in her turn-of-the-century gingham dress. Proudly Gus demonstrated especially successful details of the figures —a smartly freckled cheek, Grandma Jones's hair done up in a perfect bun, the clever detail of her high-button shoes . . . Fascinated,

Marge and Martin looked on from their corner of the kitchen. While he was showing off Gus never let on that he noticed the tension between Louise Kilbanky on the one hand and Marge and Martin on the other. The old woman's brittle smiles and clipped chatter were part of a difficult attempt on her part to retain a modicum of domestic normalcy for the benefit of the photographers. Actually, they were strangers to each other now. As for Bill and Fontessa, throughout the entire proceedings they were nowhere in sight. By the time Gus and Bud had finished and were sipping tea, munching cookies and making small talk with the old woman, Fontessa had faded from their memories entirely.

It was 8:00 p.m. and nearly pitch-dark before the two men persuaded themselves they had to leave. As they were going, Gus produced a simulated-metal "Golden Eagle Wall Plaque" from the truck and insisted Mrs. Kilbanky accept it as a gift from them for her friendly cooperation and as a token of their esteem. In spite of her protests they insisted the handsome "Early American" unbreakable polypropylene plaque would add drama to her front door or kitchen wall and must be accepted. It was the symbol of America and the rage of decorators everywhere, they said. Proudly they demonstrated by holding up the tacky black wrought-iron-colored bird. The wing-span of over two full feet was truly impressive, they said. Didn't Mrs. Kilbanky agree? How could they leave after taking so much of her time without thanking her in some way? The simulated look of colonial wrought-iron was a magnificent touch of Americana to enhance every decor. The bird was not only completely weatherproof and rustproof, but it would stay lovely for years and years. It would add incomparable distinction to her home, Gus insisted, and they refused to leave until she accepted it. "This bird was made in Massachusetts, where independence originated!" Bud announced, while Marge could be heard tittering in the background.

Wearily Louise accepted the plaque and Gus and Bud finally climbed into their truck and drove away. As soon as their taillights disappeared over the hill she threw the plaque into the garbage and, sweeping past Marge without a word, tramped upstairs to her room and locked herself in.

Marge walked into the parlor and noticed that the State Historical men had forgotten one of their mannequins. A freckled yokel in Lil Abner boots with a piece of straw in his mouth leaned against the mantelpiece. Apparently the farmboy was gorgotten. Gus and Bud got so carried away toward the end of their stay they had dragged a few more figures from the truck and photographed them all over the house, just for laughs.

This particular yokel startled Marge, but she was too tired to bother mentioning it to the others. She merely stopped and rubbed at the cardboard body in the vicinity of its sex, as a kind of wistful private joke, and then turned out the lights.

Completely exhausted, Marge and Martin retired shortly thereafter to Martin's room. Although there still was no sign of Bill, Marge assumed correctly that he and Fontessa had appropriated the room she and Bill Parsons previously occupied as man and wife. In the morning, she decided, she would go straightaway and collect her things. She would move in with Martin. Obviously Bill and Fontessa were determined to live together on the farm, and a minute's reflection was sufficient to convince Marge no real means existed for her to get rid of Fontessa short of imperiling her own stay. Bill could rat on them all in retaliation. Besides, Marge had come to loathe Bill to the point she now doubted they would ever sleep together again, Fontessa or no Fontessa. So what difference did it make?

"I mize well get used to the situation," she thought to herself sourly. "Maybe something'll turn up." She still detested Fontessa and felt they had a score to settle. Sooner or later she knew in fact they would.

"So now there are five people loose on this property," she mused to herself sleepily. "That's what you get when you perpetrate something underhanded . . . You broke the rules, sister, consequently you have to pay the price. Anything can happen now. You gotta make allowances for that. Open yourself up to new lanes of experience," she said to herself hopefully, growing philosophical. "Otherwise you'll just freeze up and waste away . . . The only possible way to make it through this life is constant adaptation . . . Constant change, always accepting change . . . It's the only way . . . Except for one thing," she wrinkled her forehead in dissatisfaction: "For some reason as time goes by the changes themselves get weirder and weirder . . . Why is that? . . ."

She lay back strangely unsure of herself and contemplated the ceiling. It looked white. She stared out the window. It looked black. She felt enervated and uneasy, too tired even to fall asleep. Suddenly she thought about Donnie, her big black standard poodle. She realized she hadn't seen him for days. She remembered kicking over his dish on the back porch that morning: it had not been touched at all and the dog food was foul-smelling and covered with flies. She thought nothing of it at the time, preoccupied as she was with Martin's loving, but now she began to worry. Where was Donnie? Was he alright? The poodle had seemed to adjust easily to its new life on the farm, although the roving packs of half-domesticated stray farm dogs proved to be a problem for him. They were aggressive and mean and although sometimes they seemed to accept him they always ended up turning on him. More than once Donnie charged across the fields with a half dozen dogs in close pursuit, growling and foam-flecked. . . .

Marge remembered these incidents now and grew more and more uneasy. She felt Donnie was in trouble and longed to go to the window and call out his name, but she knew all that would accomplish was to wake up the others. Somehow she knew Donnie would not respond to her calls. She contemplated the ceiling again. She could hear Martin snoring beside her in bed—that monotonous series of dull explosions was unmistakable—and with her heart skipping a beat in spite of herself she turned to look fondly at her lover as he lay sleeping. She noticed the sole survivor of that afternoon's grasshoppers climbing slowly up his neck. Outside Marge heard the sound the other grasshoppers made, moving in the night . . . Stretching into the infinity of their night, an insect carpet drifting magnetically like a needle always further and further into their night. . . .

A few seconds later she picked up the half-crumpled being off Martin's neck by its wings and flung it out the open second-story window. The grasshopper disappeared into the night. Marge buried her face in her pillow and unsuccessfully tried to sleep. She tossed and turned. But then a nude cardboard figure loomed in the white space overhead; "like a god," she thought fuzzily, although she couldn't see it clearly. It dropped down onto her almost immediately and clapped a hand over her eyes. It was then that Marge finally fell asleep.

11

The Micro World

The following morning Martin Kilbanky was awakened by a sharp pain in his heart. Shifting onto his right side he breathed regularly, in and out, listening down into himself until the pain disappeared. The pain was brief but intense, like a bubble lodged there, and this fact worried him. He took it as a sign, an omen. It was dramatic: a silver bullet suddenly lodged in a passage of his heart. He didn't like it. It popped in and would only pop back out thirty seconds later. During those thirty seconds Martin Kilbanky knew fear.

Now he peered outside, out the second-story window into the bundles of warm green elm branches. They rustled softly. He could tell it was going to be another hot day—another scorcher—but this time he looked forward to it: at least it won't be muggy, he thought. At least the sun's out, the wind's blowing, it's a clear blue day! . . . Shedding his previous mood like a skin he jumped out of bed and with mounting enthusiasm ran through a few perfunctory calisthenics, finishing with a headstand that sent the blood rushing to his scalp.

Dizzy and red he toppled onto the floor and lay there breathing heavily. Marge kicked him playfully once or twice, then put on her jeans and jersey and kicked open her overnight case. There at the very bottom lay her toothbrush. She would brush her teeth, she decided, then slip downstairs and fix breakfast for Martin and herself—hopefully before any of the others were awake. It would be tiresome and probably impossible to avoid Bill and Fontessa, but for the time being this was her course of action. The farm should be large enough to absorb them all. She was aware that Bill (and Martin too for that matter) had been ignoring his chores recently. Maybe now that Fontessa was with him he'd be able to concentrate on them. There was a lot of work to be done. Hopefully somehow they all could coordinate themselves enough to do it.

Because, otherwise, Marge was tempted in her heart to say "to hell with it." When she and Bill first moved out it had been her dream to really work that summer, to make the farm a successful operation. She hadn't forseen what would occur. She had not intended to sponge off the Kilbankys. She wanted to show she could do it. She wanted to succeed.

But things worked out differently, and now although she was willing to do her share of the work her heart was no longer in it. She didn't feel the urgency anymore. Someone else would have to provide the impetus, and it didn't take too much hard thinking to arrive at the conclusion that no one besides herself was capable of furnishing that —certainly not Fontessa, certainly not Martin or Mrs. Kilbanky. It remained to be seen whether Bill still possessed the pride and self-discipline necessary to channel his energies in that one direction; to sacrifice his time and give freely of his labor. But even while she pondered Marge knew it was hopeless. So many things had happened to encourage his aimlessness and lethargy—their own growing out of love (to put it mildly), for one; and Martin's loss of the Kilbanky inheritance money; and Fontessa's growing importance in his life . . . In view of all this Marge didn't see how the farm could continue to be productive.

But at the very least, she hoped, Bill and Martin will work enough to keep the truck garden going. They all had a right to expect a few summer vegetables—lettuce, squash, corn, tomatoes and so on. As she brushed her teeth it occurred to her for the first time that the farm might simply deteriorate until they were forced to abandon it. Or something unforeseen might occur: Mrs. Kilbanky have a heart attack, for instance, or Martin go legally insane. . . .

Marge shuddered. These thoughts spooked her, and it was with a tragic resolve to make the most of whatever time remained of her newfound love that she turned to look at Martin as he picked the sleep out of his eyes. Sighing heavily she insisted to herself that Bill and Fontessa's presence must not curtail their lovemaking. They must be together always as they had been these past two days. Sad vague words like "fate" and "destiny" surfaced in her mind. How could she know how much more time they would have with each other in this life? The tears welling up in her eyes, the lump enlarging in her throat, Marge resolved to give her lover only the best during the unknown parcel of time allotted to them. It might be twenty minutes or twenty years, she reflected fearfully, but while it lasted only the best was good enough. She must love and honor and respect him—look after him and encourage him in his dreams and plans, wherever they may lead. She must provide the critical eye he seemed to lack, but do so in such a way as not to check his enthusiasm. Previously when he brought up his architectural schemes she had tried to discourage him—they now had very little money left, they must be careful, etc. She succeeded in restraining his impulse to build but his eyes had dimmed tragically, the spring had gone out of his walk. Now she vowed with tears in her eyes that she would never discourage him again. Who cares, she thought recklessly, if we run out of money? Who cares if the farm has to be sold to pay off its debts, and we're forced back on our own naked resources in order to survive? Who cares, she whispered to herself defiantly . . . Our stay on earth is so brief and uncertain—from this day on I'm gonna make damn sure Martin does what he wants. Let him build his house! What kinds of lives are the rest of us leading? What are we doing that's so important he must restrain himself on our account? She looked at herself and Bill and Fontessa in this light and laughed contemptuously. "Nothing," she hissed, answering her own question.

The tears in her eyes made them glimmer heroically as she crept downstairs to fix Martin breakfast.

"I'll give him as much food as he wants," she said to herself, and while Martin sat at the kitchen table sipping tea Marge proceeded to fry up six eggs, and great strips of bacon and helpings of hot greasy batter-bread. Martin ate and ate. His stomach swelled to the size of a basketball. When he was finished she fixed herself a little toast and tea. She then squeezed his member and kissed him passionately but also persuading him to do a little work that morning.

"Nobody's been working the garden for nearly two weeks, honey," she purred. "It needs to be weeded something awful. Why don't you go on out and work it awhile? I'll have the *nicest* lunch ready for you when you're done." She winked lasciviously, and although he failed to catch the meaning of the wink he returned it.

"I'll do whatever you say," he chirped, winking repeatedly, and before any of the others were awake he found himself on his knees in the weed-infested earth, digging and tugging and chopping.

For a time Marge sat on the porch watching him work, a clandestine cup of instant coffee in her hand. The morning sun beat down pleasurably on her shoulders and knees. When the others finally stirred inside the house she threw the coffee into the weeds and stood up. It wouldn't do for her to appear too soft and mellow in front of Fontessa. She had to keep her guard up. She had to hang tough.

With a sigh she altered to a more aggressive demeanor. Frowning and growling to herself she flexed her biceps and threw several punches at the air. She continued this show of hostility as long as she heard Bill and Fontessa getting their breakfast directly behind her in the kitchen. Only an open screen door separated them but never once did she turn to say hello.

Martin tugged and chopped industriously. It felt good to be working again and he was happy. The sun beat down on his shoulder blades as he dug into the furrows. Little voices, like far-off children babbling, came and went in his head as he worked, but Martin felt so contented he hardly noticed them at first . . . Tiny voices as of an approaching children's army . . . Delicate and mysterious, although at the moment he simply could not be bothered . . . Miniature bagpipes and micro-flutes. Flags of all nations mounted on tiny wooden pegs obscured the view . . . Next came pans of hot melted butter alternating with cool white whipped cream clouds, in that peripheral field of vision located just along the edge of the simultaneously projected "real" landscape and view that Martin and all the rest of us normally see. At that periphery—dancing along the very rim—a world perpetually takes shape as lively and full of biophysical day-by-day detail as this world is, but reduced in scale to the infinitely miniature; and more bubbly, more carefree and bicarbonated. Martin caught glimpses of that world—sudden glimpses that wavered like faces and bodies painted on a canvas sail perpetually rippling in the wind *just out of reach*, rippling along the borders of his vision like a dream. An intermittently seen barrel of brightly-painted images, alive and transforming their details continuously as the barrel is rotated—two barrels, actually, one far to the left and one far to the right—constantly rotated like prayer wheels by unseen hands . . . Great shafts of sunlight slashed across these images at all times, however, partially obscuring them: life in the forefront, comprised of the details and objects of every day, was much too hardy and violent and assertive, all but drowning out the peripheral world that surrounded it, a world that as a consequence of this relentless pressure was pulverized and made perishable and passive. Few people that were unlike Martin Kilbanky were more than subliminally aware of it . . . It floated, perpetually out of reach, insubstantial as a maniac or a kiss . . . And even Martin, who had already seen brief instants and pieces of this other world whir alongside him before, treated them as totally unimportant—exactly the way he treated his dreams, in fact, which he looked upon with the disinterested attention one brings to peering out an automobile window at the whizzing billboard roadside in the rain.

Nevertheless that world existed; and as he dug between the rows of lettuce and radish plants he was aware of it, although to him it was a tiny sideshow. Half uncaring he watched out of the corner of his eye as tiny white elves built themselves igloos of facial cream. Then the scene changed and huge tufts of crabgrass obscured rows and rows of miniature Inca or Aymara maidens dancing gravely to music Martin could faintly hear only if he stopped what he was doing and listened intently. Only once did he in fact do this, and it was just a few minutes before he was interrupted by Marge approaching behind him in the garden—but when he did, what he saw and heard enchanted him. A crowd of pubescent virgins dressed in sparkling white robes and long ceremonial headdresses of beaten gold that flashed in the sun suddenly appeared over the crest of a hill, beating their breasts and stamping their feet to haunting Andean foothill music produced by a variety of strange aboriginal reed instruments—enormous bamboo trumpets over ten feet long honked on by boys on stilts, as well as a throng of smaller wooden flutes. Flanking them a half-dozen circular stationary drums like upended fifty-gallon barrels were being slugged and pounded and tapped in a complicated serial fashion by groups of warriors. Flags and pennants flapped in the wind, a prince in a golden litter sat suspended nearby in the branches of an ancient willow tree, ten feet off the ground, carefully watching the virgins dance with super-prescient eyes as he stuffed brightly-colored psychotropic mushrooms into his mouth and flexed all the muscles in his body one by one according to some sort of ritualistic gymnastic formula. The scarlet mushroom juice ran down his chin as he sat,

161

chewing steadily, never taking his eyes off the dancers . . . Great queenly birds like herons but much larger and all dazzling white with intricate filigrees of specialized feathers projecting from their crowns wheeled slowly in and out of the picture above the enraptured prince's head . . . Attendants stood perfectly still nearby, mesmerized in the sunlight . . . Occasionally one of them moved forward with a long feathered whisk and touched the prince's cheek . . . Time seemed to spin like a wheel in the sun, suddenly becoming motionless . . . For a few precious seconds Martin's garden tools slid from his grip and he sat transfixed by this vision that hovered and coalesced at each side of his visibility. At his left the prince—or whoever he was —and his attendants; the willows and the great, wheeling birds. At his right the virgins assembled and danced, the musicians played, the fine ceremonial breastplates and costumes rustled in the wind.

Above him Martin could feel luminous discrete clouds sailing through a hard blue altiplano sky. Without looking up he sensed those were the exact same clouds floating through the exact same sky as encapsulated the tiny prince and maidens that surrounded him. For a few timeless seconds he floated, equally in both worlds: the sky above Winosha and the sky above the unknown dancers of the Andes were the same. He accepted that as an amazing fact. He accepted as a fact without questioning it that the dancers were real in the same way he himself was real, although he also knew that in a few seconds or minutes at most they would be gone—vanished forever—and that another, completely unrelated episode would take its place. In its turn that scene too would disappear, never to reoccur, replaced by another. Sometimes two scenes took place at once, one to the left and one to the right, both unrelated to each other and both soon to vanish from his sight. Martin paid sufficient attention to these "worlds" to sense that although their histories vanished never to return, *they themselves* were not fragmentary or disrupted in nature. He felt intuitively that they continued uninterrupted their narrative sequences at an always steady rate of transformation even though for Martin the partial stories he saw vanished from view never to reappear. Life went on perfectly normally in each one of these worlds. Therefore an inexhaustible number of them must exist simultaneously, he reasoned, worlds that were mutually encapsulated and unaware of each other as they motivated themselves through time . . . And although he never could have put it into words Martin realized all this. The prospect of these numberless situations unwinding endlessly all around him, each oblivious to the others, first sent him to the heights of euphoria and then made him dizzy, eventually leaving him over-excited and strangely insecure: was all this really going on around him? He was afraid to ask anyone else—even Marge—if they had ever seen these things too. He was afraid they would laugh at him. Make fun of him.

Yet the hardest fact to bear was that Martin knew—he positively *knew*—that these sequences did exist. He guessed sadly that others glimpsed these worlds too, or had seen bits of them at one time or another—but refused to admit them. Or rather refused to encourage them, since they were in every way like plants, like a garden that had to be cared for and watered, a garden that had to be met on its own terms if it was to survive. It was a wavering presence, very vulnerable and easily overwhelmed and crushed by the intimidating reality of everyday life that clamored constantly for attention like a two-year old baby among the crabgrass and garden tools. It was an insatiable reality that soon reduced those other worlds—so charming and full of life—to featureless mayonnaise. Mayonnaise! (For a second the tubular face of Eugene Sisley, County Prosecutor, rudely superposed itself upon the garden tools, but with one violent snort Martin made the unwelcome visitor disappear.)

Martin hated mayonnaise! He flinched with resentment that these events should be so frail in comparison to the everyday world. Why weren't they front and center like everything else? Why did keeping them in focus require so much effort? Why didn't anyone else admit seeing or experiencing them? Why should he alone have to deal with them?

He answered these questions by not answering them—by affecting nonchalance and unconcern. He usually made no attempt to detain the images which appeared so infrequently, showing little interest when or if they came and went. This morning was an exception, the first time in months he had dropped everything he was doing to watch them at the edges of his vision. The tiny dancers were so beautiful and mysterious, the prince and his retenue so majestic, the big white birds so lovely and at the same time so fearful as they swept across the scene—

"Fucking whore! Fucking shit!"

Martin's heart popped in and out of place. He gulped in fright at these booming obscenities, staring around wildly off balance.

"I don't see how I'm gonna stand it, honey. Jes hearing Fontessa's voice in that kitchen getting her breakfast makes me wanna rush inside and stab her full of goddamn holes! I never hated anybody so much in my whole damn entire life!"

"Wug . . . gug?" he burbled. Marge had strolled up behind him undetected and her first words, spat from between her teeth with such vehemence, sent him reeling. He rolled over backwards, exhaling streams of tiny white bubbles from his nose and crushing nearby radish shoots and tomato plants, as well as several of the new corn plants whose stalks up until then had in some cases grown over two feet tall. Unintentionally he snapped and lacerated several of these proud young corn stalks before regaining control. Marge's voice had intruded so harshly on his delicate double universe that for a moment Martin found himself feeling irritated and uncertain about her, wondering whether he and Marge were really suited for each other after all . . . Maybe he should remain alone; maybe she was a stranger too, like all the others . . . Her strident vocalisms often unnerved him and her spells of hatred seemed nothing but a waste of time.

This rudimentary reflection soon crumbled, however, and in no time she was shrieking playfully for him to stop embracing her as they rolled together over the radish plants, while at the very same instant the inviolate prince and his maidens and musicians continued unraveling their lives forever without him. Martin would never see them again, though sometime soon another fragile unrelated human episode would roll in to take their place.

The bubbles reflected in the light. A thousand tiny windows and a thousand tiny doors and chairs and faces—especially faces. A thousand faces of people he did not know, people he did not want to know. They chattered and smiled at each other pleasantly but he knew they were dissimulating. He knew they were lying. They all wore masks, significant expressions and gestures that fit the occasion. They joked and talked gaily among themselves as if for all the world they were kids again, opening bottles of soda pop on a picnic! But while they talked and looked—especially looked—that way, he sensed that underneath or behind all of that lurked danger. The smiling, chattering faces spelled danger. He didn't understand what or how, but he knew they were a threat. And he knew also—he was *positive* of it and it was this more than anything that traumatized him—he knew that all these people *themselves knew* they were lying, he could see it in their faces now as plain as day. And they knew everyone else was lying, and knew that everyone else knew they were lying, and still they went on lying, still they went on chattering and joking and smiling—and it was this he couldn't stand. It terrified him and froze him to the spot, which also happened to be the precise location he was in when he realized this—namely, at precisely the instant during which, seated at the dining room table as a gang of strangers mobbed the room and his mother attempted to be hospitable, Martin leaned over his steaming cup of tea with a teaspoon of sugar in his hand. At that precise instant he caught sight of a thousand faces in the bubbles on the surface of the tea in the teacup. Thousands of bubbles formed and re-formed, piling up and breaking against the rim, reflecting off their round surfaces the ceaseless but precise explosion of faces whose expressions suddenly and hypnotically caught his eye and filled him with revulsion.

Gagging on the hot tea he attempted to look away, but each time the teacup drew him back and he found himself staring down at the bubbles, scrutinizing the reflections of the people in the bubbles, holding onto the seat of his pants with his hands in order not to panic, in order not to embarrass his mother or Marge. Manfully gritting his teeth he determined not to give himself away. He refused to break down. If all these people were liars then he could be a liar too.

Breathing deeply he decided to start lying right then. His impending panic would not allow him to act otherwise. Another minute of it was a minute more than he could take.

So he summoned all his courage and tore his eyes away from the cup. He looked up at the people surrounding him in the room and smiled. He looked at the others standing in the hallway and smiled at them as well.

Soon he had an automatic smile for whoever came his way.

What had happened was this:

Eventually they rolled apart in the garden: Marge looked up from their horseplay to see a car approaching the house from the road. A big automobile with five men inside. Five big, strange men. Her heart skipped twice and sank. Looking closer, however, she thought she recognized two or three of the men, guys about Bill's age from in town; in fact they were probably the guys Bill had been hanging out with lately, shooting pool and so on, Marge thought, and her fear gave way to irritation. "They probly come out to get him and go huntin or something," she reflected crossly. She had told Bill over and over again to keep their presence at the farm a secret, but she knew he couldn't resist mentioning it to some of his buddies, in addition to telling Fontessa all about it, of course. That was the most Marge had learned she could expect of Bill. Hopefully these "buddies" could keep their mouths shut. She wondered just how long it might be before someone with a grudge or a nose for money found out about their living arrangement and decided to press them on it. It was constant mounting pressure such as this—the anxious foreboding that had taken the place of her previous bossy self-reliance—that was propelling her with such abandon into Martin Kilbanky's arms. She had become melancholy, fatalistic. She saw they were balanced like little china dolls in the bearpaws of destiny, and this revelation coupled with her passion for Martin forced her to give herself to him totally, without compunction. Any day, she thought tragically, may be their last.

Since she was in full view of the car she did not attempt to hide but rather walked out to greet the men who sat inside it. Several puffed on cigarettes, while the man behind the wheel, older than the others, smoked a cigar. Hopefully Bill would appear soon and they'd all drive away together. She suppressed a smile as she visualized what was certain to occur between herself and Fontessa the minute Bill left the premises . . . What a monumental cat fight! She saw her cousin's gouged-out eyeballs bouncing along the ground . . . But anybody could see that would happen, Bill included; in which case he might send the men away without him or—gulp!—invite them in for a beer. Marge was unable to visualize the scene that would take place if they decided to be neighborly and stay awhile. The people at the house were already so estranged from each other that she doubted they'd all fit into one room without uncontrollable squabbling.

When Bill did not appear on the porch, however, Marge walked up to the driver's side of the car, a big late-model Buick, and sang out "Hello!" She had a bright smile on her face. Martin remained more or less somnolent, stretched out among the radishes.

Though dusty from the drive the royal blue Buick was in mint condition. No expense had been spared to outfit it to the owner's specifications. Whitewalls, chrome mudguards, supplemental rear view mirrors, fancy headlight-eyelids made of chrome, additional strips and chevrons, and the final touch in this distinguished elder citizen's version of a hot rod: the so-called "Continental Kit" affixed to the Buick's rear end. The Kit was a gleaming extension of steel, paint and chrome available at custom car shops that mimicked the rear section of a swanky Lincoln Continental—actually was a forty pound replica of it affixed to the rear of any car to give it that luxury look.

"Hi!" Marge repeated gaily.

"Howdy, howdy—and how are *you* folks?" the large, easy-going man behind the wheel drawled good-naturedly, and at that moment with a sigh of relief she recognized who the man was . . . Old Doc Rice from in town . . . Dr. Rice! . . . Rimless spectacles and crumpled black suits. He always seemed so old-fashioned, Marge never imagined he drove a car like this! "Another secret goat," she thought with a smirk. She had even gone to him once for a sore throat and remembered now that he had opened her mouth long enough to peer inside and say "Five dollars, please" to her tonsils. But the sore throat *had* gone away. . . .

The Doc eyed Marge quizzically. He came right to the point.

"You're Marge Parsons, ain't ya? So y'all done moved out here now?" he asked, smiling broadly. But the glint of sunlight across his eyeglasses sent a shiver down Marge's spine.

There followed in the back seat laughter and a jostling of seats. Marge recognized Billy "Trenchmouth" Williams and Dee Wagoner —or was that Marvin Staples? . . . Yes it was Marvin Staples, alright, and his younger brother Sonny, too. But was that other fellow Trenchmouth?

These were some of the "tough guys" Bill had been hanging out with recently. Lazy assholes, Marge knew, fellows who never would amount to anything as men, who had been wise guys and punks in high school and now seemed to be stuck reluctantly in a rut. Marge herself did not grow up in Winosha Falls, but she had seen enough of these boys since her marriage to know what they were like. She had met a few of them previous to her marriage as well, during visits with her cousin Fontessa while in high school. One or two had tried to date her, but she would have nothing to do with the local talent. Until Bill came along, that is. Looking back on it now she could not believe she had ever fallen for Bill in the first place; seen something different in him. After Bill was dismissed from the army he came back to Winosha very cool and stand-offish. He acted like a snob, wouldn't talk to any of his old high school buddies and of course avoided his old friend Martin Kilbanky like the plague. He pretended the army had made a man out of him and bragged about his exploits abroad, promising to "make it big" now that he was back in the States. He had returned to Winosha only temporarily, he said: scouting out the business opportunities. Everyone in town was aware that all his talk was just hot air, however; they knew he had been kicked out of the army rather than released with honor, though the precise reason for his dismissal was never discovered. As a result, of course, Bill had gone nowhere. The banks refused to advance any credit for his vague schemes and before long he was backsliding, hanging out with the boys and getting in Marge's hair. Several years went by in this manner. . . .

Marge swallowed as she tried to put her marriage out of her mind. All that took place long before her new life with Martin. Thinking about the women she knew she felt lucky to have been given a second chance: not many were. Girls married to deadbeats quickly found themselves with two or three screaming brats and little else. Luckily Marge had always been firm about not having children and Bill was indifferent. She was free to fall into Martin's arms when the time came for that without a bad conscience . . . Scenes of their lovemaking flashed before her eyes. With a shudder Marge wondered if any of these men in the car knew about their forty-eight hours of intercourse. Had anyone seen them fucking? Suddenly she remembered Mrs. Kilbanky's warning about being seen from the road and how she and Martin had laughed it off at the time. Now her face went crimson. Had any of these brutes in the back seat seen them? Was that why Dr. Rice was here?

She searched the eyes of the men in the car, her stomach sinking, but they seemed calm and normal—Doc Rice gazing up at her good-naturedly, the boys in back socking each other around, laughing and joking.

No, she guessed not. She didn't see how they could have been seen from the road, anyway. They had been careful, hadn't they? She tried to visualize their scenes in the front yard but her customary accurate recall failed her. The best she could manage was an emotional wash of her and Martin melting into each other's arms, and this sent her swooning back against the side of the car with a thud. The Buick rocked slightly.

Dr. Rice opened the door and got out in concern.

"Are you alright, young lady?" he asked paternally, putting an arm around her.

"Y-Yes . . . It must be the heat . . . I ain't used to working out on a farm," she laughed, then bit her tongue in consternation at what she had said. "What's wrong with me: I shouldn't have said that, for Christ sake!"

She pinched herself in several places and slapped her own cheeks in an effort to clear out the cobwebs and pay attention. Dr. Rice saw this, however, and wrinkled his brow in thought. "Is this girl drugged?" flashed through his mind, but then he concluded she was not. "Still," he thought to himself, as Bill finally appeared on the porch steps and Marge rushed up to join him, "that girl's got something bothering her. I wonder what it is?"

He moved up smiling to shake Bill's hand.

"Howdy, Bill."

"Howdy, Doc," he said as he stuffed his shirt into his jeans and hopped down the steps. He shook the big hand.

"What brings you out here, anyway?" he added casually. "Are you sick about somethin?" He laughed at his own feeble joke. Then he looked over and spied Marvin Staples sitting in the back seat.

"Hey, Marvin," he shouted enthusiastically. "Yore sure ridin in style today, ain't ya, ha ha."

Marvin and the others laughed at this in an exaggerated fashion until the car started rocking again. Doc Rice turned to them and motioned with his big hand.

"Y'all get out of there, now, or I won't have a car left to drive home in!"

The other four men got out then, and stood in the yard stretching their frames and limbering up, looking around.

"Just decided to come out and pay you a visit," Marvin announced.

"Nice spread you got here, Bill," one of the men Marge didn't recognize said with a hint of sarcasm, and Marge felt Bill go tense momentarily under his shirt. "I didn't know you was a *landowner* now," the same voice added with deeper sarcasm.

"Ha ha ha," everyone said.

There was an awkward silence. Marge happened to look up and saw Mrs. Kilbanky above her, peering down at the scene from her second-story bedroom window. Without stopping to think if the old lady was sufficiently in possession of herself to carry on friendly chit-chat conversation she beckoned up at her, waving at her to come down. The head instantly drew away from the window, and ten full minutes went by during which time Marge was uncertain whether the old woman would ever make an appearance. Doc Rice and the rest saw her signal Mrs. Kilbanky, which Marge did on impulse, and so as the interval lengthened during which she did not appear they became suspicious, though they tried not to show it. After the topics of sore muscles and the weather had been exhausted, however, Doc Rice could not resist getting down to business.

"Exactly what are you and your wife doing here?" he asked, rather more directly than he intended. Bill gulped and caught his breath.

"Workin out here," he finally croaked.

"Workin," Rice pursued, trying to be casual.

"Yeah—and what the hell are *you* doin here, Doctor?" Bill blurted back, so comically arrogant that everyone took the insolence for a joke and laughed.

"Actually," Bill continued, "Martin and Mrs. Kilbanky invited us out here last month to help em run the farm." He swept his arm around the farmyard. "It's too much for them to handle alone since old Ike died. We do plowin, keep the house together, feed the animals...."

Bill spoke in such a way that although he was being perfectly cordial Rice knew he would not be able to pursue the topic further without seeming downright suspicious, so he accepted it with a friendly smile of congratulation.

"I'm damn glad to hear it, Bill," he said, clapping him on the back. "Damn glad. It's good to know Bill Parsons is a working man at last," he announced, winking at the others. "Now maybe he can pay me for them six stitches I put in him way back before he went into the army!"

Everyone laughed on cue, and at that moment Mrs. Kilbanky finally appeared above them at the top of the porch stairs in one of her best silk dresses, navy blue with hundreds of equidistant white polka dots. Rouge and powder left almost no trace of the red-rimmed eyes caused by her suffering the past few days, though if one caught her glance and looked her in the eye one saw the sadness, one saw the despair. As a consequence she avoided looking at anyone directly as she stepped down from the porch to assume the role of hostess. Marge, who had been afraid Louise would not show her face at all that morning, looked on in amazement at the fortitude of this brave little woman. Marge understood how much she was suffering and she marveled at her bravery: which, however, she knew to be occasioned exclusively by her determination to protect her son. To protect her son, Marge realized, she would also protect Marge and Bill. She would act as if they were the valuable hands they pretended to be. With tears of gratitude in her eyes she went to the old lady's side and offered an arm of support.

Graciously Louise accepted Marge's arm as the most natural thing in the world. They seemed the best of friends. Even Bill was impressed by this impromptu performance.

As for Dr. Rice, he was completely convinced. Solicitously he inquired after Mrs. Kilbanky's health, sympathizing with her over the loss of her husband in spite of having paid his respects at the funeral some months earlier.

But he and Louise Kilbanky were of the same generation. They had grown up together, gone to the same school, along with Ike Kilbanky himself and Bill and Digger's mother and father too, for that matter. Although they were quite dissimilar people, moving in different circles and in fact seeing little of each other over the years, yet they were of the same generation. This in itself was now a sort of bond between them. They had been aware of each other for sixty years! Merely as survivors of a time they both experienced they had something in common, though personally Doc Rice and Ike Kilbanky had never been close. Louise remembered Ike had always called Tom Rice a "smoothie," a "sharpie." Still, Louise thought, when you get to be our age just seeing someone else who's been around as long as you have draws you toward him.

She extended her hand to the doctor, and she could tell by the way he gripped it that he was touched.

"Won't you please come in?" she said, so simply and openly that Marge nearly wept.

"Why, thank you, ma'am," the old fellow answered, captivated now for the first time by this woman he had known but not noticed all his life.

Together they led the way up the porch stairs. Marge and Bill and then the other four men followed.

From out in the garden Martin lay on his stomach watching them. He hoped he could lie like that all day. He decided as soon as he saw Marge talking to the men inside the car that he did not like the situation. Now that they were all inside the house he breathed easier. He resolved to stay outside until the men left in their car. He ran a hand through his grey hair, humming to himself, talking under his breath and singing.

As they grouped and draped themselves in the parlor Mrs. Kilbanky walked off to scare up some tea and cookies and there was another awkward silence. While it filled the room Marge had ample time in which to reflect about the identities of these five new men.

One was Dr. Rice, of course; the little black bag he always carried with him was incontestable proof of that, though he made a point of leaving it in the car for now. This was a social call.

Then there were the Staples brothers—Marvin and his little brother Sonny. Marvin was twenty-six or so at the time and his brother a stolid twenty-three, but to everyone in the area Sonny remained "Marvin's little brother": all through childhood and school he had endured this form of automatic ranking, but actually Sonny didn't mind. He didn't care one way or the other. A little slow in the head though good-natured, he usually let his more explosive older brother speak for him. He let Marvin take the lead, being content to go along for the ride. Though the ride had included much delinquency and car-stealing during their high school years, lately it had settled down to no more than an insignificant purr inside the well-oiled social hierarchy of the town. The Staples preferred to hang out at Sonny's, but they hung out at Shorty's too.

Fourthly there was "Trenchmouth" Williams, Marge thought to herself with a shudder: though in truth she had so little contact with many of the boys from Winosha that she wasn't sure if it was "Trenchmouth" or not. Subsequently she learned from Bill she had been mistaken. It was a pale blond fellow, quiet and attractive really, to whom Bill himself was a perfect stranger. His name was "Dutch" Fecter, he had just moved to Winosha Falls earlier that week from out of state, and he had somehow found himself purely by accident coming along for the ride. Before two more hours were up he would in fact excuse himself, saying he had to hitchhike back to town right away to help his wife unpack and get accustomed to their new home, one of the unpainted cinderblock two-story houses lately erected on the outskirts of town. Marvin surprised Bill by apologizing *sotto voce* for bringing Dutch along: he had simply appeared by the side of the car as they were about to leave the vicinity of Shorty's pool room and Dr. Rice for some reason felt like inviting him along. Rumor had it that Dutch was a good carpenter and an experienced electrician, which if so would put him in direct competition with Marvin Staples's cousin Alvin Upton, at present Winosha's only licensed electrician. As a consequence of this indirect threat Marvin felt himself obliged to snub Dutch and during their drive out to the Kilbanky farm he teased and tested the stranger in the eyes of the others. Dutch's hopes for a friendly welcome to Winosha Falls were dealt a hard blow by this car ride. Marvin was certain he had made an enemy for life, he confided to Bill afterwards with a short laugh and a snort.

That left one man—or boy—yet to be identified, but of him Marge suddenly now felt certain. At least she knew who he was: Roger Yancey, fat Mrs. Yancey's son, the golden boy with the cynical smile. Three years before, when she first came to Winosha to stay, Marge had had a crush on Roger Yancey. He was a cool hard-muscled pretty-boy athlete, big, blond and good-looking. Almost immediately, however, Roger had gone off on a football scholarship to S.M.U. and only returned to Winosha last year after having torn a ligament and failed his language courses at the same time, whereupon he was summarily bounced out of S.M.U. (or wherever—Marge wasn't sure which college it was).

Roger was still big and good-looking and when she finally recognized him Marge experienced a pang directly related to her old heart-throb. But after taking a good look at him she changed her mind. Though outwardly as cute and strong as ever, Roger appeared on closer examination to have suffered some unknown psychic puncture or laceration deep in his being. He seemed to Marge to be *creased*: that was the word! she thought excitedly as she studied him on the sly across the parlor . . . His very soul had been creased and crinkled! Marge shivered as she deduced that in some way Roger Yancey was already middle-aged. The openness, the carefree dream, the youth in his eyes was gone. Extinguished forever. Not yet twenty-four years of age and already just a cynical hanger-on, another guy who would never know what to do with himself and who secretly resented it. Behind his bright mischievous smile and pearly white teeth lurked bitterness and erosion! Marge swooned and tried to hide her feelings. Poor Roger Yancey, she thought: it had taken her five minutes to recognize him. And the most interesting thing of all was that if she hadn't plunged head over heels into her unusual affair with Martin she probably would not have noticed *any* of these changes in Roger Yancey. On the contrary she probably would have seen substantially the same boy she'd had a crush on three years before, and then proceeded to make a play for him as well. Whereas now she just recoiled.

The gobs of ointment hung from Marge's fingers. The scars of bugs and lovemaking after some fifty-six hours straight rolling around in the grass and weeds and planks had left her skin raw and chapped. Abrasive cuts covered her back and legs. In addition she had apparently contracted some kind of patchy skin irritation that itched and burned and was driving her near crazy. The ointment—crushed roots and herbs suspended in a special translucent blue cold cream—was a home-made salve originally of her grandmother's manufacture. Grandma Facit had learned how to prepare it as a girl on a farm in Willamette, Ohio before the turn of the century. Marge kept a small tub of it in the pantry under a perpetual damp towel so its balance of enzymes and fungus would not veer. The effect was lovely, though, creamy and efficacious. Marge dabbed and rubbed in the cool blue salve, closing her eyes and purring softly to herself as she massaged it back and forth into her skin. Back and forth, back and forth, back and forth.

The five new men in the room watched in fascination. Bill followed her every move as well. Marge seemed to be floating off right before their eyes. She began rocking back and forth, her eyes narrowed down to slits, her tongue appearing at the corner of her mouth. It was an odd neglect of ceremony on her part—a weird lapse of manners—and the men seemed mesmerized by it.

They looked on half-dazed, gradually reaching a point where they were unable to keep their eyes open, though unaware of it, like a movie turned down to four-fifths speed. Big houseflies hurled themselves with a characteristic thud against the window screens. Time passed slowly. Outside could be heard the numberless, discrete, unimportant sounds of their rural surroundings. Birds chirped in trees, branches creaked and hushed against each other, a nearby mouth could be heard grazing loudly in the grass. Off in the distance a farm machine of some kind grated and grrrred. The machine changed gears five or six times; probably a thresher being tested academically, since threshers would not be used until the autumn harvest—a strange thing for a farmer to be doing this time of year. The men wondered vaguely whether the thresher sound came from Dowd Farms or from the Jakes place. They attempted to make a mental note of it . . . They fought against the strange colloidal torpor that was overwhelming them. . . .

But one by one heads nodded out onto chests. Chins met collarbones. Soon all the men were sleeping where they sat, hands folded neatly in their laps but sleeping nonetheless. Only Marge remained awake. She looked up from rubbing the ointment into her skin with a gasp. All these men have simply dropped off! she realized, and a chill ran down her spine. She never thought to connect it with her hypnotic massage, and in general Marge was forgetful of the power of suggestion she naturally possessed.

"God almighty!" she whispered aloud.

At that moment Mrs. Kilbanky appeared in the doorway, frozen and transfixed by the sight of the sleeping men arrayed before her in the room. She stood suspended on tiptoe, holding a big pewter tray laden with steaming teapot, cups and saucers, cookies and bread, and some ramps and ham for sandwiches. She had thought it only proper to serve the men lunch. She was uncertain what these men wanted of her, if indeed they wanted anything, but fuzzily uncertain: so that although she felt ill at ease with them she also was genuinely overjoyed to see some new faces in the house. Since they had taken the trouble to pay her a visit the least she could do was serve them lunch. Secretly grateful to be able to carry out normal interpersonal activity after so much irregular storm and trauma, her customary vitality returned miraculously. With these visitors, at least, she had the joy of knowing precisely what to do—serve refreshments and chat neighborly-like with them. And also of knowing that they in turn knew exactly what they had to do—carry on conversation graciously and good-humoredly, inquire after her solicitously, stroll around the grounds a bit and then leave. She looked forward to all this predictable activity. In fact she craved it, and so it was with a jolting eerie shock that she ran up against a sudden roomful of sleeping men. The six of them—including Bill—lay slumped on the sofa and in various chairs, two of them even standing—and all were asleep. Snoring steadily but lightly, as if any moment they might wake up and continue talking. But they did not wake up.

The two women looked on astounded and could not move. It was an uncanny moment frozen in time, a gleaming droplet of time that hung suspended and hung suspended. Marge refused to believe her eyes. The men were in a trance. Finally Mrs. Kilbanky's voice broke the silence.

"And why don't they sleep forever, the poor babies? Why can't they sleep forever? Oh, poor babies!" she cried sadly to herself as she stood at that point in mid-air, poised on the balls of her feet with the heavy tray of food balanced on her outstretched right palm and fingers. Tears were in her eyes, and she knew without turning to look that tears must be in Marge's eyes as well. There was a mysterious bond with this woman, momentary but deep. The two women looked on longingly at the scene. They hungered for the same oblivion, to be able to join the men. Tears ran down their cheeks. The men hung suspended in their sleep. The same solitary monster black housefly kept flying directly into one of the windows on the south side of the house, smacking repeatedly against the screen.

The two women were transfixed.

Then the fly bounded off the screen and buzzed across the room at top speed, smacking loudly into Dr. Rice's ear. Whap! Rice fell off his chair onto the floor and awoke with a strangled grunt, whereupon, like a bubble bursting, the two sleeping men who were standing (Bill and Little Sonny) collapsed onto the floor and awoke. Soon they were all awake, rubbing their eyes sheepishly and staring around, but actually not aware that they had been asleep. None of the men suspected what had taken place. None of them had the faintest memory of the scene, or of the tears shed by Mrs. Kilbanky. They shook their heads and cleared their throats.

Marge and Louise exchanged glances briefly as the previous situation resumed. They looked into each other's eyes but saw nothing. Soon they would forget that astonishing interlude, no matter how hard they fought to retain its image in their hearts. The moment had caught itself on something, some strange obstruction in the river of time, but now it was gone. The bubbles resumed floating up to the rim and breaking. So what if one bubble had hung suspended there for a few minutes longer than its destiny decreed? The river's force was far greater. The rivers of tea poured down six gullets. Ham sandwiches were prepared and eaten. Ramps were served. A couple of the men asked if great big flies had been in the room. The women chuckled to themselves and replied, "Yes, yes. . . ."

"Well, what happened to them?" Dr. Rice demanded as he tried to straighten his vest and sip his tea all at once. Some of the hot tea washed over the rim of the saucer into his lap.

"Goddamnit to hell!" he exploded, then looked up. "Oh, scuse me, ladies. . . ."

Marge handed him a napkin.

Mrs. Kilbanky sat back after distributing the lunch and turned to him with a winning smile.

"And what brings you folks out in these parts, Doctor?" she queried smoothly. Marge tried not to appear nosey as she craned her neck listening for Rice's reply.

It never came, however, because meanwhile Bill happened to look down at the floor in front of him as he stood tucking in his shirt and saw, perfectly clearly, a leg projecting along the baseboard from behind the sofa. A human leg. He stared fixedly at it for a second and then let out a bloodcurdling shriek, practically jumping out of his socks in fright.

"Aaahh, yaaahh—what is that!" he yowled, and everyone in the room sneezed hot tea. A horror-stricken interval elapsed during which Bill was *certain* the leg belonged to Martin. He hadn't seen him all morning. Somehow Martin had been murdered in his sleep! Bill jumped to this conclusion without thinking and soon regretted it.

He regretted it as soon as he knelt down and fearfully touched the outstretched leg. It was cardboard.

In consternation he yanked the figure out from behind the sofa: the cardboard mannequin yokel forgotten the night before by the State Historical Society men! Obviously Marge or Mrs. Kilbanky had stored it temporarily behind the sofa. No one told *him* about the damn thing. Bill's face turned red as he pulled the freckle-faced life-size yokel out from behind the sofa and stood him up against the mantelpiece.

Everyone else in the room broke into gales of laughter, bumping against one another in riotous amusement as they thrust their tonsils up into the light. Bill felt like disappearing into the woodwork. Everyone looked from him to the yokel and back again, dissolving in tears.

"Bill, boy, you sure are a sight for sore eyes," Dr. Rice drawled sarcastically, and the room erupted again.

"Yes, he's just a natural-born clown," Marge couldn't resist adding, and the room shook.

Bill felt like a fool. He glowered at Marge. From upstairs where she was in hiding, Fontessa heard almost every word. She bristled with hate at the way Marge was treating her man. She longed to close her hands around her cousin's throat. From two steps inside the bedroom door her heart went out to Bill. She was powerless, however. She must not make her presence known to the visitors. There was nothing Fontessa could do.

The men finished their sandwiches and tea. Louise Kilbanky collected the plates with a madly beating heart, for she sensed something momentous was about to occur. Why had Tom Rice shown up at the farm, anyway? She searched her mind but found no answer.

Bill and Marge, for their part, looked on with a secret sense of dread. Was it possible they simply were going to sit around and make talk, and then the men would leave? For a while it seemed so. Marge felt relieved.

Dr. Rice stretched his legs pleasurably, as if his shoes and socks were gone, and looked for all the world like he had the rest of the day off. Dutch Fecter, the new man in town, paced around nervously and then went to the window. Everyone was acting a little unfriendly and he felt ostracized. He was wondering about how he might be able to return to Winosha without having to hitchhike, when he looked out one of the east windows and happened to spy the cement mixer, upended beside the pond behind the house. The huge red truck looked ridiculous.

"What in the world is *that*?" Dutch asked incredulously. They all turned to look. Marvin and Sonny Staples came to the window and let out barks of surprise. Marvin had heard vague gossip in town over the past few weeks about Martin Kilbanky's insane building plans, but the story about the abandoned cement truck he had dismissed as hogwash. Seeing it out there in broad daylight surrounded by a large pool of cement made his head spin, and he turned without thinking to Doc Rice for an explanation. The mood in the room became tense. He was about to ask something, as his younger brother stood snickering beside him, when Rice signaled him with a movement of his hand to be silent. The only trouble was that everyone in the room had been watching, so that Bill, Marge and Louise tensed, and their bodies snapped anxiously alert. They all saw Rice signal briefly with his hand. They saw Marvin Staples break off in mid-syllable and turn away from the group to look out the window once again. What's more, it appeared certain that the wily old doctor himself knew the three had seen him signal. It almost seemed as if he had *wanted* to be seen. . . .

Marge didn't like it at all. She felt herself becoming defensive. Her body stiffened. Bill fidgeted with his hands and Louise began trembling in spite of herself, like a leaf. Everyone seemed to be waiting for Dr. Rice to resolve the situation. They all became conscious of the sound of water dripping in the kitchen sink down the hallway.

The doctor chuckled to himself mysteriously and looked down at his lap. There, in the folds of his pants, his thumbs were twiddling. He watched them closely for a few seconds, then chuckled again.

"So . . . Y'all probably ain't heard about the basketball game yet, have you?" he finally said with a wink, and immediately everyone breathed easier. Apparently some sort of story was going to be told. At least the topic of the cement truck had been dropped.

"Huh?" said Bill.

"The basketball game—the semi-pro league game last night over at the high school gymnasium," he explained, as Marvin and Little Sonny turned back into the room and Roger Yancey let out a congested rebel yell that stirred everyone's blood.

"You people are so busy workin out here you probably don't even know anything about it," Rice resumed. Roger's cold eyes gleamed in eager anticipation of a tale to be told—in fact a whopper to be recounted by one of the best storytellers in the county. "Man, I wouldn't have missed that damn game for the whole world!" the Yancey boy interjected.

"You mean the semi-pro league that the Winosha Ford-Lords play in?" Bill asked contemptuously. He couldn't believe his ears. The Winosha team, financed by Neil Lord's Ford automobile agency, was notorious for losing. It was a mediocre team at best and hardly anyone went to watch them play anymore, especially since the weather was so hot now and the season nearly over. The Ford-Lord players—even the starting five—were all overweight mechanics and truck drivers, incipient beerbellies. Bill had difficulty believing a first-class athlete like Roger Yancey—or rather, a once upon a time first-class athlete like Roger Yancey—would even stoop to attend a Ford-Lords game, much less praise one.

"The Ford-Lords are bullshit," Bill announced categorically. "I personally have plenty more to do than go watch those losers play. You guys sure must be hard up."

Marvin cut in. "But Bill, man, last night was *different*. First of all, the Ford-Lords won! And then—"

"So what if they won? You gotta be jokin. Most of the teams they play are just as bad as they are, anyway. It's *painful*," Bill was getting himself worked up. "*Painful—*"

"Yes, it was painful, alright, but not in the way you mean the word, Bill," Doc Rice spoke up, and unconsciously everyone else found themselves gathering in a semicircle around the old man. He had their undivided attention.

". . . Painful but not the way you mean the word . . . You see, Bill, last night was the last basketball game of the season and the Ford-Lords were determined to improve upon their season's record of four games won and forty-nine lost . . . Actually, lots of people showed up; that goddamn gym was packed, ain't that right, boys?"

Roger, Marvin and Sonny all agreed. Dutch Fecter merely looked and listened. He himself had not attended the game the night before since he had not known about it. The Winosha Ford-Lords and their semi-pro league were news to him. Dutch loved to play basketball, however, and even determined on the spot to try out for a starting position on the Ford-Lords as soon as possible. Obviously they were not a good team, in which case he was assured of winning a starting position. Happily he relished the prospect of playing for the Ford-Lords and thereby ingratiating himself with all the new guys in Winosha who at present were studiously ignoring him. Unknown to them, Dutch had been an all-state guard in high school, a legendary hot shooter who had to give up the dream of his life (professional basketball) and become an electrician because of his size. All five feet six inches of Dutch Fecter listened carefully as Doc Rice continued talking.

"Yep, lots of people showed up for the game, but even that ain't the big news. The big news is all on account of the team they played."

"The team they played?" Bill was becoming incredulous again.

"Yep . . . Because the Ford-Lords played the JCC Blue-Stars . . . Know who they are, Bill?"

"The JCC Blue-Stars . . . Lemme see. . . No I don't, actually."

"The JCC Blue-Stars," Doc Rice announced after a momentous pause, "is a traveling Jewish basketball team. It's a semi-pro basketball team made up entirely of J-e-e-w-ws," he said triumphantly, drawing out the word *Jews* until everyone laughed. "Now ain't that somethin? Ain't that somethin? Nobody had the slightest idea what JCC Blue-Stars stood for, until right before game time this team trots out on the court in white jerseys with big old blue stars on em . . . Jewish stars, you know? Star of David, I think they call it. Can you imagine that?"

Everyone laughed whole-heartedly.

"Little guys with big noses and wiry black hair, you know?"

A few seconds of silence elapsed and then Bill spoke up. "Well, thank God Winosha done won it, that's all I can say!" and everyone laughed once more. "It'd be the living end if we got whupped by a bunch of kikes."

"Yep . . . Well, it was a close one, I can tell you that. Most of the time it looked dead sure we was gonna lose, you know. The Ford-Lords were down twelve points or somethin like that eight minutes into the fourth quarter!"

"Really?" Bill was becoming interested. The Ford-Lords usually never scored more than thirty points in a whole game, so it must have been some comeback. "They must a played some damn good basketball to catch up, then."

"Waaal . . ." Doc Rice drawled, "Yes and no."

Roger Yancey snorted aloud.

"What do you mean, yes and no?" Mrs. Kilbanky spoke up. It seemed to her Tom Rice couldn't even tell a simple story without getting sneaky.

"Waaal . . . Y'see, Louise, the Ford-Lords had a little extracurricular help from some of the folks in the stands."

"Oh, my goodness!"

At that point the Staples brothers could contain themselves no longer and broke into howls, slapping their knees and punching each other in glee. "Man, it was the greatest thing you ever saw in your entire life!" Marvin shouted sloppily. "Ain't that the truth, Doctor Rice?"

"Waaal, it certainly was un-ex-pec-ted," he quipped, drawing out the syllables. "Especially for them J-e-e-w-i-s-h players, I reckon. And e-spec-i-ally that one little guy, remember him, Roger? Musta been one of their guards, and a pretty good little ballplayer too. That was when it started. They was ahead like I said, twelve or fifteen points, and this guy was bringing the ball downcourt as fast as he could, outrunnin poor Walt Wingo who was tryin to keep up with him, when all of a sudden Walt's baby brother Eddie, he's barely ten years old ain't that true, he bolts out of the stands and sticks his fist right up into this guy's throat as he's racing downcourt. Almost tore the fellow's throat clear off. He fell back onto the floor gagging and choking and boy you shoulda seen it—that doggone gym went wild! Everybody cheerin and hollerin. And the thing was, the referees or whatever refused to do anything. Eddie left a big old scratch down the guy's chest and even grabbed the ball away from him and threw it into his face when he came after him. The whole place broke up! And then the guy caught little Eddie and started punching him—can you imagine that? Punching a little kid like that? Hell, he was just playin around, you know . . . And when everybody saw him getting punched like that by a grown man—even if the guy was bleeding— well, nobody could take it. They started booing, and the scene got real ugly. It got real ugly real quick. The referees somehow reestablished order and the game continued, but people was running down onto the edge of the court and taunting the Jews every time they had the ball, throwin stuff at em like Coke bottles, and toward the very end of the game even interfering with the play. Whacked a few of em on the side of the head. You know young Mrs. Taggert, Lloyd's wife, that runs the dress shop? She ran up behind their bench and like to choke their coach to death. Boy, it was some show, I'm tellin you! Those Jewish fellows was terrified by the time the game was over. Cowering in the corner. They ran straight off the court into their dressing room. It was some game, boy. . . ."

"Yeah," Roger Yancey suddenly added, "it was some game, but that ain't all. A whole bunch of us went into the locker room after the game . . ." An evil glint lit his eyes and Roger leaned forward. "We caught us two of em in the shower and beat the living shit out of em," he said savagely. "We woulda killed em for sure if Sheriff Handle hadn't come in from the parking lot and their team bus hadn't pulled in right then to take em away. Boy, they owe their goddamn lives to that goddamn team bus of theirs!"

Roger then apologized for swearing in front of the ladies.

"Yes . . . Well, I don't know anything about all that, of course," Dr. Rice said evasively. "It sure was some game, though!"

Everyone laughed and savored details of the story, although Mrs. Kilbanky was quite upset by the beating Roger half-implied and half-described. She looked over at the blond Yancey boy and felt afraid. He was staring directly into her eyes. He seemed so cold and cruel.

Bravely she made her feelings known. "You should be ashamed of yourself," she said. "Beating people up like that is unfair!"

"Why, it wasn't unfair, Mizz Kilbanky," Roger deadpanned. "There was five of us against two of them."

Marvin and Sonny guffawed at this facetious reply, but Louise Kilbanky's lips narrowed. She immediately shot back: "Only cowards pick fights at those odds."

The room was dead silent as Roger leaped out of his chair. "Nobody calls me a coward, you—"

His fists clenched he stood ready for battle, but when he looked down at the terrified old woman quaking below him he came to his senses.

"I'm sorry, ma'am," he apologized. Dr. Rice icily stared him down.

"You darn well better be," the doctor said irately, and Roger skulked back to his chair and took his place. An uncomfortable silence remained. Everyone was wondering what to talk about next. The story about the basketball game had been great, but now a thick ill-humor stuck in their throats, making conversation difficult.

It was at that point that Dutch Fecter apologized to everyone and insisted he had to be leaving. He had to get back to town to help his wife move into their new house. Suddenly a crucial moment surfaced: Marge and Louise and even Bill were aware that this Fecter fellow was hoping for a ride home from Dr. Rice so he wouldn't have to hitchhike. His tone of voice clearly betrayed this. Yet he was a stranger, a newcomer, and as such he waited for Dr. Rice himself to volunteer the ride.

They had been at the farm now for nearly two hours. They had eaten lunch and carried on a conversation. In a way, it was time for them all to leave. In another way, however, the situation could just as naturally extend itself for a few hours longer. The decision was obviously up to Dr. Rice. All Marge and Louise could do was look on anxiously.

Without a word the decision was made. Dr. Rice turned to the little coffee table beside him and picked up a copy of *Life* magazine. He sat leafing through the pages. Dutch Fecter took the hint. He cleared his throat, made his goodbyes, and turned to go. Mrs. Kilbanky saw him to the door, thanking him rather abstractedly for paying them a visit. This short young man was a perfect stranger to her. Also, her mind was completely preoccupied with detecting any possible hidden meaning in Dr. Rice's decision to remain at the farm. What possible reason could he have for hanging around? In this frame of mind she watched absent-mindedly from the porch as the sandy-haired stranger disappeared down the road toward town.

Just as she turned to go back inside she saw her son Martin out of the corner of her eye, a grey-haired apparition streaking through the garden to her far right. She felt a lump in her throat as she closed the door and reentered the front room to continue the conversation. She wiped away a nervous tear and tried to appear calm and collected. Luckily Marge and Dr. Rice were discussing the weather so she had a few precious moments to compose herself before she would have to chat and chatter once again. But all she could think of was her son. She desperately hoped he would not get involved this afternoon. She prayed Dr. Rice would just leave.

At that point Martin couldn't contain his curiosity any longer. He rushed inside the house and bolted right into the front room where they all were sitting. Louise jumped as if she had been poleaxed. "Oh, Martin, what are you doing here?" she wailed. "Oh, son . . . uh," she didn't know how to proceed, how to introduce her son into the group. The poor woman kept looking at him unbelievingly, wishing he were just an apparition that would disappear. But over the past two hours Martin had become increasingly intrigued by this group of talkative visitors, and he had just worked himself up to the point where he was about to dash across the yard to a window and look inside the house when the front door had opened, scaring him half to death, and his mother had said goodbye to one of the visitors who then trotted off alone down the road. Martin nearly laughed aloud he was so nervous, but after his mother shut the door he fell to thinking and decided he had better go inside the house and confront the people for real rather than spy on them through the window. He wanted to see them in the flesh.

He decided there was no other way to do it than to open the door and rush inside. He was thirsty, he would explain, and simply came in for a glass of water. He was hungry, he would say, and wanted a pork roll sandwich . . . But the traumatic concussion unleashed by suddenly finding himself surrounded by five strange gaping men was too much. He stood in the middle of the parlor, in plain view of the group, and stuttered and turned red in the face with embarrassment. He was speechless.

"Uh—uh—uh," he stumbled pathetically. His mother was nearly weeping, as was Marge, from compassion.

As for the visitors, they were electrified beyond words by the sudden appearance of this grey-haired ghost. Each man fought to control a primitive onrush of fright that threatened to overwhelm him. Even Dr. Rice was shattered by his appearance in spite of the fact that he had seen Martin in his present condition in Gene Sisley's office and given the boy an injection. But people were uncomfortable with Martin to begin with, and the grey hair merely intensified this. The five men wished he would just go away. They felt unequal to the task of dealing with him. Martin himself was acutely sensitive to this reaction from people and it made the task of socializing that much more difficult for him. Why did people find it so hard to be open and friendly?

But it had been a long time since Martin felt so flustered when in the presence of other people as he did now. Frantically he searched for something to say and finally popped out with: "Hey, Bill!"

Dr. Rice by this time was sitting straight as a razor in his chair, and bug-eyed as well. Bill laughed stiffly, finding himself so suddenly addressed by this maniac who just jumps into the room with no warning and starts—

"What do you want, Martin?" he found himself saying, instead of what he intended to say.

"Say, Bill!" Martin warmed up, abruptly filling with energy and self-assurance as he hit on a topic that might explain his presence: "I was just outside there, out in the yard, you know? And I was thinking about the Green Bay Packers. Remember? Like used to be on TV? Whaddya say, Bill . . . Let's go see those Packers play!"

Bill was dumbstruck. For a second nothing moved, then Sonny Staples broke into a strangulated giggle. Then Roger Yancey snickered, Marvin Staples chortled, and all the men were guffawing.

Soon the laughter died down, however. The men eyed Martin curiously with everything from blatant monkey-house stares to furtive sidelong glances. His grey hair unnerved them. It gave them all upset stomachs.

Marge and Louise remained frozen, unable to speak. But Bill felt obliged to reply:

"No, Martin, I refuse to accompany you," he wisecracked. Then he condescended to explain himself: "It's *summer*, remember? They don't play football in the summer, they play it in the *winter*."

Everyone laughed dutifully but they were looking at Martin rather than listening to Bill.

Martin felt cornered. He shifted his ground abruptly. "Is there anything to eat?" he sang out. Marge flinched at the brittle tone of his voice. She could tell he was frightened and disoriented, but as she sat among this roomful of local men who identified her as Mrs. Bill Parsons it was impossible for her to go to his side, to aid and comfort him. She looked on helplessly. Tears welled in her eyes that she hurriedly wiped away.

"Is there anything for lunch? I'm hungry!" Martin announced, a trace of manic petulance in his voice. He stood in the middle of the parlor floor in full view of the men and women slouched along the perimeter. From the most comfortable chair in the room—Louise's favorite old Morris chair— Dr. Rice stroked his chin and squinted up at the boy. Martin seemed acutely uncomfortable, as if he were longing to run from the room. Rice decided now was the time to make contact.

"Been workin hard, son?" he asked with a friendly smile.

Martin swung around in his direction. He remembered the doctor from the awful day he had spent as a captive in the County Prosecutor's office the month before. He remembered the doctor's spectacles glinting in the light so his eyes were invisible as he filled a hypodermic needle with some amber-colored liquid and swiftly punched the needle into Martin's arm. This was the only memory he had of Dr. Rice but it was more than sufficient to make him distrust the big, heavyset man in the rumpled three-piece suit.

"Y-yessir, working hard in the garden is hard work!"

Marge bit her lip at this absurd tautology. "Please, oh baby please!" she prayed under her breath. "Please don't make an ass of yourself. . . ."

At that point Mrs. Kilbanky came to her son's rescue, breaking the temporary paralysis that had set in when he appeared.

"C'mon, son: there's a mess of ramps and ham in the kitchen. Let's go see if we can find it." Gamely she stepped to the center of the room and took her son's hand. It was damp and rigid.

"Ramps . . . and ham?" he echoed vacantly.

His mother tightened her grip on his forearm. "Yes, Martin. Let's go have some *lunch*," she repeated, emphasizing the word.

"Lunch!" A bulb lit up inside his head.

Bill stood nearby, deeply embarrassed to be counted a member of this household. He vowed to himself that once these nosey bastards finally left the farm he'd pack up his belongings and he and Fontessa would leave forever. One of them was sure to find work somehow. Even *poverty* could be no worse than this mortal embarrassment. He couldn't stand it.

Martin seemed substantially more divorced from reality than usual. His mother had to tug him across the room into the hallway and then propel him forward with a fist planted in the small of his back. Spittle ran down his chin when they were alone. Louise's heart swelled until she thought it would burst. She ascribed his loss of contact to the sudden confrontation with so many mocking strangers. But she was also convinced more than ever that Marge was a pernicious influence. She was certain that their filthy promiscuity over such a long period of time had released something awful in him. As she fed her son ham sandwiches and made a fresh batch of lemonade for him to drink, the fears and sorrow of the last few days came back to her with such force she trembled anew at the horrible behavior she had witnessed . . . Someone passing by on the road was *sure* to have seen them copulating . . . And in the back of her mind she dreaded that Tom Rice was aware of Marge and Martin's revolting behavior and was waiting for the right moment to accuse them of immoral acts.

Louise couldn't stand the suspense any longer, and as she stirred heaps of white sugar into the pitcher of water and lemon juice she determined to take Rice aside and plead with him to spare her son any further humiliation. She was sure he would see it her way: together, then, they could easily threaten Marge and Bill Parsons off the farm, and if Martin was able to survive that shock he and his mother would be free to start their life all over again. Free! Free! Free! The word echoed miserably in her head as she cracked the ice cube trays with vehemence against the side of the kitchen sink. Crack! Crack! Crack! The little frozen cubes shot out across the kitchen in all directions.

Laughing wildly Martin jumped up in pursuit, and soon he and his mother were down on their knees, retrieving the slippery cubes from underneath the table and behind various chairs and cartons and other objects. With a finger to her lips Louise signaled her son to be quiet and his giddy laughter immediately ceased. He was puzzled. His brow creased in vexation. Why couldn't he laugh if he wanted to?

His mother pointed wordlessly in the direction of the front parlor and shook her head again, but Martin still didn't understand. He heard the men talking and laughing: why weren't they allowed to hear *him* laugh?

Silently they gathered the cubes and washed them off under the faucet.

Martin then consumed a full quart of lemonade while his mother looked on absently. Her back ached. She was getting too old to be stooping under tables for stray ice cubes. She shivered and yawned, then looked up at the clock. 2:15 P.M. She felt exhausted. She longed to take a nap: draw the curtains and sink into darkness. Instead, all she had to look forward to was a long afternoon of aggravation and uncertainty. It was almost too much for her to contemplate . . . Why should she have to deal with these people? She resented so much her present position in life! Did she have the strength to carry on? Could she walk back into that room and face those men and boys again? And pretend Marge and Bill were part of the household—part of her family? And pretend that Martin was a strong, capable, devoted son in full possession of his faculties? And pretend everything was "just fine"? Pretend, pretend? How much longer could she go on with these lies? How much longer would she be able to live like this? Just how much more was she expected to take?—Oh, Ike, Ike! Where have you gone—Oh God, oh God, I can't go on! I can't go on!

. . . And at that point as Martin sat perfectly oblivious to his mother's frame of mind, stirring the bottom of the lemonade pitcher for the gummy yellow residue, his mouth watering in expectation, his eye wandering toward the scraps of ham and bread that remained on the table, his mind's eye wandering forever high among the clouds, his sex puttering too, endlessly bound to clamor for his attention—as all these vectors assailed him at once, from off in the momentary warm comfort of his mother's nearby presence there came a sudden gurgling and then a heart-rending, half-stifled single sob, followed by a desperate attempt to quash what soon erupted, however, into his mother's horribly distended unhappy weeping.

Martin's immediate physical reaction was to send the lemonade pitcher hurtling against one of the kitchen cabinets. His mother was crying! He sprang to her side, alarmed but also possessed of what for him was a truly miraculous presence of mind. With surprising serenity and self-assurance he knelt beside the poor bent frame and whispered in her ear, "Don't be frightened, mother. Don't be frightened. I am wonderful and I am here . . ."

Louise's mind temporarily blanked out. Were those really the words Martin was uttering? She couldn't believe her ears but then she realized it didn't matter because the important thing—the surprising thing—was the tone with which he was saying them.

His tone was clear, calm—like a bell. It soothed her immediately. At the same time he put his arm around her and squeezed: again so self-assured, she thought. Calm and sure. She stopped crying and turned to look at him with tears in her eyes. "Oh, Martin!" she wailed, in a great sad release of pent-up frustration. "Oh, Martin, Martin!"

They had been estranged from each other for days now, really estranged for the first time in their lives, and this precipitous rediscovery of their love was extremely emotional. They wept and embraced quite noisily, oblivious for a few precious moments of the other people in their house.

But soon Marge appeared in the kitchen doorway, drawn by the weeping that they had not at first heard in the front room, separated as it was from the kitchen by a long hallway, but which had become distressingly audible in the parlor not moments before, bringing a desultory conversation between Bill and Marvin Staples to a halt. Everyone stopped what they were doing and looked up. The sound of tortured weeping rushed into the room, loud and disconcerting.

Bill flinched in horror. "Can this really be happening to me? What's wrong with those damn Kilbankys, anyway?" he thought, revolted by the sound. "If this keeps up much longer we'll all be screwed to the wall! Finished!"

Marge looked over at Dr. Rice. His eyes widened as if he had been jabbed in the ass with a fork, but otherwise he preserved a strict business-as-usual demeanor. Obviously Dr. Rice was determined to act as if he heard nothing. He continued leafing through *Life* magazine.

"So the old buzzard still has some sense of decency left," Marge mistakenly thought to herself with grudging admiration, as she got up from her chair and left the room. . . .

And now she stood in the kitchen before this weeping mother and son, behind whose shivering bodies Marge saw fields of silvery-green rye stalks waving dreamily in the sun. She realized with an ironic twisted smile that it was her destiny to come between this boy and his mother, both of whom she loved in a way. "Look," she said to herself bitterly, "Look—even now I'm about to interrupt them! Whether I want to or not I'm going to break their bubble and they'll look up at me, defensive and resentful. They'll see me standing here above them, they'll hear the men's voices in the other room again, they'll know who they are and what the situation is. And even if they're not aware of it, they'll blame me for waking them. . . ."

And even as she stood in the doorway thinking this Martin looked up and saw her. His body tensed. His mother looked up, they both stopped crying, Mrs. Kilbanky's mouth tensed. The spell had been broken.

Marge smiled bitterly to herself. "I guess I'm just a fool like all the rest . . ." Humming to herself she sang a line from a country and western song she had once heard that came out of nowhere into her head: "Yes, I guess I'm just a stranger and a fool."

She turned and walked back down the hallway. No conversations were in progress in the front room: everyone seemed to be listening for further sounds from the kitchen, though there were none.

"Why, this must be the longest day of the year!" Marge exclaimed gaily as she reentered the parlor. "I'm plumb wore out!"

Mustering all her determination Marge smiled a warm open smile and let it hang there in the parlor air until it drew the attention of all the men.

She was determined to continue acting naturally.

"Mrs. Kilbanky isn't feeling well," she finally confided, "and asks to be excused for the rest of the afternoon." She pointed wordlessly at the ceiling to signify the old woman had retired for a nap. The men exchanged glances.

Marge continued. "She also begs me to invite y'all to take an afternoon nap here in the parlor—or anywhere you please. The floor's perfectly clean," she added, stooping over to pick up a stray ball of dust, "if you're accustomed to stretching out on hardwood for your siestas . . . Otherwise, the porch is mighty comfortable . . ." She trailed off. "Bill and I can bring out some stuffed chairs . . ." she concluded vaguely. "Maybe there's an old hammock someplace."

She was on edge and seemed uncharacteristically unsure of herself. Bill was annoyed that on this day of all days her usual spunk and aggressiveness appeared to be missing. He felt she was betraying him on purpose.

Dr. Rice, however, greeted her suggestion with a large smile.

"Why sure, little lady," he chirped. "If it ain't no inconvenience, that is."

He stood up. "But oughtn't I go and see if I can be of any assistance?" he asked in concern, pointing up at the ceiling and raising his eyebrows.

"Oh, no—please don't bother," Marge replied as Bill and she struggled out onto the porch with several heavy upholstered chairs. "Louise is just a bit tired, that's all. Worn out. All this unexpected activity. It's understandable. She's been that way a whole lot since Mr. Kilbanky died, you know. She tires real easy."

"So I hear, so I hear," Rice muttered, stroking his chin.

"We sleep a lot out here," Marge felt compelled to add.

Soon various chairs and pillows were arranged and the four men stretched out on the front porch. They looked up from the shady enclosure through beautiful big elms at the bright hot afternoon sky. None of them retained the faintest memory of their previous brief slumber before Dutch Fecter had left. Now they kicked off their shoes or rolled over onto their sides and before five minutes passed were sound asleep.

While they slept and the hot afternoon wore on Bill and Marge met in the hallway and stared vacantly but significantly into each other's eyes for a full five minutes. Sweat glistened on Bill's forehead. Marge's armpits burned and her stomach churned dangerously. There would be no sleep for either of them that afternoon.

They stared at each other without speaking. An indescribable magnetic current of complicity, loathing, fear and excitement flowed back and forth between them. Today seemed to be their day of reckoning. Then Bill turned away and bounded up the stairs to be with Fontessa for a few precious hours before it all reappeared.

The Kilbanky dining room had not been in use for quite some time. After Ike died Louise experienced a weighty loneliness every time she and Martin attempted to have dinner there. Soon they gave it up and ate their meals in the kitchen. Even when Ike was alive the room had been used only on Sundays and special occasions. Now its massive oak table and monumental spun glass peacock centerpiece—the secret gem of the Kilbanky collection of American authenticities and one which Louise was careful to hide from the prying eyes of the State Historical Society—lay under dusty white bedsheets. The marvelous set of eight Shaker chairs and the mahogany grandfather clock were similarly covered with sheets.

These shapes lurched out of the dimness as Marge moved through the room, opening long-shut windows and attempting to brighten up the room and air it out before it was used. She was doing this because in a secret meeting earlier with Louise—a temporary joining of arms of two foes in order to meet the greater threat—the two women had decided after much consideration to invite the men to stay for dinner.

Marge hated the idea at first and was dead set against it. Marvin and Sonny Staples, Roger Yancey: the last thing she wanted to do was cook dinner for such as them. She felt above them and sneered at Louise for suggesting the idea. But then Louise explained to her that it was precisely because she did *not* know whether the men planned to stay to dinner that she was forced to ask them to stay. Otherwise they might become suspicious. They still were sleeping on the porch and it was already past 5:00 P.M. A decision had to be made. Martin was getting hungry, and also moody and irritable: he complained to his mother about the presence of the men, and Louise feared that if she and Marge did not act now and invite them to dinner Martin might lose his temper, tromp downstairs and shout at them to leave!

Marge visualized the scene. She saw his rigid body and heard his hysterical voice telling the men to get off the farm. She flinched: it's true, it would be awful. She decided Louise was right. While they were talking she could hear Martin above them, pacing noisily up and down in Louise's bedroom. His heavy workboots made a terrific racket, actually. Marge had frowned: "Tell Martin to take off those damn workboots and put on some sneakers and I'll do it."

Louise agreed and went back upstairs to tell Martin they would be eating soon, while Marge walked into the dining room and began opening it up and cleaning it out. She shook out the sheets and folded them. Carefully she stored the fragile peacock centerpiece in a closet. She opened windows, swept up dead wasps, and double-checked silverware. She hated every second of it but saw no other way.

While she was dusting she thought of her missing dog Donnie again. Where was he? It wasn't like him to run off by himself for days on end. Again Marge worried about the packs of stray farm dogs she had seen: she was positive something had happened to Donnie that was in some way connected with the strays, but the hectic pace of the last few days had not allowed her to search for him. But the big black poodle's image came to her as she worked, and this upset her. It wavered before her eyes and then was gone. What can that mean? Marge wondered. Since she and Martin stopped making love she simply had not felt herself. Her customary aggressive energy was gone. Now for the first time she linked this, in some unexplained way, with Donnie's disappearance. What did it mean? She didn't understand it but she knew, she just *knew*, it was necessary to have her dog. Without the dog nearby she felt indecisive, uncertain of herself. This apparent link between herself and a canine disturbed more than it enlightened her, however, so that she was all the more willing to submerge herself in the present onrush of events. She resisted the pull of something she could not explain. Donnie would turn up soon enough . . . And if worse came to worst she had her aerosol cans, she had her wigs. Their powers, which she did not understand either, were already more than enough for her. . . .

Finally the room was ready, and as she joined Louise in the kitchen the men on the porch awoke. They lit cigarettes and walked off in the grass to stretch their legs and piss. It was late afternoon now, a breeze was stirring dreamily in the hot shadows. Fragrant perfumes were broadcast by flowers of all kinds from the garden by the side of the house.

Dr. Rice stood on the lawn and breathed in and out until he became dizzy. It's so great to be alive! he felt. His nostrils quivered with the scent, although actually they were so desiccated they smelled almost nothing. In reality his olfactory sense was greatly diminished in comparison to those of the youths who surrounded him, but Dr. Rice was not aware of it since many of his other senses and responses had eroded to exactly the same degree. Consequently it was almost impossible to be aware as they all gradually deteriorated. Everyone else only reinforced this by automatically assuming without thinking that he smelled the same things they did.

Roger, Marvin and Sonny cavorted on the grass, wrestling and chasing each other around the yard. Soon one of them stopped short, however. It was Sonny Staples.

"Hey—smell that, will ya!"

They stopped and sniffed the wonderful odors escaping from the

Kilbanky kitchen ten or fifteen yards away. Soon stomachs were turning and growling stubbornly, so it was no difficult task for Mrs. Kilbanky to pursuade the men to stay for dinner. When she emerged smiling from the kitchen screen door with a gravy boat in her hand, pushing back a stray lock of hair that had fallen into her mouth while she worked, the three boys immediately went down on their knees before her, mouths open and salivating in mock distress. Everyone else laughed.

"Shore we'll stay for supper," Marvin Staples practically choked. "Won't we, Doc?" he turned to Rice with a plea on his face.

Rice laughed. "It's a hard offer to refuse," he said smiling, but then paused without actually saying yes. His wire-rimmed spectacles glinted in the light. It seemed he was appraising the situation from a secret vantage point. Everyone started to feel uneasy.

Finally he spoke up. "You boys sure you ain't got anybody expecting you for dinner? What about you, Roger? I'll bet your momma's got a wall of hot dumplings steaming up the kitchen right this second!"

Roger waved his arm in disgust. "Aw, she cooks all day whether anybody's there or not. It don't mean nothin, I swear. Besides," he added with a peculiar smile, "I ain't seen hardly nothing of my buddy Bill yet. I say let's visit some more."

"It's right nice of you to ask us, Louise," Dr. Rice drawled graciously, "so I guess we'll have to say yes!" Whereupon the four of them laughed among themselves and Louise, somewhat shaken by the episode, turned back to the kitchen.

She wondered as she stirred the gravy and stripped fresh rhubarb for rhubarb compote whether she had made a mistake. Should she have invited them for dinner? What would Ike have done?

But it was too late to turn back now, and she and Marge worked until soon the various courses were ready. She and Marge worked well together, and for a moment she found herself thinking wistfully of Marge as a daughter-in-law, as Martin's wife . . . She snapped out of it when Bill suddenly sneaked into the kitchen and Marge explained the situation. He liked it even less than she did.

"You mean they ain't gonna leave?" he asked incredulously. He wasn't sure he could stand up under the added strain.

Marge lost her temper. "Listen, you jackass: if anything goes wrong around here you'll be the one to blame, for having such disgusting friends in the first place. You and that whore of yours upstairs!" she seethed.

Bill cried out and lunged for her with fists clenched but Louise jumped between them. "Stop it!" she whispered, "Stop it! Both of you are vermin," she found herself hissing, "and as soon as we get rid of these men there's going to be a change here if I have to call in the sheriff myself!"

But she had said too much and instantly regretted it. The possibility that she might forget about shielding her son to the extent that she would even *think* of calling in the sheriff filled the Parsons with alarm.

"You don't mean that!" Marge spat contemptuously. "You ain't got the guts." This electrified all three of them, but it was the only way Marge saw to call the old woman's bluff. And it worked.

Noiselessly her shoulders shook and she began to whimper. Once again Marge was the only one left to take charge. "Now listen, Louise," she said sympathetically, "I'm sorry. I didn't mean that. But we've gotta forget about ourselves for the time being and finish what we started. We have to carry through with this dinner. We have to join together."

She turned to Bill. "And *you're* gonna help, lunkhead . . ." She jabbed a batter-covered fork into his chest. "I want you to go to the dining room and set the table with the best plates while we get this food ready. And I want you to participate in the conversation at the dinner table and act like you're supposed to: Bill Parsons, the guy Mrs. Kilbanky hired to help run the farm, remember?"

Bill nodded and strode from the kitchen.

Soon dinner was on the table and eight people sat around it. Steaming platters of country-fried chicken, potato salad, green beans and white sauce tempted them. A fresh tossed salad stood on the sideboard. Rhubarb compote and cookies waited in the kitchen as dessert.

Louise Kilbanky was at the head of the table nearest the door leading down the hallway to the kitchen, while Dr. Rice sat at the opposite end. To his left and right respectively sat Roger Yancey and Sonny Staples, while Martin Kilbanky and Marvin Staples sat at Mrs. Kilbanky's left and right. In the middle facing each other were Marge and Bill: Bill between Roger and Marvin, Marge between Sonny and Martin.

Martin stared glumly at his plate as the meal began. He toyed with a chicken breast, poking it with his thumb. At first it looked like he wouldn't eat, but soon his mood changed and he was shoveling the food down at an alarming rate, communicating with downcast eyes only to his mother or to Marge. He refused to acknowledge the others or take part in the conversation—which was, admittedly, a desultory one.

Almost nothing was said as the platters were finally on the table and the people began to eat. There was a surface tension in the air that made conversation difficult; also, everyone was ravenous.

"This chicken sure is good!" Bill volunteered at one point, but no one responded.

After they had been eating for some time their hungers were satisfied but the tension remained. It was as if they were all unable to be in the same room together, which was odd since most of them had known each other for years. This fact only made them more tongue-tied, so that the only outlet remaining was the food. The potato salad was a special success and Louise had made a big tub of it.

They ate and ate and ate.

Luckily it was a very good meal, varied and delicious.

They had been eating for forty-five minutes, engrossed now in how to continue swallowing as long as possible without bursting, when suddenly the telephone rang. Before anyone else moved Marge jumped up and ran to the kitchen to answer it.

"Is this the Kilbanky residence?" Louella Jacksonburg, the local telephone operator, demanded self-importantly: "New York City calling long distance! A collect call person to person to Mrs. Louise Kilbanky from Miss Chartruse Kilbanky. Do you accept?"

Marge was stunned momentarily, until she remembered that Chartruse Kilbanky was Martin's older sister, who had left the farm—or been banished, depending on who you talked to—two or three years earlier. Marge had never met Chartruse, and since neither Martin nor Louise ever mentioned her Marge had forgotten she existed.

"Well?" Louella Jacksonburg demanded impatiently. "Is this Mrs. Kilbanky? Do you accept the call?"

"Uh, yes operator. Hold on. I'll call her to the phone."

"The party accepts the call," the operator droned to the person at the other end, and a sigh of relief could be heard.

"Louise!" Marge shouted. "Telephone! Long distance calling!" She shouted at the top of her lungs so she would be sure to be heard down the hallway. "IT'S YOUR DAUGHTER CHARTRUSE CALLING ALL THE WAY FROM NEW YORK CITY!"

Louise's eyes widened as her daughter's name sailed into the room. Martin twitched, spilling rhubarb compote onto his jeans.

"Oh, my goodness," the mother gasped. "What'll happen next!" The last she'd heard from her daughter, Chartruse had been in Baltimore.

She looked up and down the dinner table in apology. "You'll please excuse me, but my daughter's calling long distance. I won't be long, though, gentlemen: of that you can be sure." A steely glint came to her eye. Already a vein stood out in her forehead. "That tramp," she added softly as if to herself and rapidly left the room.

Dr. Rice, and for that matter everyone in the room except perhaps Sonny Staples, was well-acquainted both with Chartruse and with the trouble she had caused the Kilbankys. As a wild, sex-crazed adolescent she had been the epitome of a small-town bad girl. She had caused her parents much grief with her all-night drinking and partying, her truancy from school, her defiant promiscuity. Quitting high school midway through the tenth grade because of pregnancy she had disappeared from Winosha in shame only to return brazenly a month later after some foul abortion somewhere. None of the decent women in town would have anything to do with her after that and it wasn't too long before her parents—especially her mother—made life so miserable for her that she left one night in a huff, stealing forty dollars from Ike's pants and leaving a scribbled note saying she was headed for some big cities, that she hated everyone in Winosha except for her father, and that she would never return. Old Ike, it's true, always had a soft spot for her—he loved the girl dearly—but finally even he came around to his wife's way of looking at things, and when it came time to make out his will Louise easily persuaded him to name their son Martin as sole beneficiary.

When Ike died Chartruse had returned, tear-stained and pale with grief, to attend the funeral. But the very next morning Louise informed her daughter of the details of the will and made clear she was unwelcome in her own home. In a raw scene filled with vicious name-calling and rancor Chartruse stormed out of the house without a cent to her name, vilifying her mother and vowing never to return. "You'll never see or hear from me again!" she swore.

Nevertheless, periodically she called home in spite of herself. Cleveland, Louisville, Chicago, Pittsburgh, Baltimore—Chartruse had been through them all, and now she was in New York City. Alone in the big city, overwhelmed and abused, she barely existed doing part-time secretary work and falling victim to all sorts of strange men. Evil men, usually, men with big cocks who loved her and then stepped all over her and abandoned her. Each time she called home—ultimately to beg for money—her situation sounded more revolting to Louise than before, but the mother refused to give in. Every time she called, Chartruse had some new man she was crazy about, and this horrified Louise.

Louise Kilbanky was an intelligent, sensitive woman whose morality nevertheless was grounded firmly in the nineteenth century vision of spotless feminine virtue. To her a girl who willingly becomes a tramp and even flaunts it in public must be diseased to the very depths of her being and consequently must be abandoned without compassion. Thus each telephone call from her daughter was a mere confirmation of her opinion. Besides, she had never really loved her daughter the way she loved her son. The relationship between Martin and his mother had been special and intense since babyhood, and in the light of that relationship Chartruse suffered from the very beginning.

As for Martin, when they were children he and Chartruse behaved much as any brother and sister, mingling affection and competition equally. They were staunch playmates and fond of each other, but puberty changed all that. Chartruse seemed to become possessed by a demon when she turned thirteen years of age, and they quickly grew apart. Martin, three years younger, had no inkling of what was involved when his mother vilified Chartruse, but since he was closer to her than to his sister he automatically assumed Chartruse had done something "very bad" and virtually stopped talking to her. Chartruse still loved Martin and preserved her affection for him but as a teenager passion took precedence over playing with her increasingly childish brother, so that by the time she became pregnant and the situation reached the critical point almost no communication remained between them. By the time Martin himself finished high school his behavior was labeled definitely bizarre and his sister saw nothing unfair in this. She came to regard him as "loopy," "around the bend," and in the final struggle with her mother Martin was totally ignored. He would roll around in the mud outside while inside the two enraged females traded denunciations.

When Chartruse finally left for good Martin was sorry to see her go, but actually he was mourning the disappearance of his childhood playmate rather than the desperate tramp who swaggered off uncertainly into the unknown.

. . . Now, as Mrs. Kilbanky picked up the receiver in the kitchen and—since the connection was poor—began shouting into it, Dr. Rice sat mulling over this family history in the dining room.

While he sat mulling and everyone else began belching and picking their teeth, Marge cleared the dinner plates from the table and served up the last of the dessert, then went back to the kitchen to make a pot of tea. As she prepared the tea and carried it to the dining room she overheard Louise's end of the telephone conversation with mounting anxiety. It didn't help to have to explain to sarcastic Roger Yancey that coffee was not served on the farm.

Louise had gone to the phone determined to cut her daughter off with five words but the bad connection made her strain to hear what was being said and forced her to shout back in reply, with the result that soon she lost command of the situation and became emotional at the top of her lungs. She forgot about the visitors. Most of what she said could be heard clearly in the dining room down the hall.

The conversation apparently began as usual with Chartruse describing her new boyfriend Tommy in glowing terms and then begging Louise to send her money.

"I don't CARE if you can't find a job! I don't CARE if you're broke and downhearted in New York City!" Louise shrieked. "I don't CARE if you're sick and depressed. I don't CARE about Tommy!" Then a pause. "I don't care WHO he is." Another pause.

"What?" Another pause.

"What?"

Then Mrs. Kilbanky exploded. "How dare you! I said, HOW DARE YOU! Chartruse, you seem to forget that you are forbidden ever to set foot in this house again! Out of the question! I don't CARE if you have no one left to turn to."

"What?"

"Chartuse," she warned, turning purple in the face, "if you try to come back here I'll find Ike's gun and shoot you, I swear. I'll call the sheriff! I absolutely REFUSE to have my house smeared with any more filth. . . ."

And it was here that Marge began worrying. She ran back to the kitchen and signaled Louise to lower her voice—pointing in the direction of the dining room—but to no avail. Louise had lost possession of herself—due, apparently, to her daughter's insistence she had the right to come home with her boyfriend.

"Yes, I said filth! What?"

"Filth! Filth! . . . Do you have any IDEA what's been going on here in your absence? I said, DO YOU HAVE ANY IDEA?"

Apparently Chartruse then said something that enraged the mother because she started bellowing hysterically into the phone.

"You cheap slut. I said, YOU CHEAP SLUT! Who do you think you are, calling me a liar!" The veins stood out in the old woman's face and neck. "I tell you it's been HORRIBLE here. HORRIBLE! These AWFUL PEOPLE have FORCED their way onto the farm! FILTHY! FILTHY WOMAN COPULATING WITH YOUR BROTHER! DO YOU REMEMBER BILL PARSONS?" Here Marge was down on her knees before the old woman, begging for mercy. But Louise, who finally realized what she was doing, gulped and continued shouting with a perverse smile contorting her normally straightforward features: "Yes, here now! Here right now! And Martin's been so strange lately, we lost all our money on a cement mixer. WE WERE FORCED TO PAY FOR A USELESS TRUCK and nobody does any work around here. A CEMENT MIXER! CEMENT! AND PILES OF CEMENT! POOLS OF CEMENT! We have no money left. Nothing! And you want to pay us a visit with your new boyfriend. You want to come back here and live. Well, I won't allow it! I won't allow it!"

Exhausted, the tears clouding her eyes, she slumped into a chair at the kitchen table and whispered into the telephone: "If you come back here, Chartruse, I'll die! Do you hear me? You'll kill me! Do you want to kill me?" she whispered grotesquely. "Do you want me to die?"

"Leave us alone . . . Why can't you just leave us alone?" she whispered, not caring whether or not her voice could be heard through the static. She hung up the receiver and sat there alone, her head buried in her hands, slumped over the kitchen table, a tired frightened woman crying her heart out—crying quietly now, ashamed of herself, embarrassed beyond conception by what she had said, by what the visitors certainly must have overheard.

In the dining room the words DO YOU REMEMBER BILL PARSONS? reverberated from wall to wall, as had most of Louise's diatribe. FILTHY WOMAN COPULATING WITH YOUR BROTHER rang out perfectly clearly. Everyone sat frozen in the exact positions they were occupying since the phrase AWFUL PEOPLE first exploded in their ears. No one turned to look at anyone else. Dr. Rice's ears were red. Marvin Staples sat, spoon raised in midair. Roger Yancey's open palm was poised at Bill's back, which he just the moment before had been slapping heartily. As for Bill, he sat paralyzed, staring straight ahead at a random section of wallpaper, unable to turn his head or even move his eyes.

But Martin, who was only marginally aware of what was going on—he never really heard his mother's words—kept staring in rapt fascination at the cup of hot tea directly below him on the table. A broad smile extended itself and hung stretched across his face. While everyone else in the room was chiseled by Mrs. Kilbanky's words into a group of immobile stone faces, stone masks that did not move or breathe, Martin was preoccupied by the steaming teacup. The cockeyed smile was his attempt to seem normal and courteously in attendance at the dinner table, whereas in fact he could have been a hundred miles away.

He stared at the amber-colored liquid as if at the surface of a distant crater lake, transfixed by what he saw.

He was captivated by the bubbles in the teacup, which were surfacing in the middle of the tea. These bubbles in the middle then were pulled toward the rim of the cup by some unknown force, where they piled up against each other in geometric configurations of up to as many as twelve bubbles, whereupon they all broke. It was very dramatic as far as Martin was concerned. The bubbles started toward the rim—sometimes slowly, sometimes quickly—as soon as they popped up to the surface of the tea. Sometimes they remained in the middle for a long time until inevitably they responded to whatever force was pulling them to the collection of bubbles at the rim.

"It must be magnetism!" he thought to himself, his excitement mounting, although he remembered nothing about magnets from his high school science classes.

But above all Martin was hypnotized by the abrupt appearance of the bubbles in the middle of the tea, and the varying lengths of time it took for them to be pulled over to the side intrigued him. Some bubbles stayed in the center much longer than others. Why? Was there a correlation between the number of captive bubbles on the rim and the corresponding force exerted on the lone bubble in the middle? The more bubbles on the rim, the quicker the one in the middle surrendered? That must be it!

He leaned over into the teacup until his nose nearly sank into the brew, then drew back hurriedly. He must be careful not to break the surface . . . But then as he observed them further he came to the conclusion that the individual bubbles in the center were *not* influenced in their rate of surrender by the number of bubbles on the rim. Each bubble now seemed to obey a law of its own, operating independently of the others.

But then, as time wore on, the bubbles on the rim *did* seem to magnetize the ones appearing in the tea sea; and the more there were on shore the faster the one in the center was sucked in, until periodically the constantly shifting pile of bubbles on the rim broke and disappeared—all the bubbles gone in a flash . . . without warning!

This discrepancy confused him. He slapped his forehead and looked up at the others sitting around the table: "Hey!" he exclaimed loudly, "These bubbles don't follow any rules at all!"

He looked down again. "Now they've all gone away," he moaned, as if everyone had been following his investigation from the beginning. Apparently the bubbles ceased coming up once the tea cooled off.

. . . By this time everyone in the room except Bill stared at Martin with expressions of horror due mainly to the fact that his exclamations about bubbles were what snapped them out of their stunned condition, so that all the surprise and mortification created by Mrs. Kilbanky's telephone call were released in Martin's direction.

"Agh, you're a moron!" Roger Yancey cried out. "Agh, aaahh . . ." Sonny Staples broke out in a cold sweat, while his brother retched. Dr. Rice stood up from the table, his heart bulging in his chest. He felt a sharp pain and was certain he was having a heart attack. He cried out for help. Marge was weeping pitifully in one corner. Only Bill remained unfazed, frozen in place, his wide-open eyes seeing nothing.

Martin, upset by this excessive reaction to his words, jumped up and ran out of the room before anyone could stop him, down the hallway and out of the house, slamming the door behind him. The way everyone looked at him: it was frightening! Feeling frustrated and defensive he stomped and slashed his way through the garden and faded off into the fields. "Nobody understands me!" he cried out. It was night by now, nearly 8:30, and everyone in the dining room heard his voice clearly out of the darkness. Crickets and whippoorwills could also be heard.

An unnoticed breeze rich with the fragrance of a clear summer evening floated in through the open windows and brushed the oblivious faces.

Martin's overturned teacup dripped its contents onto the floor.

Dr. Rice sat down again and turned his attention to Bill. A smile played rudely with the corner of his mouth. Bill swiveled his head in Rice's direction in the manner of a puppet wearing a neck brace. Rice noticed that Bill's lower lip was quivering, and in an astonishing, almost ghastly exchange of glances he caught Bill staring down at his own tremulous lip and then up directly into the doctor's eyeglasses. Bill saw his own lip reflected there.

Suddenly the distant sound of crying ceased in the kitchen and Louise's unsteady footsteps were heard approaching the dining room.

The footsteps, the crickets and the weeping all rushed into Marge's head. But the weeping she heard was her own. She realized now that her game was up. It was only a matter of time. And what about Martin? she wondered dejectedly. What about their love? Their improbable affair had changed her life completely—catapulted her into a realm of deep emotion she never suspected to exist until then. Her lover was her hero! How could she ever give him up?

But as she ran through her mind what had just happened she knew it was impossible. Their love was doomed. She sat in the corner of the big "formal" dining room and let go. All restraint crumbled. Horribly depressed weeping filled the air.

Tom Rice's cryptic smile, his wire-rimmed spectacles glinting enigmatically in the overhead light, were the first things Louise saw as she lifted her gaze from the hall carpet.

His smile stayed with her as she navigated past several rigid bodies and found her chair. Wearily she surrendered to the sober simplicity of the armless Shaker chair. Her right hand flicked out across the tablecloth and began playing with pieces of bread, playing with a napkin, tapping against a water glass. She was afraid to look up.

When she finally did look up all she detected were Rice's smile, Marge's brief weeping replaced by strenuous breathing, and Bill's quivering lower lip. These three disembodied presences emerged from what otherwise was a dull grey sea of light. She literally was unable to see either of the Staples brothers or Roger Yancey, in spite of the fact that they were sitting there, just like Bill, big as life.

Rice realized as he studied her that Louise was on the verge of slipping into a state of shock. Bill, too, he thought, looked as if he might crack at any second. "He's the living prototype of a latent catatonic schizophrenic," Rice observed to himself proudly though inaccurately. He took pride in the discipline of a scientific education which had given him the ability to initiate a cool, detached appraisal of any situation, no matter how extreme. Rice had seen latent catatonic schizophrenics before—in his medical textbook back at Duke University in 1928. The identifying characteristics were unmistakable. "I'd better go easy on these people, Bill especially," he decided. He then looked over at the three local boys and nearly laughed out loud. In their stop-motion postures they reminded him of the cardboard yokel Bill had pulled out from behind the sofa in the parlor. That yokel's a riot! he thought. He must find out where they're manufactured and get one for his office. Give his poor patients a lift.

He met Mrs. Kilbanky's eyes with that same insinuating smirk, however; he was convinced that with women all one needed was unwavering self-assurance. One stern glance or determined movement at the right time and one could do with them whatever one wished . . . He smiled smugly.

But at the other end of the table, and for all the wrong reasons, Louise saw his sly smile broaden and decided Tom Rice had definitely overheard the shouting match with her daughter. In a way she welcomed it—although she was mortified with shame—because it seemed impossible for Bill and Marge to remain at the farm after what these people overheard . . . At least I'll be getting rid of those two, she reflected, a wave of hatred welling up inside. Her only concern was Martin: would he be able to survive the shock of Marge leaving him? Or (and suddenly she went grey with anxiety) would he run after her? Would he try to run away from home?

"Well, after all, what more is there to say?" Rice spoke up finally. His voice sounded warm and reassuring. It was as if he were appealing to the nobler side of their natures by not belaboring the obvious. He had come to the farm for other purposes entirely, he seemed to be implying, but if Bill and Marge wanted to go and reveal themselves to him as crooked, depraved elements that was fine with him. It would be his duty as a citizen to contact the lawful authorities immediately—well, almost immediately . . . After all, there's no hurry. Bill and Marge are sunk and I've got three strong boys along with me to prove it. They'll come in handy as witnesses if the Parsons try any funny stuff. No, there's nothing to fear from Bill or Marge Parsons, that's for sure!

He looked from one to the other of the ill-fated couple with compassion.

"They know not what they do," he quoted piously.

Louise Kilbanky's face relaxed when she heard his words. "Thank God!" she couldn't help swearing aloud, whereupon Marge let escape one final defeated whimper. An impotent inner rage made her dig her fingernails into her thighs until they drew blood. She cursed herself for her defeat, rocking back and forth in her chair, biting her tongue and rolling her eyes.

"How ironic!" she gasped bitterly. She seemed quite hysterical now. "Ha, ha, ha . . ." Her bitter laughter, however, was somehow misinterpreted by Mrs. Kilbanky. In an access of pent-up resentment she turned on the younger woman savagely, punching and scratching with all the strength she possessed.

"You shameless creature!" she whispered horribly. "Have you no dignity?" Dr. Rice was on his feet in a flash, positioning himself between the two women and stiff-arming them back into their chairs.

"Now, ladies, this is no time for name-calling," he said sanctimoniously. Then he turned: "Hey, Roger! You, boy! Marvin! Sonny! Let's go, boy! Let's wake up!" He clapped his hands. "C'mon, damn it. Snap out of it!"

Slowly they came around, rubbing their eyes and shaking their heads. Bill, as well, could no longer avoid a confrontation with the everyday. In spite of himself and the troubles he faced he came out of it, and soon sat grimly staring down at his hands. He thought of Fontessa upstairs and hoped she had enough sense to stay hidden.

He refused to speak when spoken to, even after Dr. Rice rapped him across the knuckles with the flat side of a bread knife. Bill was the object of derision now.

"What's the matter, Bill?" Rice added sarcastically. "Not feeling well? Do you need a doctor? Somebody sew your lips together by mistake?"

The newly-awakened townies joined together behind Bill's seated figure, prodding him and slapping the back of his head. His neck turned red but he refused to speak.

"Do you remember Bill Parsons?" Marvin mercilessly addressed the back of his head, and everyone but Marge and Louise burst out laughing.

These taunts succeeded only in driving Bill back into his previous state of paralysis. He sat perfectly motionless. His nostrils flared regularly in the harsh overhead light. He looked straight ahead but did not see.

Martin ran disconnectedly into the moonless, starry night. As he crashed through the looming rye stalks, that were as firm as bamboo by now and resisted his movement, his head spun and he couldn't see what was in front of him. He was profoundly disturbed. Rapidly proliferating red dots and huge satin-blue globules sprang up in his line of sight interfering with his vision.

Not that he cared if he could see or not, though . . . As he slogged through the damp, narrow gullies that ran between the towering stalks of rye he felt melancholy and disoriented. He was depressed by the hostile reception his words had been given at the dinner table earlier. Every move he made as he struggled among the stalks seemed to portray clearly to him his plight as a small, defensive creature in an alien world. He felt as if he were suffocating, and then became frightened by the scene that stretched before him as he stopped and wiped the rye dust from his burning eyes. In the moonless darkness there at the bottom of the rye he barely discerned the infinity of closely-seeded stalks like roots of human hair that closed in over him, breathing and alive in every direction at once. It was alive! Crackling noises intensified as the wind whistled by above him. I'm buried alive in a sea of hair! he gasped, and in a flash saw himself struggling for his life in the tangled, matted greasy hair of an unknown giant buried in the earth, whose scalp this was.

Panicky by now, Martin arbitrarily pointed himself in one direction and began fighting through the tangle in what he thought of as a straight line. In reality it was the curve of an ellipse, but after getting very nervous he finally broke through the rye and burst across a few yards of grass and open bushes, staggering up an incline and collapsing on his back out of breath. As he lay there panting he could hear his heart gallop madly in his chest. He put a hand over his heart and looked down, and in the darkness he had to strain until he saw the hand, bouncing up and down rapidly. He watched the hand in fascination. It bounced up and down on his T-shirt like a little man. The man in fact was gripping the chest to keep from being thrown off, washed away. Suddenly Martin flashed that the man on his chest was a man clinging to the side of a house as the house rolled off, certain to be swept away in a raging flood. Martin looked down, awestruck. Slowly the chest quieted down, until at last the man stood up and, testing his legs once or twice, brushed himself off and walked away....

Martin giggled. He lay back on the grass and looked up at the stars. What a wonderful night! He'd forgot all about the stars! There were thousands of them, he now noticed, in all directions. It was a very clear night, and since there was no moon the stars were visible as rarely before. The Milky Way, distinct and startling, seemed to choke the sky with its thick cascade of light. Martin became ecstatic. He marveled at the endless combinations of the stars, the endless configurations in the night. Besides the Milky Way he recognized the Little Dipper, Orion, the Great Bear and the Swan. His knowledge of the constellations was sketchy at best, but as he stared in rapture at the spectacle above him he began seeing other shapes that took the place of the bear and the swan—wonderful dolphins, goats and horses that took shape in the sky and cavorted there, or chased each other back and forth across the heavens. Soon other silhouettes appeared as well—a blindfolded woman in a robe, striding regally across the sky with a set of scales in her hand; a classically-attired nymph strumming her lyre; a small child reaching up to purchase a pie from a big, aproned pieman. Beings that Martin had seen once long before in high school world-history books came alive for him now even though he didn't know their names—a man-horse, a fish-woman, several young boy-dogs . . . And these were no illusions. In no way were they colorful or three-dimensional, as if delusions or hallucinations: they were the same empty, dot-connected forms as the Little Dipper or the Great Bear. That is, they were suggested by the starry night itself, by the spaces between the stars inside the night.

As he looked up at the night the lines connecting the constellations disappeared and all he saw were the stars—a thousand million pin-points of light, some wavering and blinking, some pulsing and seeming to ripple as he stared at them. So many different kinds of stars! If he stared keenly at any one particular star it soon began to gyrate, revolving slowly in place, or even drifted straight across a particular patch of sky. Martin became intrigued: was that really an ordinary star, or was it something else, a shooting star or rocket ship? Then he would break his fixed gaze to look at another star, to see if it too was moving, and if he stared fixedly at it long enough it did! Martin was flabbergasted. When he ran his eyes across the entire sky all the stars were stationary points; but if he stared fixedly at any one of these points it soon began to move across the sky.

He closed his eyes and rubbed them. He felt dizzy. A strange state of mind—elated by the night sky but also filled with uneasiness—accosted him. He could not relax. When he opened his eyes again his head happened to be swiveled parallel to the ground, so that he was looking at the abandoned cement mixer rising up out of the night, a barely visible upended hulk about a hundred yards distant. Behind it stood the pool of cement. The sight of the truck electrified him. Leaping to his feet with a shout he began running toward it: "My house, my house! Where is my house!" he sang out in despair, his voice surprisingly loud in his ears, filling him with sorrow. He'd never heard such a sorrowful voice in his whole life!

A ball of anxiety expanded in his stomach and Martin couldn't bear to look at the cement truck any longer. With a lump in his throat he turned away and ran distractedly for a few yards in the brush. Looking up at the sky the countless points of light washed over him, and as he lifted his face to the heavens and bellowed in despair one of the distant points detached itself from its string of six particular stars directly above him and began traveling rapidly down out of the sky.

In a brief ten seconds or so this specific star had already traversed a large part of the sky, and as Martin watched in amazement it grew larger and larger until he saw what appeared to be a luminous silver bullet or peanut rapidly whirl in out of the sky. It skittered from right to left across his field of vision, coming to rest after a graceful trajectory through the star-lit sky gave way to the peanut's arcing in a handsome curvilinear motion to the ground. In fact, the tiny star or spaceship—Martin couldn't tell *what* it was—came to rest, no bigger than a peanut, barely thirty feet away, in a small open clearing in the rolling brush-covered terrain.

The tiny peanut hummed and glowed and although it remained in a stationary position in the dirt (illuminating the surrounding earth and grass like a pocket flashlight) Martin had the distinct impression that it was still whirling rapidly. Whirling so rapidly, in fact, that it appeared stationary but also hurt his eyes when he looked at it. He was forced to look away.

It was a very strange situation: because the rocket vehicle was so small—almost the exact size and shape of a peanut—Martin at first was tempted to dismiss it as unimportant or slight. More precisely, he regarded it as a sort of dream-object since he was convinced a *real* spaceship would have to be much larger. He was confused: was it a real star that somehow kept its pinpoint size despite the fact that it was no longer distant from the earth? He found that hard to believe. The curious thing, though, was that this value-judgment of his in no way interfered with what was happening since it took place unconsciously, like a conditioned reflex. On the conscious level he was completely caught up in what he was seeing. . . .

For while he deliberated, the peanut had not been idle. It whirled in one spot—as stationary now as a star—and glowed. Although not very bright the nature of the light it released was such that it could not be looked at directly, at least by such a being as Martin Kilbanky. When he tried to look at the peanut directly the light attacked his eyeballs without pity. Soon they burned and ached and he had to look away. He swiveled his head thirty or forty degrees south of the peanut, where he could glimpse it out of the corner of his eye and keep track of it, but where the peanut's poisonous frontal light would not destroy his eyesight. Even now as he looked the other way his eyes ached and stung terribly, and it was only through the greatest determination to satisfy his curiosity that he kept them open at all.

After a few minutes the pain went away, however, and his eyes felt normal and rested once again. He was able to see the peanut out of the corner of his eye without actually facing it.

It was then that the light's intensity dimmed even further and the silver peanut slowed down, slowed down, slowed down—until a series of undulating lines like stripes became visible rippling along its surface. The lines moved across the peanut slowly, as if they were shadows being projected onto the surface of the peanut from within.

Finally they halted altogether, leaving several curved black lines in place on the surface of the miniature spaceship.

At the exact moment the curved lines stopped moving and locked into place the spaceship broke open and two small nuts rolled out onto the ground. They were brown and looked exactly like roasted peanuts. It occurred to Martin that the nuts were some sort of disguise to prevent detection on earth, though he had no time to follow the implications of this idea.

The two little nuts rolled out onto the ground and immediately became agitated. Seemingly riven with messages and urgent communications they trembled on the spot, dancing nervously in place. They bumped into each other and rolled apart, then bumped together once more and exploded with a tiny controlled blast of noise and smoke. The two nuts exploded simultaneously. When the smoke cleared away the two nuts and the shell were gone.

Martin gasped. He wanted to squint down at the bare patch of ground, but when he looked out of the corner of his eye he howled aloud in fear and stumbled backwards with his arms raised protectively over his face. In the vicinity where the tiny nuts exploded there now stood about a dozen spacemen—alien beings, astral wanderers, he didn't know what to call them—that advanced slowly toward him. He couldn't see them clearly out of the corner of his eye, but it was easy to see *they were much larger than the peanut*, very much larger, in fact. It was this that startled him so completely: they were a different scale from the vehicle they had arrived in. Twenty times larger! He didn't understand: how was it possible?

In spite of himself he turned to face them directly and the beings instantly transformed themselves into a dozen oblong iridescent halos in which all he could see clearly was a + or − sign, suspended about chest level and glowing in the night. The halos soon evaporated and all that remained was this series of plus and minus signs, a force field of glowing figures arrayed in mid-air in a semicircle around him and slowly drawing closer:

Martin's grey hair stood on end and he began moaning deliriously, backing away from the approaching figures in terror. The luminous tiny slits and cross-marks floated before him in the night, obviously endowed with life but totally alien and silent. He noticed they could arrange themselves at will into various sequences, like amino acids or peptide bonds. It seemed as if they were regarding him, observing him in some horribly thorough way through the slits of light. Suddenly two of the signs, a plus and a minus, broke away from the rest and approached to within a few feet of his face, where they hung in the air a second longer before beginning to rotate.

As the two signs revolved like miniature ceiling fans a series of gurgling sounds could be heard, and Martin leaned forward to listen. Obviously they were trying to communicate with him or interrogate him. The sounds they produced, however, were completely incomprehensible. All he made out was a low gurgling, like a distant stream or brook or someone gargling. Martin shivered in fright but managed to shake his head back and forth to signify that he could not understand them. The plus and minus signs continued their gurgling a while longer but when he shook his head a second time they appeared to understand and grew still. Immediately the gurgling ceased.

The other ten signs, meanwhile, hovered silently in the background.

Slowly but surely Martin's curiosity got the better of his fear once more until he realized with astonishment that he was no longer mortally afraid. He looked at the plus and minus signs gingerly, as if any moment he might turn and run away, but he found if he stood his ground and breathed calmly the fear subsided until all that remained was a rapidly skyrocketing curiosity. *What were these figures?* All of them strung together looked like an unknown polymer. He, too, tried to communicate.

"What—who are you?" he barked hoarsely, with no apparent impact.

"Who are you?" he repeated. Nothing.

But then the signs became agitated. Instead of whirling in place, this time they collided with each other. The plus struck the minus and there was a brief flash, like two pieces of flint being struck together. Martin turned away shielding his eyes, and when he looked back he saw the plus and minus signs separated as before and a piece of white paper fluttering between them to the ground. They had made a sheet of paper! He pounced on it and brought it close to his eyes. On a sheet of perfectly ordinary unlined notebook paper was the pencil drawing of a house.

Martin's fingers shook as he squinted at the drawing. The plus and minus signs drew near, plainly impatient to see what he would make of it. It was actually a simple outline or silhouette rather than a drawing, and if anything looked more like a tower than a house, as Martin studied it: an upended rectangle without a roof, unadorned except for a vertical row of three evenly spaced marks like slits that ran up the middle.

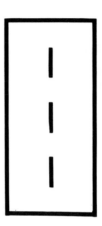

After staring at it until he thought his head would burst he finally realized the slits stood for windows. Like a medieval castle! A turret! He pointed at the slits on the paper, then turned and pointed a quarter of a mile away at the lighted windows of the farmhouse. He pointed from one to the other and looked up at the signs for corroboration. They were dancing excitedly up and down—Martin was certain this meant they were assenting to his interpretation of the drawing. Trembling with emotion he bobbed his head up and down, and the beings immediately copied the movement. They were agreeing with his interpretation! Martin couldn't believe it: he was right, it *was* a tower!

Soon all twelve plus and minus signs were bobbing up and down and he became delirious. He decided they were communicating! He tucked the sheet of paper in his pocket. Breathlessly he waited for their next move.

The two signs collided once more, and when the smoke cleared a metal plate or plaque about eight inches by six inches fell to the ground with a clunk. Martin picked it up, and saw lying next to it on the ground another object, which he also picked up. This turned out to be a spool of white cotton thread, absolutely ordinary-looking, and he was about to throw it away when one of the signs skittered frantically. Instead he stuffed the spool of thread in his jeans and gave his attention to the metal plate.

As he stared at the plate a detailed full-color image appeared on its surface and then became agitated. Martin stared down awestruck. It was beautiful, breathtaking! The color images on the surface were divided into short cinematic sequences, each of which told a story. First, a group of astral beings whose physical characteristics always remained out of focus—obviously to camouflage from him their true appearance—were shown constructing a spool of thread. They worked carefully and deliberately. Soon the spool was finished.

Next, the interior of a five-and-ten-cent store, otherwise unidentified but obviously located somewhere in the United States. A vague blur is seen approaching the sewing-materials counter and stealing a spool of thread from under the nose of an unsuspecting salesgirl. The blur then streaks out the door.

Finally a table is shown on which the spool of thread made by the beings is compared to the spool stolen from the five-and-ten-cent store. They are identical! The same partly torn red label covering one end, the same 100 yards of tightly wound white thread.

Unaware of the implications involved in this revelation Martin simply squealed with delight, and thereupon the space beings made their first mistake: they assumed he understood what they had shown him so far. The plus and minus signs danced up and down with delight.

Next, a sequence of images appeared on the metal plate which showed in the middle distance the figure of a man—a human being—building a tower. Martin looked closer: it was an exact replica of the tower in the drawing! He became extremely overexcited by this fact and neglected to pay attention to the final sequence of images, which portrayed a series of plus and minus creatures interacting at close proximity with a group of humans—presumably "shaking hands" with them in a depiction of successful communication between humans and aliens.

Martin nodded enthusiastically at this, thereby causing the creatures to commit their second error of interpretation. For them, these sequences were meant to demonstrate that their form of life had mastered earthly processes well enough to communicate, in the mistaken belief they were dealing with beings as highly organized as they themselves whose time cannot be wasted. Their perfectly accurate replica of a spool of thread was meant to be a sign to earthlings that the astral beings were conversant with earthly reality and had thereby earned the right to communicate with them. They naturally assumed that earth society was highly purposive, highly organized like theirs was, and that as a matter of course anyone they gave the spool of thread to would take it immediately to his superior who then would spirit it, plus the drawing of the tower, to the actual leaders of the planet. The leaders of the planet then would construct the tower as a sign of faith that they in turn understood and were favorably disposed to communicate further. The creatures then would reappear for further discussions wherever on the face of the earth the tower was constructed. Eventually they hoped to establish a free port on the planet where commercial trade and the exchange of ideas could take place. In reality they were surprisingly level-headed and benign creatures, considering their power, with no dark urge to conquer or enslave.

All this was perfectly clear to these strange, semivisible beings but far from clear to Martin Kilbanky. Their painstaking and ingenious plan was worthless for one simple reason: Martin completely failed to understand it.

Instead, as far as he was concerned, *he himself* was the man shown constructing the tower in the picture: the beings were showing him the picture to inspire him, to give him the confidence he needed to build. He misinterpreted the picture as a "sign" or secret revelation to him that he must build; a personal disclosure, aimed specifically at him, of what he must do. His personal destiny and immediate mission in life was revealed to him in that sequence of images.

The astral beings—the shimmering collection of plus and minus signs—confidently waited for Martin to show that he understood them. They expected to see him hastily make his way back to the farmhouse, preliminary to alerting his superiors.

When he refused to move they grew suspicious, however, and when he pointed excitedly at the upended cement truck and pool of cement some distance from the house they became perplexed and then obviously hostile. The earthling had misunderstood them. Their plan meant nothing now! Angrily the points of light swooped down on him, buzzing around his head like a swarm of bees. Amidst cries of alarm Martin saw the first pair of plus and minus signs collide on the surface of the metal plate, which he had dropped to the ground—

214

instantly it disappeared. They then attempted to dig into his pants pocket to recover the drawing and the spool of thread, buzzing furiously at his hip, but Martin wouldn't let them. His jeans were too tight and finally they gave up.

Before he knew what was happening the beings swirled together in the air and exploded in a flash of light. Wisps of smoke were illuminated by the explosion. Martin looked down and saw that the two nuts had reappeared on the ground. In spite of the blinding pain that hit his eyes he reached down attempting to grab one of the nuts, but they both rolled back into the open silver peanut shell which stood waiting nearby.

The peanut sealed itself immediately and began whirling in place. Martin couldn't get any closer to it. The black lines animating its surface seemed to seal it off from any physical contact, like some kind of reverse magnet. In a matter of seconds it lifted itself from the ground and whirled upward into the night in an ever-widening spiral. Soon it was a mere dot of light rapidly climbing into the heavens, sinking in the endless sea of stars. Martin strained his eyes in desperation but couldn't keep track of it. It was lost among the hundred million points of light above him.

Choked with emotions he didn't understand, clutching the sheet of paper and the spool of thread in his hands, he made his way back to the house. As he neared the cement mixer the kitchen door suddenly opened and Marge walked out onto the porch and stood looking up at the stars. She was alone. Martin approached her holding out the paper and the thread. His heartbeat pounded in his head.

"Marge! Marge!" Martin exclaimed in a conspiratorial whisper as he approached the back porch. "Look what I've got!" He was whispering in order not to be overheard by the visitors still inside the house.

"Look!"

He stumbled up the porch steps, both hands extended. "UFO!"

Like everyone else, Martin Kilbanky had grown up with stories about creatures from outer space, alleged "factual" sightings of flying saucers, "moonmen" in insect suits and so forth. Like everyone else he regarded these stories with little more than sarcasm. It was simply that everyone had their own lives to live: they were too busy working and playing, eating and sleeping, to give UFO tales more than amused attention. Furthermore, in some definite way Martin was convinced the creatures he had seen *were not* creatures from outer space, in the sense of being unreal or even alien. On the contrary, the points of light belonged to this world the same way as the creatures and episodes he saw in his daytime peripheral visions—like the Indian virgins and the tiny eskimos—definitely belonged to this world and no other. After all, what other world was there? As far as he was concerned the universe was happening all at once: how could there be any "outer," then? He wasn't sure that he knew what he meant or could put it into words, but he was certain no "outer space," and consequently no outer space beings, existed. It was like an optical illusion that seemed to be fitted into almost everyone's head but his!

Unfortunately he wavered in his conviction, simultaneously feeling that on the other hand there was a good chance the beings he had just seen *were* spacemen after all . . . It was all so confusing . . . In the end the word "UFO" just popped out of his mouth although he meant nothing by it.

Not only that, but Marge didn't even hear the word.

"What?" she asked.

"Look, Marge—the plus and minus signs gave these things to me!" He pointed excitedly into the night. "Back there! They came and exploded their star on the ground and gave me this picture!"

Proudly he held the crude pencil outline up to the light escaping from the kitchen:

"They want me to build!" he announced in a majestic tone, and instantly Marge knew something was wrong. His eyes were glittering and his entire muscular structure was tense. "Oh, no," she thought, and a chill ran down her spine. "Martin . . ." she implored aloud, "what on earth are you talking about?"

"See?" he continued, becoming more and more enthusiastic. "It's a tower—you know, not a house like the farmhouse but a tower . . ." He stared intently at the rectangle pierced by three slits for windows. His brow wrinkled. "But how can I make a tower out of cement?"

Then a wide smile broke his features. He was confusing what he had attempted to build months ago with what he was determined to build now. When he realized this he shouted, waving the paper in the air, "Cement was a mistake! I should have used some other material, brick or—or . . ." he faltered, straining his mind to the utmost: "Look! Look, Marge!" he pointed at the drawing, raising his voice with each word despite her warning. "Look! This tower should be built with flagstone—that's it, flagstone! You know," he explained, turning to her: "Big granite flagstones! It's just so obvious; and it'll be economical and easy to use. Not like *that* stuff," referring to the five tons of cement he had wasted.

"It'll be so easy," he repeated, his face suffused with happiness. "Don't you see?"

But apparently she did not see. Extreme dejection had forced her to excuse herself from the dinner table—around which the rest of the people still sat—and seek solace under the stars. She barely had time to take a breath of night air before Martin accosted her, and as she stood there now trying in spite of herself to make sense out of what he was saying her mouth started trembling and she had to fight to keep from bursting into tears. Everything was going wrong for her— ever since the telephone call her life had escalated into an atmosphere of betrayal and desolation from which she saw no escape. After Martin jumped up from the dinner table and ran out of the room the situation there had become more and more oppressive. Dr. Rice's cryptic smile dominated the motionless people gathered around the table. Marge felt she was suffocating and excused herself in the most humiliating manner—stuttering, barely able to stand on her feet, mortified that Rice would break the pretense of a family dinner and refuse her simple desire for fresh air.

Marge appeared to be finished, done for—a broken spirit. She had fled to the back yard in a last attempt to calm herself and possibly regain the strength to fight back—and now this was happening! The crude pencil drawing held aloft in Martin's hand seemed the height of absurdity. She still had no idea what he was talking about.

At that moment she happened to look down and saw that he was clutching something else in the other hand.

"What's that, baby?" she regretted asking as soon as the words were out of her mouth. Martin thrust the spool of thread into the light, six inches from her face.

"They gave me this, too!" he exclaimed. "I saw them make it with my own eyes. Isn't it great? They had that picture there . . ." he fumbled vaguely, already forgetting the details of his experience with the strange creatures. He was impatient to build his tower. Everything else seemed extraneous, a waste of time, in the light of his new-found mission.

"Who, Martin?" Marge persisted, becoming alarmed. She had seen him run up alone out of the darkness: no one else had been in sight.

"The—the—oh, fuck: the spacemen gave it to me, that's who! How am I supposed to know who they are?"

"What!?!"

"They came in their spaceship, Marge," he explained impatiently. "They were inside a little bitty spaceship no bigger than a bullet. It whizzed out of the sky and then it landed on the ground and exploded and they were big transparent beings like technicolor ghosts with shiny lights in the middle I couldn't look at—so painful—there were ten or twelve of them—then they changed into little lights that looked exactly like stars, only close-up, you know?"

By now Marge was backing away from him along the edge of the porch.

"And they built this spool of thread copying exactly one they stole from a five-and-dime someplace—I saw them do it. They had a picture machine, Marge! And they, they gave me this blueprint," he concluded solemnly, his voice full of emotion. "They showed a picture of me building the tower: I *have* to build it, don't you see?"

She stood blankly before him.

"Don't you believe me?"

He loved her and longed to throw his arms around her and embrace her now that they were alone, but his love was being dealt a staggering blow. She didn't believe him! If she didn't believe him, how could he continue to love her?

Tears filled Marge's eyes as he started to push past her with the obvious intention of informing his mother and the others of what he had found.

"*Martin, don't!*" she pleaded, becoming hysterical and pushing him off the porch into the back yard. "They'll all think you're crazy, Martin—please don't!" But in her deflated condition she was no match for him and in a matter of seconds he was stomping through the kitchen with Marge at his heels, the tears streaming down her face. She pulled at his shirt from behind but it was no use. He burst into the dining room just as Dr. Rice was rising from his chair.

"Why don't we all retire to the front room for a little after-dinner smoke? Maybe watch some TV?" the doctor suggested, eyeing Mrs. Kilbanky meaningfully. Everyone stood up.

Martin propelled himself into the room at that moment with such force he collided with Sonny Staples and knocked him off his feet. The Staples boy fell heavily across one of Mrs. Kilbanky's prize Shaker chairs, splintering it to pieces in an instant. Everyone gasped in surprise; it occurred so quickly after what had seemed like an eternity of perfectly motionless repose around the dinner table—paralytic and traumatic in some cases, digestive and somnolescent in others. Bill went rigid once again.

Louise shrieked in anger. Dr. Rice became cross with Sonny and was just about to berate him for his clumsiness when Martin's voice erupted in the room like a foghorn, silencing all competition.

"Look, mother!" he boomed. "Look what the creatures from the starship gave me!"

As the parlor (or "front room") was only a few steps across the hall from the dining room, however, Dr. Rice finished what he had started by leading everyone into that room and turning on the TV. Martin hurried after them, shocked that they would forget his own entrance in order to carry out Rice's suggestion—which in this light Martin realized was more an order than a suggestion. Already he was so excited that this final fact—this curious but accurate observation on his part of the group he had deserted for a period of time and thereby gained perspective upon—namely, that this doctor, this super-slick oldster, was controlling all the people in the room, nullifying his mother's power, and Bill's power, and Marge's power!—this observation catapulted Martin Kilbanky into a state of blind determination. He felt there wasn't a moment to waste, it might *already* be too late.

He lunged across the room and shouldering Rice out of the way, spun the audio knob, turning down the sound on the TV. He would have turned the set off completely but Rice was so incensed by this sudden insubordination that he barked like a terrier, flapping his arms, and Martin hopped away from the set in surprise. In the confusion that followed he dropped his spool of thread, and so the next thing he did was fall on his hands and knees and search feverishly until the spool was retrieved.

Everyone looked down at him. His sudden entrance, his incomprehensible garble and frantic agitation unnerved them.

Meanwhile, since this was taking place only in the ghostly blue glow of the television's light, since everyone had been too stunned to turn the parlor light on, the huge black picture on the set captured their attention, so that all of them including Martin found themselves looking down at it. What they saw was the immense business-suited upper frame and flat white face of a TV newscaster. It was a news report. The burly flattopped network newsman sat under a bright bank of lights and reported the evening news. Obviously nothing of great interest or importance had occurred in the world that day, for the polite but unmistakeable boredom expressed on the man's face would not go away. He looked as if he were running through the same morsel of news for the umpteenth time, and the dark alcoholic pouches under his eyes hinted plainly to what lengths the poor man had been driven in his search for distraction during his offscreen hours.

He wore a professional smile, however, and briskly narrated the day's events looking down occasionally at the sheaf of papers clutched in his left hand. It was only the super-agitated state of mind of everyone in the parlor watching the TV that revealed this about the newsman's character—that, plus the fact that the sound was turned off, thereby heightening the image.

Everyone groped and felt for seats until all the chairs in the parlor were taken and Martin and Sonny Staples were left standing. Spooky blue light filled the room. They continued looking at the TV, and it was then that one by one they gradually became aware that the sheaf of papers in the newsman's hand was a prop. Certain slips of the lip and minor discontinuities made them all, first subliminally and then consciously, aware that the sheaf of papers was blank.

At the next moment they saw why: the newscaster wasn't really looking at the camera at all. He appeared to be looking directly into the camera, addressing the audience, but in reality he was looking *slightly above* the camera's eye, not addressing the audience at all.

The older people in the room found this especially irritating.

"Obviously the man's reading his lines off a—what do you call it, anyway?" Dr. Rice asked aloud.

"What?"

"You know . . . a whatchacallit, damn it." He turned to Louise: "Whaddya call those things, people on live TV use em to read their lines from, when they forget em." As he looked at the box his irritation grew. Such obvious disregard for verisimilitude offended him. "A—a *teleprompter!* That's it . . . teleprompter . . . The box up behind the camera that has all the lines that guy's gonna say tonight," he gestured contemptuously. "That's the thing about TV that gets my goat—it's so dishonest. Pretend, pretend, pretend. It's a lie, cause they're playing for real just like us but they pretend they ain't . . ." Rice was getting more and more indignant. "Or vice versa. . . ."

"Lookit that!" The announcer was being especially sloppy now, abandoning all pretense of telling the news spontaneously and frankly glancing high above the camera to read his lines from the teleprompter.

"It's outrageous," Louise agreed. She was disgusted.

The newsman pretended to be looking the TV viewer in the eye. He spoke convincingly: sometimes with passion, sometimes with humor, sometimes solemnly. But his eyes gave him away, they were devious. While the face went through its mechanical modulations the eyes hid from view. The fact that the television's sound was off made this startlingly clear. It was an eerie sensation—everyone in the room felt uneasy and cheapened by it. Several experienced the desire to wash out their mouths, brush their teeth. Their mouths tasted flat, sour. Rising petulance, which however none understood completely, washed over them. They felt cheated by this phony image imposed upon them from afar, from deep in the sophistication of the network night.

"Let's turn this damn thing off," Rice announced as he stood up and yanked peevishly at the dial. It came off in his hand and the room was plunged into darkness. Everyone felt spooked now for real.

. . . Because as they sat there in the darkness they remembered, one by one, that Martin was there with them. His bizarre, alien entrance of a few minutes before came back to them. They sat there in their chairs and all became afraid. Sonny backed away from the middle of the room and left Martin alone, a vague hulk towering above them in the blackness, a shape that suddenly whirled and faced them all when it realized it had become the center of attention. Martin turned defensively, confronting everyone like an animal surprised in the woods, a cornered deer or beaver.

"Oh!" his mother gasped. Martin began breathing heavily and the hair raised off everyone's necks. At that moment Marge came to his rescue, springing up and flicking on the light switch. The parlor was flooded in light. Louise sighed in relief. There stood her son in the middle of the floor, still breathing heavily but fully recognizable.

Martin, however, stood there with the strangest expression on his face—as if he'd just given birth to a field mouse—and holding something in each hand. A sheet of paper and—and what was that other object? Louise leaned forward squinting. Marge swallowed and thought she was going to faint.

Suddenly Louise half remembered her son's words earlier, when he had burst into the dining room.

"What were you saying, Martin?" she asked. "What do you have in your hands? What are you holding, dear?"

He advanced toward them. He hadn't a moment to lose. He held the spool up for everyone to see.

"The creatures made this," he announced confidently. "They gave it to me. Then they tried to take it back, but I wouldn't let them."

"*Creatures?*" his mother echoed without comprehension.

Martin became defiant. "Oh, hell, I don't know what they were. What does it matter, anyway? . . . Creatures, spacemen, plus and minus signs inside a silver peanut-ball of light . . . Who cares? . . . Look, mother, the only important thing is that they made this spool and gave it to me. And they also gave me *this*!" Triumphantly he raised the piece of paper in the air. Dr. Rice leaned forward in his chair, a cautious neutral face-mask covering his intense curiosity. The boy seemed to have finally gone around the bend.

Martin waved the paper in his mother's face. "See, mother? It's a tower—a drawing of a tower!" Everyone leaned forward to look. The way he was holding the paper made it look like nothing—a crude box-shape enclosing three short lines. He straightened the crumpled paper and held it vertically.

"See? It's a tower, mother—a flagstone tower!" He turned to the others. "They gave this to me and told me to build," he proclaimed, surprisingly calm and self-assured. He didn't shout or boast: he didn't need to.

"W-wh-what!?!"

"A tower," he explained. "They showed me how to build it on this picture machine they had—in fact, they showed an actual picture of me building a tower. Don't you see, I *have* to do it. I'll need a lot of flagstone, but that's nothing. Flagstone's not expensive like the—like the—" he couldn't bring himself to say the word "cement."

While he was stuttering, however, his mother noticed something so startling that it took her mind for the time being off his sad, impossible story. When he looked down at her—when he addressed her specifically—*he wasn't looking her in the eye.*

Rice noticed this as well when Martin turned in his direction. He was staring out over the doctor's head, as if at a spot directly above and behind him. Rice even turned around briefly and checked it out, although he knew no one was there. Then it hit him:

"He's just like—" His face went grey but then he regained his composure, "he's just like the newscaster! The announcer on the television!"

Martin stared from one to the other of the rapidly blanching group. They all saw it now. Whatever he had experienced out in the fields obviously had affected him this way. Marge and Louise began whimpering, twisting their hands in their laps, while Bill blacked out again and Roger Yancey's forehead flashed in pain. They were all terrified.

Martin didn't understand. "What do you mean? What's wrong now? What are you talking about?" But no one would answer him and so in an atmosphere of proliferating suffocation he plunged ahead with his tale.

His grey hair was suddenly very noticeable to everyone in the room, as if they had just seen it for the first time. This curious effect had occurred periodically to Marge and Bill and Louise even weeks after he returned to the farm in that condition. Occasionally, and for no detectable reason, they would find themselves staring at the silvery streaks and powdery grey areas as if they had just appeared. For Dr. Rice and the Staples brothers and Roger Yancey now was one of those moments. The totality of his presence—the other-worldly stare, the insane story about a tower and creatures from outer space, the pathetic spool of white cotton thread—a perfectly ordinary-looking spool of thread—his grey hair, his unfazed determination . . . It was too much.

When he earnestly held up his treasures for inspection all Roger saw was a sheet of paper and a spool of thread. He made as if to inspect the spool more closely, and Martin thrust it up into his face. Roger looked at it, touched it, started to unravel it—then felt like a damn fool. His ears turned red.

"You're nuts, boy!" he cackled somewhat hysterically. But soon the Staples brothers and Bill too were snickering behind their hands, and abruptly the mood altered to one of derision. Martin had misunderstood the spacemen and now these people were misunderstanding him. Marge wept uncontrollably in the corner, her big athletic shoulders shaking. So much was destroyed for her now—her new home, her lover, her dream. Gone! She rocked her head from side to side, crying and gnashing her teeth. Aghast at her own defeat, humiliated by her inability to fight back, she sat and wept, abandoned by the others. No one paid the slightest attention to her now. Earlier, Martin had longed to throw his arms around her and embrace her, but now her abject behavior and her refusal to accept his experience alienated him from her.

She sat alone, bitterly denouncing herself for her failure, her impotence. She thought of Fontessa cowering upstairs in Bill's bedroom and laughed hollowly. Even Fontessa—the big bruiser, the big hustler—even she couldn't help her man . . . Both of them, so big and tough, women who thought they could take charge no matter what . . . Now look at them . . . When it came down to the final test, the big challenge of their lives, they were not equal to it. They were equal to nothing. Nothing!

Marge couldn't stand it. Letting out a howl of torment she ran out of the parlor holding her head. The others heard her run down the hall and climb the stairs but they were too preoccupied with Martin to pay her any mind.

For at that moment he was advancing upon them all, daring them to refute him, to show why he shouldn't start building his tower immediately. He stood above the seated figures, confident and out of touch. It was more than anyone was able to bear. In spite of Louise's tears Roger Yancey could restrain himself no longer.

"You're diseased, Martin. You're crazy—sick! You oughtta be locked up!" But he didn't even have the chance to cackle, because Dr. Rice cut him off immediately with a baleful stare—and in a sudden inspired flash Louise Kilbanky thought she finally understood what they had come for:

They had come to take her son away. It was obvious now. Dropping her head on her breast, her spirit broken, she went limp. They had come to take Martin away from her.

Tom Rice spoke up first.

"Now, let's not get overexcited," he said in his capacity as resident physician. "Let's look thoughtfully and objectively at the boy with the dispassionate eyes of a medical man. . . ."

Leaning forward in his chair he asked Martin to describe precisely what he had seen. But Martin was wary of the doctor—he remembered the injection in Sisley's office and his consequent loss of consciousness—and, on his guard, he refused to respond until the doctor made the supreme dramatic gesture of his short career as a soldier of fortune: he looked up piteously at the boy and shed a single, solitary tear. Martin watched the tear as it hung at the man's chin.

"Please, son," he begged, "Tell me. That's what I'm here for, Martin. I am a doctor."

Martin looked around the room suspiciously, but the three boys from town were nonchalantly studying the ceiling and his mother seemed distant, crushed—eerily beyond reach. Martin felt disoriented. Who were these men? What did they want from him?

Suddenly his confidence and determination evaporated and he found himself facing the doctor in a world that was theirs alone. Only Bill, who stood frozen in immobility against the mantelpiece, stood between them: and Bill was gone, catatonic. He stood rigidly, propped up against the very same cardboard yokel they had discovered behind the sofa earlier that day. The yokel's gay freckled face, toothy grin, and the fresh primary colors of his overalls and shirt— bright and hearty reds and blues—contrasted vividly with Bill's ashen pallor. The normally hale, muscular Parsons had lost all his color and muscle tone and looked clammy. His face was white and slack. Dr. Rice made a mental note to give Bill an injection of tranquilizer: 30 cc's of what he jokingly referred to as "cotton mouth" would certainly do the trick, he concluded. Otherwise, Bill might freeze up altogether and never say another word or take another step as long as he lived, and that would be awkward. The shock of being unmasked obviously had proved too much for him. "The exercise of psychological power is fraught with danger," Rice reflected. It was always sticky when someone you were dealing with got that way—just stopped in his tracks. People asked you how the person got that way and what were you supposed to tell them? As a doctor, you couldn't say the person in question "froze up" because he was "burned too bad" by another person, although it was the truth. That kind of terminology was too harsh for most people and merely upset them further. No, you couldn't tell people the truth—they just weren't equipped to handle it. . . .

He turned his attention to Martin Kilbanky as the poor scared boy told a disjointed story about spaceships and tiny pluses and minuses. He related the story in a brittle, nervous voice that did its credibility no good. Rice tsk-tsked to himself as the tale wore on. Martin held up his spool of thread and spread out the crumpled drawing with a tremulous air of defeat that made his story impossible to believe. Rice soon became disgusted and raised an open hand in the air. Martin's story came to a halt.

"—swarming around my head like a crowd of angry bees!" he was saying when Rice held up his hand.

"OK, Martin—OK," the doctor said softly, as if commiserating with him. Martin gulped and took a sharp breath. This is going to get worse, I just know it, he said to himself mournfully. All the time he had been telling his story his mother had not taken her eyes off her own gnarled hands that sat gripping each other in her lap. *Not once* did she look up at her son. Martin was on the verge of bursting into tears when Rice cleared his throat and began to speak.

Though looking steadily at Martin, he addressed Mrs. Kilbanky in the following terms: "Now, these are painful words for me to say, Louise, but I think that in the interest of your own well-being and the moral caliber of life in Wayne County my friends and I will be forced to spend the night here. . . ."

"We'll bed down on the floor or spare sofas, it doesn't matter," he added, waving the details aside.

"I'm forced to ask this of you, Louise, because I'm wondering if you are fully aware of the situation prevailing here in your own home . . . As I said, these are painful words—but your son is simply unfit to carry out his responsibilities as head of the household. He is a failure at farm maintenance . . . He can't run a farm . . ." The words stuck like fish hooks.

His tone became accusatory: "It's not merely general incompetence, Louise: what about that cement truck, for God's sake? What about the pool of cement, the waste? All that money down the drain! . . . You see, I heard about it in town," he explained carefully, "I was called in by the County Prosecutor when your son became unmanageable, and, in all fairness to the attending physician, Mr. Sisley was obliged to relate the particulars of the case to me. It was unavoidable. I must admit, I've never been more shocked. All Ike's hard-earned capital, the security and savings meant for *you*, Louise, after a lifetime of labor—gone, down the drain in a flash!"

He pointed from the boy to the open window outside of which, in the pitch-dark night, the abandoned cement mixer still stood tilted in the air.

Louise thought to herself in amazement: "It's true, with all the

excitement the past few weeks I plain forgot the thing was still there!"
A chill ran up the old woman's spine as she realized they had all
grown so used to the big machine that they ceased noticing its presence, as if it were a junked car. In the midst of the trauma caused by
Marge and Martin's copulation they had all more or less forgotten
about it. But in the back of her mind, of course, she never forgot
about Martin's disastrous handling of the whole affair. How could
she forget? . . . All that money . . . She felt faint . . . How should she
have handled it? Should she have seized the initiative? Gone into
town herself and dealt with Sisley? Was it her fault?

She buried her face in her hands once more.

The implacable Dr. Rice continued.

"Now, Louise, this is going to be difficult, so brace yourself . . . Do
you know, Louise, what an *encephalogram* is? It's an X-ray photograph of the brain," he explained softly. "Actually, it is also an instrument for recording brain waves on graph paper, but we're not
talking about that kind of encephalogram. . . ."

"Now, do you remember, Louise, when Martin was just a young-
ster, a mere tot, and you brought him in to my office for several tests
and X rays? He couldn't have been more than six years old at the
time but I'm sure you remember . . ." He paused and took a deep
breath. Everyone in the room suddenly seemed to be listening—even
Bill tilted forward a little.

"Well," he barked out crossly, as if it wasn't *his* fault all this had to
come out, "I've kept those encephalograms all these years and in fact
I've got them with me now—they're in my doctor's bag out in the
car!"

He leaped to his feet. Martin drew back against the wall in terror.

"Roger!" Rice barked. "Go out and fetch my black bag from the
car. I hoped I wouldn't have to show you this, Louise, but Martin's
actions and the degenerate, immoral conditions prevailing here at the
farm leave me no choice. I must protect the memory of my dear dead
friend Ike Kilbanky and the ethical interests of the county," he pon-
tificated.

Roger Yancey appeared in the doorway holding the little black
bag. A stethoscope protruded from one end.

"Bring it here, boy," Rice ordered, and Roger placed the bag in
the doctor's hands. Rice unzipped it and started pawing through the
contents until he found what he wanted. Ampules and hypodermics

fell to the floor. The others in the room looked on in hushed defer-
ence at the wonder-working implements of the trade. Their respect
was palpable.

"Goddamn it," he cursed as the large manila envelope he was
attempting to extricate snagged on one of the inside pockets. He
tugged with all his might and the envelope tore free, spilling a dozen
plastic bottles filled with various pills and capsules onto the floor.

"Pick those up!" he ordered, and Sonny Staples found himself on
his hands and knees retrieving the scattered containers. While he
scrounged around on the floor Rice turned to Mrs. Kilbanky and
continued his display.

"Now as I was saying, Louise . . ." He paused to give her a piteous
expression that drove her further into the upholstery of her Morris
chair: "Don't worry, my dear." His voice was now meant to be soft
and reassuring, a parenthetical aside meant for her alone: "It's all for
the best. . . ."

Rice's face was now briefly suffused with compassion, but his con-
fidential whisper was heard instead by Louise as a horrible rattle and
garbled whistling; for her the words were inaudible. Instead, she was
transported momentarily back to her husband's death bed—the awful
ghostly rattle, the incoherent whispering—and she cried out in fright.

"Oh Ike, Ike!" she wailed, "Why have you forsaken me?"

Everyone else but Dr. Rice turned their heads in shame, but he
became firm and comforting. Instantly he was at her side.

"Now Louise, you know that's ridiculous. . . ."

She nodded wordlessly, dabbing at her eyes with a handkerchief.
Her fingers trembled. Rice drew back and continued, his voice au-
thoritative.

"I won't mince words, Louise: Unfortunately, I believe Martin is
simply not able to function in a normal, responsible manner. What's
more, obviously this *hussy*," he spat the word in Marge's direction,
only to find that she was absent from the room—"this hussy took
advantage of your son's condition to perpetrate herself upon him in
the most disgusting manner possible in order to establish herself and
her no-good husband on your farm, to strong-arm her way onto the
farm." Here he gestured with contempt at Bill. "And in spite of how
you must have felt about them you were powerless, Louise—you
were unable to deal with it, in short. Am I right?" he demanded, his
voice rising remorselessly.

No one answered.

"So first we had this poor boy with his *house*—" his thumb stabbed in the direction of the cement mixer and pool of cement. "And now suddenly here he is demanding money for flagstone to be delivered so he might build *another* house. Not only that, but little bitty spacemen came and furnished him with the blueprint." His tone of voice was deadly.

Several voices snickered at the sheet of note paper still clutched in Martin's hand. Martin himself stood cowering against the wall. His grey hair was beginning to stand on end.

"Well, Louise, in spite of the respect I have for you and for Ike's memory, the time has come to put a stop to all this. I have asked that my associates and I be allowed to spend the night here in the interests of the moral caliber of life in our county, and now I'm going to ask—no, I'm going to *demand*—that in your own best interest and for the sake of the boy you allow me to take charge of his case. There is no alternative . . . I feel obligated to have him held under observation for certain tests at Burden State Mental Hospital . . . Only until certain things have been determined, of course . . . Now don't misunderstand me . . . For the boy's own good . . . The 'little spacemen' are a clear example of the so-called catalytic externalization phenomenon, you see . . . Apparitions and apparent materializations, unconscious projections, you know. . . ."

But Louise Kilbanky recoiled in horror. So that's what he's come for! He wants to shut Martin up. She leaped to her feet, suddenly eloquent.

"I've had to fix you food and worry after you all day—as if I didn't have enough problems and heartaches already—and now you want to take my son away. What else do you want from me? My house, my farm, my money? Take my farm, then, but at least leave me the boy!"

But he refused to be sidetracked. "Now Louise, *calm down! Trust me!* I am not going to lock your son up. I merely think that in view of—" Here he interrupted himself and made a show of his wounded pride, of genuine anger. He seemed so overcome he couldn't speak.

"OK, Louise, OK . . . Whaddya think I . . . So you have the nerve to think I've come out to your farm for personal, selfish reasons; that I would waste an entire working day of my precious time to surround myself with a bunch of incompetent, unregenerate morons and an old lady who can't cut it any longer but refuses to admit it to herself. . . ."

Here he stopped himself. Maybe he had gone too far? His last words seemed to have totally destroyed the old woman's composure. He decided he had better keep to the point.

"Look, Louise, it's very simple." He extracted the manila folder from his doctor's bag and dropped the bag to the floor with a crash in order to get everyone's attention. "I have had evidence *for years* of Martin's condition . . . *For years. . . .*"

Opening the folder with a flourish he held the big X ray up to the light. "This, Louise, is a cranial X ray. See the shape of the skull? This encephalogram of Martin's brain was taken on such-and-such a date in my office when Martin Kilbanky was six and one-half years of age, and this is what we found. This is what we've known all along!" He thrust the X ray into the light, displaying his evidence to all. "We found his brain is shaped like a house!"

He said these words perfectly seriously, yet Roger, Marvin and Sonny immediately went into hysterics. They guffawed so loudly even Bill was contaminated, and let out from between clenched teeth a short strangled laugh that clashed weirdly with the others. Roger, Sonny and Marvin by now had moved to the opposite end of the parlor from Bill. His rigid presence against the mantel next to the cardboard mannequin thoroughly spooked them. It just wasn't the same old Bill Parsons. Consequently they welcomed the opportunity to laugh once again, and the faint but unmistakable rectangular image that was visible on the X ray was just what they needed. They slapped their shanks and roared in amusement.

Rice himself smiled ever so slightly, and Martin, who was standing right next to him, was revolted by this beyond measure. It was too much for his mother as well, and she sat crumpled in her chair not even looking up. For some reason she reacted in panic to the news that her son's brain was shaped like a house—on the one hand she couldn't believe it and thought Rice was making some kind of macabre joke. But on the other hand she felt it just might be true: why else would Martin keep coming up with these crazy schemes? She knew he wasn't insane in the normal definition of the word. She had seen mentally-ill people before, gibbering at the mouth and being led around on leashes, and she knew Martin wasn't one of those. But *something* had to be compelling him to act this way.

"Now, what more is there to say?" the doctor concluded. "I can assure you that Martin will not be sequestered or locked up in any mental ward. Legal consent must be given before anything permanent like that. We merely wish to perform certain tests. He will be released in your care, Louise, of that I can assure you. But we've *got* to have a free hand if we're ever to get to the bottom of this. . . ."

His eyes half-closed and he became rhapsodic. "Psychotherapy has come a long, long way since the unavoidable excesses of its first experiments several decades ago . . . Do you realize, Louise, medical science has progressed to the point where we're able now to take a half-inch-square chunk from anywhere deep in the brain for testing and nobody is the wiser? We are not considering surgery here, of course. But did you know, just the same, that if the brain shows physical abnormality, surgery might alleviate behavior that torments the patient or threatens the safety of others?" He seemed to be reciting these words from memory—a book or scientific paper he had read, perhaps. Certainly a country doctor such as he had no first-hand or even second-hand experience of brain surgery, or knowledge for the treatment of mental disorders, though this did not curb his missionary zeal.

Mrs. Kilbanky was terrified now for good. Her head thrown back against the upholstered chair she gripped its arms in panic. Her eyes staring up at Rice nearly popped out of their sockets.

Already Martin was edging his way along the parlor wall preparatory to making his escape. He saw no other alternative.

At that moment the parlor door burst open and a bloodcurdling war-whoop split the air. The panes rattled in their frames. In a last desperate attempt to salvage the situation Marge had gone upstairs a half-hour earlier and had communed with herself, trying to reactivate the "charge" or "power" she fuzzily knew she possessed. In the midst of her hopelessness she saw a ray of light, and soon she was down on her knees among her secret bags and cartons, rummaging through her psycho-cosmetic jars and bottles and costumes in search of the right combination. It was a last-ditch attempt to save them all. Finding a box filled with face masks only compounded the difficulty and pain—which mask to use? Which wig? How could she ever decide? The swift sure-mindedness she possessed in the past seemed to have deserted her for good. She stood among the bottles and cartons paralyzed with indecision.

Finally she got hold of herself, however. There was no time to lose. She decided only the most astonishing, breathtaking, forbidding creation possible would turn the tide for herself and her lover. She looked and looked for her special snake-woman costume but couldn't locate it; then she became jittery and felt the snake-woman wouldn't be right anyway. As time was running out, she was forced to opt for classic simplicity: she would wear a single, transparent plastic face mask that pressed and distorted the facial features, thereby projecting a subliminal suggestion of personality mutation—of character alteration—or worse . . . She found the clear face mask she wanted and fit it on, then selected her most outlandish hot pink fright-wig, the very same one she had worn in her fight with Fontessa.

Simplicity itself, the face mask and the wig: classic simplicity. At the last possible moment, however, she became unsure of herself again and, panicking, began to add to the costume. Soon she stood in a sloppy amalgam that in addition to the mask and wig included a sequined leotard, two-inch false eyelashes that protruded from the transparent mask, and black net stockings. In her right hand she held an aerosol can labeled FRIGHT SPRAY. The overall effect was atrocious.

In another culture Marge might have been a shamaness, since she had the natural talent, but as it was she was conscious of only a small part of her power. A victim to urges of costume and cosmetics that she didn't understand, she was as unaware of her limitations as of her true abilities. She never even suspected the kind of control she was capable of exercising. Her power was not in tune with anything because it was not recognized by anyone else. The denizens of the community in which she lived did not recognize such powers as even existing, of course. Shamanism was not even within the realm of conjecture. So that as a result she was not hooked into anything, there was no context for her secret ability to take root in. Her gifts merely flourished blindly, to be blown away on the wind . . . *Marge as the girl she never even knew. . . .*

Now, as she paced along the upstairs hallway trying to build up her confidence, Fontessa spied her through the open bedroom door and came out on the landing to look. First she gasped, but soon she was giggling behind her hand in a vicious attempt to cut Marge down to size. Marge noticed her at that point and stared at her with such hatred that Fontessa flinched and retreated.

But the fateful moment had arrived. Taking a deep breath and clutching the aerosol can Marge bounded down the stairs with a bloodcurdling whoop. All five feet nine inches and one hundred forty pounds of her burst into the front room without warning. Everyone squealed with alarm, and in the sixty seconds or so before she was recognized Marge was queen. Roger Yancey and the Staples brothers cringed against the wall, pleading for mercy. Foam appeared on Dr. Rice's lips. His waistcoat buttons snapped and his watch-chain broke. The heirloom timepiece fell to the floor and was promptly spiked to smithereens by one of Marge's nasty lion-tamer boots. Rice overturned his easy chair in his haste to escape from the room, his tongue lolling uncontrollably from his mouth. Marge laughed wildly when she saw this. He's scared out of his wits! she exulted. Blocking the exit from the room and growling grotesquely, she loomed up over the yellow figure of the doctor down on his knees begging for mercy and sunk her teeth into his neck. Rice howled in pain and lashed out instinctively to protect himself. In doing so he tore off one of Marge's eyelashes and set the wig askew. In a flash he realized what this nameless vortex was.

Leaping to his feet he turned to the others and shouted, "Roger: look! Marvin! Sonny! Look! That's Marge Parsons! Marge Parsons!"

They all surrounded her, and although she struggled furiously, punching Marvin Staples squarely on the nose and breaking it in two places, she finally was subdued. She was finished. Sonny and Dr. Rice each held an arm while Roger easily and mockingly tore the mask from her face. Her brave attempt at a voodoo she didn't understand had failed miserably. Roger yanked the wig from her head and slapped her face for good measure. Her aerosol can clattered to the floor. She was finished. Rolling her eyes to the ceiling she collapsed onto the floor in tears. From where she lay she looked up at the hostile male bodies surrounding her and tried to push their legs aside. "Martin, Martin!" she wailed, then began weeping again. "Where is my lover, where is my friend?"

They all spun around but Martin was gone.

"Martin!" Marge howled.

Finally they heard a distant reply from somewhere outside the house. "I have to be free to build!" he boomed. His words ricocheted off the walls and sank rapidly into the silence of the rural night. They all listened but heard not one word more. With a smack Marge's forehead hit the floor.

Under Rice's supervision, after they had recovered from the shock, the three boys from town picked Marge off the floor and dropped her into an upholstered chair. By now—except for Fontessa who still hid upstairs—the remaining members of the Kilbanky household were in various degrees of immobility, frozen in set postures due to stress and defeat. Bill seemed catatonic; Marge was immobilized; and Mrs. Kilbanky had collapsed from exhaustion, fear and unhappiness. Inanimate and limp, they remained like the Historical Society yokel, or sacks of flour, to be carried around at will or stacked away for the night by Roger, Marvin and Sonny.

Dr. Rice directed the operation. They found ropes and stacked them together, storing them in the kitchen. Rice looked up at the wall-clock—nearly 11:30! No wonder he was so tired. His voice cracked as he spoke.

"Let's find out where the bedrooms are located and go to sleep. We'll take care of this mess in the morning."

Wearily he looked around him and sighed. "And don't worry about Martin. He'll be here bright and early tomorrow morning like the rest of us, eating breakfast. We can apprehend him then. He's only out there dreaming somewhere now," he added, pointing out the window into the darkness as he looked around the parlor once more and snapped off the parlor light.

"He's just outside somewhere. . . ."

12

Martin's Dream

Martin marched in the darkness directly across the yard to the cement truck. The encrusted, upturned vehicle loomed out of the night. Kicking the big left rear tire, he satisfied himself that it was still filled with air and immediately he started to scale it. Lifting himself up by the numerous toggles and cranks that projected from underneath the huge cone-shaped mixer above the rear wheel, he hoisted himself onto the rim of the girders that supported the mixer and began crawling upward along the length of the truck.

He reached the cab and opened the door on the driver's side, using all his strength to push the door vertically into the night, since the entire truck was tilted at a forty-five degree angle upward. At last he was able to pry it open sufficiently to squeeze inside. The door slammed shut. He worried at first whether the frozen glob of cement cascading from the rear of the mixer would support his added weight, but the truck seemed anchored to the spot. He bounced up and down on the dusty, long-neglected seat but the frame didn't budge.

Exhausted by the day's events he looked up through the windshield at the stars, half-obscured by the upper limbs of three old elm trees that stirred above him. It was so quiet and peaceful all alone inside the truck after his ordeal in the house that soon his eyes dropped shut, he fell asleep, and Martin finally had his dream:

He was a very large woodland animal—a deer or a bear, he didn't know what exactly at first—climbing steadily up steep boulder-strewn terrain in broad daylight. It seemed he was climbing diagonally up the face of some high mountain pass, and although he was an animal and consequently in perfect physical shape his heart beat wildly from the strain. He must have been climbing without letup for two hours by now, and although he longed to take a rest—flop down beside one of the crystal streams he passed—something refused to let him stop. Something kept pushing him. The next moment, as he paused momentarily to sniff at the wind, he knew what that something was:

He was being followed. Other animals of some kind. He realized with a start that sent gooseflesh down his back that he was able to recognize that they were other animals *by their scents*. And he could do this so easily and automatically because he too was an animal.

Out of curiosity he leaped across several yards of open alpine meadow to where a small stream left pools of water eddying against cold yellow sand. In one of the pools he saw himself reflected: he was a beaver. A beaver! Martin gasped.

Then he looked again, walking slowly along the perimeter of the pool so he could see his whole body unfold in progression. The pool was so small compared to the size of his body that first he saw his head, then had to move his head out of the reflection in order for his chest to come into view, then move his chest in order to see his legs and tail.

He panned down the body in this fashion, like a movie-camera, and what he saw was eight feet tall with a big beaver's head, bristling blood-red whiskers, streamlined fish-scale back, swift muscular scurrier's legs, three-pronged webbed feet, and a thick scaly tail over four feet long and glowing rusty red. In addition he wore a blue and white checked hunter's shirt. A small pack was strapped to his back, and a hunter's knife at his waist. In one hand he carried a gun: it was not a particularly good gun, some sort of cheap light rifle like a twenty-two. Martin couldn't tell exactly because for some reason he was unable to verify it simply by looking down at himself. Something prevented him from looking down at his body. He could only see himself—feel and sense himself as well—by looking in the reflection in the pool.

Just as curiously, Martin was aware of one more thing. It was a piece of information lodged in his head—namely, that he had acquired his flannel hunter's shirt, red sweater (packed away now) and knife and gun, from a hunter "a day or two before," sometime in the recent past. It was nothing more specific than that, he couldn't remember the details, only that a heavy physical oppression settled over him when he *did* try to remember. It forced him to forget. Because in the back of his mind he was afraid he had murdered the hunter—killed him for his gun and clothes. He vaguely remembered, for instance, the hunter's tail: the hunter was ring-tailed, white ring around darker fur, and so must have been a ringtailed cat or a raccoon. Martin shivered as this lone detail surfaced in his memory. If he was able to remember this detail then he must have killed the hunter, he decided. There was no other explanation. Most likely the poor thing never had a chance, for Martin himself was a monstrous animal-amalgam, a creature of immense strength over eight feet tall. He was a king of the wilderness, of that he was certain, and only old age or illness, or some emergency the nature of which he couldn't quite grasp, would compel him to come down out of his mountain remoteness and attack a lesser being.

For he was king of the wilderness, the forbidding mountain terrain of immense fractured granite shelves, precipitous cliffs and sudden tortuous valley walls. It was true wilderness country, the home of the eagle and the mountain goat, both above and below the treeline at about 10,000 feet. It was country totally unlike the low rolling farmland around Winosha Falls where he actually lived, but country that he was familiar with nonetheless from a hunting trip as a small boy with his father: now in the dream, however, the dry barren days of the hawk and the cold, wind-lashed nights on unprotected boulders towering out over the void were all he knew.

It was the 24th of July in the dream. He had been up above the borderline hunting down mountain goat and sinking them on the run, roasting them whole under a flashlight-white moon, running high and heady with summer, even at this altitude, as he vaulted across the rims and cuts and sank his teeth into a leg, or sprocketed down through the frog's heart at the bottom of mindless quivering little alpine ponds, or sank the heavy owl and slapped the swift antelope dead on the run. He was an enormous beaver with an iguana's trunk and tail, and versatile webbed feet. He was king of the wilderness, but for some reason now he was running scared.

He was running and running, as fast as he could, and he was

scared—traumatized to such an extent that only by involvement in the physical act of running could he remain in control of himself. Fear drove him further and further up the steep granite slopes. He stopped now and then only to listen, to sniff and listen.

He was being followed. His big beaver's face became sleek and wet from concentration. It was a bright sunny day, the vivid cobalt blue of the high mountain skies testified to that, and glaring shafts of sunlight reflected off Martin's big buck teeth, his incisors. His dark, scaly reptilian back and tail absorbed the light to a fantastic degree, but he decided he would have to find some way to camouflage the teeth or else their reflection in the brilliant sunlight might give him away to whoever was tracking him on the slopes below.

He knelt down on the spot and rapidly untied the knapsack, spilling its contents onto the ground: scissors, sterilized gauze pads, snakebite kit, peanuts, raisins, pemmican, penknife, pencils, a few family snapshots of raccoons, and a spiral notebook in which the previous owner had been keeping a diary in pencil. Martin's curiosity was stung by a scribbled page that fell open to view and he longed to read what was written in the diary, but something—some physical force—prevented him from reaching down and picking it up.

A few other survival objects fell out including a ball of twine, a box of rifle shells, a few fish hooks and nylon line, and a roll of black cloth-backed tape. There seemed to be other things in the pack as well—a small bag of marshmallows and a tin of dehydrated wood by-products—but he had found what he needed. He picked up the roll of black tape and hurriedly cut off several long pieces using his razor-sharp incisors. Then he replaced everything in the knapsack, tied the pack on his back, and carefully wound the sections of tape around each of the protruding teeth. Now they wouldn't reflect in the sunlight and give him away. Immediately he leaped to his feet and continued climbing. A new urgency made itself felt: there wasn't a moment to lose. He still couldn't actually hear his followers but he knew they were there. He could smell them, a thousand yards below him on the slopes. His immediate task was to maintain this distance between them. Otherwise it was only a matter of time until they came into sight.

He turned his gaze upward and resumed climbing. The air thinned as the altitude increased until soon he was huffing and puffing to keep his breath. In spite of the breakneck pace with which he pawed and vaulted across the rocky screes and canyon walls the distance separating Martin from his trackers decreased steadily until soon, when he paused for a moment and looked back down the giddy incline, something bright red appeared moving among the fir trees and, abruptly and before he realized it, a tiny figure emerged in a clearing three or four hundred yards below him. Martin hid behind a boulder and, straining his eyes, tried to identify his pursuer. It looked like a hunter with a gun, though the figure was so small at this point he couldn't be sure. The figure then emerged completely into view and although it was still small Martin saw that indeed it was a hunter: he paused, obviously out of breath himself, and tossing some sort of hat he was wearing to the ground, began mopping his brow. He sat down on a boulder to catch his breath. Directly below the hunter Martin saw the sheer drop thousands of feet back down the mountainside: a spectacular sight.

Then other shirts and parts of bodies began appearing in miniature at that distance behind the first hunter, and Martin turned and resumed his ascent. The terrain got rougher and more difficult to climb as the altitude increased. Soon Martin was above the tree line. His heart pounded in his chest. Just when he thought he would give out the terrain reached a sort of plateau, treeless except for small bush-like growths of some kind. The land leveled off to the extent that he was running on more or less level ground rather than vertically, though in fact he was still gaining altitude. The effort it took to run at this altitude more than made up for the lack of steep ground, so that soon he was out of breath again, holding his aching side and looking back down the brush-covered, boulder-strewn slope.

He barely had time to roll behind a boulder for cover before the same hunter he had seen previously emerged at the mouth of the plateau, not more than two hundred yards below him. Martin gasped and stretched out on his belly, trying to fold his enormous tail between some rocks so that it wouldn't spring up into view. The tail already had given him much trouble while climbing, and he wondered vaguely at this point in the dream why he was handicapped with such a big tail. When he stood motionless on his hind legs the strong, muscular tail served a purpose in providing balance for the bulky body, but when climbing it was worse than useless. Martin just didn't understand. He began to resent his body rather than feel proud of it. He didn't remember feeling this way before and it made him depressed. He was being tracked, hunted down, of that he was sure, and the tail merely made it more difficult to outdistance his pursuers.

In fact, even as he lay there pondering his situation they were drawing closer. He now had the distinct feeling they were "all around" him. He craned his neck desperately in every direction, then became disgusted with his loss of composure and looked back down the slope.

They were there, slowly advancing through the brush and boulders. One by one they emerged from cover then disappeared again as each one searched painstakingly the immediate area around him. Martin saw what appeared to be men with guns in the bushes, but then they were not men but animals like himself—enormous (eight or nine feet tall) bear and deer and foxes, raccoons and groundhogs —all the common woodland variety of mammals. They shouted merrily among themselves as they beat the bushes in the hunt.

Martin turned and ran.

After what seemed like another half hour or so he stopped again gasping for breath, and saw with a start that they were gaining ground no matter how hard he ran. Martin became alarmed. His black buck teeth shook nervously in the cold mountain air. The animals were definitely closer now and seemed to be closing in on him from several directions at once. Obviously he had been spotted by one of them. He saw a fox point more or less in his direction.

The foxes, who seemed to be in the majority, sported scarves and caps and carried guns, just like the others. Only instead of shouting merrily among each other as they beat the bushes in the hunt, these eight foot foxes clicked like castanets among themselves as their form of communication. They beat among the bushes and stunted trees with their whisks and staves. Rat-a-tat-tat, rat-a-tat-tat went their rows and tiers of teeth, and Martin was terrified. Dry twigs and branches snapped loudly under their feet.

Some of the animal-hunters were oddly distinguished-looking, especially the foxes, a few of whom looked positively British in their red velveteen hunting jackets and black twill britches. And it was precisely the foxes whose merry, prankish facial expressions mortified him, since the other animals mustered only dull or blank expressions. But the huge red foxes with their patent-leather boots and snappy, two-way visor caps looked diabolical as they beat the field with their staves and overturned big boulders with a twist of one paw. And it was always one of the foxes that caught sight of Martin and redirected the chase toward him as he fled higher and higher among the rocks . . . For the plateau he had been traversing suddenly disappeared, and he found himself climbing steeply as before. Terrible vistas yawned beneath him—the startling clarity of an alpine meadow three thousand feet below, the vision of a diamond-like glacier lake far below, glittering with amazing purity in the sunlight.

Martin breathed the thin mountain air and his head reeled. He stumbled over to a rock to rest. As he sat looking down on the tortuous slopes he had just climbed, trying to catch his breath and plan his next move, one of the foxes suddenly emerged in a clearing not two hundred feet below him, panting and out of breath.

Martin froze. His heart stopped. He knew if he moved from where he sat the fox surely would see him—freezing in place, crouching perfectly still, was his only hope. "Maybe," he thought desperately, "if I can really freeze, the fox won't see me; I'll blend into the rocks." Deep inside he knew this to be wishful thinking, however: his enormous bulk and bizarre amalgam of contrasting mammal˙and reptile body parts was sure to give him away. Martin frozen in place not because he thought the strategy would work but because the fox had caught him by surprise and there was nothing else he could do.

He saw the fox's gun. It gleamed dully in the otherwise sparkling mountain atmosphere. It was a heavy, brutal-looking gun, with a thick stock and professional scope and lens. Martin knew the fox must be a great marksman. He swallowed and nearly choked in fear. His stomach sank and a miserable hopelessness overtook him. He had never felt worse—ever, in his entire life. He felt sure the fox would see him and shoot before he could move. He heard the other hunters climbing up the slope, beating the rocks and grunting, drawing nearer.

The fox finally caught his breath and, shading his eyes from the sun, started scanning the slope above him with his methodical hunter's eye. His head swung back and forth, back and forth, like a doll's on a spring.

The fox stopped short, glowing bright red. He raised his rifle until it pointed where Martin sat. The other animals emerged from below and joined the fox. They belched and grunted horribly, clicking to each other like insects and pointing Martin out to each other high up among the rocks.

They all began advancing. The fox cocked his trigger. Why didn't he shoot? Martin couldn't stand it any longer. He let out an awful, tortured howl, raising his beaver's teeth to the sky. His eyes ran with tears as he beseeched the deep blue crystal above him.

When no shot rang out, however, Martin decided he had a chance to survive after all: he decided to throw himself at the mercy of his pursuers. He jumped up and started running and tripping down the slope toward the animals, all the while shielding his eyes with his paws in spite of himself, still certain that at any second they would shoot and cut him down.

Running pell-mell as he was, with his hands over his eyes, his visibility was impaired to the point that he stumbled and fell more than once, gashing himself on sharp rocks and tripping over his own tail. He lost his gun and knapsack.

As he ran along he felt more and more uncomfortable, until he temporarily forgot the big animals waiting for him below. He felt imprisoned in his awkward animal body, hindered by its bulk and contradictory elements. This sensation amazed him, since he had never experienced it before. Oblivious now to his tormentors, he stopped on the spot and began tugging with both paws in the vicinity of his throat.

Suddenly his beaver's face lit up and he shook with joy: Martin had found a zipper! His body was so bulky because it was a costume! He was wearing a costume! Feverishly he yanked at the zipper until finally it tore free and he pulled it down past his stomach to his legs. The cool mountain air rushed inside the costume like an ice-cold shower. Liberation! Martin struggled out of the bulky, sweat-soaked costume and rolled free onto the ground, exhilarated beyond belief by the loss of all that dead weight. The top-heavy costume toppled over onto the ground, shapeless now except for the two tape-wrapped tusks.

Dressed as usual, in a white T-shirt and Levi's, Martin Kilbanky now possessed his normal size and shape, though he could barely contain his excitement at feeling so sleek and light and fresh.

By now the big animals were no more than thirty feet away, laughing and pointing derisively at him. Martin was shocked by their behavior. Didn't they realize who he was? Didn't they understand?

He rushed up to their leader—the fox who originally spotted him —and reached for the hunter's throat, all the time shouting something about a zipper. He had to stand on a boulder in order to reach the throat that was now three feet higher than him. His fingers closed around the throat searching feverishly through the golden fur for the zipper, but none could be found. There was no zipper.

The fox, momentarily stunned by Martin's strange appearance and

242

behavior, regained possession of himself and with one swipe of his paw sent him reeling. All the animals now approached him and began striking him with their staves and laughing at him.

Martin rolled free of them and stood up. The huge flannel-shirted animals regarded him maliciously out of sharp red eyes. They drew closer, beating their staves and guns in the brush. They paused not more than five feet away from him, beating the brush in unison.